Par for the Course

To Lillian,

Be careful! you never know where the next "trip" might take you. Enjoy!

Janet Elaine Smith

Other books by Janet Elaine Smith

Dunnottar
Marylebone

The Patrick and Grace Mystery Series
  In St. Patrick's Custody
  Recipe for Murder
  Old Habits Die Hard

ISBN 1-932993-52-5   ISBN13: 978-1-932993-52-3   LCCN: 2006931892

Cover Photograph Credit: www.where2golf.com

Star Publish
http://starpublish.com
2nd. Edition Published in 2006 by Star Publish

To Mechi,
A real sweetheart
And a perfect example of what a
"Sam's Club" employee should be.
And to Holly,
A very dear friend,
And the most dedicated
Golfer I know.

Par for the Course

Chapter I

"Life isn't fair!" the red-haired actress on the TV said, banging her fists on the wall.

Mechi Jeanotte stared at the screen. She always watched *Another World*, but she didn't even seem conscious that she had *General Hospital* on instead. Maybe it was fate. It certainly echoed her own experiences over the past few days.

In less than one week her father had died, she had moved clear across the country to begin her first job as a golf pro at St. Andrew's Golf Course, just outside Aberdeen, Maryland, and the only boy—no, man—she had ever dated told her he was getting married. And it wasn't to her!

"You're damned tootin' life's not fair!" she shouted back at the portable screen. "Not this one, anyway!"

She had practiced so hard to get rid of her Texas twang, but it came through loud and clear now. She didn't care. The only good thing she could find to think about was that so many things had been fouled up that it couldn't get any worse.

"Dad!" she cried out, knowing he couldn't hear her.

It had all been so sudden. One minute he was there talking to her at the breakfast table, and the next minute he was gone. *Gone*! Forever! There wasn't any solace in the fact that he had at least stuck around for the first twenty-three years of her life, unlike her mother who died when she was almost too young to remember her.

Sensing the futility of her plea to her missing father, she turned her focus to Robert Pearson. If she admitted the truth to herself, she knew that part of her life, at least, was for the best, having ended as abruptly as her father's life. She tried to imagine the rest of her life with him. It sent cold shivers up and down her spine. He was the dullest, most boring, spoiled, arrogant person she had ever known. What had she ever seen in him, anyway?

The truth of the matter was, nobody else had ever paid her the slightest bit of attention. She had always suspected that the only reason he liked her was so he could ride the thoroughbred horses she and her father raised on their ranch in Paris, Texas. She had seen him plenty of times, trotting through town, the girls swooning over his shiny black hair and his slim, trim body. He acted like that horse was his! The nerve of it, she thought, suddenly overwhelmed with relief that she wasn't there anymore and that he didn't have any interest in following her to the ends of the earth. Shoot! He didn't even follow her to the end of the block after he told her he was going to marry Helen Jean Berkeley. Well, let him try to make his way in *her world* of society balls, oil tycoons' meetings and fancy shindigs. They'd all find out in a hurry what a fraud he was and she would dump him as fast as he had just dumped Mechi. She had known Helen Jean all her life, and she was nobody's fool. She'd end up taking him for a ride; she was sure of it. Served him right, too.

She had made a clean break with everything as soon as her father's funeral was over. Now, she was determined to make a fresh start. She had a new job, a wonderful apartment, the glistening pink 1957 Cadillac convertible she had always dreamed of owning . . . Maybe life wasn't fair, but it wasn't all that bad, either.

"B-r-r-r-ing!"

Mechi jumped at the sound of the phone. She quickly reached to grab it.

"It must be the club," she reasoned aloud. "Nobody else has my number yet."

"Hello."

"Mechi?" came the deep male voice she knew so well. "Are you okay? I feel really bad that I didn't make it back in time for Dad's funeral. Can you ever forgive me? I know it wasn't fair to leave you with everything to do…"

"Hold it, little bro!" Mechi yelled into the phone, interrupting Brian, her older brother.

She couldn't find it in her heart to tell him that it had been so long since she had seen him that she had almost forgotten she even had a brother. After all, they had never been real close. He was twelve years older than she was, and he went off to join the Navy when she was just a little girl. On the few occasions when he had come home on a furlough, he had seemed more like a stranger than a brother. Now, with the death of their father—their only link—she found true solace in the sound of his voice.

"I really mean it," he insisted, continuing as if she hadn't said a word. "You know I would have been there if I could have."

'I know," Mechi said, sarcasm running rampant in her voice. "Just like you were when Mom died. Or when I was in the school play. Or when Dad had his heart attack a few years ago. Oh, sure. I understand perfectly. It was never your fault. Blame it on good old Uncle Sam! He doesn't have a heart. Well, sometimes I think you don't, either."

"Jeez!" Brian said, breathing a deep sigh of relief that she had finally stopped. "Try to apologize to some people!"

"I'm sorry," Mechi said slowly. "I didn't mean to get on your case. It is just that it's been a really rough week." She swallowed hard, hoping the lump in her throat would disappear before she broke out in hysterical sobs.

"I know," Brian said. "I really am sorry I wasn't there for you. I mean, we're all we've got left. It's just you and me, kid. The two of us against the big old ugly world."

"I'll make it on my own," she said. *I don't need your help, either!* she wanted to add, but decided against it. "By the way, where are you calling from?"

"Oh!" Brian answered excitedly. "I almost forgot. We just docked in South Carolina. The ship will be in port for about a week. I've managed to get a few days free, 'cuz of Dad and all, you know. I'll catch a bus tonight. I'll be in Aberdeen early tomorrow morning. Suppose you could meet your big brother at the bus depot? That is, if it's not too early for you. If it is, I can just wait it out until you get up."

"Don't worry about it," Mechi said. "I'll be there. What time does it get in?" She wasn't going to tell him that she hadn't been sleeping, anyway, so she might just as well be there to pick him up. At least it gave her something different to look forward to.

"Six-fifteen," he said. When she was silent he added, "I told you it was early."

"No," she said. "I'll be there." She hesitated a few moments, then added, "It will be good to see you. *Honest!*"

"You, too," he said. "See you tomorrow, then."

Mechi heard the *click* of his receiver, but held hers in her hand for a few minutes before setting it back in its cradle. She meant it. It would be good to have her brother there with her, even if it was only for a few days. Like he said, all they had left was each other.

Mechi suddenly began to laugh. Yeah, she was going to make it. She would show dear old Robert that he was the last thing in the world she needed. Nobody with an ounce of love or compassion would walk out on the girl he claimed to love the same week her father died! It was unthinkable! Revolting! Utterly uncouth! No, she didn't need the likes of Robert Pearson. What an old stuffed shirt, anyway! Imagine! He wouldn't even let her call him Bob, or Robbie, or anything else. He was so formal even the girl he claimed he was going to marry had to call him *Robert*! And he had told her time after time that he *loved* her!

Love! The word seemed to have barbs sticking out of it on all sides. Robert Pearson didn't have the foggiest idea what love was all about. The only thing he loved was himself. She should have seen it coming, but she was as blind as a bat.

Was she really that desperate? Well, no more. She was sure her mother ahd loved her, but she had gone and left her. She *knew* her father loved her. Oh, he didn't come out and say so, but his actions told her countless times. She was the apple of his eye. Yes, she knew what love felt like, but she would probably spend her whole life searching for that kind of love and never find it.

She yawned and stretched, then glanced at her watch. She hadn't realized that it was so late: nearly midnight. If she was going to get an early start in the morning, she should turn in for the night and at least try to get some sleep. If only she could keep from having those awful nightmares. Visions of people dressed in old fashioned costumes kept coming to take her away with them. She didn't know who they were, or where they were going or what it all meant, but she always woke up in a cold sweat afterwards. But, in some strange, inexplicable way she felt like she belonged with them. Like it was the only place that really held any peace for her any more. Especially the big, virile man who scooped her up in his arms as she fell and carried her off—to safety, she hoped.

None of it makes any sense, she thought as she climbed into bed. She reached up and switched off the lamp which sat on the table beside her bed.

"B-r-r-ring!"

Mechi groped around in the dark for the phone. It must be Brian. Nobody from the club would call her this late at night. She should have known as much. He was canceling out again. The ship had to leave earlier than they planned.

"Hello," she said softly into the phone.

"Miss Jeanotte? Michelle?"

A strange-sounding English-accented woman spoke into the phone.

"Yes," Mechi said cautiously. "Who is this?" It sure wasn't Brian. Or anyone else she recognized, either.

Chapter II

Mechi tossed and turned fitfully for hours. She kept going over and over the conversation with the strange English lady. No one had ever sounded so desperate—and for what? One lousy golf lesson?

She pulled the clock radio around so she could see the green glow-in-the dark numbers. Four-thirty-two. She pondered getting up; after all, she had to be at the bus depot in less than an hour and a half. No, her legs didn't seem to want to lift her out of her bed.

"Seven-thirty, *sharp*!" the strange woman had said. "Oh, and my name is Liz. Liz Stewart."

Something about the woman gave Mechi the creeps, like the *monster in the closet* used to do when she was a tiny tot. She wanted to avoid meeting her, but the mystique of her voice nudged her to respond.

Finally, as the first rays of dawn began to creep through the tiny slits in the vertical blinds on the windows, Mechi dozed off.

She sat bolt upright in bed, once more the sweat pouring off her forehead and down her face. It was the same as before. Those people—all decked out in their finest duds like they were going to a ball.

It must be a masquerade ball, Mechi reasoned. But why was she going with them? And why wasn't she in costume? She was, like always, wearing her blue jeans and a sweatshirt.

They talked with a thick foreign accent which made her think of her mother's brother, David. He was from the Scottish side of her family. It was his fault Mechi had become nearly obsessed with British history. She had three loves in her life: history, horses and golf. Well, she had had her fill of horses, living on the ranch with her father. Now that she was in Maryland, she still had her favorite, *Prince*, boarded nearby so she could ride him daily. Her new position as the golf pro at St. Andrew's Country Club gave her plenty of time to indulge herself in her passion of the game. The only thing lacking was a way to pursue her interest in history.

As soon as I have a free day, she told herself sleepily, I am going to start visiting the museums and historical sights. The area was full of such delights. It was only a few miles to the country's capitol, and she had never even seen the White House.

That must be it, she realized. My stupid dream is just a way to live out the other part of my wishes. How many times did I tell Uncle David that I wished I could have lived back then? He claimed they were direct descendants of King James the Sixth—or the First—depending on which country you were from. "On his father's side, of course," he would entone, the "r's" rolling thickly off his tongue.

Yes, that was the only thing that made any sense out of this whole dream—or nightmare—business at all. It was Mechi's subconscious effort to link up with family. Any family. Well, in just a few minutes she would be with Brian. Then the whole dream scene could just disappear. *He* was her family now; she didn't need some old-time ghost from the past.

"Over here, Sis!" Mechi recognized Brian's voice immediately. She ran to greet him, throwing her arms around his neck. The fact that he was too late for his own father's funeral didn't matter now. He was here, and that was the important thing.

"It's good to see you, too," he said with a wink. "I can't remember the last time I had such a welcome."

"Let me look at you," she said, pushing him back to an arm's length away from her. "You look good," she said, nodding her approval.

"Did you expect me to be a pile of skin and bones?" he asked, laughing. "Uncle Sam does feed us, you know."

"Sure, but what?" Mechi asked, remembering his letters about the "mess" they served up on board the ships. It was easy to see where the name came from, judging by his descriptions.

Changing the subject abruptly he said, "So you're a real pro now, huh? I always knew you'd make good use of your talents some way. Think you could give me a few pointers while I'm in town?"

"Sure," Mechi said. "Seems funny, me trying to teach you anything. I didn't think there was anything I could do better than you."

"Are you kidding?" Brian asked. "According to Pops, you were just about the most perfect thing that ever set foot on the earth."

"What do you mean?" Mechi asked. "All my life I have heard 'Brian did it this way,' or 'Brian would have said this,' or 'Brian would know what to do.' I never thought I would be able to teach you anything, not even how to play golf."

"This is crazy!" Brian exclaimed. "Here we are arguing about which one of us

Pops thought was the best. I think he loved us both."

"You're right," Mechi said, a tear trickling down her cheek.

"God, I'm going to miss him!" Brian said with a deep sigh. "Even when I was gone, if I had a problem or I didn't know what to do, I knew he was just a phone call away. He was always there when I needed him."

"Yeah," Mechi said, wiping her face with the back of her sweatshirt sleeve. "Me, too."

She glanced at her watch. "We'd better get going. I've got an early appointment at the club. Do you want to just wait it out there? It shouldn't take too long."

"They start you out this early in the morning?" he asked in surprise. "The slave drivers! Maybe I should have a talk with your boss."

"I can take care of myself, thank you very much. In case you hadn't noticed, I'm a big girl now."

"Yes, I did notice, although it's hard to tell what is underneath that big old baggy sweatshirt," Brian teased.

"Besides," Mechi continued to explain as they walked out the door of the bus station towards her car, "this one is kind of unusual. I'll tell you all about it on the way back to the club."

Brian looked around, waving his arms in the air like he was doing the Australian crawl.

"Is the fog always this bad?" he asked, pretending to push it out of the way so they could see where they were going.

"No," Mechi said, snickering. "Sometimes it's even worse."

They walked to her car, and Brian pulled his sunglasses from his pocket and put them on.

"Whew!" he said. "Even in this pea soup you can make that one out. That's bright, Sis! Almost florescent! Are you trying to tell me something? That you are clamoring for recognition? That you want to be noticed? Okay, I noticed!"

"Just get in!" Mechi grumbled. "This is my dream machine."

"Some nightmare!" Brian said.

They got into the car and when Mechi turned the key, the music began to blare loudly. "This is your oldies but goodies station," the announcer said when the song ended. "All your favorite tunes from the fifties and sixties. Hope you're having a good day."

Brian laughed. "You always have loved the junk from back then, haven't you?"

"Bite your tongue!" Mechi shouted. "That's almost sacreligious—calling the good stuff from that era *junk*. But you are right about one thing. I think I was born at the wrong time—totally. The stuff from back then meant something People had feelings. Life was better. Sometimes I feel like I don't belong here at all."

"What about this golf lesson?" Brian asked, his curiosity riding high. "Who is so special, and why?"

"Her name is Liz Stewart," Mechi began, "and I don't know why she is special. But, she certainly seemed to think she was somebody worth something. She was so insistent, I finally gave in and agreed. Even with you here. Talk about a sacrifice!"

"Sarcasm somehow becomes you!" Brian scoffed.

Mechi told him about the strange call, what there was to tell. She really didn't know much herself, other than what the woman had told her on the phone. For some reason, she had to have the golf lesson, and it had to be this morning. She acted like it was a matter of life and death.

Mechi wheeled the car into her parking spot at the club.

"Wow!" Brian said, then let out a long slow whistle. "Your very own private parking spot. I am impressed!"

"And well you should be!" Mechi joked back, jabbing him with her elbow. "Why, we have senators, and cabinet members and really important people who are members at St. Andrew's. Even presidents have been known to put in an appearance from time to time."

"And this Liz Stewart?" Brian asked. "Is she a member too?"

"I don't really know," Mechi admitted, suddenly realizing that she should have checked that out. She shrugged her shoulders. "Guess she must be. She said she had been at St. Andrew's many times, but that she had never golfed there before." What if she was—unacceptable? Mechi realized, for the first time, that she had never seen *certain* people there. Yes, in a club like St. Andrew's there were bound to be restrictions.

"Can you wait here for a few minutes while I go out and warm up?" she asked Brian as they entered the clubhouse. "I'm sure Lori will be glad to make you comfortable, won't you, Lori?" she asked the receptionist. "Everybody loves a man in uniform."

"Sure," Lori said, batting her long dark lashes at Mechi's handsome brother. "Anything you want, soldier boy!"

"Gee, thanks!" Brian said, turning to glare at Mechi. "And it's *sailor* boy."

"Sorry," Lori said. "I never could tell one from the other."

Mechi was laughing as she headed out the door, waving to Brian. He could figure out how to handle Lori. It was obvious that it wasn't her brains that had landed her that job. But, what does a guy want at his country club, anyway? Brains, or…? Mechi had figured that one out as soon as she set eyes on Lori. Of course it wasn't always true. She was about as "plain Jane" as any girl could be; they had to have hired her for her reputation in golf.

She swung her nine iron as she groped her way through the fog. It wasn't going to be easy to teach anyone anything on a day like this, but she knew Liz would be there. From the tone of her voice, *nothing* would keep her away.

Liz looked at her watch. Seven-twenty-eight. If Liz was as prompt as she insisted on Mechi being, she should be there in two minutes. Well, a few swings of the golf club would have her ready and waiting by the time she put in an appearance.

Chapter III

Mechi took a golf ball and a tee from her jacket pocket and set them in position. As she stood up she could hardly see them through the fog, but she was determined to play them through.

She swung at the ball—time and time again, but try as she might she couldn't seem to hit it. She had never been so frustrated. The fog was no excuse.

In desperation she swung again, harder than ever. At least this time she hit it, and the ball went flying high into the air, heading towards where she knew the river was, even though she couldn't see it.

She headed off in the general direction the ball had traveled, kicking at the damp autumn leaves to try to find it. By her calculations she must be close to it.

Her foot hit something hard and round. She picked the object up, expecting it to be her golf ball. Instead, in her gloved hand she held an old, dirty sphere, the likes of which she had never seen before. It looked more like an old rotten miniature baseball than a golf ball. It was covered in mud. No, she thought as she examined it more carefully, she could see that it wasn't mud. It was more like tar. Her gloves were covered in the thick black goo.

She clung to the ball, unexplainably, as she continued to look for her own ball. It seemed to have vanished off the face of the earth. She was sure it must have landed somewhere in this area.

She looked at her watch. She had been on her search far longer than she realized. It was only a couple of minutes before eight. Why was this Liz so late? She was the one who had insisted on this early hour of the morning.

Mechi felt her blood boil. She hated people it when people were late.

Frustrated, she decided to hit one good wallop before she returned to the clubhouse and Brian. It was obvious Liz wasn't here; they would have paged her on the speaker system if she was.

She reached into her jacket pocket for a new ball, then decided to use this odd thing she had found instead. She carefully set it on the ground and… With one swift blow to the ball she was completely enveloped in… *feathers*?

Her head began to spin around like a whirling top. She lunged forward, then felt her foot catch on the root of a tree as she fell. Farther and farther down she sank, to the ground and into unconsciousness.

Mechi rubbed her head. It ached like nothing she had ever felt before. She tried to sit up, but the world began spinning around, like giant trees flying through the sky.

"Quite a fall you took, lassie. Bad r-r-r-r-oot, that one," the voice of a stranger said to Mechi. She recognized the Scottish brogue immediately. She hadn't heard anyone speak like that since her mother's brother, Uncle David, had visited them on their ranch just outside Paris, Texas. Or since the people in her dream…

Mechi strained her neck, trying to get the stranger in her view. She could tell that he was above her. No, he was cradling her head in his lap. It was soft—like new mown grass.

Her foot hit the root she had tripped on when she went to try to find the golf ball she had lost in the fog.

"Stupid root!" she sputtered. "It's all your fault! No, actually, it's Liz's fault! Why did anyone want a golf lesson at this hour of the morning—and in such a fog?"

Mechi's mind began racing as fast as the trees appeared to move. After all, she thought, she didn't know this Liz who called her last night and insisted Mechi give her a private golf lesson at seven-thirty. What did people expect of her, anyway? Just because she, Mechi Jeanotte, happened to be the golf pro at St. Andrew's Golf Course just outside Aberdeen, Maryland?

Mechi struggled to get to her feet, but she was still far too dizzy to make it on her own.

"I dinna ken what to do with ye," the stranger said, "but perchance if we sit here a moment…"

When Mechi's vision cleared enough to make out the features of her rescuer, her heart skipped a beat. She knew she had seen this man, but for the life of her she didn't know where. He was the picture of strength, with huge muscles rippling in his neck. All she could see was his upper torso, as her head was still in his lap. He sported a course red, bristly beard, which made him look more manly than any creature she had ever seen. His long red hair, pulled back behind his neck and knotted in a leather strip, had small wisps which defied the control he tried to wield. His eyes, greener than the grass below them, were almost as bright as emeralds. His concern for her well-being showed in his eyes, but behind it there was a slight glimmer of mischief.

Suddenly something deep within her told Mechi that this was the stranger in her dream who had carried her off into a netherworld. Although she had never seen him from the front, she knew that if he turned his back to her it would be the man of her dreams.

That's it, she thought, *this is still my dream. But it has gone on this time. I didn't wake up*. Maybe *everything* had been a dream. Did Brian really call? What about crazy Liz? Was she a figment of her imagination, too? Maybe her father was still alive. Where did reality end and imagination begin? She was so confused.

She looked up again at the stranger. Maybe it would be better for her if she didn't wake up. If she had to spend an eternity lost in time, well, this guy would do just fine as part of her dream. What had seemed like a nightmare was suddenly not frightening at all. Not when she had this man with her.

She reached up to feel his face. His beard prickled her fingers, causing her to pull her hand back quickly. She ran it slowly over the rippling muscles in his arms on its way back to her lap.

"Wow!" Mechi said, letting out a most unladylike wolf whistle. "What a hunk!"

"A *hunk* indeed!" the man said. "We better get something cold on it." He continued to rub the lump, or *hunk*, as she had called it, on her head.

"And how did ye git here, lassie?" he asked. "And what's a woman doin' wearin' the likes o' yer britches?"

"These?" Mechi asked, pulling at her brand new Liz Claiborne jeans. She looked at them to see if they had been torn in her fall. She found no holes, but could see smudges of grass stain. "Drats! I'll bet that will never come out! And I just blew forty bucks on them!"

"Forty bucks?" the stranger asked, puzzled by her speech. "You paid for these with forty deer? Lassie, ye got yerself swindled!"

Mechi laughed. Who was this haunting stranger? Where was he from? Why hadn't she seen him when she first got to the golf course this morning? And where was Liz, the woman who had been so desperate for a lesson?

"Did I say somethin' strange?" the man asked, again rolling his "r" in that delightful way—like Uncle David.

"You *are* strange! Mechi exclaimed. "Who are you, anyway?"

"Why, I might ask ye the same, milady. It appears that you are the one who's a wee bit odd, if I might be so bold as to say so. Me name is R-r-r-r-obert Keith, the Viscount of Kintore. At yer service, milady. And you?"

Mechi gasped. A real live English—or was he truly Scottish, as she assumed from his speech—lord? Whatever was he doing here? One thing was sure; he was not in the least like her *other Robert*. Why, this Robert would put that old pussy-foot to shame. No, if ever she had seen a *real* Robert, this was it! Him and Robert Redford!

"M-m-m-Mechi Jeanotte," she stammered. "Actually, it is Michelle, but everyone calls me Mechi."

"A French lassie?" Lord Keith asked. "Your accent is most strange, but it did not impress me as being French."

Mechi laughed. Her great-grandfather was French, so technically she was a *French lassie,* yet her head ached too much to try to explain anything—her accent or her ancestry—to this man.

"Do you think you could help me get to the clubhouse? Maybe if I lie down for a bit my head will quit spinning."

Mechi coughed as she realized that she was asking this man, the man of her dreams, to help her like he was real. She must have lost her sanity overnight. Still, it might be fun to go on with the act and see where it took her. After all, it was *her* dream!

"I'll be glad to help ye," Lord Keith said, "but there's no *cloobhouse* nearby. There is, however, Moray's quarters. We can go there."

He supported her as she tried to stand up, but she felt her knees buckle beneath her. She wasn't sure if it was from her head, or if it was from her heart doing flip-flops being so near this—lord.

Big, strong muscle-bound arms wrapped themselves around her. Mechi had always prided herself on being independent. She never liked to rely on anyone for anything. Too many people in her past had let her down. This, she knew, was different. This man would stand by her, no matter what; she could feel it in her bones. And her bones never lied!

Before she knew what was happening, Lord Robert Keith, Viscount of Kintore, had her in his arms and was hurrying through the fog and across the green grass of the golf course to take her to Moray's abode. She rubbed her burning eyes. None of this made any sense, but it hurt her head to try to think. Besides, in her dream he always ended up carrying her off somewhere. She felt like she was going to wake up any second. This had to be the end of the dream. Part of her longed for it to go on. She felt so wonderfully safe in his arms...

"It *must* be all a dream," she mumbled.

"What did ye say, lassie?" Robert Keith asked.

"Nothing," Mechi answered. "Nothing at all."

Soon she felt him lowering her body, gently, so gently. She could hear voices all around her. Men's voices. Women's voices. Scottish voices. Then she felt her body sink into something as soft as marshmallows. When she tripped on that oak root, it must have been her demise. That was it. She must be dead. Was this heaven? It couldn't be hell! Not with the likes of Lord Robert Keith, Viscount of Kintore, beside her.

Mechi tried to focus on the figures who stood huddled over her. She could make out three men and a woman. She was relieved at the sight of another woman. At least she offered some protection. From what? Mechi wondered.

"Who are y'all?" Mechi asked, lapsing into her childhood Texas drawl she had worked so hard to lose once she got to Maryland.

It was the woman who spoke. "You know Robbie, of course. And this is James Stewart, but they call him Darnley." She nodded towards the tallest of the male trio.

"And him?" Mechi asked, pointing to the other man. She chuckled as she thought that they looked like the Three Musketeers.

"Why, that's Moray, of course. 'Tis his abode you're in."

"Then I thank you for your hospitality," Mechi said, again rubbing the bump on her head. She groaned when she touched it. Instinctively, she pulled her hand away to see if there was any blood on it, but any damage, she decided, must be internal.

Mechi stared at the woman. There was something so familiar about her, but she couldn't put her finger on what it was. She knew she had seen her in her dream, but it was more than that. Suddenly, as if she was looking a a history book, she saw a picture of Mary, Queen of Scots, playing golf at St. Andrew's near Aberdeen, Scotland. What kind of cruel joke were these people playing on her, anyway? She started out at St. Andrew's Golf Course near Aberdeen, Maryland, and she felt as if by some miracle she had been transported to another time. Another place.

She rubbed her eyes, trying to clear them. She closed them tightly. Maybe when she opened them again these strange people would all be gone. To her dismay, they were all there, and all very real. Especially Lord Robert Keith, Viscount of Kintore. Oh, yes, she could never have imagined anyone as fine a specimen as Lord Keith.

She shook her head slightly as she thought about her father. He had always warned her that some day her obsession with the three passions in her life—golf, horses and history—would be her undoing. Well, it looked like he was right. Had she somehow allowed herself to be overtaken by some weird imaginative plot to set her in some other time? Had she become a member of the Twilight Zone?

Realizing that they were not going to leave, she asked the woman, trying not to sound impolite yet overwhelmed by curiosity, "And you? Who are you, ma'am?"

"You don't know who I am?" the woman asked. She sounded, Mechi thought, almost insulted at the lack of recognition. "Who do you think I might be?"

She wondered if she dared tell them what she really thought. Was it too bizarre? Nothing ventured, nothing gained, she told herself. If these weird people want to be practical jokers, fine! I'll play along with them.

"You….with your piles of crinolines and your high, ruffled collar, you look just like…"

"Like whom?" the woman asked impatiently, pushing Mechi for an answer.

"You look, if you'll forgive my saying so," Mechi said, "just like the pictures I've seen of Mary, Queen of Scots."

"Well!" the woman said, applauding loudly. "You're not as ill-bred as one might think. 'Tis a fact; I am she. But for the life of me, I cannot understand why someone who has access to paintings of the Queen of Scotland would clothe herself in the likes of—this!"

As she spoke, she pulled at Mechi's nylon windbreaker. "Why, lassie, you're as wet as a salmon from the loch!"

The queen placed her hand on Mechi's forehead.

"Moray! Fetch a pitcher of cool water. The poor child is burning up with a fever! The fall must have done her more harm than we thought."

As she freed Mechi's arms from the jacket, the queen began to laugh, pointing at Mechi's sweatshirt.

"Guess?" she said. "Look, her garment says 'Guess.' So she wants to play games with us, does she?"

A fleeting inspiration hit Mechi. She had read in the paper that there was a British theater troupe touring the area, putting on Shakespeare plays. *That's it!* She thought, relieved that she wasn't completely crazy. These were just actors, and they had gotten a little carried away. They had obviously been playing their parts far too long. Maybe they actually believed they had become the characters they were portraying. Well, if she was among the loonies, she might as well play along with them. It was probably safer that way. Who knew what they might do if she tried to tell them they were all crazy? She wasn't about to find out. Not with that dagger in the side of Lord Keith's belt.

Soon there were many more people buzzing around Mechi. As she fell into a deep sleep, or a coma, or whatever it was, she pondered the fact that she was having her head bathed by the Queen of Scotland! And the incredibly handsome Lord Robert Keith, Viscount of Kintore, was sitting at her side, telling her of some place called Dunnottar—a place that sounded like a fairy book castle. And then she was gone.

As she drifted in and out of consciousness, Mechi's mind ran like a VCR tape. The events of the past few hours played over and over and over. The phone call from the strange young woman, Liz, who was so insistent on having a golfing lesson at seven- thirty in the morning. The drive to St. Andrew's Golf Course through the fog. The frustrating wait, while Liz never showed up. The attempt at hitting a golf ball and losing it near the river. The feathers flying everywhere. The fall. That infernal fall. The roots of the old oak tree. The fall. The roots… The fall… She felt herself falling, over and over again. The rest of it, when she came to with her head on the lap of the Viscount of Kintore, seemed to be a blur on the tape. Like the cable had gone out and the only thing there was the sound…

The sound. She could hear voices—those very Scottish voices—all around her, yet they seemed so far away. Like she was watching a drive-in movie from across the field like she used to do when she was a little girl in Paris, Texas, when her dad forbid her to go. Like she was in a dream…

Chapter IV

As she slept, Mechi was subconsciously aware of the people hovering over her and talking. And of the cool, refreshing water being rubbed on her head. Even though she could hear, she could not distinguish things clearly. If she had somehow traveled to another time and another place, it must have been to the State of Confusion.

When she finally awoke, to everyone's relief, she immediately began to ask questions.

"Would someone mind telling me where we are? I seem to be a ... bit confused."

Ha! If *that* isn't the understatement of the year!

"We are in Moray's abode," the one who claimed to be Queen Mary said.

"And where exactly is that?" Mechi asked.

"Why, at St. Andrew's Golf Course, of course!" Moray said, smiling at the quaint repetition of the words.

"Near Aberdeen?" Mechi asked.

"Certainly, 'tis near Aberdeen," Moray said, frustrated at the ignorance of this woman. "Unless it's been moved and they forgot to inform me."

"And Aberdeen is ... " Mechi hesitated momentarily ... "in Scotland?"

"You're bloody right we're in Scotland!" he shouted. "And don't you go thinking just because you're some French tart that you can get by with your little innocent act. We just got over a war with France, so recently I'm not even sure yet who won, and for all I know you could be a bloody spy!"

Mechi laughed. She had been accused of being a lot of things in her life, but a spy was not one of them. At least not that she could remember.

"And you are Moray?" Mechi asked. "And he is Lord Darnley? And she— she is truly Mary, Queen of the Scots?"

Mechi thought maybe if she kept questioning them long enough they would admit who they *really* were.

"Yes, milady. We have already made that quite clear to you."

This was completely nuts. Mechi wondered what she had to do to wake up. This had gone on long enough—too long. She was ready for reality. For Brian. For crazy Liz. She would even be glad to see Robert! Now that was a frightening thought. It showed just how desperate she really was.

Mechi tried to retrace history in her mind. She had always been fascinated by the subject, especially British history. She got that from her mother. Even though she had died when Mechi was quite young, she could still hear her mother's claims to be descended from King James I.

Ha! Mechi thought. A lot of good that would do her now! If she remembered her facts right, Queen Mary was James I's mother. And here she was, sitting with the very same woman who vowed she was Mary, Queen of the Scots.

As her mind raced ahead, Mechi realized that Mary, this woman who had taken her in and bathed her fevered brow—if she somehow *was* Queen Mary— would quite literally lose her head before too long. And Darnley? He married the queen. And his fate …

Was history right? Was it really Queen Mary who had Darnley, her own husband, put to death?

"*You* are Darnley?" Mechi cried out in shock. If he was, he was doomed. His days were numbered. "*Lord* Darnley? The man who will wed Queen Mary?"

"Hush!" he ordered, then almost violently placed his hand over her mouth to silence her. "You must not speak of this to anyone. We shall discuss it later." He looked around nervously, hoping no one else had heard her question. Fortunately, the others seemed to be discussing Mechi's plight, so it was possible her question had gone unnoticed. "How did you know?" he whispered to her.

Darnley had worked hard to set his plan in motion. Queen Elizabeth of England, Mary's cousin, thought he had come to Scotland to help her achieve her goals. She had heard that Mary wanted to take over the rule of both Scotland and England, and she had vowed it would never happen. So, she sent Lord Darnley, whom she trusted implicitly, to deal with Mary.

"I—I can't tell you," Mechi said. "Just trust me, please. If you will let me help you, I can save your life. But you must not wed Queen Mary!"

"And by what authority do you presume to tell me what to do?"

Oh, my! Mechi thought. Now what do I do? I don't know how it has happened, but if this is actually my life—not a dream—then somehow I have found my way back to the year—let's see. Mary appears to be quite young. She has not yet married Lord Darnley. It must be… Somewhere… around… could it be? About 1560? Impossible!

She searched in vain for Robert Keith. Perhaps, if they could be alone, she could try to explain it all to him. For some strange reason, she felt he *might* understand. How absurd! Where would she begin? How could she tell him? None of this made any sense; not even to her.

Mechi's entire countenance went completely pale. Soon she had Lord Darnley's arms around her, trying to support her, as she fainted dead away.

"Your majesty!" Darnley called out. "Come quickly! The—Mechi—has collapsed! Perhaps she is dead!"

Queen Mary and the other men were soon at her side, all fanning her quite vigorously.

"What did you do to her?" Queen Mary demanded of Darnley. "What harm have you caused her?"

"None, your majesty," Darnley said in his own defense. "I swear, I did nothing to her."

Mechi began to moan as soon as she regained consciousness. When the queen saw that she was adequately revived, she said, "Moray, fetch the carriage! Quickly! We must get this poor creature to the palace at once. Surely my physician will be able to minister to her needs."

Mechi tried to focus on her surroundings as Robert Keith carried her to the coach. If only, she thought, I could be in his arms under different circumstances. Queen Mary ordered him to set her on one seat, and she assumed the facing seat. She placed a cover over her and instructed the driver, "To Holyrood! Quickly, but carefully. Be off!"

Through a fog of her own mind far denser than that on the golf course, Mechi heard Robert Keith's deep sexy voice.

"Why don't we take her to our place instead? It's so much closer than Edinburgh."

"A splendid idea!" Mary agreed. "And I'm sure the Marischal won't mind. I haven't yet seen him since my return, and it's high time I pay homage to him."

Mechi wondered at her choice of words. Who was this *marshall*? Was this *home* the Dunnottar he had described to her? Was it really a castle? She smiled as she thought that today—or tomorrow—or whenever—centuries later, men still considered their home their castle. And why, she wondered, would the queen, if indeed she was the queen, want to pay homage to some mere man? Or was he someone special? And if so, what made him special? Surely it was for something more than fathering Robert Keith, but then perhaps that was enough to make him special. Certainly, she had already decided that Robert Keith was special! Let *that other Robert* stay in his own little world. He certainly couldn't hold a candlestick to *this* Robert!

Mechi clung to her head, the questions causing the pain to increase until it became almost unbearable. She felt like screaming, but the noise would probably only make it worse.

The carriage bumped and swayed over the pathway. The constant *clip-clop* of the horses pulling them sounded like a beating drum as they went. She wanted to understand all of this, but not now. All she wanted to do was get to a nice soft bed, get a good hot bath and a good night's sleep. She would try to fit the pieces together tomorrow. Or, maybe when she woke up the whole thing would be all over.

Mechi slept, fitfully and restlessly, as the coach jogged along. Mary sat, watching her, wondering exactly who or what this strange woman was. She had never seen anyone quite like her. She smiled when Mechi awoke and tried to assume an upright position.

Mechi still cradled her head, hoping beyond hope, that somehow everything she had just seen was nothing more than the rest of her dream. It couldn't be reality. Nothing this far-fetched. She rubbed her eyes and looked around.

"You're still here?" she asked the now-familiar woman seated across from her.

"Of course," Mary answered. "With the coach still moving towards Dunnottar, where else would I be?"

"And Lord Keith?" Mechi asked.

Mechi saw a mischievous light in her eyes. She wondered if she could trust this woman. *This crazy woman who thinks she is Queen Mary*! For the moment, she saw no alternative.

Seeing that the stranger was indeed her captive, Mary decided it was her turn to question her.

"You said your name is Mechi?" she asked.

"Yes," Mechi said. "Actually, it is Michelle. Michelle Jeanotte, but I prefer Mechi."

"Michelle Jeanotte?" Mary asked, a spark of pleasure evident in her eyes. "You are French, no? *Parlez vous francais*?"

"No," Mechi said, understanding the phrase, but that was about the extent of her knowledge of the language. "My great-grandfather was reared in France, but that is the extent of my French connection."

'Your name is *Michelle Jeanotte*," Mary said with a stiff French accent, "but you speak no French?"

"That is quite right," Mechi said. Suddenly, she wondered, if this really is Queen Mary, shouldn't I be addressing her as "Your majesty?"

"You have lived in Scotland all your life?" Mary asked, continuing her interrogation. "Near here?"

"Actually, no," Mechi said, trying to make sense of her answers as well as of her thoughts. "I grew up on a large ranch. My father raised cattle and horses."

"And where was that?" Mary asked.

Before she considered how it would appear, she replied. "The ranch was just outside a small town just across the border." She stopped. If this was about 1560, there was no such place as Texas yet. No Mexican border. How could she effectively explain what she was referring to? In desperation she blurted out the name of the small Texas town which was closest to the ranch. "Paris!" She realized immediately that she had just made a gross error.

Mary looked puzzled. She shook her head, wondering if this woman was mad, or if part of her mind was missing, to say the very least.

"Your name is Michelle Jeanotte, which certainly sounds French. Your wearing apparel is quite unlike any I have ever seen. You say you are not French, yet you grew up in Paris." She threw her hands up in despair. "Lady, Mechi, Michelle Jeanotte, whoever you are, you are the most insane person I have ever met in my life! And believe me, I have seen more than my share of mad people!"

"You may be quite right," Mechi agreed. "I have no explanation for my presence here, nor how I came to be."

Speaking softly, she confided in Mechi. "I had so hoped we could be friends. You no doubt know that I just returned from France myself. After the death of the dauphin, God rest his soul, I was so alone. I thought it would be different when I returned to my homeland. Yet there have been none who have truly befriended me. The closest thing I have to a friend is Darnley. Oh, of of course Moray, but he is my cousin."

For no apparent reason, Mechi giggled.

"I do not find it amusing!" Queen Mary snapped.

"I'm sorry," Mechi said apologetically. More to see her reaction than from royal etiquette—about which she knew nothing—she added, "Your majesty."

Much to Mechi's surprise, Mary did not so much as flinch an eye at the address. She seemed, Mechi thought, quite accustomed to it. More and more Mechi was becoming convinced that this really was Mary Stuart, the Queen of the Scots. Yes, it appeared that she was actually in Scotland. In…

"Could you tell me, please, your majesty, what the date is? I—seem to have lost track of time."

Lost track of time! Right! That wasn't the only thing she had lost track of. Her own sanity came to mind.

"'Tis the twelfth of October," Mary answered matter-of-factly.

Mechi hesitated, then asked, "And the year?"

Now Mary laughed. She could understand someone not knowing the day it was, but to falter over the year?

"You can't be serious," Mary said.

"Oh, but, your majesty, I have never been more serious in my life!"

Seeing that she was indeed troubled over the issue, Mary hastened to reply. "My dear, it is the year of our Lord one thousand five hundred and sixty one. Now, surely that does not surprise you."

You can't imagine how much of a surprise that is, Mechi wanted to say, but hoping to avoid questions simply thanked the queen for the information.

"As I asked, might we be friends?" Queen Mary repeated.

"I'd like that," Mechi said. "I think I might need a friend, too." She knew that if what she suspected was true, that she had somehow entered the fog in nineteen-ninety-seven and come out of the fog in fifteen-sixty-one, the one thing she needed more than anything else was a friend. Someone who, even though they didn't understand her, would accept her for who she was. For that matter, time would soon prove, if she remembered her history right, Queen Mary was going to be in urgent need of a friend.

As the carriage bumped along on its way to... Mechi wondered where this intriguing, handsome man came from. He had called it *Dunnottar.* Why did she feel such a strong pull towards him? She was drawn to him like iron to a magnet. Was it just his handsome face? His masculine muscular physique? Or was it those incredible green eyes which danced with mischief?

"This man who offered to take us to his home," Mechi began to question Queen Mary.

Sensing her question, Mary said, laughing, "You mean Robert? Little Robbie? Why, from Dunnottar, of course. He's a Keith!"

As if on cue once again, Robert Keith rode up on his horse alongside them.

"I'll go on ahead and tell Mums you're coming," he called out to them. As he disappeared, Mechi wished she could get out and ride with him. Maybe, if she was on a horse, she could feel some sense of belonging. Oh, yes! If she was mounted on a horse with her arms around Lord Robert Keith, Viscount of Kintore, she could

"Dunnottar?" Mechi asked, trying to pick the conversation with Mary up where definitely feel like she belonged!they had left off. It sounds...wonderful." As the name rolled off her tongue, there was something as magical about the name as there was about Robbie Keith himself.

Robbie! It brought a smile to her lips. She could not imagine anyone daring to call her *other Robert* Robbie! He would turn over in his grave! Ha! It would be centuries before he would even be born.

"Aye, it is," Queen Mary exclaimed. "And the lot of the Keith family is the most divine. Sir William, Robbie's father, is my guardian. He's known to be the wealthiest man in all of Scotland, yet I should love him as a father were he completely penniless."

Queen Mary broke into laughter at the very idea of *any* Keith being poor. They were far too cunning and wise to ever face such a destiny.

"Sir William—he's a laird of a multitude of residents, you know—is the kindest man…" She hesitated, her eyes rolling about as she thought of him. "He's said to be so kind to his charges that they pay him taxes, even when there are none owed him."

Mechi stared out the side window of the carriage, trying to take everything in at once. The scenery was beautiful, breathtaking, too much to absorb in one brief glance.

"There!" Queen Mary shouted excitedly. "Look to the other side!"

Mechi turned to see the view out the other window. Her eyes grew as big as frisbees at what she saw. There, looming closer and closer, was a high, stony cliff. At the top stood a stone wall, giving the impression of an old fort.

"Wow!" Mechi exclaimed. "That makes the Alamo look like—an ant farm! What is it?"

Mary laughed at Mechi's enthusiasm. She felt their kindred spirits as they gazed, in awe, together. No matter how many times she saw this massive site, it would always amaze her, just as it did Mechi.

"That, my dear Mechi, is Dunnottar."

Mechi's mouth was agape. "That—that is the Keith's *home*?" she stammered in disbelief. "They *live* there?"

"Yes," Mary replied. "Although I do not understand what you mean by the *Alamo*. What is that?"

Mechi hedged. She still couldn't explain Texas, let alone the Alamo, to this monarch.

"It's—a shrine near my home."

"Near Paris?" Mary asked, puzzled.

Mechi nodded.

"But I've never seen it," Mary said. "Nor even, I'm quite sure, heard of it."

"I'm sure you haven't," Mechi said softly, but the queen was quick to hear her in spite of the low volume.

"And why is that?" Mary asked.

Again Mechi hesitated. "It's not a well-known shrine," she hurried to explain. "Sort of a religious monument."

"Well," Mary said, "it sounds intriguing. Next time I travel to Paris I shall be certain to look for it."

Yes, Mechi thought, *you do that. And see how far you get! I dare you.*

The horses strained as they pulled the carriage up the steep pathway, through dark tunnels which seemed to be hollowed out of the very rock itself, up to the top of the islet, which protruded out into the sea, causing a most eerie feeling to flow through Mechi's veins. She pinched herself to make sure she was awake. She winced from the hurt.

As they rode, veering from side to side, Mary began to tell Mechi some of the history of the Keith family. All-too-soon they were at the top. A soldier or guard, clad in strange woolen knickers and a tweed jacket and who toted a sword, bowed before the coach, allowing them entry through the opening in the wall.

"Stop the coach!" Mechi cried out.

"What is it?" Mary asked, afraid of the look on Mechi's face. Thinking it was one of recognition she said, "So you have been here before."

"No!" Mechi assured her. "Never! I have never seen anything like this in my life. Not even in the movies."

"Movies?" Mary asked.

Mechi gave a wave of her hand. "I'll tell you about them some other time." Under her breath she added, "maybe."

"It is…" Mechi gasped. She was speechless. There were no words to describe it. Robert's attempts paled by comparison to the real thing.

"Wonderful?" Mary asked, trying to help Mechi put her feelings into words. "Grand?"

"Oh, yes!" Mechi said. "And so much more!"

"May we proceed now?" Mary asked.

"Of course," Mechi said. "I'm sorry. It's just…"

"I know," Mary said sympathetically. "It is hard to take it all in at once, is it not?"

"Yes, he is," Mechi said absent-mindedly, seeing Lord Robert Keith, Viscount of Kintore, there to welcome them.

At St. Andrew's Country Club near Aberdeen, Maryland, Liz went to the information desk for the umpteenth time.

"Still no word from Ms. Jeanotte?" she asked.

"I'm sorry, ma'am," the attendant said. "We have sent someone out to try to find her. She was here, earlier. In fact, she was quite upset that you were late."

A young man came back into the clubhouse, panting breathlessly.

"I've looked everywhere," he said. "She seems to have disappeared completely. All that is left of her is this."

In his hand he held a golf ball and a No. 9 iron.

"I know this is hers," he said. "No one else has one like it."

"Do you want to wait to see if she comes back?" the attendant asked Liz.

"We can keep paging her."

"No," Liz answered nervously. "I really have to get back home."

She fiddled nervously with her fingers.

"Is her jacket here?" Liz queried. "The one she wore yesterday? The green one?"

Liz had spent time secretly studying Mechi yesterday. It was the reason Liz *had* to find Mechi. Mechi had not even noticed when she had slipped the ring into her pocket from behind her to keep it away from that thief who had threatened her.

"I don't think so," Lori said. "She had it on when she went out on the greens this morning. Why do you ask?"

"I…um…accidentally put something in it by mistake last night. I have to have it back. I can't survive without it!"

"I don't know what to tell you," Lori said. "I'm sure she will be back eventually. I will ask her about it as soon as she comes back in."

Before she had finished the statement, the crazy Liz was out the door.

"Look!" the attendant called out. "She left a book on the table! Go catch her!"

The young man ran to the door and looked in every direction. There was no sign of the woman.

"She's gone, too," he said, shrugging his shoulders in bewilderment. "Just like Mechi, she disappeared."

Lori went and got the book.

"*Garner Garton's Needle*," she read from the cover. "Ever hear of it?"

"Not me," he said, then went about his work.

The attendant opened the book. Her eyes filled with wonder as she saw the signature of the author, "To my dear friend and beloved sovereign, Liz. Nicholas Udall." The date under his name was 8 May, 1559.

"Weird!" she exclaimed. She carefully ran her fingers along the outer edges of the pages. "It looks brand new."

Brian sat there, sipping on his hot cup of tea, shaking his head.

"I feel just like I've walked into the Twilight Zone. Mechi, Mechi! Come out, come out, wherever you are!"

Like he suspected, no one appeared.

Chapter V

As a horde of people of all ages came rushing at them, Mechi tried to sort the images out, but they all seemed to blend together into one fuzzy being.

"Please come inside," someone said. Mechi turned towards the voice, relieved to see that it belonged to her spell-binding Robert Keith. *Queen Mary is right,* she thought as she studied him. *"Robbie" does seem to fit.*

She gladly took his extended hand and climbed out of the coach. They made their way through the crowd to the huge, old overpowering stone building. He pushed the door open and waited for her to pass through it.

As she entered the house, which was indeed a castle, she realized that she had indeed become part of another time zone. *If ever there was a time warp,* she thought, *this is the ultimate one.* She rubbed her eyes, hoping to see things differently if they were cleared, yet afraid if she did, Robbie would disappear.

"I told Mums you were coming," Robbie said, his voice soft with compassion and concern.

Mechi smiled faintly. She wondered what else he had told his "Mums" about her. Surely Robbie Keith found her as strange as she found all of them.

"She has the solar readied," he said, leading her through a long, narrow corridor.

Mechi stared at the room. There was a warm, inviting flame in the fireplace. It seemed to cast mystical, magical images around as it danced freely hither and yon.

"Come," Robbie invited. "Why don't you lie down? It appears that whatever has happened to you, it has caused quite a blow."

She watched Robbie as he made his way carefully to a candle and lit it. With more light, she could easily see the pieces of furniture which occupied the room. What had he called it? A solar?

"My god!" Mechi exclaimed. "you've brought me to your bedroom!"

Robbie smiled, a clever, almost sinister grin. He was quite drawn to this—creature. He could think of more terrible things than to have her in his *bedroom.* But he was, after all, a gentleman, and he knew his place, and for the moment, at least, it was with this woman in his bedroom.

"I'm afraid you've assumed a wee bit too much, lassie," he said, a twinkle peeking through the corner of his eye. "You are in a *bedroom*, but I'm fearful 'tis not mine."

"Pity," Mechi said, then smiled.

Robbie returned the smile. It was the first time he had seen her with that impish grin. True, she was not like anything he had ever seen before, but she was definitely worth finding out about.

Mechi was relieved when he did not reply. She knew she should not have said it. She had to watch how she spoke to him. After all, he *was* a lord.

Before she realized what was happening, she felt his arms gently go around her waist as he helped her to the huge canopy bed. As he released her, she sank into the deep, thick layers of feather and down comforters and sensed that it was soft clear to the floor.

Gazing up, Mechi saw the rich tapestry which covered the canopy frame on the top of the bed. She had never been in such a bed. She thought of her childhood friend, Pam. Pam had a white canopy bed—the kind you buy from the Sears catalog—with dainty pink ruffled bedspreads and covers. That was the closest thing this bed resembled. She remembered thinking that it wasn't fair when Pam had moved away; she would never be able to sleep in such a bed again. But that was before she knew about *this* bed!

"I'll be leavin' ye on your own so you can rest a mite," Rbobie said.

Mechi looked up at him, her eyes pleading for him to stay. She suddenly felt very alone. Like she felt when her father died. She had no one close to her in her *other world*, so if she was really here—if this wasn't a dream—there was no one she would rather have near her than Lord Robbie Keith.

"Robbie?" she asked shyly.

"Yes, lassie," he said, looking at her tenderly. "What is it?"

"Would you mind terribly staying here with me? I mean, things seem so strange."

Robbie threw his head back, his long red hair flowing and shimmering in the firelight, and laughed heartily.

"You think things seem strange?" he asked. "I don't mean to be speakin' ill of ye, lassie, but ye seem a wee bit odd yourself."

Mechi felt the color rise in her face. Of course she must seem strange to him. One thing was certain: he was not apt to run into another person just like her. No, considering her present circumstances, she was definitely one of a kind.

He continued speaking, studying her intensely. "I'll be glad to stay at your side, as long as ye wish," he said.

Mechi felt slightly uncomfortable at his offer. Had he read more into her request than she intended? She would have to set him straight, but that could be done later. For the moment, she really was tired. After all, it's a long, long way…

"To Tipperary," she sang softly as her eyes closed in sleep.

"Most peculiar lassie," Robbie said, pulling a chair up along side the bed. "But truly fascinating." And he sat, his eyes glued to her face, watching her as she slept.

Mechi began to wake up, then put her head back down on her pillow.

"That's the craziest dream I've ever had," she mumbled, rubbing her eyes to get them to focus on her surroundings. Once she could see them clearly, her dream did not disappear. Was she still asleep? Was that really Lord Robert Keith sitting beside the monster of a bed? She could hear his voice—too clearly. Who was he talking to?

"Ssh!" she heard a woman say. "We mustn't frighten the poor little thing."

Mechi lay with her eyes closed, her ears straining to hear what they said.

"Do you know what happened to her?" the woman asked. "Or who she is? Or where she's from?"

"Nay," Robbie answered softly. "She did not tell us a thing. Although Queen Mary did say she said she was reared in Paris."

"So she's French?" the woman, whom Mechi assumed was most likely Robbie Keith's *Mums,* asked.

"Not so's you'd notice," Robbie said. "True, she does have a strange accent to her speech, but it's not like any French I've ever heard. And Queen Mary, she says when she asked her if she spoke French, she said 'Not a word.' It's the oddest thing, Mums, but I find myself completely taken with the lassie."

"Ye'd best be takin' things a wee bit slow, least 'til we know somethin' more 'bout the lass. I must admit, I've never in all my life seen anyone quite like her. She looks to have some breeding, but her attire is—why, it's worse than the poor who come to fetch their vittles for the day."

"Now, Mums," Robbie said, laughing slightly as he spoke, "isn't it true that it's been you who've sought a wife for me for the last four years? Now that I've found me a woman who could offer the intrigue and excitement I've sought all the while, you're tellin' me that I must watch my step? Women! I'll never understand the lot o' ye if I live to be a hundred-and-three!"

"And well you might," Mrs. Keith said. "Why, your grandpapa, since he got over his blight, he just seems to get stronger and stubborner with each passin' day. While it's true there's two dates entered in the church records for his christening, still he's well past ninety. And to watch him, he's not fixin' to kick up his heels for a good long while yet."

"Reckon as how that'll give me about enough time to figure this one out," Robbie said. "Let's see, I'm twenty-seven now, and if I live to be a hundred-and-three, that's…"

"Seventy-six years," Mechi volunteered. "Think that's long enough to *figure me out?*"

Robbie went over to the side of the bed and stared down at the stranger. He was pleased that the impish grin he had seen on one previous occasion was still there.

"Aye," he said, smiling down at her, "I tell ye, Mums, she's more excitin' than a wee whisp o' any fool Irish leprechaun."

Mechi tried to sit up, but she did so slowly, just in case she felt faint again. She was always a tough little number, and she had never fainted in her life. Until today. But then she'd never had another day quite like this one before, either.

"I should be getting home," Mechi said before she realized that she didn't have a home to go to. "I don't want to be a burden to you. You've already been too kind."

"Don't be ridiculous," the countess said. "You are no bother. Besides, you in no condition to be traveling anywhere."

Mechi was suddenly overcome with fear. What if this kind-hearted woman *had* turned her away? Where would she go? What would she do? The only other person she knew, even the slightest, was Queen Mary. Even with her lack of knowledge about protocol, she realized you don't just invite yourself to sponge off the reigning monarch of the country.

Mechi laughed, softly at first, then hilariously. She thought of the homeless who had camped outside the White House in nearby Washington, D.C. Well, if they could set up camp in the president's front yard, maybe she *could* do the same at the royal palace in Scotland. Maybe it wasn't so far fetched after all.

"Something we said?" Robbie asked, puzzled by her outburst.

"No," Mechi assured him. "I was just thinking. When I left—home this morning, I sure didn't know what was in store for the day."

Countess Keith smiled at the strange young woman. She always had a soft heart towards an outcast. Was this Mechi left to herself, given a cold shoulder by her family for some unknown reason? If so, she needed a mother. Every young woman needed a mother, no matter how old and independent they proclaimed to be.

"Queen Mary says you were reared in Paris," the countess said. It was more a question than a statement.

"Yes," Mechi said. "However, it is not the umm well-known Paris. This one is far away from the one where the Eiffel Tower stands. It is a very small town."

Mechi noticed that both Robert and his mother eyed her quizzically. Try as she might, she couldn't remember when the Eiffel Tower was built, but from the look on their faces, she knew it was well beyond the year 1561.

"She does speak in riddles, as you said," Lady Keith said, turning towards Robert, as if Mechi was not there.

Mechi wondered if perhaps she had suddenly become invisible. Then Robbie turned to her, smiling warmly, and she knew he could see her.

A helpless, confused young woman is what he saw. Ever since he had been a wee tot, he had taken pity on the less fortunate than himself. He recalled the time he brought a wounded fawn home from a hunting trip with his father. He had nursed him back to health, then turned him loose, only to have Lord Edzell from nearby shoot him. And the gall! To invite the Keiths to sup with them to partake of the poor critter.

Mechi reminded him terribly of the young deer. Perhaps he could help nurse her back to health, too, but this time he was older and much, much wiser. This time he knew he would have to protect her from the evil forces of the outside world— those who might want to steal her away or harm her.

Mechi sat up and put her legs over the side of the bed.

So far so good, she thought. Test the waters, something seemed to tell her. Slowly, carefully, she stood. She walked to the tiny window and looked out.

Water! All she could see was water. She wondered if they were on a deserted island. Everything seemed so foggy in her mind. Fog! She remembered the fog.

Well, she thought, *if this is an island I guess there is no one I've ever met I would rather be marooned with than the handsome, beguiling Lord Robbie Keith.*

"Do you like the view?" Robert asked.

"It's beautiful!" Mechi exclaimed, meaning it. The water was so pure, so clean, so bright.

"It's as if the fog lifted just for you," Robert said. "It was as thick as porridge before you appeared. As soon as you set foot on the fiddlehead it became as clear as a bell."

"Fiddlehead?" Mechi asked.

"Aye," Lady Keith said. "'Tis what they call this place."

"But I thought Mary—her majesty—said it is called *Dunnottar*."

"Aye," Lady Keith explained, "the castle itself is called Dunnottar, but the land it's set on is called a fiddlehead. See?" She pointed towards the mainland. "It is connected by one small neck to the mother soil."

Mechi did not hear the door open as Queen Mary quietly entered the solar. She was just in time to hear Mechi say, "There are so many things I do not know. Thank you kindly for your patience, Mrs. Keith."

Mary snickered, tucking her chin down into her high pleated collar to try to hide it.

"Mary!" Mechi exclaimed. "I didn't hear you come in. You should warn a guy before you sneak up on 'em. Now, would you mind telling me what is so funny?"

"It's just," Mary said, hiding her mouth behind her hand, "I have never heard anyone call the countess *Mrs. Keith*!"

Mechi swallowed hard. How many gaffes would she make before her time here was at an end? Or would it ever end? Was there a way out of this dilemma? And if there was, did she want it?

"Um, your majesty?" she asked, eyeing Robbie's *Mums* to see if that was correct. She was greeted with a firm shaking of the woman's head.

"That refers only to the queen," she said.

"Would someone just tell me before I make a complete jackass out of myself?" Mechi shouted.

"Why, I never!" the countess said, slapping her hands over her ears to prevent her from hearing any more such language from a—lady? It was doubtful that anyone who would have such a vocabulary was a *lady*.

"Begging your pardon, ma'am," Mechi said, "but I do seem to be a bit confused by the surroundings. I really can't explain how I happened to get here in the first place. I didn't mean any disrespect."

"None taken," Lady Keith replied. "At least if you cease speaking with such a vile tongue there will be no offense taken. Why, if you were *my* daughter, I should wash out your mouth with lye!"

"Yuck!" Mechi sputtered, making an awful face. "I wouldn't like that."

"Then you shall speak like a lady," the countess said. "As to how you should address me, since my husband is the earl marischal, he is to be referred to as 'My Lord.' As his wife, the countess, you may call me 'My Lady.' Robert here," she said, nodding to her son, "is our eldest son, so he is automatically dubbed a viscount and you may call him 'Lord.'"

Mechi turned to the handsome gentleman she had become very fond of in such a few short hours. She winked at him as she bowed, then said, "I would like to take this opportunity to express my gratitude for your concern and aid in my— time of trial, *Lord Robbie*."

The room filled with snickers. Never had anyone ever called Sir Robert Keith, Viscount of Kintore, *Lord Robbie*, but somehow it seemed to fit him quite well.

"Have you no recollection at all of what happened to you?" Lady Keith asked when she regained her composure. "Queen Mary and Robert said you seemed most shaken when they came upon you. They said you stated that you were to have an appointment with Elizabeth."

"That's right," Mechi said, trying to remember just what had occurred earlier in the day. She should have known when that crazy Liz woman called and was so insistent that this wouldn't be a normal day.

"Someone called me and asked me to meet them at the golf course. She wanted me to give her an emergency lesson."

"A lesson in golfing?" Robert asked. "From a woman?"

"You find that strange?" Queen Mary asked. She was, after all, on the golf course herself when Mechi had come to them. "I know, I know. A woman can do ontly the things a man deems proper for her. Well, I shall tell you right here and now that I shall choose to do whatever *I* deem proper! And I am quite certain that Mechi will do the same."

Robert glanced at Mechi. Yes, he was sure she would do whatever she pleased. He knew nothing of the women's liberation movement, but if he had, he would have selected Mechi as its CEO.

"Enough!" Lady Keith scolded. "Let the poor girl rest. It is obvious she is suffering from—something. Why, anyone with their wits about them would know you could not stand on the links at St. Andrews and *call* Elizabeth and expect her to hear. That is absurd!"

A look of discovery spread across Lady Keith's face. *Much like a lightbulb above the image of a cartoon character*, Mechi thought. She smiled as she pictured, instead, a lighted candle above the countess's head. Yes, given the circumstances it was much more appropriate.

"I know!" Lady Keith exclaimed. "She has been stricken! The poor lass is hysterical! She has no memory of her past."

Lady Keith went to Mechi's side and stroked her hair like you would that of a little child.

She thinks I have amnesia, Mechi thought, *except that they have obviously never heard of that malady, either. Instead, they attribute the loss of one's memory to hysteria. Well, I am not hysterical, although God knows I have plenty of reason to be.* She laughed inwardly as she thought that *historical* would be a better way to describe her than *hysterical.* To be cast back in years like she had been was something straight out of a Steven Spielberg film. She wondered, if and when she returned to 1997, if the strange Liz would still be waiting for her at St. Andrew's Country Club, just outside Aberdeen, Maryland, to welcome her "Back to the Future."

Her thoughts were interrupted as the door swung open and a very plain-looking woman entered, carrying a tray of cups, scones and a teapot.

"Tea time," she announced, setting the tray on a small table near Mechi.

"That's what got me into this mess!" Mechi sputtered under her breath. "Tee time!"

Chapter VI

A woman hurried into the solar, her arms laden with tons of petticoats and a brilliant red frock slung over her arm. Her hands were outstretched directly in front of her, and were bearing an old-fashioned corset. The strings from the garment were trailing on the floor, and just as she came through the door her foot caught on one of the ties and she fell flat on her face, the clothes flying in every direction as if they were spring-propelled.

"Oh, my lady!" she exclaimed. "I'm ever so sorry, ma'am." Her face was crimson and she burst into tears. "I've went and done it again, haven't I, ma'am? Oh, you'll be sendin' me away 'fore the week's out, and then whatever shall I do?"

Mechi stifled a laugh as she watched the scene. It reminded her of something that would have occurred in *Alice in Wonderland*. That thought caused her to ponder the well-known story written by Lewis Carroll. Had it even been written yet? She shrugged her shoulders and quietly said to herself, "Probably not."

Lady Keith smiled tenderly at the young woman, who was struggling to get to her feet and gather the strewn items up again.

"Don't you go fretting about it, Ann," she said. "I'm sure you're just nervous yet. It's a new place, a new post and all. Why, in no time at all you'll be serving the queen herself."

"Oh, no, my lady!" Ann protested. "I shan't never be able to do the likes o' that. Why, I just know I'd pour the tea all of the front o' her highness."

They were all laughing at the girl by now. She was the epitome of gracelessness.

"A real *klutz*!" Mechi remarked.

Robert turned to look at her. "What is a *klutz*?" he asked. "Can't say as I've heard of one before."

A *klutz* is a … Oh!" she cried out in exasperation. "I don't know! *I'm* a *klutz*!"

"In that case," Robert said, "you are a very lucky young lass, Ann. If the—

Mechi— is a *klutz,* you are most fortunate, indeed. I cannot imagine her to be anything terrible."

He grinned broadly at Mechi as he spoke. The Cheshire pussycat, Mechi thought. Perhaps she was in indeed in the land of Alice. If not, Lewis Carroll no doubt know about these people when he formulated his own characters.

"*The* Mechi," Robert had called her. That was at least the second time that she had heard him call her that. Mechi bit her tongue. The only other person she had ever heard of being called *the anybody* was Donald Trump, the mega-millionaire who nearly went broke in Atlantic City. Ivana, his ex-wife, always called him *the Donald.* Maybe that was her forte, too, to be known as *the Mechi.* For some reason it made her feel safe. She smiled at him, speaking a silent word of thanks for his compassion. He was right, she knew. She was as strange to them as they were to her. Perhaps even stranger.

That whole world seemed so far away now. Mechi wondered if she had ever really existed there, or was that all a dream? Or was this a dream? Or were both lives a nightmare? Perhaps she was just a figment of someone's imagination. Maybe that imagination was strong enough to cause her to be.

"Robert," Lady Keith said, interrupting Mechi's pensive mood and taking her son by the arm as she pulled him towards the door. "We should leave Ann here alone to help our guest prepare to sup with us."

Robert obediently followed his mother, but out of the corner of her eye Mechi saw him turn to take one last peek at her before he pulled the door shut.

Mechi felt Ann's piercing eyes on her as she lifted the garment onto the bed and began laying them out in order. She held the corset out first.

"Most times, lady, I'd have a bath drawed for ya, but there's not much time now or we'll be late to dine. You slept a long while. Must have been some trip you took."

Yes, Mechi thought, *it sure was a trip! That damned root*!

"Let's get you out o' the—whatever ya call them *things* you're sportin'," Ann said, glaring at the jeans and GUESS sweatshirt Mechi still had on. "I've never seen the likes o' it. 'Tis a wonder Lord Robert even brought ya' home, much less took to ya like 'e did."

Mechi felt the color rise to her cheeks. She had felt an undeniable attraction to the younger Keith man, but she was sure someone of his obvious status had no interest in the likes of her. Why, she was certainly not royalty. Not even close to it. She would have to set him straight…

An alarm went off inside Mechi's brain. There was, she was sure, more to Lord Robbie Keith than met the eye. She couldn't put her finger on it, but there was something almost devious—even deceptive—about this Scotsman who seemed too good to be true. She remembered her father telling her, "If something seems too good to be true, it usually is." So, was that the case with Lord Robbie Keith, Viscount of Kintore? It was just a sudden feeling she had, with no logical explanation, but then why, oh why, should anything here be logical?

Mechi laughed. What would she tell him? If she told him the truth, as she knew it, he would have her hauled away to a dungeon or some such thing. Maybe he'd have her head cut off for being a witch. No, she couldn't risk the consequences of *coming clean* with anyone. At least not yet. Perhaps in time.

"Come on, missy," Ann said, holding the corset out for Mechi. "Time's a wastin'."

"You expect me to get into that thing?" Mechi asked.

"Yes, 'm," Ann answered. She did not leave any room for argument, just went over to Mechi and began to pull at her sweatshirt. In no time at all it was off and she stood there in her jeans and bra.

"Now that's about the craziest contraption I ever seen," Ann said, covering her mouth to hide the gasp that escaped despite her efforts. "Why, it don't half cover nothin'."

"Never mind that," Mechi said. "Let's just get on with it."

"Yer not one o' them—*wicked ladies*—are ya?"

"You mean a whore?" Mechi said, laughing at the mere idea. "No, I assure you, Ann, I am not a whore. I have never been *kept* by a man."

"Whew!" she breathed out. "I was afeard fer Lord Robert. Why, he's a fine young lad. He deserves the best, and if it's you he's set his mind about, then I'll see to it that yer worthy o' him."

"Hold your horses!" Mechi said, exasperated at the assumption of a mere servant girl. "I have just barely met the man. You don't need to go getting any ideas about us. I'm sure Robbie—*Lord* Robbie—has plenty of eligible young women who have their sights set on him."

"I s'pects as how yer right, ma'am," Ann said, curtsying to Mechi. "I didn't have no business talkin' out o'turn like that. I'll not do it again, ya can be sure."

Mechi saw the sparks of fire that danced about in Ann's eyes as she talked about Robert Keith. It was obvious to Mechi that Ann *had the hots* for the lord of the castle.

"Isn't there any way you can just make an excuse for me to Lord and Lady Keith?" she asked Ann. "Just say I'm still very tired. Or that I don't feel well. I'm not sure I can…"

She stopped. She was about to say "pull it off," but that was another no-no. *Oh, dear, what have you gotten yourself into?*

"They're expectin' ya," Ann said. "let's get ya outa them—things ya got on—so's you can get dressed like a proper lady. Why, if I didn't know better, I'd think ya must o' been tryin' ta pass yerself off as a lad."

"It was nothing of the kind," Mechi said, unzipping her jeans and wiggling out of them.

She looked at the corset Ann was still holding out for her to put on. Lord, she sure never thought she'd end up in one of those outfits! She wasn't even sure how to begin putting it on.

"Give it here," she ordered Ann, who obeyed immediately. Mechi pulled the strings and ties out as far as they could go so it would be easier to get into it. Each tie was pulled through a tiny hole, worse than the high top riding boots she used to wear on the ranch.

She stepped into the loosened garment than began to pull it up—first over her legs, then her hips, and finally it was in place. It wasn't nearly as bad as she had feared. Actually, it felt much like the brace she had worn when she hurt her back when Commanche had thrown her several years ago. Or was it several hundred years ahead? She grabbed hold of her head, trying to sort things out, then trying to forget them. "Take one thing at a time," she heard her father's voice as he gave her that piece of advice over and over again when she was growing up. At least for the time being she didn't seem to have any other options.

Mechi unhooked her bra and removed it. She then began to pull the ties on the corset slightly and formed a careful bow at the top of her bust.

"Oh, no, ma'am," Ann said, shocked at her actions. "Ya mean ta tell me, ya don't know how to fix the rig? Here, let me give you a hand."

Ann untied the bow and began tugging as hard as she could, forcing the garment tighter and tighter.

Mechi felt the stiff stays poke into her ribs, causing her to cry out in pain.

"Stop!" she yelled. "That's enough!"

"Oh, no, ma'am," Ann argued. "Ye've only just begun."

Mechi hummed a few bars of the song she knew so well. "You've only just begun - to say you're sorry." The words came popping into her mind as she sang. Whoever wrote that song sure never imagined anything like this. Whatever the poor sucker was sorry for, it couldn't have been as bad as this.

Ann took hold of one of the ties and wrapped it around the poster on the big bed, securing it tightly in place. She then grabbed onto the other end of the tie and pulled, first on the tie itself and then on Mechi.

"That's enough!" Mechi screamed again. "It can't get any tighter! I'm not made that way!"

Ann stepped back, the tie wrapped around her wrist so she wouldn't lose any of the ground she had gained.

"Yes, ma'am, you'll be a sight for sore eyes now," she said. "Here, look fer yerself." She pointed to a mirror.

Mechi turned, straining against the end of the tie which was still fastened to the bed post, and stared at her image in the fuzzy mirror. It was not shiny and bright like a modern mirror, but she could definitely see what she looked like.

Wow! She never imagined she would ever look like that! The corset had pulled her waist in so it was smaller than Dolly Parton's. Even more amazing, it had forced the excess up to her bosom, creating a bust equally as impressive as Dolly's. Talk about an hourglass figure! The gang back home would never believe this. All her life she had been self-conscious because she had the smallest upstairs of anyone in her gym class. They should see her now!

"I'll just secure it fer ya so's it won't bust somethin' when you eat," Ann said.

Mechi gasped. She was supposed to *eat* with this thing on? There was no room for any food! She'd just have to fake it. Do the best she could. She could always use the excuse that she still didn't have much of an appetite since her… well, whatever it was that happened to her.

Mechi turned to the mirror and stared at herself. Ann had helped her into the pantaloons, the petticoats—all six of them—and finally the bright red dress. *A fitting color, considering she thinks I'm a whore*, Mechi mused.

The neckline plunged—about halfway to her navel, Mechi realized as she looked down. She wished she had one of Queen Mary's outfits with the high, pleated collar that framed her face. As she thought about it, every picture she could ever remember seeing of Queen Mary showed her with a collar like that. And Mary, she was sure, must have a corset, too. At least her figure, even as tall as she was, was quite shapely.

Mechi thought about their earlier encounter on the golf course. How in the world could *anybody* play golf in a get-up like this?

"Sit here," Ann said, pulling a stool out into the center of the room. "I'll tend to yer tresses."

Mechi walked to the stool, then groaned as she struggled to bend at the waist. In a sort of half-seated position, she sat stiffly as Ann brushed her hair.

"Not much o' it there," Ann remarked. "Why, there's less o' it than a man has. Did ya have the cooties?"

Mechi laughed. She supposed that if a person had the *cooties*, the only way to get rid of them would be to shave your head.

"No," she said. "I've never had the cooties. I just happen to like my hair this way. There's no fuss and bother with it."

"Guess yer right about that," Ann said, shaking her head in bewilderment.

"I'll show ya to the hall," Ann said, smiling at her handiwork. "I dare say, if Lord Robert had eyes fer ya afore, he'll be struck dumb at the sights o' ya now."

"I told you," Mechi warned, "no matchmaking."

"We'll see," Ann said simply. "Truth o' the matter is, even if there's somethin' strange 'bout ya, I kinda like ya. If'n he's got to find a lady, might as well have it be one I like."

"Thank you," Mechi said, then hastily added, "I think."

Mechi kept her eyes glued to Robbie as she made her grand entry. His eyes got as big as a silver dollar. Ha! He wouldn't have the foggiest idea of what a silver dollar looked like! *Foggy idea!* That stupid fog was what got her into this whole mess in the beginning.

"I must say," he said, coming towards her and extending his arm to escort her to the table, "you do not look the least bit strange now. Why, you are the most beautiful sight I have ever laid me eyes on."

He bowed deeply to her. She bowed in return, then realized that they obviously assumed that she was a proper lady; she should curtsy. She did so, quite well, in spite of the corset.

Mechi was sure she saw the countess give an evil eye to Lord Keith and shake her head at Robbie in warning. So, if she was going to capture the heart of the young lord she would have to get past his mother first.

Times really haven't changed that much, she thought, remembering Brad Gibbons, the young man who had taken her to the prom when she was a junior in high school. Her father warned her about "guys like him." She saw the same look on Mums Keith's face.

Mechi quickly scanned the room. Lord and Lady Keith were there, of course, as well as Queen Mary, Lord Darnley, the one they called Moray and several other young people. She knew instinctively they must be other members of the Keith clan; they all had the same piercing green eyes and the same bouncing red curls.

"The table is laid," a servant said, entering the room from a huge oak door.

With no further ado, Lord and Lady Keith led the way to the huge hall, followed by Queen Mary, who was on the arm of Darnley, then Moray with one of the Keith women on his arm, then Robbie and Mechi, and finally the other members of the family.

Mechi coughed, trying to catch her breath, as she viewed the long banquet table. What a spread!

She strained to sit on the chair Robbie gallantly pulled out for her. *At least chivalry started before this,* she thought. And it definitely wasn't dead.

As she sat at the table, she was terribly aware of the plunging neckline that had been chosen for her. She looked at Queen Mary and again wished she had her collar in preference to her own gown. She smiled when she saw the queen looking back at her.

"Are you feeling better, child?" the earl marischal asked. The warmth in his voice showed genuine concern. Perhaps she had an ally in him. She decided to put her best foot forward, hoping to impress him with her sincerity, and hope he wouldn't catch on to some *faux pas* she might make in her conversation.

"Yes, my lord," she said, dropping her eyes to the plate in front of her nervously. "I can't explain what came over me today at St. Andrews."

"Not to worry," he said, smiling at her. "I'm sure it will pass. You will spend the night here with us at Dunnottar. Perhaps by tomorrow you will feel well enough to
travel to Edinburgh. Mary—her majesty—is dead set on taking you there with her, although I tried my best to persuade her to allow you to stay here a while longer, until you are stronger."

Mechi saw Robbie studying her carefully. She wondered how she could persuade him to accompany them to Edinburgh. With him nearby she felt safe. Strange, yes, yet protected.

Mechi shivered, although she felt quite warm. Perhaps it was the thought of leaving Robbie that left her cold!

"Poor girl," Lady Keith said, seeing the shiver. "You must have caught a chill. You must avoid the grippe." She sounded her knife against the pewter plate, summoning a servant.

"Yes, my lady," the girl said, curtsying at Lady Keith's side. "You called for me?"

"Yes, Beth," she said. "Our guest seems to have a chill. Would you fetch her a shawl?"

"Right away, my lady," the girl said, again curtsying as she backed away. In no time at all she was back, wrapping a heavy woolen blanket around Mechi's shoulders.

"That should warm you nicely," Lady Keith said. She was not aware that Mechi heard her add, "And keep Robert's eyes off you as well."

Before she realized that she had done so, she winked at Robert, who was seated directly across the table from her. He winked back, playfully.

Mechi stared at his eyes. Never had she seen such intense, piercing eyes. It was as if he could look into her heart and see the pangs of desire she felt for him. There was definitely something mysterious behind those deep emerald eyes. What kind of a secret lay buried beneath them? A strong, driving force told her she *must* know more about this wonderful Scot, no matter what the cost.

Stop it! She warned herself. *There is no way you can get hooked on some dude from this—insane asylum. Sure, you never met anyone like him. How could you? Men like that don't exist anymore! Besides, as soon as you let yourself go, you'd end up being sent back to the twentieth century and you'd never see him again.*

She was suddenly aware of the conversation that was taking place between Queen Mary, Lord Keith, Darnley and Moray. They were discussing Queen Elizabeth.

It took a few moments for Mechi to figure out what was happening. Queen Elizabeth was the Queen of Great Britain when she—left. Oh, but of course! That was Queen Elizabeth the Second. They were talking about the *first* Queen Elizabeth.

She listened intensely as they discussed the politics of the day. Men! Maybe they weren't so different after all. It was, however, reassuring to realize that Queen Mary was doing an excellent job of holding her own in the conversation. Why, she was a true *women's libber*, just a few centuries ahead of her time.

She thought again of the fact that Queen Mary would eventually marry Darnley and then have him killed. At least that was the assumption which followed down through history, even though it seemed to her that Mary's involvement was never really proven.

She watched Lord Keith carefully. Could she trust him? *Really* trust him? She had to let someone know that they had to keep an eye on Queen Mary. Mary had said that Lord Keith was her guardian. It was perfect.

After they finished dining, which she did very sparingly to keep from breaking the ties on her corset and the seams of her gown, she would approach him. She must talk to him privately. She had to find a way to convince him to go to Edinburgh with them. He had to protect—who? Queen Mary? Darnley? All of them?

Mechi listened as Moray spoke. There was something so fascinating about the man. His speech was slow. Not a stutter, but more of a drawl. It was the kind of oration that when he said something you wanted to reach into his throat and pull the words out. She had heard any number of people who spoke that way, but with him it was something more. *Deja vu*, she thought, then smiled as she realized that she knew a least a few more French words than she had realized.

Find out more about him, she said silently, making a mental note on her brain. *See if you can figure out who he reminds you of.* As she continued studying him, even his movements and gestures seemed familiar.

Finally, when they had finished dining, they rose from the table. As the maid began to clear the table, Lady Keith remarked, "Be sure to guard the morsels for the poor."

Mechi went to Lord Keith's side, waiting for an opportunity to speak to him. When the others were busily engaged in heavy conversation, she pulled him down so she could whisper in his ear.

"My lord," she said softly, "I must speak with you in private."

He glared at her.

"That is most unusual," he said.

"I know, my lord, and I wouldn't ask, except that it is really important. It may be a matter of life and death."

"Very well," he said. "I will send for you after everyone has retired. Please listen for me."

Mechi sighed, pleased that she could confide in him. She felt as safe with him as she had with her own father. The only thing that would make it better would be if she could figure out some way for Robbie to go to Edinburgh, too.

Chapter VII

With the candles in the sconces extinguished, except for a few in the corridor which were well-protected by their surrounding iron casings, Mechi stood with the door to her chamber just slightly ajar. She looked up and down, as if to spot the ghost she felt might jump out at her at any moment. She slowly closed the door and went to the chair by the window. As she gazed out into the night, the moon cast an eerie shadow on the water below the fiddlehead.

She jumped when she heard a very light tap-tap-tap on the door. Even though she was expecting Lord Keith to send someone for her, the sound startled her.

Mechi hurried to pull the robe Ann had given her tight around her frame. The embers were still red in the fireplace, making it look like the room was filled with a blacklight. She went to the door and opened it, carefully, expecting to find one of the servants who would show her to Lord Keith's whereabouts.

"Please, let me come in. No one must see me here. This is most improper, but you sounded so…"

"Desperate?" Mechi asked, finishing his sentence. She had not expected Lord Keith himself to come to her quarters. But, he was here, and there was nothing to do but let him in to discuss the important issues at hand.

Lord Keith quietly crept inside, closing the door tightly behind him. He studied the young woman who stood in front of him. There was something disturbing about her. Perhaps his wife was right. They both sensed Robert fancied her, yet they must look out for his well-being. She was, he decided as he watched her, someone to be avoided. Still he knew he must find out what it was that she wanted to tell him. She had indeed sounded desperate.

Robert Keith heard someone moving about in the corridor. He went to the door from his own chamber and opened it just a crack to see who was out and about so late at night. It was most unusual, as the castle chilled quickly in the darkness, except for inside the individual room which each contained its own fireplace.

Sensing that it was the stranger, perhaps lost in the obscurity of the night, he wondered if he dared to offer her some assistance. If no one else was around… just to protect her… His mind raced ahead of his thoughts, knowing that he would like to follow her to her quarters if she was out there, but knowing he ought not do anything so bold.

His eyes popped open, his mouth fell agape as he saw his father. Whatever was he doing wandering about at this hour? He could not remember his father ever acting like this. He watched carefully, silently, as his father softly rapped on the stranger's door, then hastened to enter her abode.

Never would he dare tell anyone of this. He was positive his father had never been unfaithful to his mother, yet what could he be doing? He could not address the matter with his father. He certainly could not whisper his suspicions to his mother!

He admitted to himself that the peculiar young lassie had captivated him. But his father…?

Robert longed to go set his ear to the door, straining to hear what they could be discussing. Or were they discussing anything? No! There had to be a logical explanation for his father's behavior, but for the life of him he couldn't imagine what it might be. Fearing he would be caught spying, he opted for pulling a chair up close to his own door, waiting to see when—or if—his father left her.

"I know I am putting you in an awkward position," Mechi said to Lord Keith.

"Right you are," Lord Keith said irritably. "Just my very presence here with you is *most* improper! Now, speak quickly, lest someone find us out."

Mechi tried not to snicker. Surely no one would think she and the earl marischal were having a secret tryst. What she had to tell him, the things she must convince him of, were definitely not matters which would lead them to a romantic rendezvous.

She thought of her apartment in Aberdeen, Maryland. If a handsome man— and yes, she decided as she studied him in the weak light from the fire that he was indeed handsome—came to call on her at night, no one would give it a second thought. They could come in broad daylight and no one would pay any attention.

"It is the queen," Mechi began slowly. "I know you are her guardian."

"How do you know that?" Lord Keith asked, as if it was a secret, which Mechi was sure it was not.

"Why, she told me herself," Mechi said.

The earl sighed. Why was he so suspicious of this woman? He couldn't answer that for himself, but she gave him a very uneasy feeling.

"How well do you know Mary—her majesty?" Lord Keith asked. "She said you were from near Paris, yet you speak no French."

"She's right," Mechi said, not wanting to discuss it further. She didn't want to try to explain her own plight to the earl.

Lord Keith shrugged his shoulders. "So what is it you wish to discuss about the queen? You know, of course, that my loyalty always lies with her."

"I know," Mechi said. "That is why I felt I could confide in you." She stopped for a few moments, then continued. "Mary—her majesty—is in grave danger."

Shock came over his face. He thought that since she had returned from France, the Scots were all too pleased to have her back where she belonged. She never should have been sent to France in the first place, he felt.

"Danger?" he asked suspiciously. "From whom?"

"From Queen Elizabeth," Mechi stated.

"I know the English spinster has no use for Mary," Lord Keith said, his voice filled with scorn as he discussed the *other* monarch. "But surely she would do her no physical harm."

"Not directly," Mechi said, trying to reach into the far corners of her head to remember what history she could. Oh, how she wished she had paid more close attention in school. She loved history, but the details seemed so sketchy. "She has, however, sent Darnley to carry out her desires towards Mary—*Queen* Mary."

"Darnley? But Darnley is devoted to Mary. I've seen it when they talk. They can discuss the most important of matters, or the triflest of things, and he nearly crawls on his hands and knees to do her bidding."

"Sure," Mechi admitted, "but it's all an act."

"An act?" Lord Keith asked. "I do not understand."

"Yes, an act!" Mechi said. "Don't you see? He has his eye set on her for himself. He pledged his loyalty to Queen Elizabeth, then promises to Mary that he'll be true to her, while all the time he wants to satisfy his own selfish desires."

"And just how does he propose to fulfill his own desires?" the earl asked.

"He will marry Mary," Mechi replied.

"Marry Mary? No!" the earl said in disbelief. "I cannot imagine such a thing. How do you know this? Surely Darnley has not taken you into his confidence."

"No," Mechi said, laughing quietly. "I know because..." She hesitated, then answered, "Because he is the only man around who is taller than the queen!"

"That is ridiculous! I have never heard anything so absurd. You had better have a better reason than that. Go on."

"I can't explain how I know. You wouldn't understand. But please, you must trust me. For Mary's sake. For Scotland's sake. And certainly for Darnley's sake."

"None of this makes any sense at all," Lord Keith said, shaking his head as if to clear it of all her nonsense. "You appear like something out of a bad dream, claiming you have the power to see into the future, and expect me to believe you.

You must be some kind of a witch! I want nothing further to do with you. Tomorrow I want you out of the castle. I want you out of our lives. And I want you to stay far, far awy from Queen Mary!"

"But I can't..." Mechi began to protest, but was interrupted by the earl.

"Furthermore, I want you to stay far away from my son! I forbid you to see him or speak to him again!"

Mechi gasped. Why would he think she would have anything more to do with his son? Had her feelings for the handsome red-headed viscount been that visible? She had never been so stricken by anyone before.

She smiled at the earl as she saw him not as a powerful member of the nobility, but as an all-too-typical father, concerned for his own son's well-being. Still, she was sure that if she could lure Robbie Keith to her cause he was as much a man in himself as his father was, and there would be a battle royal if the two of them ever came to blows.

"And I want you to go to Edinburgh with queen, to stand guard for her, to be her protectorate—her guardian, as you claim to be."

The earl jumped back. Who did she think she was to demand his obedience? *No one* gave orders to the earl marischal! Well, with the possible exception of Queen Mary herself. If *she* had come and asked him to offer her his protection, he would not have hesitated for a second, even if it meant leaving his beloved Dunnottar and his family.

A gleam of hope occurred to Lord Keith. If he should decide to accompany the queen to Holyrood Palace, he could persuade the strange Mechi to stay within his sight much of the time. Perhaps, if he could observe her more carefully, he could determine exactly who or what she was. Also, it would keep her away from Robert.

Elizabeth, his wife, was right as usual. She was sure that Robert had designs on the young woman, and the earl agreed when he saw the way Robert looked at her. Yes, if he went to Edinburgh he could protect two people he cared for deeply: Queen Mary and Robert, his oldest son.

"If I were to believe you," Lord Keith said, "what would become of Dunnottar? Who would keep the tower? Who would keep the keep?"

Mechi giggled. She had heard people here talk about "the keep," but she wasn't certain exactly which part of the fascinating castle layout they referred to. If Lord Keith went with Mary, perhaps she could stay on at Dunnottar and be of some assistance to them in the earl's absence.

How absurd! she thought. He would not think that anything she had to offer would be of any value to the Keith clan. There were countless servants, governors, and people of all descriptions moving about constantly during the day. Then, too, the countess seemed quite capable of controlling the staff. And the children all seemed to have their part to play in the daily rituals. And no doubt Robert had been properly groomed by his father to take over in case of an emergency, such as war.

She longed to get outside the castle proper and investigate, but she knew it would have to wait at least until the daylight. If she were allowed to stay here, she would have plenty of time to familiarize herself with the surroundings.

"I'm sure Robbie could keep the tower and the keep," she said, still laughing at the sound of *keeping the keep*. "He seems a very capable young man."

"He is capable," Lord Keith barked at her. "He is capable of many things. Some good, some not so good."

Mechi wondered if the earl had had trouble with his son. Did he have hopes and dreams for his son that he had chosen to cast aside? Was he, like so many modern sons, a disappointment to his father? If so, what had he done?

"Perhaps I could stay on at Dunnottar while you are away," Mechi suggested.

"No!" Lord Keith yelled, then covered his own mouth to silence himself lest someone else should hear him. They would not understand his presence here, alone with Mechi.

"I already warned you; stay away from my son!"

"I didn't mean…" Mechi said.

"I don't care what you meant!" Lord Keith said. "If I am to go to Edinburgh, so be it. But you shall also go to Edinburgh. I do not trust you, and I don't mind telling you that. You shall never again set foot on the fiddlehead! Never! If I find out that you tricked me, for whatever reason, I shall have you hanged."

"Well," Mechi said sarcastically, "that's so much better than having my head cut off!"

"Perhaps I should have your tongue cut out!" the earl said as he headed for the door. "It seems to get you into a great deal of trouble. Well, no more! You shall answer to me for your every move. And that is the final word I have to say on the matter!"

The earl stomped out of the room, slamming the door behind him.

Robert watched his father quietly sneak back to his own solar. He didn't know what they had discussed, or done, but the encounter had obviously ended in a disagreement. He longed to go to her, to comfort her if necessary. He loved his father dearly, and respected him greatly, but he also knew that he could be extremely stubborn and unreasonable.

The earl tossed and turned most of the night, sleeping only a few minutes at a time. What if Mechi was right? It was impossible for her to foresee the future. He had never believed in such nonsense. Still, if anything should happen to the queen and he could have prevented it…

How would he explain his departure to the rest of the family? At least Elizabeth would have her wish; the peculiar Mechi would be safely away from Robert. Perhaps that was worth something.

And then there was the matter of Agnes, his oldest daughter. She was being courted by the earl of Moray. He supposed she could do far worse, but he had always hoped that Viscount Lindsay from the neighboring Edzell Castle would show some initiative where Agnes was concerned. If she was there, he could keep an eye on her much easier than if she was off in Edinburgh with Moray. Besides, Viscount Lindsay had a much better personality than Moray. He was such a pain! He hated to think of his daughter spending a lifetime being bored to death while waiting for her husband to speak at least one or two civil words a day.

The Keiths were all known for their quick wit. Agnes, if she fell prey to the wiles of Moray, would have to entertain herself to maintain her sanity.

Mechi scurried underneath the covers, feeling the chill of the room and, even worse, the chill of the earl. She didn't know how she ever got into such an awful mess. She wracked her brain, trying to figure out if she had done anything so terrible to someone that she was being punished. Or, was she sent here for the express purpose of protecting the people in power? If so, why had *she* been chosen? Oh, if only there was some way of escape. Perhaps back at St. Andrews. If only she could get back there. Maybe then she would have a chance to return to her normal life.

Her thoughts turned to the woman who had enticed her to the early morning golf lesson at St. Andrew's, back in Aberdeen, Maryland. What was her name? Liz Stewart. *Liz Stewart*! Elizabeth Stewart! Queen Elizabeth the First? Now *nothing* made sense. Had there been some strange connection between the two Liz Stewarts? Was she trying to get a message back to the past to Queen Mary through her?

And if so, why? Was the queen's name Elizabeth Stewart? Or was it something different? It didn't sound right, but if it wasn't Stewart, what was it? "Think!" she ordered herself aloud. Whatever it was, she knew that one Liz had something to do with the other Liz.

Mechi laughed, then her laughter turned to sobs. She never asked to come here. She'd always been a simple girl. The daughter of a rancher. The thing she loved the most in the whole world was golf. And horses. She longed for her father. She missed him so much. When she was on the ranch just outside Paris, *Texas*, if all else failed she could go talk to the horses. They always seemed to understand her. But here— here she had no one, not even a horse!

Robert stood outside the door, listening to her cry. He longed to go in, take her in his arms and comfort her. He had never met anyone who pulled at his heart strings like this Mechi.

His mind battled within. Go in. Your father can be so cruel, even if he doesn't mean to. You don't dare; what if someone caught you in with her? But if father could go in to her, then what is to stop me? At least I am not doing something behind a wife's back! He had no business in there.

He opened the door quietly and walked to the bed. He gently laid a hand on her shoulder. She sobbed ever harder. What had his father done to her? And why was she here? Would he ever know the answers to the mystery that surrounded the—Mechi?

Chapter VIII

Mechi rubbed her eyes when she awoke in the morning, hoping she had dreamed this whole thing. As soon as she absorbed her surroundings—the old, damp stone walls, the cold extinguished ashes in the fireplace and the huge four poster bed she still lay in—she knew one of two things: either she was still asleep or *this* was reality.

The sun peeked in through the tiny diamond-shaped window, sparkling on the dust beams as it entered the room. At least it isn't so foggy, she mused. Then an idea struck her. Suppose it was foggy again. Suppose she found her way back to St. Andrews. Suppose she hit her head again. Would that take her back to Maryland? It would be worth a try, she decided, but it would have to wait for another day. Today, even in Scotland, the fog was nowhere to be found.

Suddenly she remembered Robbie Keith sitting on the bed beside her. Had she imagined that, too? Wished so hard that he was there with her that she thought it really happened?

She glanced around the room, hoping to find a sign of his presence last night. He had been so kind, so tender. Did anyone else know he had come to her? And, she wondered, did Robbie know that his father had been there just a few minutes before he appeared? If so, he had not mentioned it.

There was a gentle knocking at her door, giving her a slight start.

"Come in," she called out softly.

Ann, Lady Keith's maiden, entered the room and went immediately to the fireplace, moving the ashes around and finally, taking the candle she had brought with her, lit a small piece of kindling and soon a warm glow filled the room. The early morning sun was still shining, but the fire felt good in the cool dampness which lingered from the night.

"Mornin', Lady Mechi," Ann said cheerfully.

Mechi grimaced. She hated people who were so happy as soon as they woke up. She had no idea that Ann had already been working for several hours.

Mechi smiled as she thought of Liz, the woman who had called her to St.

Andrew's in Maryland. She had kept Mechi waiting. There was a certain amount of pleasure in knowing that she was probably sitting there, still waiting for her to show up. She knew the receptionist had seen her come, and she wondered how they were explaining her mysterious disappearance. How long would they wait for her? Surely Liz had more important things in her life than sitting there waiting for a woman who had gone. Mechi thought with surprising humor, *was she ever gone! She was really gone!*

Mechi snickered. Nobody had ever called her *Lady* anything before. Something within her told her that she could learn to like it. For the first time in her life she felt like she was somebody important. Why, if her mind wasn't playing tricks on her just yesterday the Queen of Scotland had asked *her* to be her friend! What could be more important than that? She wondered if Queen Elizabeth—the second one, that is—had any personal friends. For that matter, she couldn't imagine the *first* Queen Elizabeth having any close friends, either. *The virgin queen*, she reflected, pleased that the history she had learned so long ago—no, so far in the future…

"Oh!" she sputtered aloud, "I don't know when I learned anything!"

"Beggin' your pardon, Lady Mechi?" Ann asked, not understanding any of what she was carrying on about.

"Nothing," Mechi said. "You wouldn't understand."

"You're probably right," Ann said agreeably. "Now, I've drawed a bath for you. I'll help you into it, then I've got some of Lady Agnes's frocks for you to choose from. She seemed quite taken with you. Said there was something strange which drawed you to herself." Ann shrugged. "Don't see as how you're no different than any one of the rest of us. You're a woman." Recalling the clothes Mechi had been wearing when she arrived she asked, her eyebrow arched in question, "Ye are, ain't ya?"

"A woman?" Mechi asked, laughing. "Yes, Ann. Rest assured, I am all woman."

"I guess I knowed that," Ann said, remembering her struggle to get Mechi into her corset the night before. "Even out o' your corset, ye were sure enough all woman."

Mechi's heart skipped a beat as she thought of Robbie. A sash from his night robe had somehow gotten wrapped around the post on her bed when he left. Mechi smiled, acknowledging that he was indeed there with her last night. At least she hadn't lost her mind completely. *No*, she thought, *only my heart.*

Robert Keith sat on the edge of his bed, looking outside.

"It's like a miracle," he said, gazing steadily at a bird who lit on his window sill and gaily cheeped its morning song to him. "Aye, 'tis the first time in weeks, perhaps even months, that the sun has shone upon the highlands. It must be the coming of the— Mechi."

He could not deny that the mere sight of her when she arrived at St. Andrews caused the sunshine to creep into the corners of his own heart. He had never felt like this. Was this, he wondered cautiously, what being in love meant? If so, no wonder his mother tried so hard to encourage him to find a mate. Well, she should be pleased now. He vowed to begin his pursuit of Mechi immediately. Perhaps, with any luck, she would stay around Dunnottar for awhile. He would try to convince his mother that she was not strong enough yet to travel. She did, after all, appear quite frail and ill when they found her yesterday.

The image of Mechi in her gown at the table when they dined last evening brought a smile to his face and a twinkle to his eye. How astute his mother had been; asking for a shawl to cover her shoulders. It was obvious she had seen his eyes fixed on her.

He played the scene in her *bedroom* over and over in his mind. He had prattled on and on about the Keith clan and their close relationship to the Scottish throne, both past and present. At first it had seemed odd that she knew nothing of the Keiths. They were, after all, not exactly hidden peoples in the countryside. Nearly everyone in the land had heard of the Keith clan, in one way or another. Then he recalled that Mary had said she was from somewhere near Paris. It hurt his pride to admit it, but perhaps the fame of the Keiths had not yet reached the continent.

Mechi had seemed extremely interested in the tales he spun of the Keiths as he stayed with her last night. She did, he realized, not offer any information on her own family. As he told her about the twins, he admitted that the Earl of Moray had set his sights on Agnes, the younger of his twin brother and sister. She had laughed, her eyes filled with sparkles like starlight on a clear, dark night, when he told her that her twin brother was Angus.

"Agnes and Angus," she had said. "Sounds like something my dad would have named a cow and a bull!" It was the only hint she gave to her fanily. Someplace she had a father, and he bred cattle. And then, in a few minutes, while he was still prattling on about the great exploits of the Keith clan at war, she was sound asleep.

Robert's mind returned to the night visit his father had paid their guest. It still confused him. She had not mentioned it during their own tryst, but it had obviously upset her. She *was* in tears when he found her. Even though she insisted that it was because she was so tired and everything around her was so strange, he felt it had something to do with his father. Surely he, of all people, would not have forced himself on her, no matter how lovely and enticing she was. No, it had to be something else. He knew his father; he would *never* do that to a woman. His father respected his mother far too much for such actions.

"I tell you," Elizabeth Keith told William. "I don't like it. Did you see the way he was ogling her at the table last eve?"

William Keith, the earl marischal, laughed at his wife.

"You will never make any sense to me, no matter how long we live together," he told his wife, patting her leg tenderly. "One moment you are moaning and complaining because he doesn't pay any attention to the girls around here, even though they all fawn over him constantly. Then when he finally does give an eye to a young lady—and a very beautiful one at that—you turn into an overly protective mother, afraid that you will lose the first of your children."

"There is nothing wrong with that!" Lady Keith huffed. "It is just… I can't help it that I'm a mother! But you mark my words; that girl is trouble through and through. Just the sheer garments she was clad in were the most scandalous things I have ever seen! She appeared more of a man than a woman. And her hair! It is like a sheep after it's been shorn. Ann whispered that perhaps she had been infected with cooties! Imagine!"

Lord Keith continued to laugh. "She appears to be a most delightful, although I too must admit that she is a bit odd, young woman."

He passed over the strange warning she had issued him about the queen and Darnley in her chambers the night before. He knew he dared not speak of it to his wife, as she would never understand. He didn't understand, himself, yet something told him to put his attention to what she had said.

"What would you say to my accompanying Mary to Edinburgh?" he asked hesitantly.

Elizabeth turned to look at her husband. His expression was serious, like trouble lying on the horizon. She usually picked up on his signals; living together did that to a woman. But this came as a complete surprise.

"Why would you do that?" she asked. "She has both Darnley and Moray with her. Surely they are capable of tending her needs on the journey."

"Of course they are," he said. "I know this will all seem strange to you. It does to me as well. But I have been informed that Darnley is not to be trusted."

"Darnley?" Elizabeth asked in surprise. "The information must be wrong!"

"He has been sent by Queen Elizabeth," he explained, "to try to keep Mary from claiming the crown of the entire British monarchy. I am her guardian, and I cannot shirk my responsibility as such. No, I must go with her."

"For how long?" Elizabeth asked softly. She hated it when he was gone. No matter how long they were together, each time he had to leave it was as if half of her heart was being torn from her.

"No longer than need be," he said, trying to sound reassuring. "As soon as I can get to the bottom of things, I shall return."

"And the stranger?" Lady Keith asked.

Lord Keith laughed at his wife. He should know by now that it was impossible to fool her.

"What makes you think this has anything to do with the stranger?" he asked, a twinkle in his eye.

"Nothing," she said. "It just seems odd that all of this occurred at the same time as she appeared."

"But it is also the first time Mary has been with us since her return from France. Does it not seem reasonable to assume that she might have her own fears about Darnley?"

"Whatever you say," Lady Keith said, shrugging her shoulders in consignment to his words, then kissing her husband tenderly on the cheek. "If that is what you choose for me to believe, then that is what I believe."

"Ha!" he scoffed. He knew she intuitively sensed the mystery—perhaps even danger—he felt. "And I don't believe you for one moment."

"We really should be getting down to break the fast. By now the rest of the family will no doubt be gathered. They will wonder what we are doing here."

His eyes danced with mischief. Elizabeth Keith, in spite of herself, blushed at the attention he paid her, even when they were alone. How she would miss him while he was away.

The Keith clan was gathered at the huge rough wooden table when Mechi entered the dining hall. She had assumed the entire family had been present when she had supped with them last evening, but the amount of them now was overwhelming.

"Good morn," Robert greeted her, rushing to her side. "Slept well, I trust?"

"I did," Mechi said, wondering if he was offended by her falling asleep while he was still talking. *It was delightful*, she thought, *to fall asleep to the sound of his deep resonant voice.* She could get used to falling asleep with him very easily. Too easily.

Mechi jerked her head slightly. Her thoughts surprised even her. She had never entertained a suggestion, no matter how small, of spending a night with a man. Not even with *the other Robert*. She had always dreamed that some day the right man would put in an appearance, but why did it have to be some man from a different world? One to which she didn't belong.

"You kept me awake half the night with your night talkin'," she could hear her dad say. What if she had talked in her sleep last night? Oh, how she hoped it wasn't so! If she had babbled on, what had she told him? How much of herself had she revealed?

"Very well," Mechi said, smiling warmly at him. *You should know*, she thought. "I guess I was more tired than I realized."

She turned towards Robbie, with her back clearly to the others. There, in plain daylight yet hidden, she coyly reached into her bodice and withdrew his sash, which he had so carelessly left behind last night, from between her breasts. She slyly placed it, tightly rolled into a little coil like a snake ready to strike, into his hand.

Robbie's eyes filled with excitement at the warmth of the tie. The warmth that he knew came from her bosom. If only he had been able to extract it himself!

Snapping himself back to reality, the color rising in his face and surprisingly, his manhood rising equally, he longed to engage her in meaningless drivel.

"You had a very—troublesome—day," the earl said, hoping he had chosen the right word.

"I don't know what came over me," Mechi said honestly. "I don't remember ever having a day quite like it before."

"How did you come to be at St. Andrews?" Agnes Keith asked. She had always loved a mystery, and the only woman she had ever heard of who frequented the links at St. Andrews was the queen.

"Hush!" Lady Keith scolded. "You must not be impolite."

"I, for one, would like to hear the tale as well," the man called Moray said, his voice no less of a slow drawl than it had been the night before.

That voice! Mechi's head screamed at her. It was just like—*oh, if only she could figure it out.*

"I will try to explain it to you," Mechi said, not sure at all what she would tell them. "But first, my lord, I don't believe I caught your name. Mary called you *Moray?*"

"Yes," Mary said, looking as if she was enjoying this whole mess. "He is called Moray. He is, in fact, the earl of Moray. My cousin. But his real name is…"

Mechi laughed out loud as she heard the queen finish her sentence.

"… James Stewart!"

Of course! He had the same slow speech that dozens of comedians copied day after day. Any one could recognize the sound of *Jimmy Stewart*! She had watched his movies over and over again.

Moray shifted about on his chair uneasily. He was not accustomed to anyone making light of his name. He knew he was not the most popular man in the kingdom, but this! This was utterly uncouth!

"I'm sorry," Mechi said, cupping her hand over her mouth to try to stifle her laughter. "It is not you I'm laughing at, my lord. It is just that I once knew another James Stewart. They called him *Jimmy.* He was such a clown!"

"A clown?" Agnes asked.

"Yes," Queen Mary said. "A jester."

The entire Keith clan, and the queen as well, began to laugh with Mechi. James Stewart, the earl of Moray, was certainly anything but a clown—or jester—or whatever it was. He was so serious. His face looked like it would crack around the edges of his mouth if he dared to smile.

Mechi looked pityingly at Agnes. If she should marry this man, she was indeed in for a most unhappy life. She would probably die of sheer boredom.

Mechi pondered what it would be like to be married to the *real* Jimmy Stewart. The one she knew and everyone loved. It could be just as frustrating, listening to him, with his stammering hesitations and her "er's" every time he spoke. But, it could not have been that bad. There were several children who had come from that marriage.

Finally, Agnes came to Moray's defense.

"I'm certain Lady Mechi meant no harm," she said, placing her hand on his arm. "No one would ever accuse you of being a clown!"

"Amen to that!" Lord Keith said. "You may be a lot of things, Moray, but a *clown* you're not. A fool, perhaps, but one whom my daughter quite obviously adores."

Moray's face became quite red. He had shown some interest in Agnes, of course, but he had not made his intentions known to anyone. Not even to Agnes!

"You're embarrassing the poor lad," Lady Keith said.

"So?" the earl commented. ""Perhaps he needs a shove in the right direction. If he does not make a move before too long, surely she will flee elsewhere for a mate."

Moray knew the earl marischal had hopes of Agnes turning to the Lindsay lad from Edzel. *Perhaps tonight*, he thought, *I will ask for her hand. I do not want to lose her. Yes, tonight it shall be.*

As they ate together, all chatting merrily away, Mechi's head seemed to be spinning like a top. There was so much to try to comprehend, and it was all happening so fast. She heard them all talking, but it seemed like a bunch of bees all buzzing together. It was as if she was in the middle of something, but she wasn't really there. She had never known a feeling like this.

"So are you ready to leave for Holyrood with us?" Lord Keith asked. "We shall be on our way shortly."

"I still think she is too weak to travel," Mechi heard Robbie say. "It would be better if she stayed here for a few days, then I could transport her to Edinburgh."

Mechi tried to smile at him. She wondered if he felt the same closeness to her that she felt to him, or if he was just worried that she might become ill from the trip.

"She will go with us!" Lord Keith said sternly.

"Then I shall accompany you," Robbie said, "so you do not have to make the return trek alone."

"You will stay here to attend your mother!" Lord Keith ordered. "Besides, I have business to attend to in Edinburgh. I might be gone a few days."

Or more, Lady Keith thought. *But please, William, not too long.*

Before she knew it, Mechi was once again in Queen Mary's coach, this time on the road to Edinburgh. As she turned and looked behind her, she could see Lady Keith and Robbie watching them as they rode away. She couldn't explain the empty void— the knot—she felt in the pit of her stomach as they disappeared from view.

Chapter IX

Mechi awoke, sat up on the edge of her bed, and looked around her. She pondered the events of the past few days and was surprised that she felt so at home in her strange surroundings.

Queen Mary had made her extremely welcome at Holyrood. She had even provided her own lady-in-waiting for Mechi. *Phoebe*! Mechi had never even known a Phoebe before, much less had one of her very own.

Mechi looked at the row of garments which had been provided for her. While they hung on hooks on the wall, along with the piles of crinolines and farthingales, their brilliant colors sparkled as the first rays of sunlight fell on them. If only they were not all so revealing. What was Mary trying to make of her? And why?

Her eyes caught a glimpse of her GUESS sweatshirt, her green nylon windbreaker and her Levi's, which were neatly folded and set on the shelf under the stand which held the ornate pitcher and laver.

As she grabbed a bright red gown, the color of rubies, she cavorted around the room singing *"If they could see me now ..."* to the familiar show tune she knew so well. *"Eatin' fancy food and drinkin' fancy wine ..."*

She dropped onto the bed, the dress tumbling on top of her, as she ended with a vociferous *"If my friends could see me now!"*

Her mind conjured up a vision of the scene from "Sweet Charity," where she had heard this same song countless times. "Eat your heart out, Shirley MacLaine!" she said, laughing out loud.

"You're in right good spirits this mornin', m'lady," Phoebe said. "That's what you'll be a wearin' today?"

"I suppose I should dress for the occasion," Mechi said.

"Today is somethin' special, m'lady?" Phoebe asked.

"I don't know," Mechi replied. "But, I suppose if we decide to make it something special, then it *will be* special!"

Phoebe giggled behind her hand. "Oh, m'lady, you're such a hoot!"

Mechi laughed. "Who knows what today might bring? If we play our cards right, it might bring something special for both of us."

Phoebe looked at her, puzzled at Mechi suggesting they play cards. She had heard of such games of chance being played by men, but never by the likes of Lady Mechi.

Mechi's mind went back automatically to Robbie Keith. It had been only a few days since they had parted ways, but it seemed like an eternity. If it were not for Queen Mary referring to him quite often, and the earl marischal himself also being at Holyrood, she might be tempted to think she had dreamed him up. That he was noting more than the imaginary ideal man. Her *Mister Right*.

When Mechi was prepared to go to meet the others, she took a deep breath. She had always jumped up and gotten into the shower and in less than ten minutes was ready to face the day on the greens at St. Andrews. Now it took more than an hour to get roped into her corset, don her layers of petticoats and put her dress on. The only thing which still took very little time was brushing her hair. This was, to Phoebe's dismay, a "most unfit mode for a lady, Lady!"

"Good morn', Lady Mechi," Queen Mary greeted her with a smile. They had become close friends, much to Mechi's delight. At times it seemed to Mechi that perhaps her *other life* was what had been a dream. It was only such things as the sight of her old clothes which had caused the only disagreement she and the queen had encountered, which indicated that really was a transplant here.

Lord Keith nodded at her, but did not speak. He had made it his business to study her carefully. If he was not mistaken, his son had designs on her. Was she a fit match for him? He smiled, admitting that Robert did have an eye for beauty if his suspicions were true. There was no denying she was a dapper young lass, with her dark brown hair and deep hazel eyes which defied description—not blue and not brown. Full of mystery, like the lass herself. *Oh, yes, he must convince Elizabeth that this Mechi was indeed worthy of thei firstborn son.*

Since her warning, he had also kept a close eye on Darnley, but he had not noticed anything truly questionable, even though he had to admit that something about the man made him extremely nervous. He vowed that today he would question Mechi further to see if she had perhaps learned anything new about Darnley's plot.

As Mechi looked around the table, she saw that Moray had joined them for the first time since they had arrived in Edinburgh. Now that she knew who he really was— Jimmy Stewart—she found it hard to concentrate on what he said. He was the epitome of the late great—yet very much alive, at least to Mechi's knowledge—Jimmy Stewart. She fully expected him at any moment to leap to his feet and shout "It's a wonderful, wonderful life!"

"I say, Lady Mechi," the earl marischal said quite loudly, bringing her back to her senses, "Queen Mary tells us you seem to be quite the hand at the game of golf."

"I do play the sport some," Mechi admitted timidly.

"She says you appear to be an expert on the matter," Lord Keith said, studying her carefully. She was, as Lady Keith had said, a most peculiar lass. At times she seemed almost normal, yet on other occasions she could easily have been from some other world.

"I know a great deal about many things and I am sure some of them would come as a great surprise to you, my lord," Mechi said, a glitter in her eyes as she teased the great earl marischal.

"Such as?" Lord Keith asked.

"Well, for one thing," Mechi said, hoping to hit him where his interest was the most intense, "I noticed when we were at Dunnottar you seem to have a lot of horses around."

"But of course!" the earl said, his chest puffed with pride. "It is for the famed horses at Dunnottar that we have been dubbed *the marischals*."

Mechi caught herself just in time. She almost made a comment about the massive Clydesdale horses—the type from Dunnottar—which were the symbol of Budweiser beer.

"I was raised on a ranch—er, a farm—with horses as well," she said instead. "I have always loved horses. They have been my closest friends."

Queen Mary clucked her tongue. "What a pity, my dear child, to have to resort to playing with mere creatures. Had you no brothers or sisters?"

"No," Mechi said. No sense in trying to explain about Brian at a time like this, she reasoned. "I am afraid I must admit to being a spoiled brat. My father, bless him, let me do almost anything I wanted to."

"And your mother?" Lord Keith inquired.

"I'm afraid she died when I was very young. My father raised me by himself."

"Darnley, isn't that dreadful?" Mary asked, noticing that he seemed lost to the conversation.

"What?" Darnley asked in surprise. "Oh, yes, I suppose so," he said, not all sure what he was agreeing to.

"What would your life have been like without all those others running around all the time?" Mary continued asking Darnley.

"I'm sure it would have been much more comfortable," Darnley said, hoping he had cued in to the right reply in the discussion.

"But surely you would have missed them!" Mary quipped.

"What?" Darnley asked. "Oh, but of course."

Lord Keith realized that Mary was very conscious of the lack of interest Darnley had been taking in the whole matter. Had she also honed in on the feeling that Darnley was up to no good? Or had Mechi warned her, as she had done to him? He must find a way to confront Mechi later in the day, when they were alone and could visit in private.

The talk and chatter continued during the meal, with the earl marischal relating tales of joy and pleasure of life at Dunnottar with myriads of children always on hand.

Mechi, much to her own chagrin, found her thoughts centering more and more on young Robbie Keith. In the past few days she had been able to limit him to fleeting moments of remembrances, but now he seemed to be taking complete dominion of her mind. Was there no escaping him? And if not, how could she ever get back to him? It was all too obvious that his father was bent on keeping them apart.

A messenger appeared in the room. All conversation came to an abrupt end. Such anxiety as filled the messenger's face could only mean trouble at hand.

Queen Mary's face paled. The country had been at rest. She was not ready to deal with a war, yet she knew that if the bloody Elizabeth had her way, her supporters would do anything in their power to get rid of Mary, thus eliminating the possibility of Mary usurping her throne.

"I have a message for Lord William Keith, the earl marischal," the messenger said, handing a scroll to the earl.

Lord Keith took the roll and unwrapped it, reading it slowly and carefully.

"No!" he cried out. "They are our very life! It can't be!"

"What is it?" Queen Mary asked, relieved that it did not pertain to her. "Is it the family?"

"No!" Lord Keith replied. "It is the horses. There seems to be an epidemic of some sort. They are dying, one by one. I must go to them, but I know not what I can do."

"Perhaps I could be of some help," Mechi suggested hesitantly. "I did tell you that I have a great deal of experience dealing with the beasts."

'What could you do that I couldn't?" the earl marischal asked, laughing at the mere idea.

"What are the symptoms?" Mechi asked. "Does your message say?"

Lord Keith read the message aloud, causing Darnley to beg for permission to leave, as the graphic details made him quite ill.

Mechi recognized the signs of the dreaded anthrax. She wondered if anyone had even given the disease a name yet. Not that it mattered.

She reached into the recesses of her mind, trying to remember what her father had done when the same ailment hit John Mason's ranch next to their own, just outside Paris, Texas.

"Penicillin!" she exclaimed.

"What?" Lord Keith asked.

On, no! Mechi thought. *No one knows anything about penicillin. It hasn't been discovered yet. Penicillin is nothing more than a form of mold,* she reasoned.

"I must go to Dunnottar!" she demanded.

"Over my dead body!" Lord Keith insisted.

"Yours or the horses!" Mechi snarled. "The choice is yours."

"I forbid it!" the earl marischal said. "I will depart this afternoon and somehow I shall handle it. The last thing I need is the interference of a mere woman!"

"So much for women's lib!" Mechi sputtered as she rose from her chair and stormed out of the room.

"Do you have any idea what she is talking about?" Lord Keith asked Queen Mary.

"Not in the least," Mary admitted. "But whatever it is, I'm sure it will pass. Just leave her alone for awhile."

Robert Keith, Viscount of Kintore and chief of Dunnottar Castle in his father's absence, wiped the sweat from his face. His vision was blurred from the salty brine which poured over him.

"Fill the bucket again!" he ordered the servants who stood nearby, waiting and willing to help, but not knowing what to do.

Darvon, one of the servants, perched atop the wall that surrounded the castle, hastened to lower the bucket over the outer edge of the wall to the sea. As soon as it was full he grabbed the rope, which was tied tightly around the turret.

"Hyar ye be, m'lord," Darvon said excitedly as he handed the bucket, causing it to slosh over the rim, to Robert. "Thar by anythin' else?"

"Not for the moment," Robert answered. "But be ready with another bucketful."

"Aye, m'lord," Darvon said, watching with steadfast eyes as Robert carefully bathed the horses, trying to reduce their fevers.

"'Tis only a miracle can save 'em," Robert mumbled. "If only we could hope for one to arrive."

Mechi struggled to free herself of the cumbersome garb she was wearing. When the back hooks would not come loose, she pulled and strained at them until finally they gave way, tearing the fabric. As soon as she was free of the dress and petticoats, she grabbed her jeans and sweatshirt from the corner under the stand. She hurried into them, anxious to be on her way. After the corset, even her jeans offered a sense of the loss of restraint.

She slipped into her windbreaker and ran from the room, looking up and down the corridor to see if anyone was about, then hurried to the servants' stairway. She raced down the steps, the long black cape which Mary had given her flying in the wind as she sneaked out the back entry.

Again, she quickly glanced about to see if anyone was watching her. She saw that everybody was either preoccupied with their own affairs or going in another direction, so she crept into the stables, where she jumped astride the first horse she came to.

It was only Darnley who saw her as she sped away, her cape behind her like the wings of a raven. He breathed a sigh of relief. He couldn't explain why, but he felt extremely uncomfortable around Lady Mechi. She seemed to know far too much about him. He found her watching him at every turn and twist in his life. Finally, she was gone! He had no idea where she was going, but it didn't matter. Not as long as she didn't return. He had Mary to deal with, and one woman at a time was enough of a challenge for any man!

Chapter X

Mechi rode through the streets of Edinburgh, passing the wide gates at Holyrood before anyone could stop her. As she came to Holyrood Park, she expertly jumped the small stone vaultings. Up the byway to the Canongate and on through the winding pathways of the Royal Mile they sped.

Mechi turned to look behind her as she escaped from the city.

"Good!" she said, tossing her head to the wind. "Nobody saw me leave." She wondered, however, how long it would be before they would miss her. Surely someone would check on her. If she had a good head start, perhaps she could evade them until she arrived safely at Dunnottar.

She looked up, feeling a few sprinkles of rain as she rode. The sky was threatening, but it was too late to stop now. She had a mission to accomplish and nothing would deter her.

She studied the surroundings as she rode, not stopping lest she lose precious moments. She recognized certain landmarks to the north from the trip which had brought her to Edinburgh from Dunnottar. She veered the horse in that direction, hoping it was right. Her head had not been very clear on the day of that journey.

Before long she was running through the forest. The huge oaks were cold and bare. She recognized the signs of the approaching winter and wondered what the weather in Scotland would be like. She imagined the countryside full of snow, like the pictures of Dickens' *Christmas Carol.* The pines, which were a deep fulL green, provided a sharp contrast to the oaks, which had long since shed their leaves.

The rain began to fall harder, faster, causing her to shiver as the cold torrent covered her. She grabbed the reins with one hand and pulled the hood of her cape up around her head, struggling to tuck it in as tight as she could to fend off the chill of the day.

She wanted to get to Dunnottar as soon as she could, yet she recalled that it had taken two days on the trip to Edinburgh. At lEast, she thought, I will get as far as I can before nightfall.

From time-to-time, she imagined she heard hoofbeats behind her and she turned to see if she could spot anyone following her. So far so good. She laughed, wondering what *Lord Keith* was doing now. She knew that they would surely have missed her long before this, and she wished she could be a mouse in the corner to hear their conversation.

"What do you mean, she's gone?" Queen Mary demanded of Phoebe. "What did she say?"

"She didn't say nothin' to me, yer majesty," Phoebe said. "I'm most frightful sorry, but I don't have no idea what she's up and done. She's a strange one, that Lady Mechi."

"What's this about Lady Mechi?" Lord Keith asked as he walked into the room, overhearing the women talking. "Where is she?"

"Don't rightly know, m'lord," Phoebe said. "She must have left in an awful hurry, she did. She even tore the dress right off her. It's upstairs on her bed and it'll take a fair piece of work to put it back together again. Pulled the hooks right off the goods, she did."

Lord Keith and Queen Mary exchanged a worried glance. Their thoughts channeled in the same direction; she had threatened to go to Dunnottar. Surely, with the weather as bad as it was, she would never attempt such a trip. And not alone.

"I'm going to the mews," the earl marischal announced. "If she went, she would have had to get a carriage first."

Lord Keith went out to the stables and began to question the hands.

"Don't know nothin' about it, m'lord."

Ha'n't seen her, m'lord."

"The carriages are all accounted for, m'lord."

"Only Ponder is missing, m'lord."

"Ponder?" Lord Keith asked. "Who is Ponder?"

"It's one o' the horses, m'lord," came the reply. "The fastest we've got. If she took him, she'll be far ahead of anyone else before you know it."

"I've got to have a horse immediately," the earl said. "Get one ready while I go inform Mary—her majesty."

"Yes, m'lord."

Lord Keith headed for the castle and found Queen Mary pacing back and forth, back and forth, in the great hall.

"Did you find her?" she asked anxiously.

"Seems she's taken Ponder and left already," he answered. "I don't have any idea how long she's been gone. I have them preparing a horse for me so I can go search for her. She doesn't appear to know her way here. If she gets out in the woods…"

His voice broke off, not daring to think what could happen to her. He didn't particularly like the lass. He certainly didn't trust her. Yet he didn't wish her any ill, either.

"Go, and godspeed," Mary said, embracing her guardian warmly. "It is a terrible day, but you must do what you think best."

"I shall be careful," the earl assured her. "I know the closest route, and with any luck I shall encounter her before too long."

Queen Mary stood at the window, watching Lord Keith ride away. She was barely able to make out his image, as the rain was by now pouring down heavily and the air was filled with a thick fog. "God be with you," she said softly, crossing herself as she watched them disappear.

The countess marischal wrapped herself in her cape and ran out into the cold, driving rain. Her arms laden with warm blankets, she slipped on the mud but recovered her balance before she fell.

"You should not have come," Robert said to his mother.

"And leave you alone to tend the dying mares? It is the least I can do."

She handed the blankets to Robert and he began setting them on top of each horse, tucking them in firmly around each animal.

"Do you think any of them will survive?" Lady Keith asked her son hesitantly.

"We can only hope," he said, his face drawn and tired from fighting the terrible disease of the horses.

"And pray for a miracle," Lady Keith added, placing her hand tenderly on Robert's.

"I thought that meself, earlier," Robert confessed. "Such foolery. As if such things still existed."

"If they do anywhere," Lady Keith said, "it is at Dunnottar. Your father should have word by now of our plight. Surely he will be here before long."

"And what can he do?" Robert asked. He yawned as he spoke, making it hard for his mother to understand him.

"What did you say?" she asked.

"I merely asked what Father can do that we cannot," Robert repeated. "It is not like he has some magic potion to bring with him from Edinburgh."

"Do not be too hasty," Lady Keith said. "Love is the magic of miracles, and your father does love his horses."

"Nearly as much as he loves you," Robert said, causing his mother to blush slightly, in spite of the rain and cold.

"I pray that some day you shall have someone to love as I love him," Lady Keith said.

Robert's mind, for the first time since the attack on the horses had struck, turned to Mechi. Thoughts of her at Holyrood danced in his head. He would have given anything to have gone with his father—and the Mechi. But, he had to admit that he was needed here. He could not imagine his mother handling this mess with the horses by herself.

"Before long it will be dark. I suppose your father will stop at Dundee for the night. It is difficult enough to travel in such weather as this in the daylight, much less at night. I do hope he is careful."

"You know Father is always careful," Robert said, trying to comfort and assure his mother. "By tomorrow eve surely he will be here with us."

As dusk settled in and it was impossible to see any more, Mechi once again stopped at a small house, as she had done frequently on her ride, to make sure she was still headed for Dunnottar. Everyone, she soon learned, knew the reputation of the Keith clan. When she explained that she was needed there, they all provided her with food and an offer to house her for the night. Still, she continued on as long as she could.

"Just ahead lies St. Andrews," the lady of the small, crude shanty with its thatched straw roof told her. "You would do well to stay the night. There is always room at the inn." She studied Mechi carefully, then added, "Though it's likely they'll question a young lass like yourself ridin' alone." The woman waited, hoping an explanation would follow. She, too, while too polite to ask, was curious.

"Thank you," Mechi said, then made her way to her horse. It was not the horse she had left Holyrood with, as the laird at one stop most graciously allowed her to take a fresh steed when he saw how tired her horse was. In a flash she was gone. Back into the cold and the rain, but with the welcome thought of Robert Keith awaiting her.

As she rode into St. Andrews, she immediately chose sanctuary at the cathedral, rather than at the local inn. There were apt to be less questions, should anyone discover her there, and if she was real lucky she might even last the night sleeping on a bench without anyone seeing her.

She sneaked quietly into the sanctuary and looked around. Near the front of the church, kneeling at the altar, was an old stooped woman, her head covered with a black cloth. She wept openly as she prayed.

Mechi listened, but could not make out the words.

"Invasion of privacy anyway," she mumbled to herself. "It's against the law." She bit her lip as she chuckled silently. "Well, maybe not yet."

Soon she was alone with only the candles burning on the altar and the rain pounding steadily on the ground outside. Even through the thick stone walls, she could hear it. The dampness seemed to fill every corner of the church.

Mechi had never been particularly religious, but now she felt a strange closeness to her unknown "Saint Andrew." Maybe, she thought, he was the patron saint of all golfers and that was the connection she felt for him.

"Bless me, Saint Andrew," she prayed as her eyes closed. Finally, exhausted from the long, hard ride of the day, she slept—alone. So alone.

He was struggling with the sick horses. Mechi watched as he slaved over them, trying to save as many as he could. She felt so close to him, yet when she spoke he ignored her, as if he didn't hear a word she said. She reached out to push the curly red hair from his forehead, but she couldn't touch him. In frustration she screamed at him, but he continued to act as if she didn't exist.

Mechi sat up, rubbing her eyes. She strained to see what was there in the near darkness. The flames from the candles flickered eerily, sending shivers up and down her spine. She struggled to remember where she was. At last she recalled entering the cathedral.

She shook her head, trying to awaken herself from the strange dream she had just had. It had to be a dream. All of it. Robbie Keith. Queen Mary. The earl marischal. The sick horses. Even the church.

She set her hand down and ran it across the surface beneath her. There was no mistaking it; it definitely wasn't her own bed. Could it be possible that she really was in St. Andrews, Scotland, in 1561? If this was a dream, it was the most real one she had ever had.

Her mind wandered back to Robbie Keith. "Lord Robbie," she said with a smile. She hoped he wasn't a figment of her imagination. Granted, he was too good to be true, but as soon as it was daylight she would be on her way to rescue him, just as he rescued her. If only there was some way to telephone or telegraph a message ahead to him to let him know that she was coming to save the day.

She pressed her fingers against the sides of her head. Maybe, if she concentrated hard enough, she could get the message through to him on the airwaves.

She laughed. "I know what's wrong with you," she said aloud. "You have flipped your lid. You've lost it, kiddo. You are ready for the men to come and carry you away, safely wrapped in a little white straight jacket."

"Are you all right, my child?"

Mechi had thought she was alone. Now she was face to face with a priest. And she wasn't even Catholic! In the dark shadows he looked more like something out of a horror movie than a man of the cloth.

"I am fine, Father," Mechi answered. "I was on a journey to Dunnottar Castle, and I had to find shelter for the night. I didn't think you would mind."

The priest's face was filled with compassion. "You are welcome to stay as long as you deem it necessary," he assured her. "It is God's house, not mine."

"Thank you," Mechi said. "I will be on my way as soon as it is light."

"At least you can travel better in the morn. The rain has ceased."

Mechi had not even noticed the quietness that filled the air. There was no rain, no wind. She wondered, since she was in St. Andrews again, if it would be foggy in the morning. She looked at her watch, pushing the tiny button to light it, and realized that it was already morning. *Five twenty-five* the digital numbers read. She smiled at the priest as he watched her. She wondered what he would think of such a contraption. *The only thing he has is probably a sun dial*, she thought.

"I shall leave you to sleep, child," the priest said.

"If you don't mind," Mechi said. "I would rather talk. I have to admit that I've never been to confession, but I've got something on my mind I've got to get off. I cannot tell anyone else, so if you've got a minute, I'd like to spill my guts to you."

The priest gave a slight shudder at such vulgar language from a lady. Even in the semi-darkness he sensed that there was something odd about her.

"I shall hear your confession," he said.

Mechi told him her whole, incredible story. When she was finished, she watched him closely to see his reaction.

The priest said nothing, but simply turned and went and knelt before the cross at the front of the church. For the second time that night Mechi strained her ears to hear what was being spoken to God. The word were clear and melodious, but they held no meaning for her. Finally she realized that he was praying in Gaelic. She could only imagine what he might be saying to his Divine Master. No doubt he was telling Him that he had a mad woman in the church. She realized her plight was too much for anyone to comprehend—perhaps even God.

Visual images seemed to appear as out of nowhere before her eyes. Again, as in her dream, she saw Robbie—*Lord* Robbie—kneeling by the horses, trying desperately to save them.

Without being noticed, she quietly slipped from the sanctuary and untied her horse. She quickly mounted it and disappeared into the almost-dawn. As it had been the day she first arrived in St. Andrews, the air was heavy with fog. She glanced briefly towards the golf grounds, but continued on. Even if she could return to the future, today there was no time to try such an experiment. No, today there were more important things at hand. Today she was needed.

"Hang on!" she called out to the wind, as if Robbie could hear her. "I'm coming, and together we can lick the world."

Chapter XI

Mechi shuddered as she rode up to the castle at Dunnottar. The sentinels, recognizing her, did nothing to try to hinder her entry. Safely inside the mighty fortress, she headed immediately for the stables. There, kneeling on the ground, soothing a weak, sick mare, was Robbie. It was like she was looking at a photograph; it was the exact image she had seen in her dream at the cathedral.

She jumped off her horse, letting the reins drop freely, without thought. In a moment she was standing behind Robbie, her hand resting gently on his shoulder. Also, as in her dream, he seemed unaware of her presence.

Mechi blinked and looked long and hard at him. Was this whole, absurd thing just something she had imagined? Maybe she wasn't really here. Maybe they couldn't see her. Maybe she was lost out in space somewhere and it was just her soul which was present here in another time.

Dispelling any doubt of her visibility, Lady Keith burst upon the scene, a pot of warm water in her hands, screaming at Mechi.

"You witch! Look what you have brought upon us!"

The idea that someone would blame her for the evils which befell the Keith clan at Dunnottar had never crossed Mechi's mind. She never wished any ill on them, nor on anyone else. In fact, more and more she was becoming convinced that the sole reason she had been sent back in time was to offer protection to Mary, and to warn her of the danger she was facing.

Now, suddenly conscious that she was there, Robbie spoke softly and kindly to her.

"You have come to help?"

"How absurd!" Lady Keith said sharply. "And just what, pray tell, do you think she can do?"

"I don't know, Mums," Robbie said, the sweat pouring down his face and off his arms in spite of the cool air of the day. The sick mare's head was resting on his lap and Robbie stroked her tenderly, as if his touch would work magic. "We both said we needed a miracle, and then she appears."

"She's nothing but borrowed trouble," Lady Keith said. "I warned you to stay away from her."

Mechi ignored the barbs and said, "Do you have any old bread around? Some that is quite stale?"

Lady Keith stared at her in bewilderment.

"Why, yes, I suppose so. There always seems to be some lying about in the kitchen."

"Bring it to me," Mechi ordered. "Now!"

As if she could not stop herself, Lady Keith made her way to the kitchen, which stood across the yard from the castle proper. She could not explain why she was doing this, but a force far greater than her own will commanded her to obey.

"Is this enough?" she asked Mechi as she returned, running across the grounds. "It is all I could find."

"It will do for a start," Mechi said. "Sprinkle it with water and then set it out in the sun for a time."

To their astonishment, although they had not noticed, the sun was now shining. Robbie shook his head. That was twice now that the sunshine had followed the mysterious young lass to the dark and shadowy highlands of Scotland. Yes, perhaps she was a miracle!

Mechi helped Lady Keith spread the bread out, hoping that it would soon develop mold. She wasn't at all sure it would work, but, she reasoned, penicillin is basically simple mold. Since she couldn't go to the corner drug store and buy some of the antibiotics, this would have to work. It was the only thing she knew to try.

"Please, St. Andrew," she prayed quietly.

Mechi was sitting on the ground, tending one of the horses, when Lord William Keith approached.

"You!" he shouted. "I have chased you all the way from Edinburgh! How dare you? Get away from my horses!"

"Father," Robbie said, "Mechi has been most helpful. In fact, she has some bread setting in the sun for them now. Perhaps you should go and check it."

Lord Keith, as his wife had done earlier, went as told to check on the bread. Why, he wondered as he went in the direction Robbie had pointed, did he feel compelled to do as she said? What magical powers did she hold over him? Over all of them? Perhaps Elizabeth was right. She should be avoided at any cost.

"It is rotten," he said as he returned to them. "I instructed Darvon to dispose of it. It is all covered with a horrible gray mold."

"Thank you," Mechi said, lifting her eyes heavenward. "Please, tell him to bring it to me immediately."

Again, as before, Lord Keith did as she bid him. When he came back again, his arms were laden with the moldy bread.

"Feed it to them," she ordered.

"Never!" Lord Keith protested. "It will kill them!"

"On the contrary," Mechi said, hoping she could explain the modern medical miracle to these people who were still living in the dark ages. "The bacteria—little tiny animals which live in the mold—will eat the bad bacteria which is making the horses sick. It is a medicine—a potion—which has been tried and proven."

As she watched their blank expressions, she added "In Paris it is quite acceptable now. I'm sure Queen Mary has heard of it."

How glad she was that the queen was quite safely back in Edinburgh. Of course she, like them, had never heard of such a thing as penicillin. But for the moment her story was safe. And if it worked, what difference would it make?

They all watched as she made her way from one horse to another, gently prodding them to eat the bread. *Crude*, she thought, *but the best chance they have*.

When she had completed the task, she sat down beside Robbie.

"Now what do we do?" he asked.

"Wait," she said simply. "And pray."

"I've done more than my share of that, I must admit, on the ride here from Edinburgh," Lord Keith admitted. "I feel as helpless with them as I did with little Genevieve," he said, his voice cracking with emotion.

Mechi made a mental note of the name, Genevieve, and decided she would ask someone about her later. For the time being, they all had their hands full with the problems at hand.

"Why don't you go inside?" Lord Keith suggested to his wife. "There is no need for you to wait out here in the cold."

Lady Keith wondered if he felt as uneasy about this strange Mechi as she did. No, as long as this lass was nearby, she intended to stick firmly by her side. She was not to be trusted. Especially not where her son was concerned. He was too vulnerable. As she watched Mechi, she looked for her beauty. The beauty Robert seemed to see in her. No, she decided, she is not beautiful. It is more—nymph-like. Yes, that was it! She was like the wood nymphs her Grandfather Hay had told her about when she was a little girl.

"I'm quite content here as long as I am by your side," she said, looking fondly at Lord Keith.

Mechi caught the glance. She was sure open displays of affection in this early age must be a rarity, yet she could sense the deep love that obviously existed between these two people. She wondered if she would ever have such a relationship with Robbie.

She shook her head, trying to clear her thoughts of such nonsense. He probably wanted nothing to do with her. After all, he knew nothing about her. And if he did, if she told him the truth, then he would most assuredly want nothing to do with her. No, it was just wishful thinking on her part. Like blowing out the candles on a birthday cake. But, she admitted reluctantly, she had never felt the way she did about Lord Robbie Keith, Viscount of Kintore, before in her life. And she really didn't want to feel that way about anyone else. Not now; not ever.

It seemed like hours had passed, yet Mechi's watch told her that it had been less than an hour since she had fed the horses the moldy bread. The mare which was resting on Robbie's lap suddenly twisted her head and looked up at him. Her tongue popped out of her mouth and she began to lick his hand. Soon she was trying to get to her feet.

Lord Keith was already beside the horse, helping her stand. Slowly, unsteady, yet with more strength than she had shown for hours, the horse was upright. She continued licking Robbie, who took a clump of greens from his pocket and began to feed her. She ate it with great relish, then walked quite briskly over beside Lady Keith and began licking her face.

To Mechi's surprise, Lady Keith—the most proper dowager of the castle—smiled warmly at the horse and patted her head.

Seeing that the crisis was past, Lord Keith walked over to Mechi and said, "I do not know what to say. I don't know how you did it, but somehow you have worked wonders on these animals. It is almost like magic."

Robbie shrugged his shoulders and grinned gleefully at Mechi. "See, Mums," he said, "I told you I asked for a miracle. Looks like she arrived just in a knick of time."

With all eyes fixed on them, Robbie took Mechi firmly by the arms, turned her towards him and kissed her—passionately, brazenly, his lips wet with the warmth of the sweat which had poured over him as he worked feverishly on the animals, the lifeblood of the Keith clan at Dunnottar Castle.

Mechi felt her knees go weak. This time it was not from the fever she had experienced when she had been cast back in time. No, this time she knew the cause. And if this was what it felt like to be swept off her feet, well, she would gladly spend the rest of her life lying on the ground in front of Lord Robbie Keith.

Sensing the loss of her strength, Robbie quickly placed his arms under her and gathered her up. When Mechi awoke, she was once again in the huge canopy bed with Robbie seated beside her.

"This is getting to be a habit," he said jokingly.

"One I rather like," Mechi said. She did not give voice to the rest of her thoughts, but to herself she admitted that she would like very much to spend the rest of her life waking up in Lord Robbie's bed with him at her side. Yes, she could think of a much worse fate in life.

Mechi glanced around the room. She was not sure if she was relieved or worried that she and Robbie were quite alone. Even Lady Keith, whom Mechi was sure didn't trust her, was absent. If Robbie wanted to take advantage of her, this was his chance. It surprised her that she wouldn't object if he did. As she recalled, once a respectable young woman of this day was *violated*, the man owed her a certain debt. Yes, if he wanted her half as much as she wanted him, their energy would be spent in something far more productive than fighting each other.

"Are you all right?" Robbie asked. Mechi felt his hand rubbing hers.

"Yes," she replied. "I don't know what came over me. Maybe it was the long ride. Or the rain."

"Maybe you aren't as tough as you pretend to be," Robbie said, winking at her. "It is as though you wanted to be in my arms, and if you succumbed, Mums would have no argument to my rescuing you."

"Are you accusing me of using my feminine wiles to entice you?" she asked playfully. "Why I never…"

"Oh, but in due time I suspect that you shall!"

In spite of the threat, he made no further advances towards her. Instead, he turned on his heel and headed out the door. Just before he left he said, "I have some business which is long overdue. I must attend to it. However, I shall return shortly. Meanwhile, I shall send Ann up to see to your needs." That devilish gleam was once again in those piercing green eyes. "I must admit, I much prefer you in one of Agnes's gowns. There is something far more appealing about your rosy orbs peeking out above the plunging necklines than to have your body hidden in that—whatever you call that garb."

He waved good-bye to her, and as he closed the door behind him she heard him mutter, "I wonder what other hidden treasure lie behind that shirt. GUESS! Indeed!"

Chapter XII

Everyone was hustling and bustling around Mechi. Even Lady Keith seemed unusually warm towards her. Mechi turned away from her so she would not see the self-satisfied grin on her face. Imagine! Who'd have thought some old moldy bread would cause such a ruckus.

Ann came in, her arms laden with various gowns. This time she did not trip. Instead, she stood in front of Mechi, who was sitting up on the side of the bed, and curtsied deeply to her. Agnes was close behind her, and she too curtsied. Mechi felt the color rise to her cheeks. She was not accustomed to such attention.

"Choose which one you would like to wear to sup with us," Agnes said cheerfully. "If none of them strikes your fancy, why then I'll just skitter off to bring some more."

"I'm quite sure any of them will be fine," Mechi said, watching carefully as Ann held one after another up for her inspection. She studied each one, looking for one which was not as revealing as the ones Agnes seemed to wear most of the time. Seeing that they were all quite daring, she marveled silently that Agnes had to settle for the likes of Moray. Could it be, she wondered, that the poor girl actually loved him? What a pity! She was really quite striking, with the same red curly locks that Robbie sported, but lacking the depth and intensity of his sharp green eyes.

"I do rather like the gold one," Mechi said, running her fingers over the fine satin of the gown.

"It will look lovely on you, dear, with your dark hair."

Mechi blinked. Was she hearing things? Lady Keith had entered, and she had called her *dear*! Was it possible that the woman was beginning to like her? All because of horses and moldy bread! God, how grateful she was that her father had raised her right. Proper? Probably not. But definitely right!

Mechi was tempted to test her farther, asking if she thought Robbie would approve of her choice, but decided not to press her luck.

"Come," Lady Keith said to the others in the room. "Let's leave Ann to ready

Mechi. I'm sure she can manage quite well without the rest of us gawking wildly at her."

As Ann and Mechi struggled once again to force her into that dreadful corset, Mechi seized the opportunity to learn more about Lord Robert Keith, Viscount of Kintore. In all actuality, his name and title were almost all she knew about him. Instinct told her that Ann knew as much about Robbie as anyone. Even if she must realize that a relationship could never exist between them, Mechi was certain that Ann had her fantasies about him. *Poor girl!* she thought. *How awful to love somebody and know that there is no hope of ever having that love returned.* At least she had a fighting chance with him.

Mechi jumped slightly, startled by the idea that she might love Lord Robbie. She had never been truly committed to anyone before, except for Robert Pearson, the ultimate bore. That seemed like a lifetime ago.

"When Lord Robbie left," Mechi said to Ann, "he said there was something he had to do. Do you know what his business was?"

Ann fidgeted nervously. She knew a great deal about the Keith clan, but as a confidante to them all she must be careful not to spill any of the family secrets. She had not been with the Keiths long, but she had quickly become privy to their ways. Obviously Robert had not wanted Mechi to know about his whereabouts or he would have confided in her.

"No, Lady Mechi," Ann answered. She hoped it wasn't too noticeable that she was lying. She had never been very good at tooting a tale. Her mother had always been able to tell immediately when she was trying to hide something.

Sensing her nervousness, Mechi knew instinctively that Ann would never tell her what she knew about the Keith clan. She giggled as she glanced at Ann's nose to see if it grew with the telling of each fib—like Pinnochio's. What would these people think of such a story as a wooden doll whose probiscus extended with each little white lie he told?

"Does he leave like that often?" Mechi asked, undaunted by Ann's vague reply.

"As the viscount," Ann explained, "he has many matters to attend to. I do not make it my business to follow him about."

Mechi sensed the warning in Ann's voice. If Ann, who had no doubt been taken into the confidence of many matters of the Keiths, didn't stick her nose in their business, Mechi was being warned not to do so either. But this was different. She felt that Robbie was as drawn to her as she was to him. She had heard about *soulmates*, but she never dreamed she would find hers in another time zone. In another world.

Mechi laughed as she remembered that the only soap opera she had ever watched was "Another World!" How appropriate! Funny, that was the only one that had ever appealed to her. She tried to imagine these people's reaction if she could import a television set to her solar at this very moment. Of course it would do no good, as Ben Franklin had not yet attached his famous key to the end of his kite. No, electricity was as foreign to this time and place as she ws.

She suddenly realized that without any forewarning she had come to feel more at home in these surroundings that she ever did in her own world. If she were to be transported back to the time she had escaped, would she ever feel like she belonged there again? No, something here was far more inviting and exciting that her former life. Or her future life. Or whatever.

Robert Keith sat astride his huge deep brown horse, whistling into the wind as he rode through the forest. The air was brisk and invigorating, causing him to hurry more than usual.

His whistling ceased and his head tilted back as he laughed—a deep, throaty laugh. If he was going to be honest with himself, he had to admit that it was not the cool air that was making him hurry. No, it was Mechi who caused him to hurry. The faster he finished his business, the sooner he could return to her.

He tried to explain the fascination she held. Was it the way she had first come to him? As if out of a dream? Or her strange garb? Or her loss of bearings when she first awoke—in his arms? Or the playful glimmer of light that sparkled in her eyes when she teased him mercilessly? No doubt it was all these things—and more—all wrapped up in one tiny package called Mechi Jeanotte.

He pulled on the reins, turning into the deep forest of Boscobel. He slowed the horse's gait to avoid any accidents. He knew the roots and branches could catch either him or the horse off guard, and he didn't want any unnecessary delays.

He thought of the first time he found Mechi, after she had tripped over the root of that big old oak tree at St. Andrews. Perhaps the dangers of the forest were not always bad; that had certainly been his lucky day. He seemed to be able to almost sense her head in his lap, as it had been when she regained consciousness.

He wondered if he would ever be able to claim the strange Mechi as his bride. He had been sought after long and hard throughout all of Scotland, yet he had never had any real interest in any of the women who pursued him. He wished he could explain the wonderful fascination Mechi held for him. He knew his mother was not fond of her, yet she did seem to be warming somewhat to her. And even his father...

Robert's mind wandered back to the night he had seen his father make his way into her chambers. He shook his head vigorously. He knew his suspicions had to be wrong, but he had never seen his father behave as he did that night. Had they had a rendezvous of their own? Could he ever trust a woman who would be bed by his very own father? If that was not what had occurred, then why was his father so secretive about such a meeting? What else could they have possibly had to discuss?

His heart told him, as he rode, his hot blood coursing through his veins and causing all sorts of feelings he had never known before, that he could trust her. But why, then, did she seem to know about so many things that were so odd to them? Like the rotten bread and the way she healed the horses! Was she, as his mother warned him, a witch? Or was she, like she seemed to him, someone magical and wonderful?

Before he knew it, a tiny thatched shanty came into view. He jabbed his heels into the horse's side, causing it to hurry. As he neared the tiny house, he alit and secured the rope around a tree. He hurried into the house, the door closing securely behind him.

He dreaded these visits. He wondered if Mechi would have anything more to do with him if she knew the truth behind these trips to Boscobel. In the midst of the fame and fortune of the Keith clan, they had their own shame. His heart ached as he watched her. Could Mechi's magic, if she knew, undo the terrible wrong that affected the family? Would he dare tell her, hoping that she would be able to change the course of history?

Mechi was entertained by the Keiths quite royally while they passed the day. She listened each time she heard someone enter the castle, for the sound of Robbie's voice. She felt strangely ill-at-ease, knowing he was not there. Would he return before the evening meal? If not, how long would he stay away? And where had he gone in such haste?

Trying to occupy her mind with other thoughts, she turned her attention to Queen Mary. She hoped Lord Keith had sent word to her that she had arrived safely at Dunnottar. The queen had been so kind to her, she didn't intend to be unappreciative for her hospitality. But, a gal's gotta do what a gal's gotta do.

What if he is in danger? She wondered suddenly. *He*, of course, was Lord Robbie. Maybe he wasn't as innocent and perfect as he seemed. "When something seems too good to be true, it usually is." The words echoed in her ears in her father's voice. He had told her that countless times. Was he trying to prepare her for the likes of Lord Robbie? Was *he* too good to be true? He did seem almost perfect. Not just his physical attributes, which were certainly splendid to a fault. His long red hair, his neat red beard, his muscles, which made her feel so safe when he held her, his eyes… Oh, those eyes! She could almost see them now, as she cleared her own eyes to fix his green orbs in the vision of her memory. Oh, what those eyes could do to you! They could melt a heart of stone. If the CIA had those eyes, they could uncover the hidden secrets of the world!

"Yes, Lady Mechi?" she heard a serving girl ask her, bringing her sharply back to reality.

"Yes, thank you," she said, accepting the fragile cup graciously.

Mechi smiled as she sipped slowly on the cup of hot brew. If she tried *really* hard, she might be able to grow accustomed to such a life as this. People waiting on her hand and foot. People to do her bidding, going to fetch whatever she wanted.

"An encyclopedia," she said, unaware that she had spoke audibly.

"An encyclopedia?" Lady Keith asked, a puzzled look on her face. "What is an encyclopedia?"

Mechi stumbled about in her mind, trying to discern how to describe such a book to these people. Surely the Encyclopedia Britannica, which she assumed was the earliest of its kind, had not been written yet. Not even the first edition.

"It is a book they have in France," she explained, hoping they would not think to ask Queen Mary about it at some later time, "which relates the history of many things. It is a most invaluable book."

"I should think it would be!" Angus said. He was, Mechi had noticed, the most studious of the Keith offspring. "I wonder why no one in Scotland has ever thought to write such a book. Or even in London, to my knowledge."

"I'm sure that one day it will be done in England, too," Mechi said,, pleased that she knew this prediction would come to pass and that it would be the most widely accepted source of factual information ever to be found on the shelves of every library in the world.

"And for what purpose do you wish such a book—an encyclopedia?" Angus asked.

Mechi blinked at the question. She could not tell them, "To read about Queen Mary. To learn exactly what she did to Darnley and what they eventually did to her. To see if I can prevent such a tragedy from occurring." No, she could not tell them the truth. No more than Ann would tell her the truth about where Lord Robbie had gone.

"I find history fascinating," Mechi said simply, hoping her answer would be satisfactory. Besides, that was true. Especially now that she was *living* history. Yes, her former intrigue with history had, as her father had warned her, been her undoing. He always said it would be one of her three loves which would "do her in." Golf, history and horses. She realized that in the past few days, all three of her passions had nearly destroyed her. Or was it that love that had given her a new love? The love of a good man, which her father had so urged her to seek. Or was this all a dream and she just couldn't wake up from it? She still wasn't sure.

"I, too, find it most exciting!" Angus said enthusiastically. "Perhaps I could spend some time with you, telling you of the great feats the Keiths have done in our many wars."

"I would like that very much," Mechi said, her voice filled with genuine interest.

Lady Keith sat on the sidelines, watching another of her sons being taken in by this strange young woman. She must speak to William! She could not allow this to happen. Not to one of her sons, and certainly not to two of them!

"Fetch me Darnley! Quickly!" Queen Elizabeth ordered. "I must speak to him at once!"

"But, your majesty," the page said, bowing deeply to his queen, "surely you remember that you sent him to keep an eye on your cousin, Mary."

"Oh, yes, of course I remember it!" What did he take her for? A fool? After all, it was perfectly normal for her to be slightly confused. She had just returned form another of her journeys.

"Then bring me Lord Cecil!" she demanded. "I seem to have lost my sapphire ring!"

"I shall send for him immediately," the page replied, then trying to make the matter seem less upsetting, added, "But it is only a jewel, your majesty. And you have so many."

Queen Elizabeth flew into a rage. "You fool! You bloody, damned fool! You don't understand at all! It is my very favorite jewel! My amulet! My way of escape! Without it… Oh, forget it! Just go find Cecil! Away with you!"

The queen sat, staring into space, her heart longing for someone with whom she could share her strange, mysterious travels. But she knew of no one who would understand. She could imagine Cecil when she told him she had lost her favorite jeweled ring. He knew how fond of it she was, but he had no idea why. And, of course, he would not understand; after all, he still had those valuable figurines from China propping the door open in the upstairs bedroom at Theopolds. The stupidity of the man! He had no sense of value whatsoever! Still, he did seem to be an invaluable voice in so many of the affairs of state.

"Yes?" Cecil asked as he entered the salon where the queen awaited him. "What do you want?"

Queen Elizabeth, frustrated by everything at the moment, hated his informality with her—today more than usual.

"Bow!" she ordered. And Cecil's head nearly hit the floor as he stooped before his sovereign.

Chapter XIII

The day was spent with the various Keiths skittering about hither and yon as they busied themselves with various tasks. Mechi watched them uneasily, feeling that she should find something constructive to do, but not having the faintest idea of what it might be. Finally, Lady Keith came and sat on the velvet chair, seeming frightfully fragile as Mechi watched her rest her arms on the massive carved arms.

"One should think," Lady Keith said, "that we must be a very boring lot to the likes of you. Mary—*Queen* Mary—tells me you are as avid a golfer as she is. And your performance with the horses! Why, my! You are certainly a creature full of surprises!"

Mechi smiled. She couldn't remember anyone ever referring to her as a *creature* before. Like one of the animals who were kept outside. Did Lady Keith wish she could evict her to the outer stables, like one of them? She sensed that she was quite uncomfortable with her, in spite of her effort to be a good hostess.

"I find your family anything but boring," Mechi admitted honestly. "In fact, I find them all—you all—very fascinating." *Especially Lord Robbie*, she admitted to herself.

"When you first arrived," Lady Keith said, "what did you discuss with my husband?"

Mechi felt the color rise to her cheeks. She assumed that Lord Keith would certainly have waited until she was asleep before he had come to her bedroom. And if Lady Keith was awake, or awoke to find him absent from their bed, why hadn't she questioned him? Surely she didn't expect there to have been any amorous encounter between them. Or was this family not as perfect as it seemed? Had he perhaps strayed at some time in the past, giving her reason to doubt his faithfulness?

"You knew?" was all Mechi could manage to get out.

"So you don't deny it?" Lady Keith asked, daggers shooting from her eyes. Eyes which, Mechi noticed for the first time, had the same fire and strength in them that Robbie's eyes had.

Mechi knew she could never lie to anyone who looked at her with those eyes, be it Robbie or his mother. She would have to try to explain what had happened the best she could, yet still not tell her the *whole* truth. No one could comprehend the whole truth. Not even herself.

"I felt that I must warn him," Mechi began.

"Warn him?" Lady Keith asked, her voice sharp with distrust. "Warn him of what? The witch you really are?"

"No," Mechi replied. "I know I must seem strange to you…"

Lady Keith laughed loudly. "If that isn't the daffiest thing I've ever heard! You show up here out of nowhere. You capture the heart of my son. No, of two of my sons. But you are not satisfied. No! You want more! You lure my husband to your solar in the deep of the night, and you say it was to *warn him*! You witch! I do not trust you now! I shall never trust you! And in spite of the way you have captured my son, you shall never have my blessing! Never! Do you hear me? Never!"

Before Mechi could utter a word in her own defense, Lord Keith came running into the room.

"Darling!" he said, going to his wife and taking her in his arms. "Whatever has she done to upset you so?"

Lady Keith sobbed as she beat her head against his chest.

"You have the audacity to ask what she has done? When you have done it with her? Nay, I shall not forgive you. I cannot. But I shall fight for you to the bitter end. She shall not have a single Keith for her own!"

With that she pulled out of his arms and ran from the room, leaving both of them looking at each other, stunned by such behavior.

Lord Keith hesitated. Should he follow his wife and try to offer her an explanation? Or would his protests just serve to reinforce her doubts and suspicions?

"Go to her!" Mechi demanded. "Tell her—about Mary. About Darnley. About the whole thing."

"But how can I explain it?" he asked. "I don't understand it myself."

Mechi shrugged her shoulders. "She already thinks I am a witch with supernatural powers. Let her think what she wants, but don't lose her for my sake."

Lord Keith hurried up the wide stairway after his beloved wife. He knew Mechi was right. Nothing was as important to him as she was. He must not lose the trust they had always had in each other.

Mechi watched him as he climbed the steps, two at a time, the long tails of his coat flapping behind him. As she sat in the great hall, she wished Robbie was there. He had been gone only a few hours, yet it seemed like an eternity had passed. Suddenly, she felt alone. More alone than she had been since the day her father had died. She needed Robbie. Desperately. She closed her eyes and tried to remember how it had felt to be in his arms, his strength pouring into her from his big, muscular body.

The horses! If she went to them, at least they might make her feel a sense of belonging. Yes, they had always been her friends. She needed someone to trust her, even if it was just an animal.

She rose and went outside, heading straight for the stables. She smiled as she saw that some of the horses had recovered enough to graze. Her smile quickly changed to panic as she realized that it must have been the grass which had caused the anthrax.

"Quick!" she commanded the stable boys. "Get the horses out of the pasture!"

The boys practically worshipped Mechi, after observing her cure of their charges. They would obey her, even if she told them to jump off the high cliff which harbored Dunnottar.

One timid young lad approached her. "Why?" he asked.

"It is probably something from the grass which made them sick in the first place," she explained. "For a few days, until it has cleared up, just feed them on oats and hay. Don't allow them to graze."

"Yes, Lady Mechi," the boy said, bowing to her.

Mechi glanced towards a young colt which was lying in the corner of the stable. She was worried about it, since it was not nearly as strong as the older, bigger horses. She walked towards it and sat down on the hay beside it. She took the colt's head and placed it gently on her lap. She began to stroke it, and was soon rewarded with a tiny whinny and a smile—if horses can smile. She had always been convinced they could and did.

She was oblivious to Robbie's entry into the stable. He grinned widely at her. She looked like she belonged, even though his mother would undoubtedly explode if she could see her on the ground with a horse in her lap, clad in one of Agnes's finest frocks. She seemed unaware that it was not normal for a young woman of her position to be in the stables at all, much less wearing a shimmering gold silk gown. The crinolines were sticking up all around the horse's head, giving Robbie a glimpse of her shapely legs which were normally hidden from his view. They made him hunger to see more of her.

He stood silently for several minutes, debating about whether he should speak, or just leave, or if he should see how long it would take for her to notice him there.

Mechi talked softly to the colt, offering words of encouragement and feeding it tiny handfuls of cracked oats. Finally, he spoke.

"Is he going to be all right?" he asked, going over and squatting down beside her.

Mechi jumped. She lifted her head and looked up to find herself face to face with those huge green piercing eyes. They went through her like a sharply pointed arrow.

"I—I think so," she stammered. "Yes, I'm sure he will. His fever has gone down and he is not fighting any more." Her eyes sparkled as she said, "In a short time he should be ready to ride."

Robbie laughed at her ignorance. She seemed so knowledgeable about these creatures, but this one would not be ready to mount until it was considerably older and stronger.

"Only if the rider is a very small child," he said, winking at her. "Even you, Lady Mechi, would be too much for his wobbly legs for some time yet."

"I didn't mean…" Mechi said, realizing the blunder she had made. She felt a strange sensation at his use of her name. It sent a tingle through her body clear to her toes. If only he would drop the *Lady*.

"There is no need to defend yourself," he answered warmly. He reached out and began to slowly and tenderly rub her shoulders.

"You are very tense," he said, continuing the massage. "There is a bad draft in here. You really should go inside. You have done quite enough around here. Why, the horses are our livelihood and you have preserved them for us."

Mechi liked the confidence and appreciation his voice conveyed, but the sense of his fingers on her bare skin was even more pleasant.

"Why did you come out here?" he asked. "Were the horses worse?"

"No," Mechi replied. She knew she could not tell him of his mother's accusations. Nor could she confide in him about the meeting she and Lord Keith had had that night in her solar. Hastening for a logical explanation she said, "I wanted to check on them. In case any of them needed my attention."

"And this one did?" he asked, a gleam in his eye.

"Yes," she said simply. "He seemed quite frail and weak yet. Talking to them helps, you know, just as it does with plants."

"You talk to plants?" he asked, obviously confused.

Mechi laughed. "Only if they are sick and need nurturing."

Suddenly Robbie doubled over, grabbing his stomach and emitting loud groans.

"What is it?" she asked, suddenly afraid that he was going to die. She had heard of people who had contracted anthrax from the cattle or horses. Was it possible? Did he have the fever, too? What could she do? Would he respond to the moldy break like the horses had? Panic gripped every part of her being. "Are you sick? Please, don't die on me! You are the only true friend I have here in this world. You and Queen Mary. No, you can't do this to me!"

Robbie burst into loud peals of laughter. His ploy had worked. He had wanted at least as much sympathy and attention as the horses had gotten from her, and he had certainly gotten it.

"It does work!" he said, jumping to his feet and pulling her with him, causing the poor colt's head to fall *kerplunk* onto the ground. "You talked to me, and suddenly I am healed! It is a miracle! I knew you were a miracle the very first time I laid eyes on you. The day I found you at St. Andrews with your head quite knocked up by the oak tree."

Now it was Mechi's turn to laugh. She was absolutely positive poor Lord Robbie Keith had no idea of what the modern term "knocked up" meant. She hadn't heard that expression since Laurie Miller had been forced to drop out of high school in disgrace because she was pregnant. "She got herself *knocked up!*" her father, who was on the school board, informed her. Well, if Mechi Jeanotte had traveled back in time more than four hundred years, she sure wanted to get *knocked up* by something a whole lot more exciting than an old oak root!

Such a thought caused her to shake her head vehemently. She had never really thought much about sex. Oh, of course she had studied all about it in health class, and she was nobody's dummy as to what it was all about, but she never could figure out why something like sex caused so many people to get so worked up about. It really held no appeal to her at all. Until, that is, Lord Robbie Keith. Now, the idea of having sex with this big strong hunk of the past produced feelings she never thought herself capable of having.

Rather than admitting, even to herself, what she was thinking, she began pounding on Robbie's chest and arms.

"What are you doing that for?" Robbie asked, grabbing hold of her arms to stop her.

"You—you *meanie!*" she shouted. "You scared me half to death! I thought you were dying! I thought you got sick from the horses. Don't you ever do anything like that again!"

She broke into loud sobs. He put his arms around her, offering her solace and comfort in his powerful embrace. And that is how they were when Lord and Lady Keith came in search of them. At her husband's insistence, Lady Keith had come to find her to apologize for thinking that she would do anything at all to try to entice her husband. Or that her husband would be less than faithful to her.

Losing all self-control, Lady Keith began to scream at Mechi, pulling her away from her son.

"I told you to leave my men alone!" she yelled. "Not only my husband, but my sons as well! Go! Away with you! Get to your quarters, and don't you dare leave them until I have made arrangements for you to return to Edinburgh! If you behave as badly with Queen Mary, she will no doubt have you beheaded!"

Mechi gathered her long skirts in her hands and held them up as she ran across the courtyard to the castle. She ran up the steps, nearly tripping on her crinolines, and into her room. She slid the heavy iron rod across the door, wishing for a way of escape.

"If only I could get back to St. Andrews," she lamented. "If only there was a way out."

Chapter XIV

Mechi could hear the entire Keith clan milling about on the lower floor of the castle, but she felt no desire to join them. She had been chastened, accused, frightened and abused by enough of the family for one day. For a lifetime.

She gazed out the window longingly. She wished for escape, but there was none. She could always steal one of the horses and head back to Edinburgh. Surely Mary would offer her protection. Or, she could stop midway at St. Andrews and hope for a repeat performance of the plight which had brought her here.

Robbie would help me, she thought, *if only I could get a message to him.* She knew the blood of the Scottish clan ran thicker than the highland fog, and that he might not defy his mother's orders, even if she could reach him.

She was sure by now they had eaten the evening meal, and no one had bothered to come for her. They had not even had one of the servants bring the scraps up to her room. Not that she was hungry; she could not have eaten anything they brought her. Especially not that horrible delicacy they called "haggis." Just the thought of the ugly mass of meat and vegetables stuffed into the lining of a sheep's stomach made her feel like she was going to vomit.

Darkness reigned outside the castle. It was a cloudy night; she could not see the sparkle of the stars on the water. In fact, she could not even see the water below. It was far too steep a cliff for her to consider jumping to the safety of the sea. Even if she survived such a jump, she had nowhere to go once she was away from the castle.

In despair, she threw herself on the huge four poster bed and sobbed. Finally, exhausted, she fell asleep.

At the sound of a light tapping on her door, she rolled over and pulled the coverlet tighter up against her head. Convinced that she was again dreaming, she tried to return to sleep for whatever escape she could find from the reality of her situation, but the knocking persisted.

She sat up in bed, straining her ears to see if there really was someone there. She heard a slight whisper.

"Lady Mechi, open up. It's me, Robert."

Mechi hurried from the bed. She had been so lost in her thoughts she had not bothered to remove her clothes. Now, as she tried to move, every muscle in her body ached.

"Stupid corset!" she grumbled, trying to move as fast as she could for fear Robbie would decide she was asleep. Surely then he would leave, and she desperately wanted him there with her.

"I'm coming," she called out softly as she struggled to remove the bar from the door. When it was finally free, it began to slip from her hands. She quickly caught it, sighing deeply. Such a loud noise as it would have made would certainly have summoned someone, and she had all the company she wanted standing there looking at her.

"May I enter?" Robbie asked.

"Oh, yes," she said, grabbing him by the arm and pulling him inside. Sheer instinct caused her to replace the rod on the doorway.

"Afraid I might get away?" he asked playfully.

"No," she replied. "I'm afraid you might disappear. Like I did from St. Andrew's."

The words were no sooner out of her mouth than she regretted saying them. Robbie gave her a puzzled look.

"But you didn't disappear from St. Andrews," he said. "That's exactly where we found you. What do you mean?"

"It's much too late to try to explain," Mechi said. "Maybe some other day."

And maybe not, she thought, knowing he would never understand.

"Are you all right?" he asked, the concern for her well-being registering in his eyes. "I mean, did Mums send you up any vittles?"

"No," Mechi said, "but I wasn't hungry anyway."

Mechi sat on the edge of the bed, twisting this way and that from the discomfort of her corset.

"Wouldn't you like to sit down, too?" she asked.

"Aye," Robbie said, then plopped down, his legs crossed in front of him, on the floor in front of her.

"There is a chair there," Mechi said, smiling.

"I'd rather the floor," he said, "unless it bothers you."

Mechi shook her head. He could sit anywhere he wanted to, as long as he stayed with her.

"I've always preferred the floor to a chair," he explained. "Ever since I was a little boy. I know it makes no sense, but when I was on the floor I always felt like I could see better. Especially when I was happy or pleased. I could..." He hesitated. "... be in the middle of everyone else, yet still be alone. Does that sound quite daft?"

Mechi laughed. "Nothing you could ever do would seem *daft* to me." She studied him carefully, looking down into his handsome face. Sitting there, below her, he seemed almost like a little boy. So secure. So confident. She longed to tell him about her strange *trip* at St. Andrew's that had cast her into another world—another time—but she stopped herself.

"You would think *I* was the one who was daft," she said softly. "If only you knew."

"Knew what?" he asked.

"Nothing," she said, hoping to steer the conversation in another direction. "Where did you go earlier when you left me in such a hurry?"

He ran his fingers through his bushy red beard, which she noticed he always did when he was nervous.

"I—um—I just had some business to tend to." His eyes pleaded with her not to question him any more. "For my father," he added quickly.

"Business?" she asked, her curiosity getting the best of her. She was determined to learn everything she could about Lord Robbie Keith, Viscount of Kintore. "What kind of business?"

"Personal business," Robbie said, still playing with his beard. "Private business. Things you would never understand. Things which must be kept secret."

His admission of something seemingly off color surprised Mechi. She had assumed that the Keith clan was far above anything which might even hint at a scandal, yet she smelled something very amiss about Robbie's *business*.

"You don't trust me," she said, her lower lip curling into a pout. He had no reason to trust her, yet she had felt that he did. That they were kindred spirits. That they could be open and honest with each other. Yet she had not confided in him as to her lot in life. But that was quite different. He couldn't be a *transplant*, too.

Robbie reached up to her and pulled her onto his lap. His arms encircled her. Her breath came in short, hurried gasps. He was probably just trying to reassure her of the safety Dunnottar offered, she reasoned. Why, then, was her heart pounding like it would break through her skin at any moment? Why were her eyes blurred? Why did she feel like her forehead was drenched in sweat?

Before she could answer any of her heart's questions, his lips were pressed tightly against hers, drawing the rest of her breath away.

"Do you still doubt my trust?" he asked when he finally released her.

"I—I don't doubt—anything!" she mumbled. *I've never been so sure of anything in my life!* she thought. *I love you, Lord Robbie Keith, Viscount of Kintore.*

Mechi jerked her head, trying to knock some sense into it. She couldn't love this man. He represented everything she had always wanted in the perfect mate. He was strong. He was handsome. He was brave. He was tender, warm and compassionate. He was everything any woman could possibly dream of. On top of everything else, he was even rich!

"No!" she shouted.

Robbie clasped his hand over her mouth.

"Hush!" he warned. "We mustn't let anyone discover us here." Sensing that she was uneasy with his actions, he apologized.

"I'm sorry," he said. "Truly I am. I don't know what came over me. I'm—not usually so bloody brazen."

So, Mechi thought, it was as new for him as it was for her. That's impossible. He had certainly had his share of young women chasing after him. Still, maybe he enjoyed playing hard-to-get. A handsome devil like him, surely he wasn't a virgin!

The idea caused Mechi to smile.

"You find it amusing? A Scotsman begging forgiveness of a young maiden?"

"No," Mechi said, color rising in her cheeks. "I find *you* amusing."

"I'm not certain I'm flattered," Robbie said, returning her smile. "Should I be?"

"Definitely," Mechi said. "I must admit I'm quite flattered by your attention."

"And my kiss?" he asked, that ever-present gleam in his eyes, even in the near darkness.

"That too," she admitted.

"'Tis good," he said, taking her hand in his. "I dinna think I felt too much resistance."

Mechi turned her head away quickly. She couldn't let this happen. They were from two different worlds. Two different times. As much as she yearned to belong to him, she knew it could never be. She couldn't lead him on. What if she were cast back to her own life as suddenly and unexplainably as she had entered his? No, she had to put a rein on her heart.

The only trouble was, there was no way to reason with her feelings. They were running rampant. She had to put a stop to this immediately.

"You have to leave!" she ordered, climbing off his lap. "Now. Please, just leave."

Shocked, he stared at her open-mouthed. He was so sure she felt the same way about him as he did about her. Could he have been so wrong?

"I don't understand," he protested without moving.

"Please leave. This can't happen. We must stop it."

"I can't leave," he insisted. "Not until you tell me what is going on. You felt the same thing I did when we kissed. I could feel it. It wasn't just a kiss. Oh, yes, I must admit I've had my fair share of kisses. But none of them made the hair on my toes inside me boots stand up on end."

Mechi bit her lip. She didn't dare laugh, but the image of Robbie's red hair on his toes standing up on end was more than she could bear.

"That's better," he said, standing up and moving to the bed. He pulled her down beside him.

She didn't try to get away, nor did she continue with this crazy game of sending him running from her room like a hunted grouse in the forest.

"You must explain," he begged. "I know you will find this hard to believe, but I have never felt this way before. I have heard of two people being in love, but I never imagined it would be like this."

"But we hardly know each other," Mechi said.

"So? We have a lifetime to get to know each others little habits and pits."

"You don't understand," Mechi said.

"You're quite right. Do you find me so appalling to look at?"

"Oh, no, my lord!" she said, trying to gain some distance between them by assuming a formal air. "Quite the opposite. I find you extremely handsome."

"Then you do not like my voice?" he asked.

"Your voice is as melodic as a nightingale in a tree," Mechi said, remembering an old poem she had learned in school years ago.

"Probably hasn't been written yet," she mused under her breath.

"What's not been written?" Robbie asked.

"A poem," she answered. "A certain poem."

"Then I shall write it for you," he said, that impish twinkle in his eyes dancing about.

"There is nothing about you which I dislike," Mechi said. "It is just that we cannot allow this to happen. We are from two different worlds."

"Of course," Robbie said. "I am from the crags of Scotland and you are from the magic land of France."

"I told you before," Mechi insisted, "I am not from France."

"But you said you are from near Paris."

"Yes," Mechi said, knowing it was hopeless to try to explain this whole mess to him. She decided she would have to try to play out the charade the best she could.

"I was sent here on a special mission," she began. "Queen Mary is in grave danger, and I have been asked to come to deliver a warning to her and to protect her from Darnley."

Robbie stared at her, not knowing what to say. He knew Mary had devout followers in France. After all, she had been *their* queen a short time ago. But now she belonged to Scotland. She belonged to her own people. If Mechi's words were true— and he had no reason to doubt them—his allegiance also lay with Mary.

"You are an emissary for the French to protect Mary?" he asked. "They sent a woman to do such an important and dangerous job?"

"They took what they had," she said. "They knew I was devoted to Mary. I never did like that wretch she was married to! They knew they could trust me. So, here I am."

Mechi held her breath. Would he buy her story? Would he believe her? If not, what else could she do to convince him that she was telling the truth?

The truth! Well, this was at least a partial truth. She had not been able to shake the feeling that she had been sent back to this place at this particular time for the express purpose of protecting Mary. Besides, she had warned Lord Keith of it. If worse came to worse she could tell Robbie to ask his father about it.

"And just how do you intend to protect the queen?" he asked, anxious to hear her explanation.

"I asked your father for his help," Mechi said.

Robbie's mind went back to the night he had seen his father sneak into her quarters. Was that what they were doing? They were plotting ways to protect Queen Mary?

He sighed deeply. He hated to admit, even to himself, the thoughts that had gone through his head when he had seen his father enter her room. He could not bear the thought of a romantic tryst; a plot to destroy the queen was much easier to accept.

"If you are determined to protect our queen," he said, pulling her tightly against his hard, warm body, "then I shall vow to protect you."

Again, he kissed her. Only this time he knew what he was getting into. Or so he thought!

Chapter XV

"Did you hear from Lady Mechi?" Darnley asked Queen Mary as they sat at the table to break the fast of the night. "Or anyone who might have seen her?"

"Aye," Mary replied. "William sent word that she had returned to Dunnottar, as he suspected."

"And is he returning her to you?" Darnley asked.

Mary laughed at him. "She's not a possession—to be handed about from one person to another. I suspect our little lass Mechi is quite capable of caring for herself."

"She does seem an independent sort," Darnley agreed. "Was there anything else Sir William's messenger relayed?"

"Oh, yes," Mary said. "He was quite full of praise for our young miss. Seems she's quite a hero back on the fiddlehead."

"How so?" Darnley inquired.

"We knew the horses had a malady. When Lady Mechi got there, she fed them moldy bread."

"Moldy bread?" Darnley asked, obviously puzzled.

"Aye, so the man said. And the astonishing thing is, the horses began to heal. Almost immediately! Like a form of miracle."

"Or witchcraft?" Darnley suggested.

"Nay, she cannot be a witch," Mary said. "She's much too pretty for that."

Darnley shrugged his shoulders. Women had never made any sense to him, and this one was no exception. But, he would have to pay close heed to her every move and wish if he was to claim her as his wife, as he fully intended to do.

His thoughts wandered to Queen Elizabeth, back in London. He still had to report to her of Mary's intentions on the throne. No way was she going to surrender her crown to her cousin. Not even for Darnley!

"I must ride into the moors today," Darnley announced. "Malcolm is expecting me."

"Then go," Mary said, suddenly irritated by his wishy-washy attitude. He had a mind of his own. Or did he? Her blood boiled at the mere presence of the man.

Never shall I succomb to such a one as Darnley! She promised herself. No, if she was ever to wed a man, it would be one which would suit her own purposes. And Darnley didn't suit a thing she desired. Not personally, nor for the kingdom. He would never be true to Scotland, as she was. She looked at him in disgust.

"If you must go," she said, trying to sound concerned and interested, "then it is best you be on your way early. You must not delay, as it is a lengthy ride. I shall have a steed prepared for you."

"Thank you," Darnley said, bowing to the queen. As he left, he gathered some of the morsels still on the table and stuffed them greedily into his pockets for the journey.

As you might expect, Mary thought, *his greed reaches to every corner of his being.*

Mechi awoke in the morning. She went to the tiny window and looked out. Again, as most mornings, it was foggy. She rubbed her eyes sleepily, pushed her hair back with her fingers, stretched and yawned.

"Do you hold the key to my escape?" she asked, knowing there was no one near enough to hear her, nor to provide the answer she wasn't sure she wanted. Life was so much simpler back in Aberdeen, Maryland. There was no monarch to protect. No ailing horses. And she had all the modern conveniences she missed here. Why, she couldn't even sit and watch an hour of TV! But, there was one drawback: most of all, there was no Lord Robbie Keith, Viscount of Kintore, awaiting her if she left.

"I don't know if that's an asset or a deficit," she muttered softly.

"Ye're up and about?" Ann asked as she opened the door a smidgen.

"Yes," Mechi replied. "Just barely."

"If I might set about fixin' ye fer the day?" she asked.

"If I'm going to have to wear one of Agnes's damnable gowns again, I'll certainly need your help." She sighed. "What I wouldn't give to put on something comfortable and take off through the woods on one of the horses."

"Ye like to ride, do ye?" Ann asked.

"I grew up riding," Mechi explained. "My father bred horses, much as the Keith's do."

"I dinna know," Ann said, smiling. "No wonder you and the bonnie Robert get on so well together."

"You think we do?" Mechi asked, blushing slightly.

"Aye, 'tis a fool what cannot see ye fits together like a quill and ink."

Quaint, Mechi thought, *but I like the analogy.*

"He likes ye, ya know," Ann said, winking at Mechi. "Ye can see it in his eyes."

"Those eyes!" Mechi exclaimed. "Have you ever seen anything like them before in your life?"

"No, I cannot say as I have," Ann admitted.

Mechi shifted about nervously as she remembered discovering that Ann was extremely fond of young Robbie Keith. It must bother her to see him paying attention to someone else.

"Does it bother you?" Mechi asked.

"Does what bother me?" Ann asked.

"To see Robbie with me?"

"Nay," she said, turning her face away from Mechi so she couldn't see the hurt in her eyes. "If there's anythin' in the world what will make my Robert happy, then that is what I wish for him."

Mechi debated about pursuing the conversation, but decided against it. In a way, it was as if Ann was giving them her blessing. Not that they needed it, but it meant a great deal to Mechi.

"And a good mornin' to you," Robert greeted Mechi, a grin on his face as he recalled the kiss they had shared the night before.

"Good morning, my lord," Mechi said, curtsying and hoping she was using the right title for him. She had never had a lord and master before, but if she could choose one…

"And to you, my lord and lady," she said, again curtsying to Lord and Lady Keith.

Lord Keith returned a warm greeting, and Lady Keith mumbled something—too low for Mechi to hear.

Mechi had so hoped she was winning Lady Keith over, but their encounters had certainly done nothing towards that end. She wondered if she would ever welcome her into their household.

What a ridiculous idea! she thought. She had to keep reminding herself that she didn't belong here. She had been sent for a specific purpose, and she was sure that once that goal had been achieved she would find herself back in the twentieth century.

During the night, she had stayed awake for hours, thinking. How much should she tell Robbie? Would he have her locked away and declared mad if she told him too much? Was she perhaps crazy? Was this all still some crazy mixed up dream? But, if she really was here, and *this* was reality, would she be able to thwart

Darnley's attempts to undo Queen Mary? And could she stop Mary from killing him, even if it was for her own self-preservation? And how could she stop Queen Mary from being beheaded?

"Something troubling you this morn?" Lord Keith asked Mechi as he studied her mood.

"No," Mechi said. "It is just the fog. It makes me sad."

"There is no fog in Paris?" Lady Keith asked, trying to sound polite by entering into the conversation.

"Not often," Mechi replied. "Not like it is here."

"Then perhaps you should desire to return to Paris," Lady Keith suggested.

That would suit you just fine, wouldn't it? Mechi thought disgustedly. *Then you wouldn't have to worry about me stealing your beloved son.*

"Is there something which might lighten your mood?" Lord Keith asked. As he watched her, Mechi sensed that he was thinking of the warning she had given him about Queen Mary. "Perhaps you might like to return to Holyrood?"

Mechi was torn. If she truly had a mission to protect Mary, then she should certainly be there with her. But her heart longed to stay here with Robbie.

"Perhaps soon," Mechi said, causing Lady Keith to smile. "But there is one thing I should enjoy doing."

"And what might that be?" Lord Keith asked.

"You know, of course, that my father had a ranch—that he raised horses near Paris, too."

"So you've said," Lord Keith replied.

"I do feel quite lost without being able to ride," she said. "If it wouldn't be too much trouble, I would really like to take one of the horses and go for a ride. Not a long ride, but just to feel at home."

"And how can we be sure you won't run away?" Lord Keith asked pointedly.

"Like I did from Edinburgh?" she asked, laughing. "I have not heard of any other ailing horses, so I assure you I will behave myself and be back before long."

"Pity!" Lady Keith sputtered. She jumped as Lord Keith kicked her beneath the table.

"I'll be glad to accompany her," Robert offered—too quickly to please his mother. Seeing her stern look, he hastened to add, "Just to assure that she does return."

"I think that is a wise decision," Lord Keith said.

Mechi smiled at Lady Keith. She might hold a certain power over her husband's head, but it was plain to see that he definitely wore the pants in the family.

"I promise," Mechi said, trying to set her mind at ease, "I'll be good."

As she looked at Robbie from the corner of her eye, she caught his devilish wink. She wondered if Robbie intended to do the same. She could always hope…

As Mechi departed, going to her room to don her one set of clothes that was appropriate for riding, she realized she was being followed. She turned to see Agnes right on her heels as she climbed the stairs.

"I'll fetch you a riding skirt," she said. "You could not possibly ride in a gown."

"You're right about that," Mechi said, glad for someone who seemed to understand a little of the complications of life in such a time as 1561.

"But Mums really does not approve of the—*things*— you were clad in when you arrived."

"No," Mechi said. "And I really do not want to alienate her."

"No," Agnes said, "not if you want to win her approval. For Robbie's sake, try to tread carefully around her."

"For Robbie's sake?" Mechi asked.

"Of course," Agnes said. "Anyone can see he is smitten."

Mechi blushed. *Smitten*! Such a quaint, old-fashioned word! Besides, just because he had kissed her once. Well, twice. Or was it three times? She found it hard to sort through the exchanges they had known.

"Would you mind a word of advice from a caring sister?" Agnes asked.

"Not at all," Mechi said. "I'd welcome it."

"Don't try to push him. He's had more than his share of chances at anyone he wants. But, he wants you. Just let him think he's pursuing you. Not the other way around."

"But I haven't…" Mechi protested.

"I know," Agnes said, smiling warmly at her. "You play the game very well."

Mechi knew she wasn't talking about golf. After all, Agnes had convinced Moray to propose to her just a few days ago. Yes, they were kindred spirits, too, over the ages. They could both *play the game.*

"As do you," Mechi said. "And we both play to win."

Chapter XVI

Mechi hurried to don her riding apparel, then raced off to the stables. For the first time since she arrived, she felt truly free. She knew that if she was mounted on the back of one of Dunnottar's great stallions, she could ride to her heart's content. The only thing that could improve on such a scenario was to have Robbie riding beside her. And now that was to be, too.

She laughed as she ran. If anyone had told her a week ago that she would be riding through the forests and trails of Scotland with Lord Robbie Keith, Viscount of Kintore, she would have declared them insane. So, she reasoned, if this is insanity— welcome! She had never been so delightfully happy in her entire life.

"Ready?" Robbie asked as she came towards him.

"You bet!" she said, her voice full of enthusiasm and her eyes sparkling like the dew on the morning grass when the first rays of sunlight hit it.

He walked over beside her, helping her mount. She smiled as she wondered if they ever used stirrups, or if they had not yet been invented. There were two woven blankets on the horse's back. She was glad for the use of Agnes's riding skirt. *Culottes*, she thought, or a *divided skirt*. Why can't these people call anything what it really is? She wanted full control of the horse, and she knew she could never manage it with a flowing skirt which would force her to ride side saddle.

Before Robbie was even astride his horse, she was off and running. As he mounted, he smiled admiringly at her. She was as good a horsewoman when she was riding as she had proven to be when she was tending them in their bout of illness.

"You are a wild one!" he called out as he pulled up beside her.

"You got a problem with that?" Mechi asked, not slowing but challenging him to keep apace with her.

"None," Robbie answered, then pulled out ahead of her.

She joyfully accepted the challenge and soon passed him. For some time they continued this way; first one ahead, then the other. Finally, Mechi pulled on the reins, bringing the horse to a complete stand still.

"Had your fill?" Robbie asked as he joined her.

"No," Mechi replied. "But I don't want to tire the horse too much." She stroked its neck gently and tenderly.

"Follow me," Robbie said, trotting his horse slowly.

"To the ends of the earth," Mechi said softly, as she did exactly as he instructed.

Soon a clearing came into view. Robbie alit from his horse and tied it to a tree at the edge of the field. Mechi followed suit. Her back was still turned to him when she felt his arms wrap around her waist.

She wriggled within his embrace until she was facing him. He was so-o-o-o close! She was completely enveloped by him. Not just his arms, which felt so secure—so right—but his manly smell, the gaze of those piercing eyes, the warmth of his breath on her face.

"How is it you do this?" Robbie asked.

"Do what?" she asked innocently. "I didn't do anything."

"I know," Robbie said. "That's just it. You simply stand still, or move, or even breathe and I am completely in your power. Maybe Mums is right. Maybe you are a witch."

Mechi felt her eyes well up with tears. *Not now*! She told herself. *He is just teasing*. Her head said that was the case; her heart cried out to believe it.

"I'm sorry," Robbie said, running his fingers through her short curly brown hair. "I didn't really mean that."

"Are you sure?" Mechi asked. She tried not to sound offended; she hated whiny people. "Because if you don't treat me right, I might cast a spell over you. Maybe I will turn you into a frog!"

Robbie laughed. "Even witches don't have such powers as that!" he said. "Do they?"

Mechi impulsively lifted her head to his and kissed him. When she came up for air, she grinned at him and said, "You tell me."

For the life of him, he didn't have an answer. If she told him to start croaking "Ribbit," he would have done so without question.

"Let's go sit on the grass," he said, taking her by the hand and leading her out into the open field.

Mechi sat down and Robbie reclined, placing his head in her lap. He gazed up at the sky, a blade of grass stuck between his teeth.

"They are so beautiful," Robbie said. "It is not often we get such a clear picture of the clouds. So much of the time it is so overcast you cannot make them out."

He looked up at Mechi, his eyes full of devotion. "Since you arrived we have seen more sunlight and more beautiful clouds than we have for years. It is as if you are enchanted."

"I feel enchanted," Mechi replied honestly. "I have never known a place like Dunnottar. Nor a family like the Keiths."

"Aye," Robbie said. "We be quite a clan, don't we?"

"To say the least," Mechi said. She looked serious.

"What is it?" Robbie asked, trying to read her change of mood.

"It is your mother," Mechi said. "If only I could get her to like me."

"Mums?" Robbie asked, laughing. "Don't let her fool you. She will come around to our side of the sea. You must just give her time. Why, she absolutely abhors Moray, yet when Agnes announced that he had finally proposed to her, did you not see how happy she was?"

With no forewarning at all, Mechi jumped to her feet, leaving Robbie's head to collapse onto the ground.

"Ouch!" he yelled, rubbing his head. "What are you doing?"

"I can't do this!" Mechi called back to him, heading towards her horse.

"No, you don't!" Robbie shouted, racing after her. He grabbed her by the arm before she could get the horse untied and whirled her around to face him. "Not without an explanation."

"What's to explain?" she asked.

"A whole lot," he insisted, lifting her in his arms and carrying her back into the field. "And if you try that again, I'll tie *you* up. You are far worse to train than the meanest steed."

Mechi sat down, staring at her lap, her hands nervously tracing the weave in the fabric of her riding skirt. How could she possibly explain to Robbie what she knew she must. She could not "string him along," knowing full well that she could leave this present world for her own at any moment.

"I'm waiting," Robbie said.

Her mind spun at a million miles an hour. She could not tell this man who had rescued her just a few days ago that she was hopelessly in love with him, but that she was from some future era that he could not possibly imagine.

"Well?" he asked again, trying to be patient, but gradually losing control.

"What do you want to know?" she finally asked. If she tried real hard, maybe she could think of some other story that might be feasible. Ha! She knew such a tale didn't exist. She certainly couldn't tell him the truth!

"To begin," he said, "are you truly from Paris?"

That one is easy, she thought. "Of course. Well, actually, from a small area near there. I told you that."

"But I don't understand why you don't speak French."

"It was a remote area," she said, biting her tongue as she spoke. She hated lying—especially to him.

"What did you speak?" he asked.

She hesitated. The only *foreign language* she knew was Pig Latin! Well, anything for a good cause!

"A dialect spoken by only a few people," she explained.

"Say something to me," he asked.

She gulped. Would he be able to decipher her feeble attempt at some strange language? Maybe, if she threw in enough modern slang...

"Go ahead," he pleaded.

She swallowed hard again, then said, "Iay inkthay outay areay ethay rooviestgay anmay Iay avehay everay etmay."

He laughed at the strange sounding words. "What does that mean?" he asked.

She smiled at him, realizing that he had not been able to pick out the English in it.

"It means I like you a lot," she said, the color again rising in her cheeks.

He took her hand tenderly. "I like you, too."

She pulled away immediately.

"I'm sorry," he said. "I don't mean to rush you. But I have never known anyone like you."

You don't know how true that is! she thought.

"Tell me more about yourself," he said. "Do you have any family?"

"Not really," she admitted. Well, that part of it was true, she told herself, soothing her troubled conscience. Even Brian didn't count now. In 1561 he definitely was not in the picture.

"You poor, poor foundling," he said, rubbing his big strong hands up and down over her arm, causing the hair on the back of her neck to stand on end.

"It wasn't that bad," she said. "My father died just a few years ago. He did a good job of raising me alone."

"Aye, that he did," Robbie said, nodding his head in agreement. "He'd be mighty proud of the way you turned out. You're a fine, fine lassie."

Mechi hid her eyes from him. She could not bear to look at him, knowing that much of her story would be—well, a little less than the whole truth.

"And your mother?" he asked.

"She died when I was quite young. I hardly remember her. Only bits and pieces here and there."

"Every child needs a mother," he said. Mechi thought he looked like he was going to cry. "I kinna imagine life without me Mums."

They sat in silence for several minutes before Robbie asked, "And ye dinna have any brothers or sisters? No other bairns?"

"One," Mechi said, her mind turning to Brian. Was he still waiting for her at St.

Andrew's in Maryland? "We aren't close. He's much older than me." She smiled as she added, "I was like an only child. A spoiled brat."

"You dinna look so spoiled to me," he said, not understanding the meaning of her words at all. He had no idea what a *brat* was, but she was certainly not so old she was no good, which is what spoiled conveyed to him.

"And ye have no other kin?" he asked.

Suddenly a light bulb went off in Mechi's head. She smiled at the image. Robbie had never seen a light bulb. She wondered what he would do if he were to flip one little switch and have the whole room fill with radiance. What if this whole drama was reversed and he had been transported to the twentieth century, instead of her coming back here? The thought was almost more than she could imagine.

"I have an Uncle David McKenzie," she said. "He's on my mother's side."

"And where is your Uncle David McKenzie?" Robbie asked.

"I don't know," Mechi said, trying to look as sad as she could. "The last time we heard from him he was somewhere near Aberdeen."

She waited for the impact of what she said to sink in. It took only a few seconds when Robbie said, "Aye, now I see! You came here in search of your uncle. Why ever didn't you say so, lassie? I'm certain we can find him."

"I don't know," Mechi said. "I guess it was the fall at St. Andrews. Until just now, I had completely forgotten about Uncle David."

She said a silent "thank you" to her Uncle David McKenzie. As she recalled, he was near Aberdeen, Scotland the last letter they had from him. But, if Lord Robbie Keith, Viscount of Kintore in 1561 went searcing for him, he would have quite a time finding him. Unless … Did he perhaps have an ancestor named David McKenzie who lived there in 1561? It was, she supposed, entirely possible. Imagine his shock if she showed up on his doorstep—with her claiming he was her only living family member!

"Tell me more of your life," Robbie begged. "I bored you one night with all the sordid tales of the Keith clan. Surely you can do me the honor of reviewing your life." He grinned at her as he added, "I promise I won't fall asleep."

Mechi fidgeted nervously. She had not meant to fall asleep while Robbie spun the tales of the Keith clan, but she was so tired from her trip.

"My life was extremely dull," she told him. "I had no famous people like the Keiths. I was nothing but a *plain Jane…*"

Robbie studied her intensely. "That is impossible," he argued. "First of all, your name is not *Jane*, and besides, you are the most *unplain* woman I have ever met in my life."

He stared at her with those big, deep green eyes. Mechi thought that he might stare a hole right through her. She shivered, hating the charade. How she wished she could tell him the truth, but she knew he would never understand. She wouldn't have any idea where to begin.

Sensing that something was troubling her deeply, Robbie asked, "What is it? What is wrong?"

"Nothing," she lied.

"I can tell there is something you are hiding from me." He took her hands in his, grasping them firmly, offering all of his own strength and support to her. "Please tell me. You can trust me."

"I can't," Mechi said softly. "You would never understand. You wouldn't believe me. I can't believe it myself."

She lowered her head and sobbed. The tears flowed like a giant waterfall, running over her cheeks and onto her blouse.

Before she realized what was happening, she was once again in Robbie's arms. It was the only haven she had. Her heart cried out to stay there forever.

Chapter XVII

It seemed like eons passed while Mechi contemplated exactly what to tell Robbie. The truth? She couldn't. It was too risky. If she had really been sent here to try to protect Queen Mary, she was afraid she might disappear back through the fog and the inevitable would occur. Was it already too late? Was history already formed, sealing Queen Mary's fate? If she was successful, in some crazy way, of altering the facts, how would she ever know? It was too late to write new history books. People for hundreds and hundreds of years had read about Queen Mary and how she had arranged Darnley's death. Yes, it was too late for that, and surely it was senseless to think she could thwart her efforts to usurp the throne of England from her cousin, Queen Elizabeth.

Mechi's mind flipped back at incredible speed, like a cassette tape on "rewind," to the scene at the golf course. The one at St. Andrew's—Maryland, that is. What did that strange Liz Steward have to do with this whole mess? She could feel it in her bones that she was somehow linked to this whole affair.

"I'm ready," she told Robbie at last. "I will tell you what is bothering me."

"Whatever it is," he said, reassuring her with a stroke of his hand on hers sending cold chills up and down her spine, "we will face it together. I am here to help you."

"You and your father," Mechi said.

"What does my father have to do with you?" he asked, puzzled by her statement.

"Remember that first night I spent at Dunnottar? The night you came to me and found me crying?"

"Of course," he said. "You looked so alone and afraid. I couldn't imagine what my father must have done to you. I *wouldn't* imagine it. Not my father!"

Mechi was shocked by his words. Surely he didn't think his father had forced himself on her! She couldn't let him think that!

"You knew your father had been with me?" she asked, then realized how that must sound. No matter what she said, she seemed to be getting herself farther and farther in trouble. "I mean, you saw him come to me?" No, that was worse. "You heard us talking?"

"I heard someone out in the corridor. It was late, and I was afraid you had lost your way and were wandering about aimlessly. I merely wanted to come to your rescue."

"You seem to do that quite frequently," Mechi said, smiling appreciatively at him. "Thank you."

"My pleasure," he said, beaming at her. "Now, about my father. He didn't...?"

"No!" Mechi screamed. "He was a perfect gentleman. I just had to warn him."

"Warn him?" Robbie asked. This was becoming more confusing by the minute. His father went to Mechi's room in search of God know what and she tried to warn him? Of what? And why, if that was all that happened, was she crying as if her heart would break after he left?

"Yes, about Mary. Well, actually, about Darnley. He can't be trusted."

"Darnley?" Robbie asked in surprise. "But why? He doesn't have enough brains to make sweetbreads. Why would anybody have to be afraid of Darnley? And especially Queen Mary. Why, he practically worships her."

"It's all an act," Mechi said. "He plans to wed her."

"She'd never agree to that!" Robbie said, laughing at the very idea. "She's much too smart for that."

"Love is blind," Mechi said. *Unless it is with someone as wonderfully handsome as you, dreamboat*, she thought. "Mary might see ways of using Darnley to try to conquer the English throne as well as the Scottish one. After all, Queen Elizabeth trusts Darnley too, you know."

"You are trying to make me believe that Darnley will somehow put Queen Mary in danger? But how do you know this? Who told you? And why?"

"I'm telling the truth," she said, her hands forming tight fists at his doubt. "He will try to have Mary destroyed. As to who told me, you remember that I am from near Paris? Didn't Mary just return from France? Is it so hard to imagine that the French might be privy to what is happening to Mary? Remember, to many Frenchmen she is still *their* sovereign, too. Why was I chosen to bring this news to your father? I don't have the foggiest idea. Um, the least idea. That is the one part about this whole thing that I don't understand, either. I just know what I must do, and that is to protect Queen Mary—at any cost and in any way possible."

Robbie studied her carefully as she spoke. She said these absurd things with such conviction, he *had* to believe her. She could not possibly have imagined any plot as far-fetched as this.

"If what you say is true," he said, his big green eyes filled with compassion, "then I will help you in any way I can. How do you suggest we proceed?"

"I don't know," Mechi admitted. "That's the part that's driving me crazy. I don't know what to do."

"Well, two heads have always been better than one," he said. "If we combine our ideas, maybe we can figure something out."

Robbie took her hands in his again. "Thank you for trusting me enough to tell me. I am so glad you shared your secret with me. I just knew there was something you weren't telling me."

You don't know the half of it, Mechi thought. *But this is enough for one day. Perhaps someday the time will be right to tell you the whole story.* In her heart, she ached to share her strange circumstances with him, but she knew this was not the time. No, if she told him that she was some creature out of the future, he would never believe her. Not that she would blame him. But if they were truly going to protect Queen Mary, she had to have his complete trust. If she didn't, she would never be able to pull off the plan that was formulating in her mind at this very moment.

They sat in silence for a long time, Robbie with his head on her lap again, staring up at the sky. Mechi kept her eyes fixed on him, wondering what he was thinking. Did he think she was a lunatic? Maybe he was right. This was the strangest plot she'd ever seen; it was sci-fi at its best. If she could write it all down when—and if—she ever got back where she belonged, she could become a millionaire overnight.

As she watched his eyes, she realized that she *was* where she belonged. It didn't matter if she was in the sixteenth century or the twentieth century, if Lord Robbie Keith, Viscount of Kintore, was with her, that was where she truly belonged.

A strange thought danced across her mind. What if she was forced, at some point in this whole thing, to return to own era? Was there any possibility that she could take Robbie with her? It was a most intriguing idea. *If it is in the realm of possibility,* she mused, *I really should prepare him for the life he would be facing once he arrived.*

"I have an idea," Mechi said, finally breaking the silence.

"I have a few ideas of my own," he said, mischief twinkling in his eyes.

"About the queen!" Mechi retorted, slapping him playfully on his arm.

"That's what I meant," Robbie insisted. "I can't imagine what else you would have thought I intended."

"Yeah, right!" Mechi said. "No, really, this is serious business."

He rubbed his hand across his face as if to remove all hints of foolishness from his countenance. "I'm serious, too."

"It's too bad you don't know about clones," Mechi said.

"Clones?" Robbie asked. "Like James Stewart: You said he is a clone."

"No," Mechi said, terrified at the thought of more than one Moray. One of them could bore you to death; two would be complete disaster. Poor blind Agnes! "That was a *clown*. A *clone* is an exact copy of one person, so there are two people just alike."

"Like Agnes and Angus?" he asked. "You mean twins?"

Mechi laughed. "Sort of, but not exactly. In case you hadn't noticed, there are a few major differences between the two of them."

"You mean one's a he and one's a she?" Robbie asked.

"You *have* noticed!" she exclaimed sarcastically.

"Of course I noticed!" he said, taking his turn now to swat her lightly. "Angus would look positively ghastly in one of Agnes's gowns!"

"And her corset!" Mechi said, laughing at the image of any man trying to outfit themselves in the damnable contraption.

"So a clone is even closer than a twin?" Robbie asked.

Mechi nodded.

"But how do you get a clone?" he asked, completely intrigued by the subject.

"No one is quite sure yet," Mechi said, suddenly clapping her hand over her mouth. What on earth was she doing? If she kept talking like this, she was going to have to explain to him about where she came from and when and where and… She couldn't tell him that in modern laboratories scientists were capable of such marvels as test tube babies and genetic engineering. No one here even knew that people had genes. The only "genes" of any type any of them had seen was her blue denims she was wearing when she arrived on the scene.

"These *clones*, Robbie said, "if it was possible to make one, you would want to make a clone of Queen Mary?"

"Exactly!" Mechi shouted. "Don't you see? Mary is going to marry Darnley. She is going to have him killed. Then Elizabeth is going to lock her in the Tower for years and eventually she will have Mary beheaded."

Robbie jumped to his feet. He stared at Mechi, his mouth wide open. He had never heard such heresy.

"That can't be!" he shouted. "How do you know this? And this time I want the truth! All of it!"

She didn't speak. She should have known that sooner or later she would talk far more than she should. She always seemed to do that. But this time she had really made a mess of things. This time a queen's life was at stake. She would have to tell him the whole truth, no matter what he thought of her, and hope that he would somehow understand her, believe her, and most importantly trust her. If he would do that, together they might be able to protect Queen Mary. They might be able to outsmart history!

"I think you'd better sit down," Mechi said quietly. "You won't believe me, but I have to tell you everything."

"If you do, I promise I will try to comprehend it." He stared at her, his eyes filled with wonder. "Are you a witch, like Mums claims?" he asked.

"No," Mechi assured him. "I am as human as anyone. I can assure you, I am not a witch. Nor a wood nymph. Nor anything else except a woman with a purpose. A very definite purpose. But I need your help. That is why I was sent here. It really was to protect the queen. And God alone knows that no one was better suited to help me than the Keith family."

For the first time, she honestly believed that was her mission. That was why she had been sent back here. It had nothing to do with Robbie Keith. It had *everything* to do with Robbie Keith. She could not fulfill her job by herself. She needed his help … desperately. She needed *him* desperately!

"I do think you'd better sit down," she repeated, this time making it sound like an order, not a suggestion.

Chapter XVIII

Mechi's mind spun around like a top. Questions, like riddles with no answers, filled her head. How did you get here? Where did you come from? Why are you here? Will you leave again? When? How? Who sent you? What do you want? How did you get here? How did you get here?

She didn't have the slightest idea how to answer the questions. She had no answers of her own. Maybe, if she was lucky, Robbie would simply believe her. Maybe he wouldn't ask any questions.

Who was she kidding? *If* the tables were turned, would she accept her story in blind faith? *No way!* She would want a perfectly logical explanation for the whole thing. And if there wasn't one…? Well, maybe witchcraft wasn't such a far-fetched idea after all. But the things they did to witches…!

She lifted her stare from the ground to Robbie's face. He was so trusting. So kind. *So bloody good looking!*

Mechi smiled. She had spent only a few days in Scotland, yet here she was already adopting their slang as her own.

"I'm waiting," he said, plucking a blade of grass and blowing on it, making a loud whistling sound.

"I know," Mechi said. "I just don't know where to begin."

"How about at the beginning?" he asked, laughing. "That usually works best." *That shouldn't be so hard,* he thought. What little he knew!

"I was born on a little ranch—a farm—just a little ways outside Paris."

"I know that much," he said. "You've already told me that."

"Paris, Texas," she said, playing with the pleats in her riding skirt.

He sat silently, waiting for her to continue. When she didn't, he said simply, "Paris is in France."

"Not this one," Mechi said. "This Paris is in Texas. Texas is in the United States of America. Across the Atlantic."

"Which direction?" Robbie asked.

"West," Mechi replied.

He gave her a look of total confusion. "No one has been west," he said. "How could you be...?"

"Let me go on," she said.

"Please do!" he said enthusiastically. He had thought there was something strange about her. What kind of people lived west of the British Isles? Were they all like her? If so, and people found out about it, Britain stood to lose a large portion of their population. She was certainly an interesting specimen of womanhood.

"I was born on July 4th, 1971," she said, waiting for his reaction.

He seemed oblivious to the brick she had dropped on his head. Suddenly, like a whole ton of bricks, the impact of her simple statement hit him.

"Nineteen-seventy-one?" he asked. "What type of calendar do you use?"

"That's right," she said. "And we use the same kind of calendar you do. *Anno Domini*, the year of our Lord."

"But this is fifteen-hundred and sixty-one," he said, trying to figure the mathematical calculation out in his head.

"I know," Mechi said. "I was born four-hundred and ten years in the future from now."

"I don't understand," Robbie said, his eyes glassed over in fear. He jumped to his feet. "Mums is right! You *are* a witch!"

"No!" Mechi insisted, pulling at his trouser leg until he fell back down onto the ground. "I don't understand it either. Not completely." She hesitated. "You know when you found me at St. Andrews?"

"Yes," he replied slowly.

"I was at St. Andrew's Golf Course near Aberdeen, Maryland."

"Maryland?" Robbie asked. He began laughing hysterically, uncontrollably. "They renamed the shire at St. Andrews after Queen Mary? How absolutely divine! She would love that. We must tell her. She has a deep passion for the game, although it is the talk of the land. Everyone finds it most unfitting. A woman on the golf links!"

"I taught people how to play golf in Aberdeen—Maryland," Mechi said, trying to explain. "Maryland is also in America. Across the Atlantic."

"To the west?" Robbie asked, his eyes sparkling with the mystery she was unwinding.

"Yes," Mechi said, nodding, "to the west."

"But I have never been in—America," Robbie said matter-of-factly. "How did you end up with your head on my lap?"

"Damned if I know!" Mechi said. "Some dame called Liz Stewart insisted I come to the golf course early in the morning—at seven o'clock—to give her a lesson. She wouldn't take 'No' for an answer."

She paused, waiting for Robbie to digest what she was telling him. When he said nothing, just sat deep in thought, his head resting on his hands, she continued telling her tale.

"I went to meet her, but she never showed up," Mechi said, once again feeling the rage at the request this woman had made, then not even putting in an appearance. "Who did she think she was?" she grumbled.

Suddenly Robbie's face was filled with terror.

"What else did this Liz Stewart say?"

Mechi saw that his hands were shaking. She tried to recall the whole conversation. It seemed so long ago. *Think!* she ordered herself. *Think harder!*

"She said something about needing an emergency lesson so she could meet her cousin without looking like a complete fool."

"Did she tell you her cousin's name?" Robbie asked.

Mechi thought. "Yes!" she shouted, remembering how commonplace it had seemed at the time. The woman seemed to command absolute obedience, but her cousin's name was… "Mary!"

"Of course!" Robbie nearly screamed. "She *would* try to pass herself off as a Stuart! She has long been envious of the family. The reign does truly belong to Mary, but she will not accept that. Mary must rule over England as well as Scotland! It must be!"

"No!" Mechi cried out. "She cannot. We must stop her from trying to do that. It will be the death of her!"

"None of this makes any sense," Robbie said, rubbing his head which hurt from trying to figure out what kind of a devilish plot Elizabeth was trying to enact. "Yet it all makes such perfect sense."

"I don't understand," Mechi said. Suddenly she realized that this wonderful Lord Robbie Keith, Viscount of Kintore, was even stranger than Liz Stewart.

"Don't you see? It was Queen Elizabeth who came to you. She wanted help to keep Mary off the throne."

Mechi's mind flashed to Queen Elizabeth. The second, that is. It was so hard to keep things in a proper perspective when you were dealing with two different lifetimes. Why would she try to keep Queen Mary off the throne? Surely she knew Britain's history far better than Mechi did.

"But why me?" Mechi asked. "And she knew what happened to Queen Mary. It is in all the history books."

"I don't know what you mean," Robbie said, puzzled.

"Queen Elizabeth was not even a direct descendant of the Stewarts," she said, wondering how she could possibly give this man a four-hundred-year history lesson in one single setting.

"You know she was a Tudor," Robbie said, "but she would not be above trying to pass herself off as a Stuart to gain what she wanted."

"Queen Elizabeth was not a Tudor," Mechi insisted. "She was the daughter of King George the Sixth."

"England has never seen a George on the throne," Robbie protested. "Queen Elizabeth's father was Henry the Eighth."

"Of course," Mechi said, glad for the enlightenment. "You are referring to the *first* Queen Elizabeth. I am talking about the *second* one."

"There's been but one," Robbie said.

"In fifteen-sixty-one, yes," Mechi agreed. "But by nineteen-ninety-seven there have been two. And six Georges. And an Edward, and a Victoria, and an Ann and a William and Mary…"

"Stop!" Robbie yelled. "I can't take this all in at once."

Mechi realized that Robbie, while he could not comprehend what was happening, at least was not denying it. He did believe her! The mere recognition of this fact made her hands turn cold and clammy. It was more than she had dared to hope for. More than she would have been capable of if the tables had been turned.

"One thing doesn't make any sense," Mechi said. "How could Queen Elizabeth the First have been on a golf course in Aberdeen, Maryland in 1997?"

"How indeed?" Robbie asked. "Perhaps the same way you arrived on a golf course in 1651."

Mechi sat, trying to determine if anything else the strange Liz Stewart had said might shed any more light on the situation at hand.

"If I cannot conquer her on the throne," Mechi said, remembering the odd remark Liz Stewart had made, "I shall capture her on her own ground. *I must have a golfing lesson, and it must be at the earliest possible moment!*"

"Whatever are you rambling about?" Robbie asked, studying her carefully. God, she was beautiful! How he longed to pull her to himself, in spite of the danger she might impose on him. If she was a witch… Well, he could think of a much worse fate than being under her spell!

"That is what Liz Stewart—or whoever she was—said the night she called me," Mechi explained. "I don't know how she got there, but you are right. Queen Elizabeth —the first one—somehow got into the future just like I got into the past. But if she wanted my help, why would she bring me back here? Why not to her own palace? I have been sent here to protect Mary. I have felt it from the beginning."

"Maybe it was fate—or the gods—who sent you back here. Not *for* Queen Elizabeth, but *because of* her." He looked at her with those eyes that bore a hole right through her into her soul. With those eyes, she could never lie to him. "Does anyone else know about this?" he asked.

"Only your father," Mechi said. "Of course, I would be sent to the Keiths to protect Queen Mary! Your father *is* her guardian."

"'Tis true," he said. "You told my father all of this? And what was his response?"

"I didn't tell him everything," Mechi confessed. "I only told him that I knew Queen Mary was in danger, and that I had been sent to warn her."

"He accepted that?"

"He had no choice. I told him Darnley is not to be trusted."

"I've always known that," Robbie said. "He is a rotten scoundrel if ever I've known one."

"You said you knew the night your father came to me?" she asked.

"Oh, yes, I remember it well," he said, the image of her lying on the bed had haunted his thoughts and visions many times.

Mechi blushed. "The night you lost the tie to your robe… "

That and a whole lot more, he thought. Never had he known a woman who could steal his heart, his head and his every waking moment like Michelle Jeanotte, this stranger from the future.

"That is why my father went to you that night?" he asked.

"You knew?"

"I watched him," Robbie said, putting words to her suspicions. "I could not imagine what he would be doing in your solar after everyone was supposed to be asleep…"

"Surely you didn't think…?" Mechi asked, knowing she didn't have to verbalize the question.

"What was I to think?" Robbie asked, sounding angry. "After all, he is a man…"

"And I am a woman?" Mechi asked.

"Oh, yes, my lady, you are every inch a woman!"

"I wasn't sure you had noticed," Mechi said, teasing him. "Anyway, I had asked your father to come to me so I could warn him about the danger Mary was facing. I didn't tell him about the strange encounter with Liz Stewart. It didn't seem important at the time. But now, when I think about her saying she wanted me to meet her on her own ground, and she wanted a golf lesson, it all seems so… Like it might really have been…"

"So it was her," Robbie said, his voice trailing off. "You said she *called* you? I don't understand. From where?"

His mind wandered to Genevieve. There had been many times when he had felt her call. Was that what Mechi meant? He supposed he should tell her about Genevieve, but this was not the time nor the place. Maybe she would never have to know.

Mechi floundered about for the words to describe a telephone to this man who had no idea how sound traveled through the air over waves. The only thing he probably knew about waves was that it was a thing on the water when the wind was blowing.

"There are so many things I have to tell you," she said, suddenly overcome with excitement at trying to explain all the wonders of the world to him. "She *called* me on a thing we call a telephone."

Robbie sat, his mouth wide open, as Mechi described a little thing in your hand that you could put up to your mouth and your ear and talk to someone miles and miles away.

"What else have they invented?" he asked.

Mechi's mouth began to race as fast as her thoughts. "There are cars—like carriages only with no horses—that could take you from here to London in just a few hours. There are airplanes that fly through the air like giant birds, carrying hundreds of people inside them. There are microwave ovens to cook things in a few seconds with no fire. There are…"

"Stop!" Robbie shouted. "I need more time to digest all of this. Oh, how I would love to see your world!"

"And I would love to show it to you," Mechi said. She realized that he was squeezing her hand so tightly it was nearly white.

Do I dare wish for such a thing? she wondered. *If I finish my work here and I'm returned to 1997, is there any way to take Lord Robbie Keith, Viscount of Kintore, back with me? If not, do I have to return? I can't bear the thought of leaving him.*

"For right now," Robbie said, "if what you say is true…"

Mechi's mind flew into a silent rage. *I thought he believed me!* Then, as if defying her very thoughts, he added, " …we have work to do. We must protect the queen. Tell me everything you can about what happens to her. Only then can we prevent it from happening."

To change history, Mechi mused. Is it really possible? They had to take a chance on it. The risk of the awful fate of Queen Mary really happening was far too great.

"We need a plan," she said.

"Then we'll find one," Robbie said, his voice filled with confidence. "For the honor of all Scotland, we'll find one!"

Chapter XIX

"Tell me everything you know about Queen Mary," Robbie pleaded. "For her sake, please."

Mechi concentrated long and hard. It was hard to think through the idea that although he couldn't possibly understand the full impact of what she had just told him, he apparently trusted her. Finally, slowly, she began to speak.

"As I told you, she will marry Darnley." She watched Robbie for his reaction.

"No!" he shouted. "I told you, she would never do that! It can't be! We must stop her. He is such an imbicile!"

"Of course he is," Mechi agreed. "But that is how Mary hopes to gain the English throne as well as the Scottish."

"Surely they don't live together—as husband and wife?"

"I'm afraid so," Mechi said. "In fact, they had a child. His name was James."

"James?" Robbie said. "How original!" Sarcasm dripped off his every word.

"Yes, he became James the Sixth of Scotland. Then, after Queen Elizabeth died he became James the First of Great Britain. He succeeded in doing what his mother was never able to accomplish. He ruled over England, Scotland and even Ireland."

"But what of Mary?" Robbie asked. "And how do you know all this? Are you an expert?" He appeared to want to say more, but he hesitated.

"Or a witch?" Mechi asked, grinning at him.

"Nay," he said. "I dinna believe you to be a witch." He smiled at her, running his index finger sensually up and down on the back of her hand. "You are far too comely to be a witch."

"If that was a compliment," she said, "thank you."

'You're most welcome," he said, his eyes alight with the fire of passion. Even though he was convinced that she was not a witch, he still found her bewitching. She could charm the sword from a warrior.

"You asked how I know so much about Queen Mary?" she asked. "I'll tell you. My mother was a pure Scot. She claimed to be a descendant of King James the Sixth —or the First—I never could figure out which one he was."

"You are a descendant of Mary's son, James? The son who isn't born yet?" he asked in disbelief.

"So my mother claimed," Mechi said.

"Then you must be kinfolk to Mary, too," he said, trying to fit the pieces together.

"No," Mechi said, not sure how to explain what her mother had tried so many times to explain to her. "Mother always said we were descended from James's father's side."

"You are a descendant of Darnley?" Robbie cried out. "How can that be? He is so…! And you are so…! No, it can't be true!"

Mechi laughed at the preposterous irony of the situation. "Don't you see?" she said. "It is my chance to redeem the dastardly deeds of Darnley after all these years. No wonder I was chosen to right the wrongs."

"Well," Robbie said, shaking his head, "I guess there is some good in knowing that the devil had at least one redeeming quality. You certainly make up for his faults."

Mechi sat, pondering a plan. Some way to keep Mary from being beheaded. Some way to keep her from killing Darnley. If she indeed was guilty, as history had recorded. They never did find any positive proof. Except the famed Casket Letters, but many authorities questioned their authenticity.

"Do you know what?" she suddenly said excitedly.

"No," Robbie said. "I'm certain I dinna ken a thing you are about to tell me."

"After Mary is put to death…"

"She is what?" Robbie screamed, interrupting her. "We cannot allow for that to happen!"

"Okay, okay! We'll figure it all out. But just listen for a minute. Agnes will marry Moray."

"We all know that," Robbie said, exasperated at how long she could take to make any sense. "And she'll no doubt die of boredom."

"No," Mechi said, "but if I remember right, James is put on the throne as a very young child."

"So there is a regent appointed?" Robbie asked. "Do you recall who it is?"

"It is Moray," Mechi said. "I am sure of it. That means that Agnes will be an *almost queen*!"

"The closest the Keith clan shall ever come to being royalty, I presume," Robbie said, obviously delighted with the prospect. "And when James is old enough, he assumes the role himself?"

"Yes," Mechi said. "He and Queen Anne." She stopped momentarily, raised her eyes heavenward and said softly, "Thank you, Mother. I will never again complain about your long-winded stories of our family history."

"Queen Anne?" Robbie questioned.

"Yes, he married Princess Anne of Denmark." A stroke of lightening exploded within Mechi's brain. "I know where I have heard the name of Keith!" she exclaimed, jumping up and down. "A George Keith made the trip to Denmark on behalf of James to bring Princess Anne back to marry him." She hesitated, trying to remember her mother's story. She began to laugh hysterically. "It seems to me that George Keith was married by proxy to Princess Anne until they returned to Scotland."

"George?" Robbie asked, intrigued by the idea. "My brother, George?"

"I can't honestly say," Mechi said, "but it is possible."

"Oh, he will be thrilled with this news!" Robbie cried out in glee. "Just wait until I tell him."

"Just a minute," Mechi said, placing her hand on his shoulder to stop him from getting up. "I don't think that is a good idea. We will just have to keep it our secret— at least for now. He would not understand how I knew about it, before Mary is even married or has a child."

"I suppose ye're right," Robbie said, pouting like a little boy who had just had his favorite toy taken away from him. He banged his fists on his legs. "But it would be such fun! Then he would just have to sit there and wait for the years to pass before he could act it out!"

"Talk about *acting it out*," Mechi said, "we really should get busy on a plan to protect Mary."

"What was it you said once about a *clone*?" Robbie asked.

"A clone—a perfect likeness of another object or person," Mechi said, almost as if she was reading it from a dictionary. "We need a clone of Queen Mary. Someone who is truly devoted to her. One who would do anything to spare the life of her sovereign."

"And one who looks like her," Robbie suggested.

"Most importantly, one who looks like her," Mechi agreed. "Any ideas?"

He shook his head. "I haven't noticed anyone who particularly resembles the queen." He shrugged his shoulders, adding, "But then I wasn't looking about for one, either."

"Well, now you are. I want you to keep your eyes wide open. If you see anyone— *anyone at all*—who has possibilities, we must learn all we can about her before we approach her. We must not let anyone else learn about our plan."

"And Father?" Robbie asked.

Mechi shuddered. She had already confided somewhat in Lord Keith. If they were going to execute their plot, she supposed he would have to know about it. And eventually, of course, Queen Mary herself would have to be informed. It would never do to have *two* Queen Marys running around the country.

"What do you find so amusing?" Robbie asked, watching her smile deepen to a wonderfully deep laugh. Even in the face of utter danger, she still had that wonderful, infectious laugh. He loved her sense of humor. *It nearly matches my own*, he speculated.

"I was just wondering what would happen if we were to find a perfect image of Queen Mary and suddenly *two* Queen Marys appeared, running about hither and yon throughout the whole of the country?"

Robbie joined her in laughter. "Imagine what fun Queen Elizabeth would have! She thinks she can outwit one of them, but how would she ever manage with two of them? Why, one Queen Mary is quite enough to bring her to her end eventually."

Mechi's countenance changed to one of horror and fear. How could she ever convince Lord Robbie Keith, Viscount of Kintore, who adored his queen to the utmost, of the terrible end which awaited her? She could not bring herself to tell him that she would one day be beheaded by the very Queen Elizabeth he scorned. No, she would save that juicy tidbit of news for his father—when and if it became necessary for his cooperation in their plan.

"We must begin our search for the new Queen Mary at once," Robbie said.

"I will tell your father," Mechi said. "We will no doubt need his help."

"No, I shall speak with him," Robbie argued. Mechi realized that Robbie really didn't trust her with his father. Or was it his father that he didn't trust? Were there skeletons in the Keith closet? Well, that would have to wait for another time. For the moment, there were more important matters to tend to.

"We will go to him together," Mechi conceded.

"Agreed," Robbie said.

Neither of them spoke, but simultaneously they got up and went to their horses. He helped Mechi onto hers, then untied the reins from the tree. He proceeded to mount his own horse, then they rode like the wind itself to find Lord Keith. The sooner they implemented their plan, the less trouble Queen Mary would have to bear.

"Maybe we can even keep her from marrying Darnley," Mechi said to herself. "If that is all we do, that ought to be worth a place in the history books. Ych! Imagine being married to such a boor! And how much more, if we can just keep her off the gallows!"

But, Mechi thought, how would anyone know? How would *they* know if they succeeded?

Her thoughts turned back—or ahead—to her life in Aberdeen, Maryland.

How absolutely boring! She still had no idea how she ended up here, but it sure beat chasing that little white pimple-poxed white sphere around on some swanky country club green.

What if I do have to return there? she wondered, suddenly aware that she much preferred this life to that other one. Of course if she could take Robbie back with her...

Chapter XX

"I—we can't explain everything to you," Robbie said to his father. "But I am convinced that what Mechi says about the queen is quite true. We must find a way to protect her."

"So she has confided in you as well?" he asked, a bit of a twinkle in his eye. "I thought she might."

"And why is that?" Robbie asked.

"'Tis a simple fact, my son. The woman is quite taken with you."

Robbie glanced about nervously.

"As you are with her?" Lord Keith asked knowingly.

"Who's to say so?" Robbie asked.

"Are some things don't need saying," his father said. "Your mother and I can see…"

"And mother is quite upset by it?" Robbie asked, fearing the answer.

"Aye, but don't worry 'bout your mother, laddie, I'll see she comes 'round."

"Thank you," Robbie said simply, then hastened to steer the conversation back to Queen Mary. "Mechi seems to think that if we can find someone who closely resembles Mary, if we could convince her to switch places with the queen, then maybe we could thwart Darnley's plan to destroy her."

"And where should you find such a woman?" Lord Keith asked.

"I dinna ken as yet," Robbie replied, "but if it is for the sake of the queen, I'm certain one shall appear."

"You intend to take off with Lady Mechi in search of this woman?"

"Aye, Father," he said slowly. "I fear we must."

"Then God be with ye," his father said, placing his hand tenderly on his shoulder. "I've but one favor to ask of ye first."

"You know I would do anything for you, Father."

"Ye must go to visit Genevieve one final time. I fear that what you about to embark upon could be quite treacherous. She needs you."

"'Tis done, Father," he said, turning to leave. "And try not to worry about me. Whatever happens, I know it is what must be."

"God be with you," Lord Keith said, smiling at his son and studying him as if it would be the last time he would ever see the face he loved—the face of his firstborn.

Robbie had finally convinced Mechi that it would be best if he spoke to his father alone. She paced back and forth in her solar, anxiously awaiting him.

"I have spoken to Father," Robbie said to Mechi as he stood in front of her in her solar.

"And?" Mechi asked, suddenly glad he had done it alone.

"He has given us his blessing," Robbie replied.

Mechi looked up into his bright green eyes, surprise on her face. What had he told his father? Surely he only discussed poor Queen Mary's plight. He had said nothing of calling anything else to his attention.

"To try to find a *clone* for the queen," Robbie said, his eyes dancing merrily as he realized what she must have thought. "Although if I had thought of asking for his permission to ask for your hand… Well, a fool I am!"

Mechi giggled slightly. She had no right to expect anything else from this man. She had been sent here to rescue Queen Mary. No more. The end. Doing it with the dashing Lord Robbie Keith, Viscount of Kintore, was certainly a bonus. Who was she to argue with fate?

"I have a matter to attend to," he said, taking his hand in hers. "I shan't be long. When I return, we shall begin our search for Queen Mary's *clone*."

"I will go with you," Mechi said. "Then we can begin our search sooner."

"No!" he insisted. "What I have to do first I must do alone." A look of fear filled his eyes. "I promise, I will be back 'ere long."

Sensing that it was futile to argue, Mechi agreed. In a flash he was gone, and she was alone. So alone. She looked heavenward and said, silently, to her mother, "It is because of you that I am here. You and your stupid ancestor, Darnley!" The corners of her mouth turned up ever so slightly. "I don't know whether to be mad at you or to thank you."

She could have sworn she heard someone somewhere say "Thank you." She shook her head. She must be losing her mind. Or was it already gone? It must have been someone talking out in the corridor. She went to the door, pushing it open slightly, looking in both directions. There did not appear to be anyone there. She shut the door and went back inside. To wait. To dress. To ponder a life with Lord Robbie Keith, Viscount of Kintore. To ponder a life with Lord Robbie Keith, Viscount of Kintore. To try to imagine a life *without* Lord Robbie Keith, Viscount of Kintore.

She pondered Robbie's strange mood when he left her. It was, she realized, the second time he had acted so mysteriously. In search of a clue, she went to the tiny diamond-shaped window and looked out towards the stables. Her eyes were fixed on the surroundings when suddenly he appeared, mounted on a huge stallion, and disappeared over the steep slope towards the mainland.

Mechi ran from her room and grabbed the first horse she saw. She did not waste time hunting for a saddle, but—struggling with her cumbersome gown—managed to climb on bareback and followed the path Robbie had taken. Soon she was close enough to see him, but she kept her distance so he would not know she was on his trail.

Down the paths and through the woods they went, he with a purpose in his travel and she with a question in hers. After nearly an hour, Mechi could see a small clearing with a tiny thatched-roof house sitting in the middle of it. Robbie alit from his horse and fastened the reins around a post in the yard.

Mechi dismounted her horse and fastened it securely to a tree in the forest, well out of vision of the house. She too stayed hidden, watching Robbie as he approached the house and entered. He did not knock nor announce his arrival in any way. It was obvious that he had visited this home many times and that his presence was certainly not out of the ordinary.

When he was inside, she quietly worked her way up to the house to try to see and hear what was going on inside. There was only one tiny window, and she stretched up on her tiptoes, craning her neck as far as she could.

Robbie was seated on a crude wooden bench, his back towards her, with a woman beside him. Was it a woman? She looked so tiny and fragile, she seemed like a young girl.

Mechi strained her ears to try to catch some of the conversation, but it was useless. If they turned to face her, she might be able to make out some of the words from trying to read their lips.

The girl had hair the same fiery red as Robbie's. *It must be a true Scottish trait*, she told herself. She wondered if her eyes were as frightening and as hypnotic as his.

Suddenly, her heart sank. She saw him lean over her and tenderly kiss her. Was this the love of his life? Why hadn't he told her about this girl? Was he as fickle as Robert Pearson? Were all men that phony? She had been so sure she could trust Lord Robbie, yet she saw now that it was a mistake. They were all alike. If only she hadn't told him about her trip into the past. Or her life in the future. It was no wonder he had fled to his *other woman*. He no doubt thought she was crazy; maybe he was right.

She still had to find a way to save Queen Mary—with or without the help of Lord Robbie Keith. If that was why she had been sent here, she was not going to shirk her responsibility. No, she would save the queen. Even if it meant losing her own life in the process.

A third person came into view from behind a curtain which hung in the doorway. It was a woman, but she stayed in the shadows where Mechi could hardly see her. She cast a dark, foreboding silhouette in the room. She turned towards the window and saw the shadowy outline of a person.

Mechi could still not hear them, but she saw the woman point in her direction. Frightened, she ran into the woods and jumped on her horse, pulling the rope free of the tree as she mounted. She hurried off down the path they had come on, riding as fast as she could. With any luck she could outrun Robbie quite easily.

Robbie left the house, hurrying after the figure which was too quickly disappearing from his view. There was only one person he knew who could ride that well. Why had Mechi followed him? Why couldn't she leave well enough alone? If she didn't trust him any more than that, how did he know that he could believe her? After all, the tale she had spun for him was the most far-fetched thing he had ever heard. Someone from the future coming to rescue the queen! Indeed!

Still, suppose she was right? He would feel terrible if something did happen to her. Especially if he and the Mechi—that strange and wonderful being—could have prevented the monarch's demise. Just to be on the safe side, he had no choice but to believe her, odd as the whole thing seemed.

He dug his heels into the horse's side, urging him on even faster. He had no need of seeing who it was he was pursuing; that he knew. But, he had to warn her— strongly enough so she would obey his command—to stay away from what she had seen today. It would only bring shame and despair. If she learned his secret, surely she would have nothing more to do with him. And he did so want to see more of her. Even if she was a witch, as his mother said, he would not mind being bewitched by her. He could think of many fates far worse than spending his life in her spell.

"Tend the horse!" Mechi called out to the stable boy as she ran towards the castle.

She hurried up the long winding stairway, grateful that no one saw her, until she came to the door to her own solar. She ran inside, closing the door quietly behind her, then placing the heavy iron bar across it to secure it from intruders.

She had not bothered to look back on the race homeward, but instinct told her that Robbie was not far behind. Surely he would come to her, chastising her for her actions.

Someone was pushing on the door, struggling to open it. Just the sound of his breathing and the scent of his persona told her it was Robbie.

"Let me in!" he yelled at her. "Open this door, *Now*!"

Mechi, afraid of arousing the rest of the family, obeyed. There, in all his splendor, stood Lord Robbie Keith. She looked into his eyes, which revealed his innermost soul. She expected anger; she found sadness. She expected hatred; she found love.

"Come in," she said, closing the door behind him. Before she could explain her actions, she gathered him into her arms. The big, brave Scotsman stood, his head resting on her breast, and sobbed like a baby.

"What is it?" she asked. "What have I done?"

"Our secret," he said, gasping for breath between each word. "You have destroyed our secret. Now the name of Keith shall be shunned throughout all Scotland."

He lifted his head, shaking it from side to side. "I shall never again be able to show my face in public. Once everyone finds out…"

"Whatever your secret is," Mechi said, trying to assure him, "I shall guard it close to my heart. I would never do anything to harm you. But first you must tell me what it is I have seen."

Chapter XXI

Mechi waited impatiently, breathlessly for Robbie to return. He had insisted that he must speak with his father before he could tell her what had been hidden deep within the forest in that tiny house.

Thousands of questions raced through her mind. *Who was the young woman? Was it Robbie's lover? If so, was she the only one he had? Why did he keep her locked away from everyone's view? Was she a mere commoner?*

Mechi laughed. She was nothing more than a *commoner* herself. If Robbie should ever ask her to marry him, would she then join the *other woman* in that awful hole in the woods?

The thought brought an unexpected flow of tears to her eyes. She could never stand such a fate. If that ever happened, as deeply as she cared for Robbie she would have to try to find a way back to back to the future. Back to freedom, to activity, to *life*.

Was the older woman perhaps the younger one's mother? Or was it someone the Keiths had hired to care for her? At least they showed *some* responsibility for the "less fortunate" of the world. They could have left her to fend for herself, alone in the cruel, heartless world.

Mechi again chuckled, wiping her eyes on the corner of the coverlet which covered the bed where she was sitting. She jumped slightly when she realized that she might be desecrating a priceless old antique. Of course it was quite new, now. But someday…

The door opened slowly. Robbie walked inside, looking as if he had just seen a ghost. The same love and concern showed in his eyes, but there was something more. Something much deeper. *Fear!* Whatever this dreadful secret was, *he*— Lord Robbie Keith, Viscount of Kintore—was afraid! The mere hint of such a thing made Mechi cringe. He was her knight in shining armor. Her Superman. Her Clark Kent. What could be so terrible that even *he* was afraid of it?

He reached behind him, closing the door tightly. He secured it with the huge iron lock and walked towards the bed. He pulled a chair up in front of her and sat, staring into her eyes, waiting—searching for the right way to begin.

"I don't know how much you saw in Boscobel," he finally began, breaking the deafening silence.

"Boscobel?" Mechi asked, unsure of the meaning of the strange new word.

"Yes," Robbie said, taking her hands in his. He gripped them hard. Mechi had the sensation that he was trying to draw strength from her before he continued. "Boscobel is the name of the forest. The one where the house is."

Robbie waited, silently, wondering if she would voice the questions he knew she must have. When she said nothing, he asked, "Well?"

"I did not see much," Mechi said, wondering if he would stop if he thought their secret was still safe with the clan Keith. "I saw a girl—a woman—a very young, fragile woman—sitting beside you."

Her heart leapt into her throat as she said, "I—I saw you kiss her!"

Robbie threw his head back, his bright red mane flailing behind him, and laughed that wonderful, deep throaty laugh. It was contagious. In a few moments Mechi was laughing with him, although she didn't have a clue why.

"Jealous?" he asked, winking at her with his green dagger-eyes.

"No," Mechi lied. He had certainly not given her any reason to think there might be a future for them together. *A future!* How ridiculous! Her future was certainly not what Robbie would have imagined for his own future. But if he wasn't there, did she really even want a future?

"I don't believe you," Robbie replied. "And I am wonderfully flattered."

"You are?" Mechi asked in surprise.

"Aye, that I am," Robbie said. "To think that you should be jealous of one such as Genevieve. Why, she would give her whole life to be as lucky—and as pretty—as you."

"Genevieve?" Mechi asked cautiously. Well, at least now her rival had a name, one which she had heard before. "And just exactly who is Genevieve?"

"Genevieve, my dear Mechi, is our secret. We have kept her hidden away from gaping eyes since shortly after she was born."

"She—was born here at Dunnottar?"

"Of course," Robbie said, his expression turning serious. There was pain as he spoke. "Genevieve is my sister."

He waited for this fact to sink in. He studied her expression, wondering what could possibly be going through her mind.

Mechi stared at him in disbelief. Of course, she had heard of people—even during her father's lifetime—who had been hidden because of some defect or handicap that the family was ashamed of. The Keith family all seemed so warm and loving, so close-knit, she could not imagine that they would be embarrassed by such a plight. But, she had to remind herself, this was a different place, a different time. Oh, yes, things were definitely different here.

"What—what's wrong with her?" Mechi finally asked.

Robbie hesitated for a long time, then began to speak slowly and deliberately. "She is—not right," as if that would explain everything.

"Not right?" Mechi asked. "What do you mean?"

"She was born under the new moon. She is a *lunatic*."

He waited for the impact of his revelation to hit her with the full force of its meaning.

Mechi sat, stunned. She didn't know whether to laugh or cry for the poor Keith clan. She had, of course, heard many old fables about *lunatics*, but she had never given much credence to such old wives' tales. She searched his face, trying to understand exactly what he meant. He was deadly serious.

"You can't believe such nonsense," she challenged. "Just because she was born at the wrong time of the moon's cycle?"

"You don't understand," Robbie said. "It is more than that. So much more." He was still gripping Mechi's hands and she felt his muscles tighten around her own fingers, so tiny by comparison. "She is—crazy. Sometimes she gets all funny like and she goes into a fit."

Mechi saw the pain in Robbie's eyes for his sister. Surely he couldn't think it was anyone's fault. Even in 1997 there were cases of babies born mentally retarded. And, she hesitantly admitted to herself, with all the wonderful strides modern medicine had made, the best solution they had come up with was that with proper testing they could determine such conditions and could opt for an abortion. She couldn't imagine the Keiths even considering such a procedure, even if it was a viable alternative in their day and age.

"There is no shame in that," Mechi tried to assure Robbie. "It happens to many families. Why, even the Kennedys…" She snickered as she realized that Robbie Keith had no idea whatsoever about the famous Kennedy family. Still, she smiled at the irony. The Kennedys were probably on a par—both politically and financially—with the Keiths. And Rose Kennedy had never made any attempt to hide their own tragedy. And they had certainly had more than their share of heartaches.

"The Kennedys?" Robbie asked. "And who are the Kennedys?"

"They are a family in America in the 1900's who had a daughter—Rosemary—who was born mentally retarded…"

"Mentally r-r-r-retarded?" Robbie asked, rolling his tongue heavily over the "r's" in the strange sounding words. "And what does that mean?"

"It is…" Mechi floundered, searching for the best way to describe the condition.

She had never studied the condition, but she had, of course, seen people who suffered terribly. Even in 1997, she realized, people who were retarded were still shunned. It was no more accepted in 1997 than it was in 1561. So much for miracles! But this was no time for her to lose faith. If she was going to save Queen Mary's life, she needed at least one miracle.

"Aye?" Robbie asked, anxious for Mechi to continue. Was it possible that she might know something that would help Genevieve? He had never dared to hope for such luck, yet she had worked miracles with the horses. Could she do the same for Genevieve? The corners of his mouth turned upwards as he pondered such possibilities. If there was any way for Mechi to win his mother's approval, that would be it. He knew his mother loved Genevieve dearly, yet her heart weighed so heavily each time she went to visit her that Lord Keith had finally forbidden her to make her weekly treks into the woods of Boscobel. She had made Robbie vow to never reveal how many times she had made that same ride with her son when Lord Keith was otherwise occupied.

"They—they have still not found a cure," Mechi said, her eyes tracing the lines of the boards on the floor. She could not stand to look into Robbie's eyes. She knew they contained such pain without even glancing up.

"So it is hopeless?" Robbie asked. "I knew as much. I have dreamed that she was…" He searched for the right word. "…normal," he finally said. "When I was a wee laddie, I used to dream that she was at Dunnottar with the rest of us, running and playing along the wall-walk. Then I would awaken, covered in sweat. She was always perfectly healthy when we started to play. Then she would fall off, tumbling into the depths of the water below, and when Father rescued her she was—well, like she is now. I always just watched her fall. I did nothing to help her."

"But surely your father told you that it was not your fault?" Mechi asked. "That she was born that way?"

"I—I never told Father about the dream," he admitted. "I was afraid he too would know that I was to blame."

"You poor, poor thing," Mechi said, again cradling him in her arms. "I am so glad you told me." She felt honored that he trusted her with such deep personal feelings. Maybe, she thought, there was hope for them yet.

After a few moments, Robbie jerked away from her. He sat stiffly upright, ashamed for letting down his guard with Mechi. He was Lord Robert Keith, Viscount of Kintore, the eldest son of the earl mariscal. He had no business being such a melonhead.

"I should not have bothered you with such frivolous details," he said. "Please forget that it ever passed between us."

"But," Mechi protested, "I am glad that you share things with me. Both the good and the bad. It is like we are—soulmates," she declared.

"Soulmates?" Robbie asked. He shook his head. She used such strange words. If she spoke English, then why did so many of them sound so foreign?

"Yes," Mechi explained, "it is when two people come together and seem to be so in tune with one another that they are almost like one person."

Robbie laughed. "And you think we are soulmates?" he asked. The myriad of young lasses from the highlands floated past his mind's eye. He knew that many of them would have given anything to be considered his *soulmate.* But no, not for Lord Robert Keith. The gods had to reach over three hundred years into the future to find his true soulmate.

"That's better," Mechi said, smiling at him. "You look so much more handsome when you laugh."

"You think I am handsome?" he asked, that all-too familiar twinkle returning to his eyes.

"Oh, yes, my lord," Mechi said, standing and curtsying so properly before him. "You are the most dashing man I have ever laid eyes on."

"And you are the most beautiful lass I have ever seen as well," Robbie said, returning the politeness with a deep bow. He was still doubled over when Lady Keith opened the door to Mechi's solar to inform them that they were all awaiting them at the dining table.

Chapter XXII

The atmosphere at the dining table seemed unusually heavy. The Keith clan was there in its entirety, plus Mechi. The small talk and fun and games of the children were noticeably absent. Mechi could not help but wonder if Lord Keith had told all of them that their secret had been shared with a complete stranger— an outsider.

"Has anyone had word from Queen Mary recently?"

The question startled Mechi, not by its content, but because it was Lady Keith who voiced it. Had Lord Keith told her of the queen's impending danger?

"Not recently," Lord Keith replied. "I have sent word to inform her that we should like her to spend some time here at Dunnottar."

At this news, the mood seemed to lighten. It was very obvious that the entire family was very fond of their sovereign. Not just as their queen, but as their friend. Probably the only true friends she has, Mechi thought, remembering how anxious Mary had been to seek friendship from Mechi herself.

Mechi passed a knowing glance at Lord Keith, who nodded in recognition of her thoughts. If they could just keep her safe until she and Robbie could find their clone of the queen, then perhaps they could indeed thwart history.

Shortly Robbie arose and stood directly behind Mechi.

"We are going for a ride," he announced, pulling the chair out for Mechi to make her exit. He looked directly at his father, who knew what they were about. He cast a quick glance at his mother, unaware of whether she knew that Mechi was privy to the family secret or not.

Lady Keith remained stoic, her face not giving an inkling of her thoughts. One thing Mechi could determine; Lady Keith was still not particularly fond of her, nor did she trust her with her son.

"Godspeed," Lord Keith bade them, rising until they were out of the room.

"Go, put on your riding skirt and then come out to the stables. I shall ready the horses and await you there," Robbie instructed.

Mechi started up the winding staircase to her quarters.

"One thing more," Robbie said. "I have a request, albeit it might seem a mite odd to you."

"Your wish is my command," Mechi said, grinning at Lord Robbie.

"Would that it were true," he said, returning her smile. "Your…" He hesitated, not certain what to call the item he wished to discuss. "…that green garb you were clad in when I found you…"

Mechi laughed. Her nylon windbreaker? Whatever could he want with that?

"Yes," she said, nodding knowingly. "What about it?"

"I know 'tis strange," Robbie said, "but it seems somehow to be—lucky."

Mechi laughed heartily. "Who is it that believes in witchcraft?" she asked. "With all the beautiful clothes Agnes has given to me, you want me to wear my windbreaker over my riding outfit?"

"Please?" he asked, nearly begging.

"Whatever floats your boat," she said, then lapsed into an old familiar song. "Whatever pops your cork."

"That's an odd bit," Robbie said. "What does it mean?"

"I'll explain it to you on our ride," she replied. "We must hurry so we can get back again before dark."

"Yes," Robbie agreed, turning on his heel and leaving through the gigantic oak doors of the keep. "Do not make me wait too long."

"I'll hurry," Mechi said. *The sooner I can get out of this corset,* she thought, *the better I will like it.* A crazy green nylon windbreaker was all it would take to make the man of her dreams happy? How easy her life would be!

As they raced through the woods, Robbie pulled his horse ahead of hers, causing her to stop. He got off his mount and went to her, extending both hands to help her down.

Mechi did not understand why they had stopped, but she did not question him. Had he changed his mind about taking her to see Genevieve? She longed to be a part of his life—all of it. That included Genevieve. She sensed that it was not his shame as much as it was plain unadulterated fear.

"It's okay," she said, hopping down into his arms. "I know I will love her. She's a part of you."

He sat down on the damp, grassy ground and pulled her down with him. He pulled her to him, afraid that she might disappear as suddenly as she first appeared to him. It was a feeling he couldn't explain, but he somehow felt that if he shared this part of his life—the dark side—with her, they would indeed be—what had she called it? *Soulmates*?

It was something he had never shared with anyone else. Even Queen Mary did not know of the existence of his younger sister. Oh, yes, they all knew that there was to be an addition to the Keith clan at the time, but when she was born—unusual as she was—everyone was informed that the poor infant had died at birth. Even their kinfolk, the Peterhead Keiths from Inverugie Castle, did not know of her survival.

"Please don't be frightened," Mechi assured him. "It will be all right. In fact, I feel in some strange way as if today holds the key that will unlock the answer to all of our troubles."

"You mean of Queen Mary?" Robbie asked, suddenly excited by the thought that they might find a solution far sooner and easier than he had dared hope.

"Yes, that and more," Mechi said. She laughed slightly as she thought of all the mystery shows she had watched on TV. The cops always had a "gut feeling" or a "gut instinct." *Well, call it crazy if you want, that's exactly what this feels like,* she thought. Either that, or I've got the flu, or I am head over heels in love with a man out of a history book and it is simply butterflies in my stomach.

"You won't be frightened by her?" Robbie asked, not putting his sister's name into a spoken word.

"Of course not," Mechi said. She thought about the retarded man who lived a few miles down the road from them in Paris, Texas. As a young child she had been terrified, but once she got to know him she learned that he was really a sweet, harmless old man. She expected at least as much of Genevieve.

Robbie ran his fingers over the soft, satiny surface of her windbreaker.

"Still think it's lucky?" Mechi asked, teasing him.

"I think I would feel much luckier if it was off," he said. He glanced down at her legs, which were quite exposed from her riding skirt being pulled up slightly. He wondered if she looked as delicious inside her clothing as she did with her body entirely covered. Of all the women he had known, and who had pursued him, she was the first who had ever caused him to entertain such thoughts.

Mechi pulled her arms out of the sleeves of her jacket and waved it in front of him. She jumped up and ran away from him, swinging it in the air.

"Come and get it!" she taunted him.

"I'll come and get it—and you!" he declared, grabbing hold of her wrist. "Aha! Now you are my prisoner."

"Prisoner?" Mechi asked. So much for liberation! Well, if she had to be held captive by someone, who better than Lord Robbie Keith?

"Prisoner of love," Robbie said, embracing her so tightly she gasped for breath. He crushed his lips against hers, kissing her more forcefully and passionately than anyone had ever done to her before. *Eat your heart out, Robert Pearson!*

When he finally came up for air, Mechi nearly fell to the ground at the rush of emotions that had overtaken her. Had she heard him right? Did he mean that he loved her? Was it possible that he felt as strongly about her as she did about him?

"I'm sorry," Robbie said. "Perhaps I should not have been so forward."

"Perhaps you should have warned me first," Mechi said. "It was not the embrace I minded, nor the kiss, it was just that I was so unprepared."

She thought about the "Be prepared" motto of the 1990's. This was a time and age when there was no such thing as birth control. Condoms were unheard of. Aids did not exist. Could Robbie, if he ever did accompany her to the twentieth century, possibly deal with such things? Or, given the fact that there was some history of retardation, would it be too much for him to handle and would he go mad, too? Mechi knew that she could never do that to him, but she also knew that she would die of a broken heart if they had to separate.

"I do love you," Robbie said. "God help me, I know I shouldn't, but I can't stop myself. I have never felt this way about anyone in my life." He leaned forward and kissed her again, but this time it was a soft, gentle kiss on her lips, leaving her wishing for more.

"I can't imagine life without you," Mechi said, not daring to commit herself to saying she loved him, too. It would be too painful if she had to leave.

"What are you thinking about so hard?" he asked.

"What if we are successful in stopping the plot against Mary and I am sent back to my time?" she asked. She shivered at the mere thought of it.

Sensing that she was chilled, Robbie took her jacket and pulled it around her shoulders. "Here, put this on," he said.

Mechi pushed her arms into the sleeves, then stuffed her hands into the pockets. To her amazement, she felt something strange in one of them. She wrapped her fingers around the objects and pulled them out. She opened her hand and stared at—two tiny feathers and the most beautiful sapphire ring she had ever seen in her life.

"What is this?" she asked. Suddenly she knew what he was up to. He had wanted to give her a gift, so he had put the ring in the pocket before they left the castle. Of course! That was why he had been so insistent on her wearing the windbreaker. It all made perfect sense. What a sweet gesture!

"Thank you!" she exclaimed as she slipped it on her finger, then grabbed Robbie around the neck and kissed him. "It is beautiful!"

His face reddened. "I would like very much to be credited for such a gift," he said, "but the truth of the matter is, it is not of my doing."

Mechi stared at him, stunned. Speechless. Finally she managed to ask, "Then how… ?"

"I have no idea," Robbie said, "but I am quite certain that is one of the jewels of the royal collection."

"It belongs to Queen Mary?" Mechi asked, completely confused.

"Nay," Robbie said. "The English regalia. 'Tis a part of the gems of Queen Elizabeth."

They both stared at each other, their thoughts matching on an intimate level.

"Do you suppose this has something to do with that crazy Liz Stewart back in Aberdeen, Maryland?" Mechi finally asked. "But how would I have gotten it? I never even met the woman."

"I would lay you odds that somehow your *crazy Liz Stewart* is in reality Queen Elizabeth. Did she find some secret way to transport herself back and forth in time as you did?"

"An amulet!" Mechi exclaimed. "I have read of such things. I never believed in them—until now. It is some object that allows such things to occur. I read a book one time about somebody who claimed this had happened to them. I thought it was a fairy tale."

"A tale of the faeries?" Robbie asked, picturing the tiny leprechauns of the Irish folk. Nobody believed in them, either, but maybe there was some truth to that, too. Today, he knew, anything was possible.

"I don't understand any of this," Mechi said. "I really don't."

"Nor do I," Robbie said, "but I am more certain now than ever that you were sent here for a purpose. We must be very careful. Elizabeth and Darnley will most assuredly have spies all about if they suspect. If she discovers that her ring is missing..."

Mechi rubbed her fingers over the gem in the ring. Suddenly her head began to reel and she fainted dead away.

"Mechi! Mechi!" Robbie cried out, shaking her to revive her. When she didn't respond, he instinctively pulled the ring from her finger and threw it on the ground. In a few seconds she came to, her face ashen, but at least awake and alert.

"What happened?" she asked, looking up at him. Her head was resting on his lap, just as it was when she first came to at St. Andrews. Had this whole thing been a dream, as she had feared all along? Was she at St. Andrew's Country Club in Aberdeen, Maryland? The only thing she was sure of at this moment was that this was still the face of the man who had called himself Lord Robbie Keith, Viscount of Kintore, in her dream.

"Who are you?" she asked shyly.

Robbie laughed. "What a ridiculous question! Why, I am Robert Keith," he answered. "But of course you know that."

"Just checking," Mechi said. "Right now I'm not real sure of anything." She looked at her finger. The ring was gone.

"I threw it away," Robbie said. "'Tis treacherous. If Queen Elizabeth wants her way to this world and another, let her have it. I want you here with me. I need you here with me. Queen Mary may have caused you to come, but I will cause you to stay."

"Very well put," Mechi said. "For you, Lord Robbie, I would sacrifice a life in any world. As long as you are there, it is the world in which I belong."

"Let's be on our way to the cottage," he said. "If you are still sure you want to go."

"Now more than ever," Mechi said. "Whatever we must face from here on out, we will do it together."

"And as long as we are together, we can do anything," Robbie said, hoisting her up onto her horse.

"Wherever we go, whatever we do," Mechi sang, "we're gonna go through it together."

"I like your songs," Robbie said, smiling at her as they rode off.

Chapter XXIII

Robbie slowed his horse as they approached the little house and motioned to Mechi to do the same. She rubbed her fingers against the palms of her hands; the sweat was cold and clammy. She did not remember ever having been so unsure of herself. What would she find inside? Would it be a ranting maniac? Was the Keith clan right in keeping Genevieve hidden from the world? Was Genevieve happier this way than if she was in the modern world—Mechi's former world—where people still pointed, laughed and snickered behind their hands at the likes of her? Maybe the whole world would be a better place if no one ever had to face such ridicule. Such thoughts made Mechi nearly sick to her stomach; civilization had progressed so much, yet it was still as arrogant and haughty in 1997 as it had been in 1561.

"I will go in first," Robbie said, securing the reins from his horse to a tree.

"No," Mechi protested. "I want to go with you."

"I will come back and get you in just a few minutes," Robbie promised. "But it will be better this way. I will try to explain who you are to Gen first. She does frighten easily."

Mechi smiled at him. How could she argue with such compassion? She nodded, then watched as he walked slowly to the door of the cottage.

The moments seemed like hours as she sat, waiting, wondering if he had changed his mind. Was she too fragile for a visit from a total stranger?

Mechi laughed. She wondered exactly how Robbie intended to explain her to his sister and her attendant. No, it was more than that. Now that he knew her secret, when and where she came from, how could he explain her to anyone? At least the analogy is appropriate, she thought: I am a total stranger. Probably the strangest thing they have ever seen!

Sitting on a fallen log, Mechi was lost in her thoughts when Robbie returned. She jumped, startled at his presence.

"You must have been a million miles away," he teased, winking at her with his incredible green eyes. "Or a million years…"

They both laughed. They knew how close to the truth that statement might be. The lifetimes between them were incomprehensible, yet the closeness could be felt each time their eyes met.

"Are you ready?" he asked, taking her hand in his to help her to her feet.

"The question is," Mechi stated, "is Genevieve ready for me?"

"Quite," Robbie said, grinning broadly. "I told her you are like someone the faeries might have found in the woods. She was delighted. I have told her many stories of the Irish leprechauns and faeries. She thinks you are magic."

Mechi shivered. She did not want to disappoint Genevieve, but she knew there was no magic up her sleeve. To the contrary, she would have welcomed some on her own behalf. She stiffened her spine and walked boldly towards the cottage. Whatever awaited her inside, she would handle it. She had handled things much tougher than this in the last few days.

As they got closer, Mechi could see Genevieve's nose pressed tightly against the tiny window, straining to catch the first glimpse of her. Mechi instinctively smiled warmly, setting the girl at ease.

Robbie pulled the door open and stood back while Mechi entered. Mechi moved slowly. She knew if she was too impetuous, it might frighten Genevieve.

"Howdy," Genevieve said, laughing at the strange sound of the new word Robbie had just taught her.

Mechi laughed, too. "Howdy to you," she said in return.

Mechi turned and looked at Robbie, who looked as pleased as a peacock with its full plumage extended. So he had paid attention to the words she had used. The idea of this man standing on the edge of a ranch in Paris, Texas, shouting "Howdy" to passersby was almost more than she could stand, but she had to control herself—for Genevieve's sake.

Mechi curtsied to the girl. After all, she reasoned, she is still a Keith. And the Keiths are all entitled to their royal honors. Yes, even Genevieve. No, *especially* Genevieve!

"I am very pleased to meet you," Mechi said. She smiled at her again as she added, "You are very pretty."

Genevieve blushed. Mechi was sure no one had ever paid her a compliment before. It was true. She had the same red hair, which was done up in braids which were fastened atop her head, and the same sparkling green eyes as the other members of the clan.

Mechi watched her closely. She did not seem retarded at all. What a pity to keep such a perfectly normal appearing person locked away from the rest of the world. There must be something she could do. Why, when the Keith clan was as tight as it was, would they put her away?

Suddenly, with no warning, Genevieve began to thrash about. Her head flew backwards and Robbie grabbed her, trying to anchor her in her time of torment.

Mechi stood, unmoving, for a few seconds, then ran to help him. She grabbed a small piece of wood she saw lying on a table and inserted it into the girl's mouth, holding her tongue down.

In a few minutes the episode passed and Genevieve, although appearing tired, seemed to be perfectly normal again.

"How did you know to do that?" Robbie asked. He had fought with his sister in such times over and over again to keep her from biting her own tongue. Finally, in desperation, he had discovered that holding her tongue flat with a stick would help protect her from herself.

"I..." Mechi hesitated. Oh, what had she gotten herself into? She had sensed immediately that the girl was not a *lunatic*, as Robbie had claimed. No, she was certain the child had some form of epilepsy.

"...I don't know," Mechi said. "I have read about such a disease as she has."

Robbie waited for her to continue. Could it be that she could do for Genevieve what she had done for the Dunnottar horses? If she was a witch, so be it! At least she was a *good* witch!

"It is something called epilepsy," Mechi said, having no idea how to explain something so foreign to Robbie. If only she could offer him some hope. Why hadn't she become a doctor—or at least a nurse—instead of a stupid golf pro? What good was that to anyone? It seemed so unimportant now, or in her future lifetime, for that matter.

"Epilepsy?" Robbie asked. "I never heard of it."

"I don't have any idea when they first identified it," Mechi said. "I do know that ... in my day—there were medications which control it. *Epileptics*, as they call people with epilepsy, can live perfectly normal lives."

"But their spells?" Robbie asked.

"With the proper medication," Mechi said, "they do not suffer from them. They are called *seizures*."

Robbie looked at her, his eyes pleading. "Can—can you help her?"

"Oh, Robbie," Mechi said, her voice catching in her throat. "I wish I could. I don't know anything about the medicine they use. I am sorry. So sorry."

"But the horses?" he asked. "You used the bread."

"Yes," Mechi said. "The mold on the bread is a form of *penicillin*. That is useful only for infections, which is what the horses had. Epilepsy is something completely different. I am afraid penicillin would not work for Genevieve."

"Then there is nothing you can do for her?" he asked, tears forming in the corners of his eyes.

"I am afraid not," Mechi said, her eyes staring at the floor. "I truly am sorry. I would do anything for her—for you—if I could."

The only way I could help her, Mechi thought, is if I could somehow send her back—or ahead—to 1997. Her mind went back to the strange sensation she had gotten when she rubbed her fingers across the ring she had found tucked away in the pocket of her jacket. If she gave the ring to Genevieve, could the girl advance into the future where she could get help and live a normal life?

Mechi shook her head. What a stupid idea! A child from 1561 being cast into 1997 would certainly be anything but normal! She entertained the thought, momentarily, of the two of them returning together. Could she find the ring again? No, that was an impossibility, too. She could not bear to leave Lord Robbie Keith behind. Besides, she still had a job to do. They had to find a clone for Queen Mary and figure out how to pull off the scam of the century. Or how ever many centuries it might have been from now until then.

Mechi heard someone come up behind her. She knew the only other person who was there was Genevieve's caretaker. She heard her speak, but she was so busy concentrating on Genevieve's problems she didn't turn to look at her.

"Have they been more frequent?" she heard Robbie ask.

"Nay," the caretaker replied. "At least not for the last week. It seems to be more when she is excited or upset about something than at other times."

Mechi wondered if it was a mistake for her to come here. She should have listened to Lord Keith; he did not want her to see this part of their lives. Maybe he had been right. She would never have done anything intentionally to upset the child.

About thirteen or fourteen, Mechi thought. Just beginning the life of a teenager. And what fun did she have to look forward to? There would be no school ballgames to attend, no senior proms, no graduation parties… What was the matter with her? None of these things existed in 1561 anyway. Not even if she had been a *normal* child.

Mechi realized that the woman was speaking to her. She turned to face her. Mechi's mouth dropped open. How could Robbie not have seen it? The answer to their very problem was right her in front of their noses.

"Mechi?" Robbie asked. "Are you all right?"

Then, as was getting to be a habit, Mechi fell into his arms in a dead faint.

Chapter XXIV

Mechi's head was still in Lord Robbie's lap when she came to. She stared up at him, then glanced at the older woman who was fanning her.

"Robbie," Mechi said, her voice cracking. "Look at her."

Robbie turned his attention to the caretaker.

"Mrs. McGrath?" he asked. "What about her?"

"She's..." Mechi paused. "She's perfect."

"Why, thank you, my lady," Mrs. McGrath said, her face turning ten shades of red. "Not since Ian died has anyone found me so."

Mechi laughed. "Nothing personal," she said, "but that is not exactly what I meant. Robbie, she's perfect! Look at her closely."

Robbie still seemed confused. "Perfect for what?" he asked.

"Can't you see it?" Mechi said, exasperated that she was the only one to whom the solution of their problem was so obvious. "Look at her again."

Robbie inched closer to Mrs. McGrath and almost buried his nose in her face. He shook his head. He had no idea what Mechi was talking about.

Mechi, now sitting up on her own, went to Mrs. McGrath and pulled her braids from the top of her head. She quickly ran her fingers through the plaits to loosen the locks. Then she began winding the hair into curls and securing them on top of her head in large curls, using the tiny sticks which were lying on the table to fasten them.

"Oh, my!" Robbie exclaimed as he looked at her with her new coif. "If only she was taller!"

"Would someone be so good as to tell me what is happening?" Mrs. McGrath asked.

"You are quite right!" Robbie said excitedly. "She is perfect."

"For what?" Mrs. McGrath asked. She should have been enjoying the attention, but something was making her extremely uncomfortable and nervous about this strange turn of events.

"You have met Queen Mary?" Robbie asked. "Surely when she was at Dunnottar."

"Aye, I've seen her from afar several times. But what have I to do with her?"

"And you owe her your full allegiance?" Robbie asked, ignoring Mrs. McGrath's questions.

"But of course," Mrs. McGrath replied. "Ian, God rest his soul, was a member of the king's guards. My allegiance always has rested with the throne of Scotland."

"You would do anything for your monarch?" Robbie asked.

"Aye, my lord. Anything."

Robbie and Mechi exchanged a quick glance. She could not know what danger might ensue if she truly meant that. If they explained their plan to her, would she be willing to devote the rest of her life, if need be, to preserving the very soul of Mary?

Mechi poked Robbie, nodding her head to the side, indicating that she wanted to talk to him privately. He immediately retreated to a corner of the house, where they went into a very secretive session.

"Do you think we can really trust her?" Mechi asked, her voice a mere whisper.

"With our lives," Robbie said softly. "My father would never have obtained her services for Genevieve if she were not trustworthy to a fault."

"I suppose that is true," Mechi said. Still, she knew they would have to find some way to test her devotion to the queen before they implemented their plot.

"We must put her to a test," Mechi said.

"Such as?" Robbie asked.

Mechi thought a few moments, then said "The ring."

"I threw it into the forest," Robbie said. "I dinna like what it was doing to you."

"But now we need it," Mechi said. "Go and find it."

Robbie glared at her. He was not accustomed to taking orders from anyone, least of all a woman.

"Go!" Mechi ordered, her voice so loud and filled with authority that Robbie immediately marched out the front door, onto his horse and back to the spot where they had first encountered the gem in Mechi's pocket.

He sat on the ground exactly where they had been just a short time ago. He looked in the general direction where he had tossed the ring. He felt a cold shiver come over him as he thought about the jewel. Did it, as Mechi said, hold some strange magical power? What had she called it? An *armlet*? No, that was not right. An *amulet*. Yes, that was it. Well, if it did have magic powers, were they good or evil?

Immediately he knew the answer to that question. It had brought Mechi there to him—well, to Queen Mary. He just happened to be in the way at the right time. Anything that could produce something as wonderful as this stranger from another world had to be good.

He heard a fluttering in the tree directly above him. He looked up. There, tucked in the cracks of a bird's nest, was the bright shiny jewel. As if to say that he was guarding it with his life, the bird sat, chirping away, daring anyone to tread on his turf.

"Sorry, ol' chap," Robbie said to his feathered friend. "But for the good of the country, I must take it from you."

He waited for the bird to fly away, as if he understood what Robbie was asking of him. The bird sat firm.

Robbie placed his fingers together and formed a horn. He held his hands to his mouth and let out a battle cry which could be heard for miles around.

The bird seemed almost to laugh at him. He sat firm, not willing to budge an inch.

Robbie picked up a small pebble from the ground and tossed it at the bird. Still, the bird was undaunted.

Robbie pushed the leaves on the ground about until he found a larger stone. He looked up at the bird, who had perched its head at an odd angle, as if to ask Robbie what on earth he was doing. Robbie took the stone and threw it, harder, at the tiny creature. The bird sat, still not budging.

Frustrated at the bird's stubbornness, Robbie grasped one of the lower branches on the tree and began to make his way up. Branch by branch, testing each one for safety before he put his weight on it, he climbed higher, higher, until he finally arrived at the same level as his feathered adversary.

Slowly, Robbie put his hand into the nest and began to untangle the ring from the grass the bird had used to interweave it securely in place.

Peck, peck, peck. Robbie let out a shrill scream as the blood began to run from the holes the bird had put in his hand.

Whatever the secret of this ring was, he thought, even the bird must realize its importance.

Finally, he pushed the bird from its perch with his elbow and succeeded in extracting the ring. He held it up to admire it, careful not to touch the gem itself, remembering the odd effect it had had on Mechi earlier.

The sun hit the jewel, nearly blinding him. He reached up to shield his eyes from the brilliance. The shift in his weight caused him to lose his balance, sending him plummeting to the ground with a loud *thud.*

"I do hope you know what you are about, my dearest Mechi," he said aloud. "I am not sure this is worth the effort." He grinned broadly as he added, "But to be sure, ye are worth this—and more. Aye, Lady Mechi, stranger from the future, you are worth far more than all the gems in the world."

He stuffed the ring into the pouch he wore around his waist and merrily mounted his horse. It took only a few minutes until he was at the cottage. He could see Genevieve's face pressed against the window, anxiously awaiting his return. He did love his sister, in spite of her malady. And, God help him, he loved the stranger as well.

"I have it," he said to Mechi as he entered the house.

Mechi hurried to his side, her hand outstretched for the trinket.

"Oh, no you don't!" Robbie said. "I shall guard it meself. I'll not trust ye with it. Not after what it did to you a short while ago. Ye'll not touch it again."

"Whatever," Mechi said, shrugging her shoulders in surrender to his wishes.

"Have ye told her of our plan?" he asked, motioning towards Mrs. McGrath.

"No," Mechi said. "I thought it would be best coming from you. She—is more apt to trust you."

"I wonder why," Robbie said, the twinkle returning to his eye. If Mechi began spouting on and on about boxes that cook with no fire and huge birds that carry hundreds of people inside them through the sky, surely Mrs. McGrath would think poor Genevieve was not the one who was a raving lunatic.

"That's enough!" Mechi said, almost hearing his thoughts, they screamed so loudly.

"We shall tell her together," Robbie said. "I'm not sure I understand it all meself."

"But you do agree?" Mechi asked, suddenly frightened by what this whole thing could mean. The impact of what they were about to undertake was overwhelming. If they succeeded, they could change the very course of history. If they failed… She shuddered at the thought of the number of lives that could be threatened—no, lost— because of them. Because of *her*. The plan was hers and hers alone. She could find no consolation in trying to place part of the blame on Lord Robbie Keith, Viscount of Kintore, nor anyone else.

"I think you had better sit down," Mechi said to Mrs. McGrath. "We have a matter of the greatest importance to discuss with you."

"Gen," Robbie said, "would you be a dear and go outside to play?"

Genevieve would do absolutely anything for her big brother. She immediately went to the door, ran outside and sat by a tiny toadstool. Mechi smiled through the window at the girl as she watched her for a few moments before she joined Robbie and Mrs. McGrath.

"We have a grave concern for the safety of Her Majesty, Queen Mary, at hand," Robbie began, watching Mrs. McGrath closely for her reaction as the plan began to unfold.

Chapter XXV

Mechi began to tell Mrs. McGrath about the fate that awaited Queen Mary, at least what she could remember of it. She tried to picture her mother, when Mechi was just a little child, relating the stories of their ancestor.

Mrs. McGrath listened intently, trying to comprehend the whole thing. Finally she grabbed her head and began to cry.

"What is it?" Robbie asked tenderly.

"How can this be possible?" Mrs. McGrath asked. "And how do you know these things?"

Mechi glared at Robbie. They had agreed in their earlier huddle that they would not tell Mrs. McGrath the truth about Mechi's strange entrance to this world. Now, she wondered if she would be able to keep it from her.

"I have something to show you," Robbie said, slowly opening his waist pouch. He paused, then asked her, "Can ye keep a secret, Mum?"

"Aye, lassie, ye know I can. Why, have I not kept the secret of the Keiths all these years?" She looked hurt, angry. "How can ye ask such a question of me, laddie?"

"I'm sorry," Robbie said, taking her hands in his. "I dinna mean anything by what I asked. It is just that the secret we must tell you holds the future of the queen—aye, of the very land of Scotland herself—in your hands. It is the most important thing anyone has ever done for the land."

"Even more than the Bruce himself?" Mrs. McGrath asked. Robbie smiled at her, then turned to Mechi. "Mrs. McGrath is a distant kin to the Bruce," he explained. "There's no finer ruler than he in all the history of Scotland."

"So I've heard," Mechi said, contemplating how to proceed. She wished she could tell Mrs. McGrath that she too was a distant kin to one of Scotland's monarchs, but since King James had not yet been born… And since no one had any great love for Darnley…

"Here," Robbie said, reaching into his pouch and pulling out the ring, which he had carefully wrapped in leaves to keep its powers from rubbing off on him.

He allowed the ring to fall freely onto the table in front of them.

Mrs. McGrath gasped. "Oh, my!" Her eyes bulged at the sight of such a jewel. "Oh, my!" she repeated. She extended her hand towards the ring.

"No!" Mechi shouted. "Don't touch it!"

Mrs. McGrath pulled her hand back like she had touched a red hot coal. She continued to stare at the ring. Never had she seen such a treasure.

"Robbie," Mechi pleaded. "Please explain the danger to her."

"'Tis Darnley," Robbie began, hoping he could make some sense out of this whole story Mechi had told him. "He is in league with Queen Elizabeth to undo Queen Mary."

"By doin' what?" Mrs. McGrath asked.

"He's pledged to wed the Queen," Robbie explained.

"He'll wed Elizabeth?" Mrs. McGrath asked, her voice full of doubt.

"Nay," Robbie replied. "He'll marry Queen Mary."

Mrs. McGrath stared at Robbie, then at Mechi. "Such foolery!" she scoffed. "Her majesty is far too wise to fall for such a trick. Why, with her wit and good sense, she'd laugh him off the face of the earth!"

"I wish you were right," Mechi said. "But I know it for a fact."

Mrs. McGrath watched Mechi carefully. Never, she thought, had she seen such sincerity in a person. Except perhaps Genevieve. The poor child trusted Robbie implicitly. He could ask her to stand 'neath a falling branch and she would oblige him.

"Are ye quite certain?" Mrs. McGrath asked, rubbing her head as if to force such an idea to makes its way inside.

"Aye," Robbie said. "But that is not the end of it."

"I should think not!" Mrs. McGrath said indignantly. "If Henry was worthy of divorcin' ever so many fine ladies, surely Queen Mary could rid herself of one such scoundrel."

"But she will not," Mechi said. "In fact, she will be condemned for Darnley's death."

"And rightfully so!" Mrs. McGrath said. "Why, should any woman pledge herself to such a man as Darnley, 'twould be grounds for madness. If she was not mad when she wed him, a fortnight in his bed—should she last that long—would drive her to become a complete lunatic. She'd be in far worse shape than Genevieve."

"So you would not sympathize with the queen's choice, should she desire Darnley?"

"She'd not desire the beast!" Mrs. McGrath shouted. "She's a reasonable woman!"

Mechi looked at Robbie, trying to capture his attention. She cleared her throat, and when that didn't work she kicked him under the table where they were seated.

"Ouch!" Robbie yelped, rubbing his bruised leg.

"I am truly sorry, my lord," Mechi said. "Might I have a word with you?"

Robbie sat, stunned by the pain in his leg.

"Now," Mechi said. "Alone."

Robbie got to his feet and limped towards the door. Mechi playfully slugged him on the arm, which he immediately began massaging vigorously.

"You big baby!" Mechi said, laughing. "And to think I believed you were my hero!" She placed both hands over her heart and Robbie was afraid she was going to swoon again. He hurried to grab her before she collapsed.

"I like that," Mechi said, a twinkle dancing about in her eyes that would match those in Lord Robbie's any day. "You may give a repeat performance any time you like."

Robbie laughed. "Faking it?" he asked, remembering the term she had used when he had pretended to be ill when she was tending the horses back at Dunnottar. "I'm ashamed of you!"

"I learned from the master," Mechi said as they sat down on the ground outside the cottage.

"And I like the sounds of that," Robbie said. "But tell me, what did you have to tell me that you dared not speak to Mrs. McGrath?"

"She seems so right for the job," Mechi said. "Her looks are so perfect for our *clone*. Yet she is so skittish about Darnley, we could never ask her to pretend to be married to the cad."

Robbie looked at her quizzically. "*Skittish?*" he asked.

"Nervous," Mechi explained. She wondered what he would think if she said "Up tight."

"'Tis not a woman alive who would willingly marry such a man as Darnley," Robbie said.

"Now watch your tongue, laddie," Mechie teased. "Don't forget that if it wasn't for him, and my being descended from him, I probably wouldn't be here."

"For that I am eternally grateful to the rat," Robbie conceded. "But that is the only good has ever come from him."

"I must say I am inclined to agree with you," Mechi said. "I really can't stand the jerk."

Robbie gave her that *I don't get it* look again.

"Idiot!" Mechi said. "Dope. Crazy man."

"Aye," Robbie said. "On that point we agree. Indeed he is a *jer-r-r-rk.*"

Mechi laughed. She had heard many people called a jerk before, but never like the way Lord Robbie called Darnley. Even a word like jerk, when he said it, made a man seem quite acceptable.

"I dinna ken," Robbie said. "Perhaps ye're right. She does seem—*skittish* about it. Still, if we are going to protect the queen, I dinna see that we have any other course to pursue."

"I suppose you're right," Mechi agreed. "But, maybe we should go a little slow with Mrs. McGrath. What if we just leave the ring with her for now? As a sort of test. We will instruct her that she must not touch it under any circumstances. Then we can come back in a day or two to see if she has succeeded."

"And if she has?" Robbie asked.

"Then we begin with phase two," Mechi said. She felt like she was piloting a rocket to the moon. Maybe, just maybe, that would have been easier.

Chapter XXVI

Mechi and Robbie again explained the importance of guarding the ring to Mrs. McGrath, making sure they told her that strange things could happen if she tried to put the jewel on her finger.

"Aye, laddie," she said, eyeing the ring with both suspicion and desire. "I'll mind yer biddin'." Her eyes were still glued to the shiny blue sapphire. "But 'twill not be an easy task ye ask o' me."

"I know," Robbie said, placing his big work-worn hand over her tiny fragile one. "But there's not another person in the land we can trust in like we can you."

Mrs. McGrath smiled. She did so dote on the lad. Had ever since he was a wee bairn. *Such a pity*, she thought as she glanced out the window at Genevieve. *She had so much to live for, and to be in such a state as she was. There was no justice in this life.*

As if he was reading her thoughts, Robbie said, "If our plan succeeds, at least Darnley will have his just rewards."

"And Queen Mary will be preserved—safe and secure because of your help," Mechi added.

"I still cannot believe that Darnley—evil though he may be—would actually bring any harm to her majesty," Mrs. McGrath said.

"Ye must trust us," Robbie said, wondering if Mechi was right. Maybe it was too much to ask of anyone, even Mrs. McGrath.

"Aye, laddie. Ye know I do. But I dinna understand it."

"Nor do I," Robbie said. "I just know that we must do what we are called upon to do."

"'Tis a duty most distasteful," Mrs. McGrath said, wrinkling her nose as if she had smelled a foul odor.

Mechi smiled at her. The woman was right. Mechi did not know if she could pull off such a charade or not. The idea of pretending to be in love with—or at least tolerate—Darnley would be almost as bad as being married to Robert Pearson. Thank God she didn't resemble the queen! Maybe there was at least one plus to being descended from the other side of the line coming down.

Mechi's jaw dropped open. She took hold of Robbie's plaid and drew him close to her.

"We've still got a problem," she whispered in his ear.

"Just one?" he said aloud, laughing that deep infectious laugh.

"Well, at least one," Mechi said.

"And that is?" Robbie asked.

"Her height," Mechi answered. "She is far too short to pass for the queen."

"Would you please stand to your feet?" Robbie asked Mrs. McGrath. She obeyed immediately, like a servant to her master.

"Aye," Robbie said. "I see whereof you speak."

"We'll have to do something about it," Mechi said.

"Now?" Robbie asked.

"It's as good a time as any," Mechi said. She turned towards Mrs. McGrath. "May I see your shoes, please?"

Mrs. McGrath hesitated a few moments, then unstrapped the boots from first one foot, then the other, handing them to Mechi.

Mechi winced. They were already heavy. If they tried to turn them into *platforms*, how would the poor woman ever be able to set one foot in front of the other.

Absentmindedly, Mechi began singing. "Just put one foot in front of the other, and soon you'll be walkin' out the door."

"Of course I will!" Mrs. McGrath said. "Such nonsense to be singin' about."

Robbie smiled at Mechi. "She knows a lot of songs which seem strange to us," he said. "But they are a mite…"

He stopped, not knowing what word would describe the strange effect the little ditties she sang seemed to have on him.

"Catchy?" Mechi asked, hoping she had chosen the right word, then realizing from his expression that that term meant absolutely nothing to him.

"Aye," she said, surprising even herself at the use of such a Scottish expression. "That means they get stuck in your head and you can't get them out."

"Aye," Robbie said, "*catchy* they be."

Mrs. McGrath, while not verbally agreeing, gave her consent to the idea by beginning to repeat the words and the tune. "Just put one foot in front of the other, and soon you'll be walkin' out the door."

"By George, I think she's got it!" Mechi said, donning her most English accent.

"Who's George?" Robbie asked.

"Queen Elizabeth's father," Mechi said, then stepped back at such a remark. Of course he was. And he wasn't. Oh, her head hurt! How would they ever manage to do this? There were so many things that got all mixed up in her mind. And, she knew, by the time they were done with Mrs. McGrath she would be as confused as Mechi—if not more so. Poor Mrs. McGrath!

"Can you get me a chunk of wood?" Mechi asked Robbie, studying Mrs. McGrath's boots.

"Aye," he said. "But would ye mind tellin' me what for?"

"For her shoes," Mechi said, as if that would explain everything.

Robbie rubbed his head, the loose red locks catching in his fingers. He knew better than to ask for more details. Yes, he had asked Mrs. McGrath to trust him. He knew he, too, must blindly trust what Mechi said. After all, it was she who knew what the future held; not him.

He headed for the door and grabbed Genevieve's hand, pulling her along with him. She skipped gaily, glad for the time to spend with her big brother.

"Where are we going?" she asked.

"To the forest to fetch a block of wood," Robbie said.

Genevieve, fully confident of her idol's intent, never asked a thing but went ahead, picking up first one piece of wood and then another. Soon her arms were loaded down.

"Enough?" she asked.

"I should think so," Robbie said. He took the wood from her and they headed back to the cottage.

"She's funny," Genevieve said.

"Who?" Robbie asked.

"Lady Mechi," Genevieve said. "Like she's from some other place."

Robbie shook his head. How did such a little person as Genevieve detect such things? Did Mechi somehow belong in her world, too? Was there any chance at all that Mechi might be able to help his little sister? Maybe there was more than one reason this strange character had come into their lives. Did he dare hope? Aye, he decided, without hope what is there left? For Gen's sake, he would hope. He would hope until the end.

Back at the cottage, Robbie dumped the armload of wood at Mechi's feet, as if he was making an offering to a goddess.

"Will that be enough?" he asked, still not sure what she planned to do with it.

"More than enough," Mechi said, handling first one piece and then another. Finally, finding one piece which was fairly flat and smooth, she handed it to Robbie.

"Can you mark an outline of her boot on it?" she asked him.

"Gen, fetch yer big brother a few ashes from the edge o' the fire," he instructed his sister. She immediately went and did as he bid her.

Mechi watched the interaction between the two siblings. She was sure that

Genevieve would have jumped into the middle of the fire if Robbie had told her to.

Genevieve emptied the corner of her apron, where she had tucked the ashes to carry them to Robbie, onto the table in front of them. Robbie set Mrs. McGrath's boot on top of the piece of wood, then dipped his finger into the ashes and traced the outline of the shoe onto the wood. He reached into his sock and removed his *skein dhu*, the knife Mechi had only seen before on TV programs of Scotsmen doing their highland dances.

Genevieve leaned forward, watching every move her big brother made. Her head circled slowly as she traced Robbie's movements with his knife. When he was finished with the first wooden tracing of the boot, Genevieve breathed a deep sigh of relief. She was, Mechi thought, as nervous about the outcome of this strange act as if she had been yielding the blade herself.

"Now what?" Robbie asked, his own curiosity as obvious as Genevieve and Mrs. McGrath's.

"We need some glue," Mechi said.

"Glue?" Robbie asked.

Mechi puzzled over this predicament for several minutes. There wasn't any corner pharmacy or Target to run to for a bottle of Elmer's glue-all. The closest she could come would be to take some flour and water and mix it into a paste, but she knew that would never be strong enough to form the kind of bond she needed.

She snickered as she thought about the bonds she had already cemented here. She could never bear to leave Robbie behind, and as she had watched Genevieve she knew the girl was anything but dumb. She caught on to everything with great ease and confidence. No, she was sure the only thing wrong with the outcast Keith was epilepsy. If only there was some way to take both of them back to the future with her.

"Don't you think?" she heard Robbie ask when her mind popped back to the present time.

"Don't I think what?" she asked.

"We should do a matching one for the other foot," Robbie repeated.

"Yes," Mechi said. Did he understand what she was doing? She was sure none of them had ever heard of platform shoes, but maybe she could start a new trend. Not that that was her forte in life, mind you. She hardly cared what she wore herself—before—choosing jeans and a sweatshirt most days. Being a golf pro at St. Andrew's provided her the perfect opportunity to shun such things as formal wear, or even acceptable office apparel.

Robbie quickly completed the second wood block and handed them both to Mechi.

"Well?" he asked, curious as to what she intended to do next.

"Well, now we need some way to fasten them to the bottom of her boots," Mechi explained.

Genevieve, who had been observing this whole episode with great interest, scurried to a vine which was trailing from the window. She grabbed a stalk of it and went back to the table. She took the boot and wood block and began wrapping it with the vine. When she was finished, she tied the ends of the vine, stood back to admire her handiwork, then tied it a second time to be sure it was secure.

"Good girl!" Robbie said, praising his little sister and patting her on the head. "I don't know if we could do this without you."

"Do what?" Genevieve asked.

"Protect the queen," Robbie said.

Mechi watched Genevieve's eyes bulge with glee. She was not accustomed to being a part of anything, much less something this big and this important. Whatever strange power it was this Mechi person had over Robbie, Gen liked it.

When both boots were fastened to the wood blocks, Mechi took one of them and asked Mrs. McGrath to lift her foot. Mechi wiggled the boot around until it was in place on Mrs. McGrath's tiny foot.

"About a size six," Mechi said to herself.

"What is a size six?" Mrs. McGrath asked.

"Your foot," Mechi replied. "At least in America, it is." She glanced at Robbie. She had not meant to say that. She would have to watch herself more carefully. She could not afford to have Mrs. McGrath distrust her. Not now. There was too much at stake. Too much depended on them. *On her!*

When both shoes were on, Mechi took hold of Mrs. McGrath's hand and helped her up. She stood, awkwardly, afraid to move.

"Try walking," Mechi said.

Mrs. McGrath took one step. Her foot landed with a loud *kerplop!* She stopped, unsure of herself in this crazy new shoe.

"Take another step," Mechi said. Mrs. McGrath hesitated, then did as she was told.

"Just put one foot in front of the other," Robbie sang, repeating the tune Mechi had sung earlier. "Soon you'll be walkin' out the door."

Mrs. McGrath proceeded, slowly, stopping after each step to be sure she wasn't going to topple over. Just like the silly little ditty, she was through the door and standing outside.

"Bravo!" Mechi said, applauding for this great feat.

Robbie, never having heard applause, could tell from the grin on Mechi's face that she was pleased with Mrs. McGrath, so he joined her in clapping his hands together loudly. Soon Genevieve was following suit, a smile as big as all outdoors covering her face.

"That's wonderful!" Mechi exclaimed, giving Mrs. McGrath a big hug that nearly knocked her off balance. Robbie, as always, rushed to rescue the damsel in distress.

Mechi took note of his action—or was it merely a *re*action? Maybe his rescue of her when she had nearly fainted was nothing more than natural instinct for him. She knew better than to get her hopes up that they could have any kind of a future together. Anyway, that was a crazy notion. His future and her future were certainly as different as night and day. But, as she looked at him, his eyes bright with danger and joy, all wrapped up together, she knew she had to hope. It was all she had. That and her brilliant idea of creating a clone for Queen Mary. She knew, as she looked at Mrs. McGrath, that their work had only begun. It would take a lifetime to pull this off, and Queen Mary's lifetime was not that long, she reminded herself. No, they had a lot of work to do.

ChapterXXVII

Robbie began to explain their plan to Mrs. McGrath, when Mechi motioned with a sideward tip of her head towards Genevieve. Robbie, seeing the gesture, took his sister's hands in his.

"Gen," he said, "I have something very important to tell you. What we are going to tell Mrs. McGrath is the biggest secret anyone has ever had."

Genevieve's eyes focused on Robbie. She sat, not speaking, but listening intently.

"Do you understand?" he asked her. "That means you cannot tell anyone."

"Not even Father?" she asked.

"Not even Father," Robbie said, knowing that keeping a secret from their father was something neither of them had ever done. He, above all others, always seemed to understand what they were feeling. "Can you do that?"

"For you?" Genevieve asked, smiling warmly at Robbie. "I can do *anything* for you." She glanced at Mechi. "And for her," she added. "You like her, don't you?"

"Yes," Robbie admitted. He knew, considering the differences between them, that he should not like her. Not even a little bit. But, God help him, he not only liked her— he had fallen head over heels in love with the stranger from another world.

"She likes you, too," Genevieve said, winking that same impish way Robbie did when he was toying with her.

Mechi felt the color rise in her cheeks. They felt so hot, she was afraid she would burn her hand if she dared touch them. How did such a child as this, who was kept locked away from the rest of the world, sheltered from everything life had to offer— good and bad—gain such a deep insight into things? It was, she felt, a God-given talent given to "special" people to make up for what they were missing in other areas. She had seen it before, but it had never been so clear as it was now.

"I won't tell a soul," Genevieve said. "Not even Father."

"Good girl," Robbie said, patting her hand.

Mechi laughed. "Do you know what a key is?" she asked Genevieve.

She did not reply, but merely shook her head.

"I once heard a saying that if you promise to keep a secret—especially one as important as the one you are about to share in—you must take a make-believe key and lock your lips so the words can never escape."

Mechi raised her hand to her mouth, pretending to turn the key in the pretend lock on her mouth. Then she made a motion to show that she was throwing the key away, never to be found again.

Genevieve giggled. She repeated Mechi's actions. "Now," she said, "no one can make me tell. I don't have the key to unlock my mouth."

Robbie watched Mechi with great admiration. She was so different from the people of his own day. They would never have understood about Genevieve. Oh, except Mrs. McGrath, of course. But she was so devoted to the Keith family she would have given her very life for the clan. Perhaps, he realized, that is exactly what she would be doing. Only it would be for the sake of Queen Mary, not the Keiths. Still, they were so close that the queen herself almost seemed like one of them.

Robbie began to explain about needing a *clone* for Queen Mary.

"But I cannot play the part of her majesty," Mrs. McGrath protested.

"Ah, but ye can," Robbie said. "That is the wonderful part. Not only did we find someone who so closely resembles the queen, but it is someone in whom we can trust completely. The gods are with us."

"The resemblance is almost uncanny," Mechi said, reinforcing Robbie's remarks. "Once I redid your hair."

"And these?" Mrs. McGrath asked, struggling to lift her feet in the air. "That is part of your plan?"

"Aye," Robbie said. "The only problem we have with you taking on the role of the queen is that you are too short."

"Were," Mechi corrected. "With the extra wood on your boots, I would guess that if you were to stand side by side with Queen Mary, it would be hard to tell which was which."

Mrs. McGrath wrung her hands nervously. What had she gotten herself into? She had no idea how to act like the queen! She could ruin this whole thing.

"But I dinna know that much about her majesty," she argued. "I would like to help, but I think it is a bad idea. I cannot do it." She paused, then asked, "Does Queen Mary know of this plan of yours?"

"Not yet," Robbie admitted. "But as soon as we return to Dunnottar, I will leave for Edinburgh to inform her."

"And if she does not agree to it?" Mrs. McGrath asked.

"Ah, but she must!" Robbie said. "'Tis the only way to save her life."

Mechi watched Mrs. McGrath closely. What if they told her that Queen Mary was going to be put to death and the terrible manner in which it was done? Would she turn tail and run away as fast as she could? Not that anyone would blame her. They were asking far too much of her. But, if they were to protect the queen. If Mechi's purpose for traveling through time was to be fulfilled...

"Her life?" Mrs. McGrath asked timidly. "What do you know of her life? Or her death?"

"Mechi knows a great deal about a plot to have her put to death," Robbie explained. "It is a dastardly idea of Queen Elizabeth."

"But how can she know?" Mrs. McGrath asked.

Mechi realized that while Mrs. McGrath trusted Robbie implicitly, she was far more skeptical of this stranger. This outsider. What did she hope to gain by spreading such rumors?

"Mechi comes from..." Robbie hesitated. "...another place," he said. He turned to Mechi, his eyes pleading with her for help. How could he explain something he still had not been able to totally grasp in his own mind? "She was born just outside Paris."

Mrs. McGrath sat, still twisting her hands, but not saying anything. She waited for him to continue.

"You know that Queen Mary was in France for several years."

Mrs. McGrath nodded.

"There was talk in France..." Robbie explained, waiting for the meaning to sink in.

"And they talked of overthrowing Queen Mary?" Mrs. McGrath asked. "For what reason?"

"To put Elizabeth on the throne of Scotland as well as England," Mechi said. "She would do anything to reign in both lands."

Mrs. McGrath began to reach for the ring, which still sat openly on the table.

"No!" Robbie and Mechi both shouted at the same instant. They knew—or at least suspected—what could happen if Mrs. McGrath put the ring on, or even rubbed it. She was far too important in this whole scheme to risk losing her to some future generation.

Mrs. McGrath jumped, causing the ring to fall to the floor. Genevieve reached down for it.

"No!" they both shouted again. Genevieve obediently left it lay.

Robbie took a piece of cloth which was sitting nearby and picked the ring up in it, not daring to touch it himself. He set it on the table again.

"We will leave the ring here," he said, wrapping it tightly in the cloth. "But you must both promise me that you will not touch it."

Mrs. McGrath and Genevieve looked at each other. They nodded, agreeing blindly.

"We really must be on our way," Robbie said, standing up and very gallantly helping Mechi to her feet. "We will be back in a few days." He smiled at Mrs. McGrath as he added, "Perhaps with the queen."

"I'll be here," Mrs. McGrath said, feeling quite certain that Queen Mary would never grace the door of such a lowly cottage as hers. Still, if it was for the Keiths… Yes, she knew that Robbie Keith could talk anyone into doing his bidding. All he had to do was look at you with those big green eyes and he could have convinced the entire world to surrender at his feet.

Mechi got up and together they walked to the door. She turned back and looked at Mrs. McGrath and Genevieve. She wondered if they would ever have their rightful place in history. Or if history was written in stone and this whole thing was just a useless escapade. Or, if their little scheme did succeed, would anyone ever know it?

Chapter XXVIII

The ride seemed much shorter on their way back to Dunnottar, Mechi mused. She remembered when she was a little girl that the visits to her cousins' homes always seemed much longer on the way there than on the way back, too. Funny, she thought, some things never change.

As they pushed their horses to the limit, she thought that if the A.S.P.C.A. could see the treacherous ascent up to the castle they would surely have her imprisoned for cruelty to animals. The idea amused her, and Robbie caught the smile on her face. She looked almost angelic, he thought, when she smiled like that. No, angelic was not it, he decided. It was, as he had suspected before, more like one of the Irish faeries his mother had read to him about.

Of one thing he was certain; she was not a witch. Nothing evil or bad could look as wonderful as she did.

They rode, side by side, up to the stables and Robbie hurried to dismount first. He ran to Mechi and took her in his arms, helping her down from her horse. He enjoyed finding any excuse to get this close to her.

Mechi's heel caught on the hem of her riding skirt.

"Damn!" she muttered as she fell to the ground, pulling Lord Robbie with her. She was glad Lady Keith wasn't there to hear her curse again.

They were both laughing as they lay in the stiff, scratchy hay when Durston, the head stable hand, stuck his nose in through the door.

"They's not to be no horse play in the stable!" he growled. "'Tis Lady Keith's orders, it is!"

Mechi got to her feet and brushed herself off.

"I'm afraid it's my fault," she said, assuming the blame for their actions. Actually, she did not feel guilty about their accidental "tumble," but only for getting caught.

Robbie tried to explain to Durston, but he could tell his words were falling on deaf ears. Durston and Lady Keith had always had a close friendship, and he knew that the less he said, the better off he would be. In typical Durston style, he knew his tongue would soon be wagging, recounting the whole thing to Lady Keith.

"We'd best be getting' into the keep," Robbie said, pulling Mechi by the hand. "We must find Father."

Mechi looked at him nervously. They had spent much of the ride home arguing about whether they should tell Lord Keith about their plan to use Mrs. McGrath. Mechi knew that Robbie would do whatever he thought was right. After all, he had never heard of "women's lib" yet. Neither, for that matter, had anyone else. Imagine the riot she could start. All she would have to do would be to enlist Queen Mary in the quest for equality. She was a woman well ahead of her time. She grinned as she tried to picture the queen's reaction. Instinct told her that the monarch would love the concept. She could put *Lord* Darnley in his place!

"You've been gone a very long while," Lady Keith said as Mechi and Robbie came into the great hall. Her eyes shot those daggers at Mechi, accusing her without words of God-knew-what.

"Gen dinna want for us to leave," Robbie said.

Lady Keith's face went white. Mechi turned around to look behind them to see if there was a ghost there. From the appearance of her hostess, she would not have been the least bit surprised to see one, if you could see a ghost.

"You—you—you went to see Genevieve?" Lady Keith asked.

"Aye," Robbie said. "She was in a jolly good mood, she was. I do believe sometimes she may be getting better."

"Do not torture me thus," Lady Keith said. "You know there is no hope of such a miracle."

Robbie placed his hand on Mechi's shoulder. "Now, Mums, ye know we've witnessed such miracles before since Mechi arrived."

"Enough!" Lady Keith shouted. She grabbed her head, suddenly overcome with a grueling headache. "She's nothing more than a witch! She should be hanged!"

"A witch?" Robbie asked, laughing that wonderfully familiar roar Mechi had come to love. "Why, a witch would work evil spells. Mechi has brought nothing but good with her." He winked at his mother as he said, "Perhaps she is an angel sent to us by God."

"An angel indeed!" Lady Keith shouted. "I will never believe such a thing is possible."

"It is easier to believe in a witch than a messenger from God?" Robbie asked his mother.

Mechi fidgeted nervously. She had been called a lot of things in her lifetime: tomboy, crazy, butt-head, horse face. But she had never been accused of being an angel. She was sure of one thing: the thoughts that went through her head as she gazed at the muscular body of Lord Robbie Keith, Viscount of Kintore, were anything but heavenly! Well, perhaps heavenly, but certainly not holy!

"What is going on here?" Lord Keith demanded, rushing in to see what was causing such a ruckus.

"Ah, Father," Robbie said. "I am glad you are here. Mechi and I must speak to you—privately."

"He took *her* to see Genevieve!" Lady Keith said. "Our shame has been found out."

"Begging your pardon," Mechi said, trying to sound overly polite and proper. "I promise you that I will never say anything to anyone about Genevieve. You secret is safe with me." She smiled at Lady Keith. "Besides, I found her quite delightful. I liked her a lot."

"And Mums, Gen seemed to enjoy Mechi as well." He hesitated, weighing his words carefully. The subject of Genevieve was very seldom discussed, even by the Keiths. "'Tis a shame, really, that she is kept to herself all the time." He watched for her reaction. "Perhaps we should bring her back here to Dunnottar."

"For all the world to see?" Lady Keith asked, horrified at such an idea. "Never!"

Mechi wondered why that would be such a terrible idea. The Keith clan surely had enough servants that they could assign one to Genevieve. The castle was so huge, it would be easy to keep a child like Genevieve hidden from the outside world. Of course they would keep Mrs. McGrath in their employ to tend her.

"No!" Mechi said. "Robbie, for the sake of—for Queen Mary we must not bring your sister here!"

She was right, of course, Robbie conceded mentally. If they took Mrs. McGrath away from Boscobel, their entire plan of thwarting the evildoers who were out to destroy Queen Mary would come to a screeching halt.

Lord Keith placed his arm around his wife, supporting her as the foursome walked to the keep. Once inside, he called Ann to tend to Lady Keith while the rest of them discussed the matter at hand.

Inside Lord Keith's private solar, which Mechi noticed was filled with more volumes than she had imagined had been written in 1561, the master of the castle hurried to secure the door with the giant lock.

"Now," he said, "what did you discover? I can see, by the look on your face, Robert, that ye bring me good news."

Mechi looked at Robbie's expression. It did not reveal any such discoveries to her, but obviously his father had learned to read him like one of the books on the shelves.

"Aye, Father," Robbie said. "We have found us a perfect specimen to take the place of the queen."

Lord Keith waited, thumping his fingers on the huge desk in front of him.

"Think of Mrs. McGrath for a moment, Father," Robbie said.

Lord Keith leaned back in this chair, trying to conjure up a picture of the woman he knew so well. She was a wee bit on the plump side, he recalled. Small of stature. Her hair was a dark brown, and she always wore it pulled back into a bun at the nape of her neck. The possibility of her having any part in this charade was beyond his imagination.

"What I wouldn't give for a Polaroid about now!" Mechi said softly, voicing her thoughts.

"A what?" Lord Keith, having heard her, asked.

"Nothing," Mechi said, waving her hand in the air to dismiss the whole thing. Still, if he could see her with her hair piled up in curls on top of her head, standing beside Robbie after she got her platforms on, she knew he, too, would be amazed at the likeness of the two women.

"I dinna see what point it is you try to make," he said to Robbie. "What can a simple serf have to do with the preservation of the Queen of Scotland?"

"Have you ever known Mrs. McGrath to be unfaithful?" Robbie asked his father.

"Nay, laddie. Ye know I'd trust her with my life. I've trusted her with my child, and there is nothing more precious to me than me kin."

Mechi had to agree with him on that point. She wondered how often Lord Keith made his way secretly and alone out to the tiny cottage in the middle of the woods of Boscobel. Surely it was more often than any of them realized. His love for his children, or *bairns*, as he called them, was evident in his eyes.

Mechi studied the patriarch of the Keith clan carefully. He was, she guessed, nearing sixty, yet he walked with the straightness of an arrow. His hair, red like Robbie's except for the few sprinkles of gray here and there, had the same unruly lock which insisted upon hanging free over his right temple. His eyes, deep hazel orbs, lacked the greenish sparkle that were so infatuating in the younger Keith, but they had the same mischievious twinkle to them. The color of Robbie's eyes, Mechi had noted, was obviously from Lady Keith's bed of genes. She envisioned Robbie at the age of his father, with her sitting at his side, and wondered if they would be in the here and now or in the forever after—or if she even dared to hope for a life, in either time zone, with the only man whom she knew she would ever love.

Her mind sprang back to the realm of reality just in time to hear Lord Keith say, "Then you must by all means go to Edinburgh and tell Queen Mary of your plan. It does not matter what you find necessary to convince her to accompany you to Boscobel, do whatever it takes. Some day, if she survives because of it, she will thank you."

Mechi felt a cold shiver run through her body, causing the hair on the back of her neck to stand on end. So Lord Keith finally did believe her. Now the only problem was, how much had Robbie told him while she was off daydreaming in her own little fantasy world? And how would she ask him without sounding like the fool she felt like?

Chapter XXIX

"I still do not understand it," Lord Keith said. "I find it very strange that you know so much about what the future holds for her majesty."

Mechi noted the formal manner in which Lord Keith referred to Queen Mary, in spite of the way she looked up to him almost as a father. *Protocol,* she thought, reminding herself that she had an awful lot to learn yet about hobnobbing among the rich and famous.

Would Robin Leach have a ball here! Even his British accent would be far more familiar than her own Texas twang. Still, it was hard to imagine what he would think if he could see how the lifestyles of the rich and famous of 1651 differed from that of the snobbish upper crust of the 1990's. Again, she wished she had a Polaroid camera. Even one roll of film would someday serve as proof of this whole crazy experience. Without it she knew no one would ever believe her. But, maybe she would never find her way back out of this and she would not have anyone to prove anything to. Maybe, if anyone found out that she and Robbie were involved in their secret plot, they would be beheaded along with the queen. Of course, she could not remember hearing that anyone else was put to death by her side. Some comfort that was! They were not important enough to go down in history on the same page as Queen Mary.

Mechi smiled slightly as she listened to Robbie try to talk his way out of the truth, as she had told it to him. *The gospel according to Saint Mechi,* he had said when she first explained the unusual circumstances that had brought her here. Then he had called her an angel to his mother. If he knew the thoughts she entertained when she watched him walk or ride or whatever else he chose to do… She had never had fantasies about a man, but then there had never been another man like Lord Robbie Keith, Viscount of Kintore.

"And they heard about this scheme of Darnley's in France?" Lord Keith asked his son.

"So it would seem," Robbie said. "How else would Mechi know about it?"

"I suppose you are right," Lord Keith conceded. "The French have always been known for their spying abilities."

"Sneaky little devils, aren't we?" Mechi asked, winking playfully at Lord Keith.

"Indeed ye are," he agreed—too quickly, Mechi thought.

"You know what to tell Mary when you get there," he said to Robbie.

"Aye, Father," Robbie said reassuringly. "We know exactly what she must do."

"Ye have my letter?" Lord Keith asked.

"Aye, Father," Robbie repeated. "Dinna fret. It will be fine." He smiled at his father. "The queen has always had a soft spot in her heart for me, ye know."

"And I've a soft spot in me head for listening to the tale you've spun for me," Lord Keith said. "But I suppose Lady Mechi is right; 'tis far better to be safe than sorry."

Mechi wondered when that phrase first came into being. In some weird way, it seemed like he had been the first person in time to use it. Oh, why did life have to be so complicated? Maybe she should have just kept rubbing the ring. Maybe then she would have found her way through the maze out of here. Maybe then she would be… No, she did not want to be away from Robbie. Not even if it never meant having a good hot bath or a real toilet again.

"We'd best be on our way," Robbie said, helping Mechi into the coach.

As she pulled her gown, complete with all its crinolines, around her, she felt like Cinderella in her pumpkin coach on the way to the ball. She wondered if she would wake up at midnight and find out that this had all been a dream. It still seemed way outside the realm of reality.

Robbie climbed into the coach and sat facing her. He reached over and took her hand in his.

No, Mechi concluded. A dream doesn't feel like this. A dream doesn't make my heart beat in double time. A dream doesn't have curly red hair and bright green eyes.

"God be with ye," Lord Keith said as the driver whisked the lash at the horses, causing them to lunge downward through the passageways and tunnels that would take them off the fiddlehead onto the mainland.

"We'll be back soon," Robbie called to his father. "With the queen."

Robbie and Mechi were deep in conversation about how to convince the queen of the impending danger. Mechi's stomach reeled as they hit bump after bump. The last time she had traveled this road it was much easier; riding one horse instead of this confounded carriage was much more to her liking.

The topic suddenly shifted to Mrs. McGrath.

"Not likely ye'd find another as willing as she to do the queen's bidding,"

Robbie said. His eyes filled with admiration for the commoner who might one day become known by the then-known world as "Her majesty." If, that is, Mechi thought, all goes well.

"What if Darnley catches on?" Mechi asked. "After all, he does know her - intimately."

"Not yet he does not," Robbie said, glee dancing in his eyes.

Mechi laughed. She wondered what Robbie would think of the scandals that filled the tabloids of the affairs of the royals in her day, from Prince Charles and Princess Diana to Andrew and Fergie. For that matter, even Princess Margaret had her hay day in the *rags* as well.

"You find it amusing?" Robbie asked. "He could put an end to the whole thing."

"I'll agree, he cannot be trusted," Mechi said. "But that's not what I was laughing at."

"You mean to tell you were laughing at *me*?" he asked, faking a childish pout.

"Never, my lord," Mechi said, trying to stand so she could make a proper curtsy. In the attempt she banged her head. She grabbed for it, letting loose of the carriage door handle just as the vehicle hit a hole and careened to the side. She swerved and swayed, then landed with a *kerplop* directly on Lord Robbie's lap.

"If you wanted a closer friendship," he teased, "why dinna ye say so?"

"I was afraid you'd refuse me," Mechi said, returning his quick-witted quips. "I'm not used to rejection."

Except for Robert Pearson, she thought. Well, that was one relationship—if you could call it that—she was glad had come to an end. If not, who knows how she could ever have made her way back here. Back to the life she admitted was far more fulfilling than her former—or was it her future—life.

"I'm sure ye're right," Robbie said. "But, not to worry. I'll be more than happy to oblige you."

Mechi squinted as she considered the word *oblige*. She did not have any right to claim Robbie's attention, but she had certainly thought she had become more than an *obligation* to him.

"You dinna like the idea?" he asked.

"I love the idea," Mechi said. "As long as you give me your attention because you *want* to, not because it is the noble thing to do."

"But, Lady Mechi," Robbie said, his voice stiff and formal, "how could I do any less?" He threw his head back and that thunderous laughter filled the tiny carriage. "After all, my lady, I *am* a noble! Surely my title warned you."

"Of course you are," Mechi said, wondering how stupid she must seem to him. "And most noble you are, and I thank you for that." *Never know when you might need an extra noble standing by*, she mused. She could remember a time or two in her past life when she would have given her right arm for a real-life noble to come to her rescue.

"What were we discussing?" Robbie asked, seeming somewhat uneasy at the way the conversation had gone. He was used to being in control, and he was rapidly losing that control. No telling where her words would steer them next, but he was not ready to reveal the thoughts of his heart. Not yet. Not until he was sure she would not disappear on him as quickly and unexpectedly as she had first come to him.

"We were discussing Darnley," Mechi said. "You are very wise not to trust him. It is a shame he could not meet with an *accident* before the queen weds him. Or, before she murders him."

"I still do not believe that Queen Mary would murder her own husband," Robbie said. "Not even if it was Darnley."

"I can't say I'd blame her," Mechi said. Her eyes lit up as she asked, "But what about Mrs. McGrath?"

"What about her?" Robbie asked, failing to see the connection.

"Would she kill Darnley?"

"In the blink of an eye," Robbie said. "She detests the rat." He turned and looked out the window, then asked, "How did he die?"

Mechi shivered at the memory of what her mother had told her about their ancestor's death. The gruesome details were molded on her mind. It was, she recalled, Darnley they were descended from, not Mary.

"Do ye feel a chill?" Robbie asked, reaching on the seat for a wool coverlet and wrapping it around her.

Mechi blushed when she realized that she had made no attempt to leave Robbie's lap, but was still nestled quite snugly against him.

"I'm sorry," she said, moving to her own seat on the opposite side of the carriage.

"Not I," said Robbie, grinning broadly at her.

Mechi shivered again, but this time it was not from darned Darnley's memory, but from the grin and those piercing eyes that were so evident as she glanced up. He could, she knew, order her to kill Darnley herself and she would have no option but to obey. When she stared into those eyes, she would do anything for anyone—in any era.

"Thank you," she said, pulling the cover tighter around her body. It was, she realized for the first time, quite cold indeed in the carriage. It was definitely the proximity of the Viscount of Kintore which had warmed the cockles of her heart.

"About Darnley?" he asked again.

"He was found in the garden at a place just outside Edinburgh, I believe, hanged," Mechi confided.

"You dinna recall the name of the place?" Robbie asked.

"I do not," Mechi said, holding her head like she was trying to force the name of the place from inside her brain.

"Was it…?" Robbie stopped, trying to think of some logical place where it might have been.

"…Stirling?" he asked.

"No," Mechi said, sure that that was not the place. She knew a great deal about Stirling Castle, and while she didn't know where it was, she knew it *wasn't* there.

"I think it was some rather small place," Mechi said.

"Did it have a funny sounding name?" Robbie asked, trying to help her force the name from her head.

"No, I don't think so," Mechi replied. "I think it—it was something about a farm or a garden."

Robbie laughed.

God, how she loved that laugh! It could drive a woman to her knees, begging to fulfill the lord and master's every whim and fancy.

"Was it perchance Kirk o' Field?" he asked.

"That's it!" Mechi shouted. "Oh, what a wonderful team we make! We are better than Sherlock Holmes and Doctor Watson!"

"Who?" Robbie asked.

"A famous detective from Scotland Yard who lived a long time ago."

Mechi began to laugh almost hysterically. She wasn't sure, but she imagined Scotland Yard did not even exist yet. And they didn't live a long time ago, but a long time in the future. And how could she explain to a true Scotsman that Scotland Yard was in London, not in Scotland at all? And how could she explain a *private eye* to someone who frowned upon spies of any type or manner?

"We are nearing the site where we must lodge for the night," Robbie said, "so there is no time now for explanations of your time. Later we shall pursue that. Now, however, we must discuss Darnley's demise while no one is near enough to hear us."

Mechi looked out the tiny window at the carriage driver. There was no doubt in her mind that their talk was far too soft for the driver to hear a word. Besides, the horses made a loud *clip-clop, clip-clop* as they made their way over the rough terrain. Then too, the driver, obviously a cheerful sort, spent most of the trip singing strange-sounding songs in Gaelic.

"He and Mary were there," Mechi explained to the best of her sketchy memory.

"As I recall, it seems to me that Mary persuaded him to spend the night there with her, then she went to a wedding."

"Alone?" Robbie asked.

"It would be far better to go alone than with Darnley!" Mechi insisted, and Robbie nodded in agreement. "Anyway, sometime during the night the house at..."

"Kirk o'Fields?" Robbie asked, offering her some help with the name.

"Yeah," Mechi said. "There was an explosion during the night. Somebody blew the whole place up."

"If they house exploded," Robbie asked, seeming confused, "why did they hang Darnley? Why not just let him explode along with the house?"

"That I can't tell you," Mechi said. "Maybe Mary didn't want to take any chances on it not working. She probably figured that the spot where he was hanged would blow up, too."

"And Mary was behind this whole thing?" Robbie asked, finding it hard to believe. This was not the Mary he knew; not the Mary who had been such a good friend of the entire Keith clan.

"Yes," Mechi said. "At least that is what they claimed. Years after she died they found some letters she was supposed to have written."

"Letters?" Robbie asked. "And she confessed to the whole thing?"

"Well, not exactly," Mechi said. "But they definitely implicated her in the death of Darnley."

"Do you think she did it?" Robbie asked Mechi, taking her by surprise. Mechi knew that in 1561, women were not supposed to have any thoughts about politics and such like. She knew that with just a little work Lord Robbie Keith, Viscount of Kintore, could fit in quite well in the 1990's. That is, of course, if he was given the chance.

"I don't know," Mechi said. "My mother always said Mary was innocent. There was a man who was Queen Mary's secretary. I can't remember his name, but he was Italian."

Robbie shook his head. He had only recently met an Italian man, David Rizzio, who was a distant cousin of Mrs. McGrath. Rumor had it that Queen Mary was quite taken with the man.

"What about David Rizzio?" Robbie asked.

"You know him?" Mechi asked in surprise.

"I have recently met him," Robbie said. "He appears quite charming."

"Apparently Mary thinks so, too," Mechi said. "I'll just bet you that he's a far better catch than Darnley."

"On that we quite agree," Robbie said. "But what does he have to do with Darnley's death?"

"It was believed that Mary and Rizzio were in it together," Mechi explained. "He was murdered, and Mary blamed Darnley for it. I suppose the old coot was jealous of his wife and her secretary spending so much time together."

"So Mary had Darnley slain?" Robbie asked.

"Hanged," Mechi corrected.

"Okay," Robbie said, smiling at her. "Hanged it is. *Done in*, as you said the other day."

"Done in," Mechi said. "Anyway, it was the end of both David Rizzio and Darnley. And, before too long it was the end of Queen Mary herself."

Robbie's face turned white. "The end of Mary?"

"Everyone out!" the carriage driver called out as he opened the door for them to exit. They were at the inn where they would spend the night. Any explanations would have to wait.

Mechi eyed the quaint, picturesque stone inn. It would be the perfect place for a honeymoon, she thought, absent-mindedly. The only question that remained for the moment was how many vacant rooms they had for the night.

"With a little bit," she began singing. "With a little bit. With a little bit of bloomin' luck." Yeah, her and the ant. "Whoops, there goes another rubber tree… Whoops, there goes another rubber tree… Whoops, there goes another rubber tree plant."

Robbie just shook his head. He knew better than to ask her to explain another one of her silly songs to him. That too, like the fate of Queen Mary, would have to wait.

Chapter XXX

As they entered the inn, Robbie banged on the table in the entry hall. Soon a short, gray-haired little woman appeared, wiping her flour-laden hands on her skirt.

"Aye?" she asked, giving them the once-over from head to toe.

Mechi wondered what she must be thinking. *Probably wants to know if we are married*, she surmised.

"We've need of two rooms for the night," Robbie said.

"I dinna ken that we've two," the woman said, the corners of her mouth turning upward. She knew the answer already. Had they been a wedded couple they would have asked for just one room. Separate, yes, she could tell, yet their looks at one another said they wished they were as one.

"We cannot have a single room," Mechi said, trying to sound as moral as she wished she was.

"'Tis quite all right," Robbie said, motioning her to be quiet. "If ye've an extra plaid I'll make meself a bed on the floor. 'Tis warmth we're after, nothing more."

"As you like it," the woman said. Mechi chuckled. She wondered if the woman had ever heard of William Shakespeare. Probably not, she decided.

"I'll show ye to your quarters," the woman said, heading for the narrow stairway.

Mechi watched her as she went, her plump rear end wobbling back and forth with each tiny step she took. If Mechi was any judge of anything, the woman would never make it up those steep steps; her legs looked only half as long as the rise in the steps. To her surprise, the woman seemed to take a jump equal to an Olympiad and conquered the steps two at a time.

Mechi turned to Robbie, who was grinning broadly at their hostess. She was just about to say something when the woman turned back towards them and asked, "I dinna catch your name, my lord."

Mechi glowed with pride. Even though she openly admitted that she didn't know Robbie, his very character and presence presented him as a man of wealth and means.

"Lord R-r-r-r-robert Keith, Viscount of Kintore," Robbie said.

Mechi cocked her head to the side, watching him closely as he said his name. She could listen to him roll his r's forever. Something about it was absolutely infatuating.

"Of the Keiths of Dunnottar?" the woman asked.

"Aye, that I be," Robbie said.

The woman dropped to her knees right there on the steps. Mechi was sure she was going to topple forward and kill herself—or at the very least break a few bones.

"Sir William Keith, who fought with Robert the Bruce," she said, her eyes looking heavenward, "saved me very great-grandmother from a terrible death at the hand of Wallace."

"How so?" Robbie asked.

"Wallace had no care for women nor for bairns, and when he came across their home he demanded she give him food and lodging."

Mechi and Robbie waited for her to continue.

"Me granny, she refused to do as he ordered. Said she was loyal only to the Bruce, she did." Her eyes glowed with pride as she spoke. "William Keith was passing by and noticed the horses outside. Fearing trouble, and knowing that it was the home of one of his most loyal soldiers—Gordon MacLaren—he charged inside, though he was alone. Seeing the fierce look in Sir Keith's eyes, Wallace's men retreated, leaving only Wallace himself to face the king."

"And Willaim Keith was too much a man for one as weak as Wallace?" Robbie asked.

"Aye, that he was," the woman replied. "Sir William Keith, God rest his soul, was too much a man for anyone. I'll ne'er forget what he done fer me granny. It was only four months later she gave birth to me grandpa, and he was properly dubbed William Keith MacLaren."

Mechi thought she saw the glimmer of a tear in the corner of Robbie's bright green eyes, but she couldn't be sure. She smiled at him, knowing that this was just one more tale that would be told from one generation to another.

Mechi's mind returned to that first night she spent at Dunnottar Castle. It seemed like a lifetime ago. She envisioned Robbie sitting beside her bed, keeping vigil until long after she had fallen asleep. She wondered if there would be any sleep for either of them tonight. "Too close, too close for comfort," she sang unconsciously, not even aware that Robbie heard her musical incantation.

As they entered the room Mechi looked around. It was quite comfortable looking, even though the furnishings were quite sparse and meager. A fire glowed brightly in the fireplace, casting a feeling of warmth over the entire room.

"'Tis a shame to waste the room in such a spacious bed," the hostess said. She took a plaid off the back of a high wooden chair and formed it into a long roll, then placed it in the middle of the bed.

"If'n ye mind the plaid," she said, "ye'll feel much more comfortable there than on the floor. I'll not have a Keith sleepin' on the floor of me inn."

Mechi breathed a sigh of relief. Hero worship at its best, she knew, but she had entertained the thought—fleetingly—that the woman might insist that Mechi take the floor instead of the honored and revered Robert Keith.

"I'll have the sup ready in about an hour," she said as she backed out of the room, bowing to Robbie. "'Twill be the finest haggis ye've ever bit into."

Mechi coughed, the taste of the last time she had been served the terrible Scottish national dish still fresh in her throat. If she never had another bite of the awful meatloaf stuffed into a sheep's stomach, it would be far too soon for her.

Alone in the room, Robbie sat on the bed and patted the spot beside him.

"It's been a long day," he said, waiting for Mechi to join him. "Come and rest awhile."

Mechi went, all-too-willingly. She could think of nothing more wonderful than being in bed with Lord Robbie Keith, Viscount of Kintore.

"If they could see me now," she sang as she laid her head on his lap.

Robbie laughed. "I do so like your songs," he said. "Will you teach me some of them?"

"Which one?" she asked.

"Which ever one you'd like," Robbie said. He looked up at her, the ever-present sparkle in his eyes. "The one about the rubber tree?"

"Once there was a little ol' ant,
Thought he could move a rubber tree plant.
Anyone knows an ant can't
Move a rubber tree plant."

Robbie watched her as she bobbed her head back and forth to the music. He could listen to her sing all day long.

"But he's got high hopes,
He's got high hopes,
He's got high apple pie in the sky hopes.
Any time you're feelin' low,
Stead of lettin' go,
Just remember that little ant and

Whoops, there goes another rubber tree...
Whoops, there goes another rubber tree...
Whoops, there goes another rubber tree plant. "

Mechi's mind went into overdrive. She could remember when this song was a symbol of years gone by. Ha! And Brian told her she was living in the past! Little did he know!

Brian! Her head reeled. What on earth did he think had happened to her? By now he had probably called out the police and the whole U.S. Navy to search for his missing little sister. How long, in *other world* time, had she been gone?

When she came back to reality, Robbie was laughing so hard he was rolling back and forth on the bed. When he could finally speak again, he said, "That is the funniest song I've ever heard. *Anyone knows an ant can't...*"

He stopped dead still. He realized that he was speaking the words to the song. His voice bellowed melodiously as he sang, "*Anyone knows an ant can't move a rubber tree plant.* "

They laughed together. It felt better than anything she could ever remember experiencing. She knew that it didn't matter any more whether she was going to live in the 1500's or the 1900's. As long as she was with Lord Robbie Keith, Viscount of Kintore, she knew she would be deliriously happy. Yes, she could even do without indoor plumbing for the sake of Robbie Keith. *Now that,* she told herself, *was the supreme sacrifice! That and eating haggis!*

Chapter XXXI

The gong sounded, a clang so loud Mechi developed an instant headache.

"Time to sup," Robbie said, heading towards the door. He turned back for a moment to look at Mechi. He had seen the sour look on her face when she had been served haggis before, and had contemplated asking her if they did not have such a delicacy in her time in America, but had decided against it. Now, he knew, the time was right. He was a favored Scot in the home of a descendant of William Keith MacLaren, and he could not risk a tarnished reputation simply because Mechi scorned the haggis.

"Ye'll eat it with relish, will ye not?" he asked, his so-familiar twinkle sparkling in his green mesmerizing eyes.

Mechi laughed. Perhaps, she thought, it might be almost palatable with a dab of green cucumber relish on top of the awful-tasting stuff.

"I'll do my best," Mechi promised. "How did you know I didn't like it?" she asked, hoping that maybe if she didn't actually give voice to the name of the Scottish delicacy it would cease to exist.

"The look on your face, lassie, was enough to tell an imbecile that you were not disposed to the likes of our wonderful haggis."

Mechi shivered at the mere mention of the word. She knew, from her Uncle David, that years later—no centuries later—the Scotsmen were still boasting of the wonders of haggis. It was, she was sure, no better in 1990 than it had been in 1561. Certain things in life, she decided, cannot be improved upon, no matter what.

"I'm sorry," she said. "I tried. I really did."

"I know ye did," Robbie said, putting his arm around her waist as they walked down the corridor to the narrow stairway. "And I thank ye for that. I'll not let on. If ye can pretend, I'll not give away your secret."

"Thank you," she said, then giggled slightly as she asked, "Can I slip it off onto your plate when no one is looking?"

"Ye'll starve to death if ye do that," he said. "For most of the serfs, when haggis is served that's all there is for the meal. That and some bread."

"I could live on the bread very nicely," she said. "Even though the Bible says 'Man shall not live by bread alone.'"

"Ye've read the Bible?" Robbie asked, surprised by such a confession.

"Of course," Mechi said. "Hasn't everybody?"

"Ye know Latin?" he asked. "Ye'll never cease to amaze me!"

"No," Mechi said. "I'm not as smart as all that. Why would you think I know Latin?" Suddenly the truth dawned on her. The well-known standard of the Bible throughout the English-speaking world was the *King James* version. And, of course, King James was the offspring of Queen Mary and Darnley! And that, obviously, had not occurred yet.

"You've told me many a tale about the Keith clan," Mechi said. "After we finish eating, I'll spin you a yarn about the son of Mary and Darnley that will curl your hair."

Robbie reached up and felt his red locks. The one stray ringlet still insisted upon seeking its freedom from the rest.

"Why, look!" he exclaimed. "I do believe it's already worked! It feels as if it is already curled!"

They entered the dining hall, laughing gaily together, just in time to hear the innkeeper scold his wife.

"Bonny McTavish! Do ye mean to be tellin' me ye've been matchmakin' again? How many times have I told ye to leave the guests alone! Keith or no Keith, his future mate is not in your hands!"

"Perhaps it would be more persuasive if it were," Robbie said as they marched to the table and sat down. "I'm not so sure I've been successful meself. But never let it be said that I dinna die trying!"

He winked at Mrs. McTavish, who winked back at him. He knew he had an ally in her. And he could use all the help he could get, if he was going to convince Mechi to stay with him in the here-and-now.

During the meal there was friendly chatter about the great and wondrous feats of the Keith clan, from the earliest member—a William, of course—up to the current William, Robbie's father. Mechi sat spell-bound, taking it all in. This was better than Superman! If she didn't watch her step, considering Robbie's admission to Mrs. McTavish, she could become the new Lois Lane.

"Ye seem like a mighty quiet one, lassie," Mr. McTavish said when there was a brief lull in the conversation. "From Bonny's words about you, I'd have thought ye'd have more to say for yerself."

"I'm not usually known for being the strong, silent type," Mechi said. "It is just that this is all so fascinating." She stopped herself just short of admitting that in *her day* such super-doers were purely fictional.

"She's right about that," Robbie said. "If she's not talking, she's singing. And she knows some of the strangest songs."

"Like what?" Mr. McTavish asked. He loved music, and could pump out a tune as fine as anyone on the bagpipes which were hanging nearby on the wall.

Much to Mechi's amazement—and amusement—Robbie broke into a full rendition of the rubber tree song. He made it all the way through, start to finish, without missing a word.

He'd make a great actor, she thought, remembering that when she first set eyes on him that is exactly what she had thought he was: a member of a Shakespearean touring group.

She looked down at her plate, realizing that she had been so taken with the tales Robbie had been relating that she had eaten the haggis and couldn't even remember taking a bite of it. She picked up the remaining piece of bread and ate it—with relish! It was very similar to the sourdough bread Hardee's boasted on their Frisco burger. Boy, what she wouldn't give for a Hardee's or a McDonald's about now!

When they were finished with the meal, Mr. McTavish invited them to join them for some games and music for the evening. It sounded delightful to Mechi, but Robbie was quick to decline.

"We've had a full day of riding today," he explained, "and more ahead of us in the morn. I do believe we should retire early."

Mrs. McTavish gave her husband an I-told-you-so look and quickly ushered them out of the room and up the stairs. As they disappeared behind the door to their quarters, Mechi heard Mrs. McTavish say "And I dare say they won't be no sleepin' on the extra plaid on the floor in that room tonight."

"Bonny McTavish, ye're a wicked woman!" her husband chided. "And I love ye very much." He planted a warm, passionate kiss on her lips. "Perhaps the dishes can wait 'til the morn?"

Mechi and Robbie were totally oblivious to the fact that their hosts had also disappeared behind closed doors. It was, indeed, a night for romance.

"That was slightly impolite," Mechi said as they sat on the edge of the bed in their quarters.

"What?" Robbie asked innocently.

"To shun the hosts when they asked us to join them," Mechi said. "It might have been fun."

"Not as much fun as we will have," Robbie said, daggers shooting from his eyes.

"And what do you propose to do to entertain us?" Mechi asked.

"'Tis you who shall entertain me," Robbie said, grinning at her.

Mechi felt the blood rush to her cheeks. What ever had given this lord and master the idea that she was interested in playing the part of the aggressor? She had so little experience in the field of sex. No, she reminded herself, that was not entirely true. She had *no* experience! Thank God, Robert Pearson had seen to that. No, her first time would be with Lord Robbie Keith, Viscount of Kintore, and she could not imagine anything more wonderful. And, if she was reading the signs right, it would be tonight.

"The tales you promised to tell me," Robbie said, causing Mechi's blush to deepen even more. "I want to hear all about Darnley and Mary and what will become of them."

Robbie hesitated briefly, then asked what he had been afraid to ever since he first met the strange, enticing Mechi.

"Then, I want you to tell me all about life in your time. You have told me a little—so little—and there must be much more to relate. We have the whole night to exchange yarns, and I am greatly looking forward to it."

Mechi turned her head away. She didn't want him to see her disappointment. Well, if things didn't go the way she wanted them to before the end of the night, what was wrong with her being the aggressive one? It might start a whole new trend! Why couldn't history be changed? Isn't that why she had been sent here in the first place?

Robbie leaned over and pulled her close to him. He laughed his delightful laugh.

"What's so funny?" Mechi asked.

"Ye forgot to thank me," Robbie said.

"Thank you? For what?" She could think of a million things he had done that deserved her thanks, and at least a million more she could anticipate if she handled things right.

"For the haggis," he said, the bed shaking from his rolling laughter. "Ye dinna notice that I ate it all?"

Mechi laughed with him. "I thought you were such a wonderful storyteller that I ate it and didn't even notice! You ate it for me?"

"Every last bite," Robbie confessed. "And I dare say I enjoyed every one."

"In that case, I do thank you," Mechi said. "I have never had a man so noble as to eat my haggis for me. How shall I ever repay you?"

"Before the night is past, I shall think of some way," Robbie said, his eyes afire.

Mechi brightened. So maybe their thoughts were on the same wave length.

She was sure he had never heard of ESP, but he made an awfully good stab at proving he had it!

Mechi slid back on the bed, hitting her bottom on the rolled up plaid Mrs. McTavish had put in the middle of it earlier. She crossed her legs Indian-style and propped her elbows on her knees.

Now it was Robbie's turn to try to figure out what was so amusing.

"Something I said?" he asked.

"No," Mechi said. "The way I am sitting. In America they call this *Indian style.*"

Robbie ran his big strong fingers through his touseled red hair. "Indian style?" he asked, repeating her.

"Yes," Mechi said.

Robbie waited for her to explain. Finally he asked, "There are people from India in America? But isn't India in the other direction? You said America is west of Scotland and I know it to be true that India is to the east. So how did the Indians get to America?"

"They were in America when the pilgrims got there." Mechi rolled her eyes up in the top of her head. This was going to be a lot harder than she had imagined. "About sixty years from now," she added.

"The pilgrims? And they were from…?"

"Great Britain," Mechi said. "Mostly England. They were not allowed to worship the way they wanted to, so they went to the Netherlands. After several years they left the Netherlands and went to America, the new land, in search of religious freedom."

"Times have not changed so much, have they?" Robbie asked. The wrinkles in his brow told Mechi that he was having a hard time digesting everything she was telling him. "Mary—Queen Mary—the only thing my father has against her is that she is in league with the Catholic church. That is part of why Queen Elizabeth wants her off the throne."

"You're right," Mechi said. "In my lifetime—the 1990's—Israel and Egypt are still fighting a religious war."

"Okay," Robbie said. "What about these Indians?"

"There were people living in the new country —they called it New England— when the pilgrims landed at Plymouth Rock."

"And they were from India?" Robbie asked.

"No, but…" Mechi groaned, waited, then continued. "…Christopher Columbus was the man who first discovered America. He convinced Queen Isabella of Spain that the world was round, not flat, and she financed his trip to try to reach India from Spain by sailing west. He probably could have done it, except he ran into a gigantic land mass, which we now know as America. He really thought he had landed in India, so he called the people Indians."

"The whole world must have thought he was crazy!" Robbie said. "And just when did this occur?"

"In 1492," Mechi answered. "At least that is one thing that has actually happened already. A group of people went with Sir Walter Raleigh, from England, in..." She tried to remember when it was. "I don't know exactly when it was, but it must be about now. Queen Elizabeth sent him. They named the place he landed after her."

"Elizabethtown?" Robbie asked.

"Not exactly," Mechi explained. "They called it *Virginia*. Queen Elizabeth died an old maid. She was called *the Virgin Queen*."

Again Robbie laughed. "So the cousin queens both ended up—how did you say it before—*real losers*? Elizabeth got nothing and Mary got Darnley? I don't know which one got the worst."

Mechi suddenly sat up as straight as an arrow. "Hey, there's something wrong!" she said, nearly shouting.

"What?"

"If Queen Mary and Darnley got married," Mechi said, trying to get a complete picture of the situation, "and they only had one son, King James, and I am descended from Darnley...but not from Mary..."

"Then Darnley had a bastard!" Robbie said. "He had a whore of his own."

"And if he had not," Mechi reminded him, "I would not be here today."

"God bless Darnley's whore!" Robbie said, grabbing Mechi and kissing her hard and passionately. "I love her."

Mechi was almost breathless. She had never had a kiss like that! Wow! He almost knocked the wind right out of her.

"Now that we have that figured out," Robbie said, "I suppose we should warn Queen Mary when we get to Edinburgh that Darnley is unfaithful."

"Not so fast," Mechi warned. "First of all, I'm not sure we can persuade her that she will one day marry Darnley. I doubt she would give a damn if he had a child with a hundred other women. It seems to me that the only reason she ever did consent to marry him was to get Queen Elizabeth off her back. Now, if I remember my history right, Mary had a few things of her own going on."

"Such as?" Robbie asked.

"David Rizzio," Mechi reminded Robbie. "She was quite smitten with him."

"Well, and with good reason," Robbie said, enjoying every minute of this like a woman who was starving for the latest gossip. "If her husband was unfaithful to her, why should she be forced to remain true to him?"

"What a modern attitude!" Mechi said, absolutely stunned that a man of this age would have such an open mind.

"Ah, yes, and I suppose I should be flogged for thinking such a thing?"

"I'll be glad to provide the spanking," Mechi said, teasing him. To her surprise, he lay down on the bed on his stomach. "I'm ready when you are," he said, daring her.

Mechi raised her hand and gave him a tiny swat on his well-rounded, firm derriere. She felt like the heat from his body was going to burn her hand. She pulled it away like she had just hit a branding iron on their ranch back in Paris, Texas.

She knew that tonight was going to be a night to remember. But she wouldn't trade it for anything in the world—hers or Robbie's.

Chapter XXXII

"Tell me about your life—before," Robbie pleaded. The little hints of things she had already told him had only served to make his curiosity grow.

"I hardly know where to begin," Mechi said, shaking her head at the gigantic task that could entail.

"You don't have to begin," Robbie said, smiling at her. "You have already done that. You've shown me the giant bird that carries hundreds of people, and little boxes that stick in a hole in the wall and cook things with no fire…"

Mechi laughed. "We have little boxes with people in them, too."

Robbie laughed with her. "And they stick that in a little hole in the wall, too?"

"Actually," Mechi said, "they do." She tried to imagine the look on Robbie's face if he saw *anything* plugged into an electric outlet and the results of the current which flowed through each appliance. As she looked at him, she felt a similar shock run through her own body, like she had just stuck a knife blade into the toaster. It was a feeling she knew all too well; she had done that several times.

"You'd think I'd learn," she said absent-mindedly.

"Learn what?" Robbie asked, puzzled.

"Not to stick my fingers where they don't belong."

Robbie took hold of one of Mechi's small delicate hands in his big, brawny ones. He ran his fingers sensually up and down her fingers, one at a time.

"I can not imagine any place where these fingers should not be," he said, lifting them to his chest, which was heaving in and out as much as Mechi's.

Mechi gasped, not from the shock but from the sheer pleasure touching him in such a way brought her. Instinctively, she pulled her hand away, then returned it, gently inserting it into the opening in his white linen shirt. She had never had these feelings before. The coarse hair on his chest, as red as the locks on his head, curled around her fingers.

Robbie put his fingers in her short cropped hair and began to tease it. She shivered at the feel of him touching her—anyplace.

"Ye dinna mind?" he asked, afraid of frightening her.

"Mind?" Mechi asked. "Nay, my lord. I dinna mind a mite."

Robbie smiled at her use of the Scottish words and phrases. "I'll make a Scot out a ye yet," he boasted.

"You forget, my mother is Scotch. She's descended from…"

"I'll forgive ye for that," Robbie said. "And anything else your ancestors might have done without your knowin' it."

"Thank you," Mechi said, her voice coming in short gasps as Robbie's hand moved down to her bosom and began to fondle her breast.

"Anytime," Robbie said. "I aim to please."

Mechi laughed. He sounded as strange using some of her modern-day expressions as she did using his old-time ones.

"And your aim is nearly perfect, my lord," she said.

"Stop it!" Robbie said suddenly, causing Mechi to pull her hand away from him like it had been stomped on.

"I'm sorry," Mechi said, her eyes focusing on the floor. "I thought…"

"No," Robbie said, putting her hand back inside his shirt. "Not that."

"Then what…?" Mechi asked.

"Calling me *lord*," he said. "If you don't, before I know it you will be off the bed and curtsying before me."

"Yes, my lord," she said, grinning at him. "And if I leave the bed?"

"Then I shall have to return you to it." He pulled her down onto the bed, pushing the plaid roll off to the side with his foot. Before she knew what hit her, she was on her back and he was propped over her, his elbows keeping his weight off her, but feeling like she was being crushed by the mere thought of their togetherness.

"I will be gentle," Robbie said. He knew, somehow, that she was a fair maiden who had never lain with a man before. "I shall teach you things you never thought possible," he said, "not even in your day."

Mechi was sure he was capable of doing exactly that.

"No brag, just fact," she said in her best western twang.

"You got that right," Robbie said, grinning at her like a cat who was ready to pounce on a poor innocent Tweety bird.

"Your student awaits, teach," she said, returning his grin. And she was truly ready for any lessons he might have in mind.

Robbie began to caress her from head to toe, making each inch of her skin feel like it was coming alive like the first jonquils of springtime. Mechi groaned, but it was from sheer pleasure.

"Like it?" he asked.

"Um-hm," Mechi mumbled.

He kissed her, softly at first, then passionately, like the heat from the nearby fire, then gently forced his tongue inside, moving it from side to side sending sensations down to the innermost depths of Mechi's being. A Frenchman could not do a better job, she mused.

His hand unfastened the buttons on her blouse and he pulled it off her shoulders, kissing her neck, then her chest. His own breath, Mechi noticed, was becoming as heated as hers. She wasn't sure exactly when it happened, but she realized that he had also removed her camisole so her breasts, which were standing at attention like a soldier on parade, were staring him in the face.

"Beautiful," he said, tracing her protruding nipples with his fingers. "You are so beautiful."

Mechi snickered. In all the time she had known Robert Pearson, he had never once said she was *good-looking*, let alone *beautiful*. She had never thought of herself as anything but *plain*, but somehow when Lord Robbie Keith, Viscount of Kintore, said it she believed it.

"Thank you," Mechi said softly. Then, totally without warning, a tear rolled out of her eye, down her cheek and onto the bed.

"Don't be afraid, little one," Robbie said. "I will not hurt you."

"I am not afraid," Mechi said. "It is just…what if something happens and I have to return…"

"Shh!" Robbie said, placing his finger over her lips. "Do not think of that now. We have this night, and we have each other. If that is all we ever have, at least we do have it—forever."

Mechi knew he was right. If they never had a chance to love each other again, then this had to be the most perfect night of lovemaking that ever was. After all, it might have to last her for—*four hundred and fifty years?* Well, Robbie, my love, it better be good. And she knew it would be.

Mechi lay all snuggled up in Robbie's arms, the fire dancing in the fireplace and in his eyes.

"Happy?" he asked, rubbing her back tenderly.

"Happier than a clam!" she said, sending him into laughter again.

"A clam is happy?" he asked. "How can you tell?"

"I really don't know," Mechi said. "But somehow by the twentieth century somebody had figured out that it was."

"I'm glad," Robbie joked. "I'd hate to think that all the clams in the world just went running around for centuries being sad."

"You are the most sensitive man I've ever known," Mechi said. "You would make the E-R-A movement proud."

"E-R-A?" Robbie asked.

And Mechi spent the next several minutes explaining that women should be treated as equal to men.

"I don't agree with that," Robbie said.

Mechi groaned. She knew it was too good to be true.

"You don't?" she asked, afraid of the answer.

"Absolutely not," Robbie said. "I think women are far more wonderful than men. So, they should be treated better."

"I like your thinking," Mechi said. "You can spoil me anytime."

"Tell me more about your world," Robbie asked again.

And well into the wee hours of the morning, Mechi talked of things like coaches that run without any horses and steel boxes that make your bread brown and big shiny things that clean the floors—and even commodes that have water in them and wash the sewer away into big tubes under the ground.

"And McDonald's," Mechi said, yawning.

"You have McDonald's in America?" Robbie asked.

"Oh, yes, we have a McDonald's in almost every town in the country," she said. "Only they don't wear a Scotch plaid."

"What do they wear?" Robbie inquired.

Mechi laughed, yawned again, laughed some more and pictured Ronald McDonald sitting in front of the golden arches.

"They wear bright yellow suits, red and white striped socks and great big red shoes," she said, trying to paint a word picture for him. "And they all have bright red hair like yours!"

"I think I like what the McDonald's have become," he said. "Although Father would die to hear me say that. The Keiths and the McDonalds are not exactly friendly clans. In fact, they've had wars with each other."

"Then, my dear Robbie, if I return to my world—and if there is any way possible for you to accompany me—you must not tell them when we go to McDonald's that you are a Keith!"

"And why would we go to McDonald's?" he asked. "They are friends of yours?"

"They are friends of everyone," Mechi said. "They serve the most wonderful food!" And she was asleep in his arms, drooling and dreaming about a Big Mac, an order of French fries and a giant shake.

Chapter XXXIII

Mr. and Mrs. MacTavish stood in the doorway of the inn as Robbie and Mechi's carriage disappeared into the distance.

"They're a fine pair," Mr. MacTavish said, patting his wife affectionately on her plump bottom.

"Aye, that they are," Mrs. MacTavish agreed. "And I'd be willin' to lay odds on where they spent the night."

"I don't know why you can't leave people alone," Mr. MacTavish chided her. "You'd ought to have learned your lesson after the mess you made the last time you tried your matchmaking."

"Ah, but this was different," she said, waving her hand in the air as if to fan the sparks of love into a full-fledge flame.

"And how can you be so sure?" Mr. MacTavish asked.

"'Twas a perfect night for makin' love last night," she said, her eyes glistening with mischief. "You should know that."

"Aye, for us it was," he said. "But for them, who knows?"

"Ach, mon!" she said, her voice filled with exasperation. "Can you be so dumb?"

"And, I repeat, how can you be so sure?"

"Could ye not see it in their eyes?" she asked. "It was as plain as the sun up in the sky."

The carriage ride seemed terribly short, Mechi lamented, as the Holy Mile in Edinburgh came into view. She knew she had been rambling, but Robbie seemed genuinely interested and fascinated by all the modern inventions. They had run the gambit from televisions to buses to trains to birth control.

"Modern day medicine is an absolute wonder," Mechi explained as they rolled towards Holyrood, where Mary was undoubtedly residing. "I just wish there was some way Genevieve could have the benefit of the medications they have for epilepsy."

"This epilepsy," Robbie asked, "are you absolutely certain that is what Gen has?"

"After watching her," Mechi answered, "I am sure. There are pills that can control it. People drive cars and have regular jobs who have had epilepsy for years."

Robbie laughed. That wonderful, uproarious laughter that made everything in the world seem all right. Mechi could cope with anything—here or beyond—as long as she had Robbie at her side.

"Do you suppose I could ever learn to manipulate one of your *cars*?" he asked.

Mechi envisioned the big strong hunk, clad in his clan plaid, which was merely a piece of material draped about his wonderful body and which could reveal a man's claim to fame with an unforeseen gale of wind. In her mind's eye he was sitting behind the wheel of her old faithful pink Cadillac, the music of the "oldies but goodies" station blaring into the open air, and his deep resonant voice shouting to the world "*Whoops, there goes another rubber tree plant.*"

"Yes, you could," she assured him. She wondered if this meant that if at some later time in this adventure she had to return to the twentieth century that he was really disposed to go with her. The thought made her body burn. She could hardly wait to introduce Lord Robbie Keith, Viscount of Kintore, to Brian.

"Poor, poor Brian," Mechi said, shaking her head at the agony she must be causing him.

"Something is wrong with your brother?" Robbie asked.

"I would imagine it is," she said. "By now he has probably called out the entire U.S. Navy to look for me."

"Your brother could do that?" Robbie asked, obviously impressed. "He must be a very powerful man. With your father…" He hesitated. He had always hated that word. It was so final. So eternal. "…dead," he said, shuddering at the very sound of the word, "he is the chieftain of your clan, aye?"

"I suppose," Mechi said, "although in our time we do not have clans."

"The clans have seen their end?" Robbie asked, his face pale at the very idea of its demise. "Then how does the family run itself?"

"Very well," Mechi said as the carriage came to a sudden, jarring halt in front of Holyrood Palace, sending Mechi sliding across from her side directly into Robbie's welcoming arms.

Robbie laughed, his hair blowing in the wind as the driver opened the door for them.

"I've half a notion to tell him to do it again," Robbie said. "The rewards of such a sudden stop are well worth the few moments of discomfort it causes."

Mechi laughed. "When I was little," she said, recounting an early incident from her own life, "a little bird flew overhead one day. Brian looked up at the sky, and just as his head was at the most opportune angle, the bird let loose with a dropping. Right in Brian's eye!"

Robbie laughed with her at the image it conjured up.

"And it angered Brian?" Robbie asked.

"No," Mechi said. "Actually, just the opposite. He motioned to the bird, who was continuing on his aerial journey, to return. When the bird ignored him, he called out to the creature, 'Do it again, boid! Do it again!'"

Robbie stuck his head out the window and looked up at the sky.

"Just checking," he said, grabbing her hand to help her out. "The sky is clear."

"You sound like a commander from NASA," Mechi said, grinning.

"NASA?" Robbie asked, feeling like she was speaking a foreign language.

"It's a space agency," Mechi said. "They have sent men to the moon."

She grabbed her head. She was developing a terrible headache. How could she ever completely prepare him for life in her world? Just in case...

"And I thought Genevieve was a lunatic!" Robbie said, clucking his tongue in disbelief. "I wonder, my dear Mechi, if you honestly believe that, or if you are at least a little bit mad."

"Maybe I am," Mechi conceded as they began walking to the Palace. "If I ever get back where I..." She paused. She was going to say *where she belonged*, but she was not sure where that was anymore. "...came from," she continued, "I'm sure they would lock me up in the loony bin if I told them where I had been."

"The *loony bin?*" Robbie asked, delighted by the sound of another of Mechi's strange words.

"Yes," Mechi said, "the loony bin. The rubber room. The insane asylum. The nut house. Oh, Robbie, we have come so far! We have a million ways to describe someone as crazy as me!"

"And none of them do you honor," he said, taking her elbow to steady her as they climbed the rocky trail up to the palace.

"Robbie! Mechi!" Their names echoed through the mist as they approached the palace. There was no mistaking the voice. Mechi smiled as she realized that the queen of Scotland had come running out to greet them. She had never imagined herself *hobnobbing* with royalty, but she had to admit it beat living in a tiny cottage in Boscobel like Mrs. McGrath did. She was not above taking advantage of all the perks she could muster. She had done a fairly decent job of bargaining on her own behalf in Aberdeen. Maryland, that is. At St. Andrew's Golf Course. In 1997.

For the first time in a long while Mechi's head began to spin. She felt like she was going to faint—again. She hated wimps! No, she would be strong. She had to pull herself together. She was about to sit and gossip with the Queen of Scotland. This was no time to lose it.

"Have you been to St. Andrews of late?" Mary was asking her.

"I have not had a chance," Mechi said, suddenly realizing how much she missed her daily golf games. "But that's par for the course."

"That's a good one!" Queen Mary said, amused by the expression. "Par for the course. Mechi, my friend, my whole life has been *par for the course*."

"You ain't seen nothin' yet, kid," Mechi said, looking at Robbie. When they finished telling her what was to become of her, she would know she was well under par. It would be a real bogey! Mechi saw the queen's entire life disappear into a sand trap. But, like the queen said, that was par for the course!

Chapter XXXIV

Mary sat beside Mechi as they rode back towards Dunnottar. She seemed dazed, in a state of shock, at the news Mechi had given her. Robbie had finally convinced the queen that Mechi, in some unexplainable way, could see into the future. With that knowledge firmly planted in her head, she reluctantly agreed to accompany them to Dunnottar, where she would meet Mrs. McGrath.

"You do understand," Robbie said to Queen Mary, "that you will have to fill in every detail of your life to Mrs. McGrath if this is to succeed."

"Aye," Queen Mary said. "But I still cannot believe it. *Marry Darnley*? How absurd! I abhor the very sight of the man. And to listen to him drone on and on about how wonderful he is…"

She began beating her clenched fists on her lap, causing her crinolines to spring up and down with each motion. Mechi smiled, knowing that she, too, would probably opt for suicide rather than spend even one day alone in the company of the dreadful Darnley.

"Just remember," Mechi said, trying to assure her, "if our plan works it will be Mrs. McGrath who weds the darned Darnley, rather than you. She has agreed to save you from a most dreadful fate."

Even if she were not going to lose her head at the hands of your cousin, Elizabeth, Mechi thought. They had, so far, avoided dropping this bombshell on either of the two women involved in their scheme. She wondered just how far Mrs. McGrath would be willing to go for her monarch. Pretending to be another person was one thing; marrying a scoundrel like Darnley was bad enough; but it was quite another matter to lay your head on the chopping block for the sake of your country or its leader.

"If you are both sure it will work," Mary said slowly. "I'm not at all sure, myself."

"It will work," Mechi said, taking Mary's hand in her own. "You know Robbie would never do anything to endanger your life. He is a Keith, you know."

"Aye, thank God!" Mary said, sighing deeply. If she had to go through with this crazy idea, at least she felt some better knowing that at least one Keith was behind her. Yes, with a Keith at her side she would manage—somehow

When they arrived at Dunnottar Castle, Robbie handed a plaid to Queen Mary and instructed her to place it over her head, keeping out of view as much as possible.

Mary did exactly as she was told, aware of the fact that if anyone knew of her whereabouts the whole plan could fail in a moment.

The men at the gates motioned Robbie inside immediately. They did not question the identity of the extra person, as the Keiths were quite often known for trying to rescue a down-and-outer. They assumed this was nothing more than Lord Robert's latest rescue mission underway.

Safely inside, Robbie hurried Queen Mary into his father's solar, then went in search of Lord Keith. They definitely needed his help and support.

Mere moments had passed when the two handsome Keith men walked through the door to begin the next phase of the experiment.

"Are ye quite prepared to do this?" Lord Keith asked Mary. "'Twill be quite a sacrifice, ye know."

"Aye," Queen Mary acknowledged. "But what choice do I have? If what Mechi says is true, I must protect myself—and my beloved Scotland—in any way I can."

"And we'er all mighty proud o' you," Lord Keith said, going over and embracing Mary fondly. "Ye know, I'd not love ye any more were ye my own kin."

"I'd be proud to be a Keith," Mary said, smiling warmly at her guardian.

"And the whole durned clan would be proud to have ye," Lord Keith returned.

Mary's countenance turned somber.

"Are ye quite sure the lassie knows of where she speaks?" Mary asked Lord Keith. Her decision, she knew, to go forward with this plan or to desert it now depended on her protector's answer.

"I'd trust her with me own life," Lord Keith said. He laughed, much the same laugh Mechi had heard escape from Robbie's lips time after time. "The horses like her."

"Then she's to be trusted—with my life and the fate of the whole of Scotland," Mary said. She looked Mechi squarely in the eye as she said, "And if'n ye betray me, may my ghost and my spirit haunt ye for the rest o' your days, however long that might be."

Robbie looked at Mechi, winking. "That's a mighty long time," he teased.

"You said it!" Mechi responded. "Talk about a life sentence!"

"Ye'd best get a good night's sleep," Lord Keith said. "In the morn Robert will take you to the woods of Boscobel. Mrs. McGrath is expectin' you."

Mechi noticed the worried look on Lord Keith's face. She wished she could assure him that this whole thing was going to end up all right, but she honestly didn't know. Even if it did, would she be around to see it? Or, when her work was done and Queen Mary was indeed safe, would she be thrust back into the twentieth century?

Mechi thought of the ring they had left with Mrs. McGrath. Maybe Robbie was right. Maybe they should have left it out in the woods for the birds to find. What difference would it make if a sparrow from 1561 suddenly made its way to 1997? Who would be the wiser? Oh, the bird might have a bad case of *jet lag*, but it would certainly be able to adjust.

"Ye'll sleep in the same quarters with Mechi for the night," Lord Keith said. "I'll have some of my men posted by the cottage by sunup tomorrow."

"But how will you explain what is happening to them?" Robbie asked. "Surely they will suspect something is amiss."

"I've tended to that," Lord Keith said. "I've already told them of a woman in the forest who has cared for many of the Keiths over the years. They think she is being threatened because of her cousin."

"Her cousin?" Mary asked.

"Aye," Lord Keith replied. "He has, in fact, just arrived from the continent. Italy, to be precise. He is to stay with her for a time. He is the one person—the only one outside those involved directly—who knows of the plan. Mrs. McGrath assures me that he can be trusted implicitly."

"And this cousin," Mary asked, "his name is…?"

"Rizzio," Lord Keith answered. "David Rizzio."

Mechi's head went into a tailspin. If she wasn't mistaken, that was the name of Queen Mary's secretary. It was because of a suspicion Darnley had of an affair between Mary and David Rizzio that he became insanely jealous. It was because of David Rizzio that Mary and Darnley were eventually separated—until that fateful night which would change history forever. It was, Mechi was quite sure, David Rizzio who was murdered, and Mary was convinced that it was Darnley who was responsible for the murder. It was, Mechi suddenly realized, David Rizzio whom Mary really loved. Yes, it was for the murder of David Rizzio that Mary had Darnley hanged outside the house at Kirk-O'-Field.

Mechi felt herself go numb. All these years she had believed her mother and her Uncle David when they told her that Mary was not really guilty of killing Darnley. The "Casket Letters," they were convinced, were phonies. Frauds. Fakes.

Now, Mechi realized that Mary had indeed killed Darnley. Not that she blamed her, but history was right. Mary was a murderer. According to the laws of the time, she deserved to die.

Mechi wondered if she should confide in Robbie that she knew the truth. The whole truth and nothing but the truth, so help her God! Could she spare Darnley's life? *Should* she spare Darnley's life? Or, was history better off left alone. Maybe this whole trip back in time was one gigantic mistake. Maybe she should find the ring as soon as they got to the cottage in the morning and get the hell out of Dodge! But, her heart strings, which were firmly tied to one Lord Robbie Keith, Viscount of Kintore, tugged at her beyond anything she had ever known. If she had to leave him, she might just as well be hanged with Darnley or have her head chopped off with Mary.

"Mechi?" Lord Keith asked. "Are you all right? You look like you have just seen a ghost."

"Well," Mechi said, making a feeble attempt at a laugh, "didn't Queen Mary just tell us that we would be haunted by her ghost forever?"

"I dinna mean it," Mary said, taking Mechi's hand. "I swear I dinna mean it for you."

"Good!" Mechi said, wiping the sweat that had formed on her forehead. "I was getting worried."

Mechi wanted to break into song again. "*Casper, the friendly ghost, the friendliest ghost in town…*" but thought better of it. She didn't feel like any lengthy explanations to Robbie—or anyone else. Not tonight.

Tomorrow, she knew, would be another day. What it would bring was anybody's guess. When should they tell Mary and Mrs. McGrath the rest of the story? If only she could turn on her car radio and let Paul Harvey announce, "And now you know…the *rest of the story*." How much simpler life was in the twentieth century than it was in the here-and-now.

Mechi sighed. If she had only known what one simple little early morning golf lesson would lead to… She wondered, *would she have changed anything if she had known?*

She looked at Robbie. No, if she had it to do all over again she would do the exact same thing. No matter what happened, no matter where she lived the rest of her life, she knew the one night they had spent together in each other's arms was worth any price she might pay. She would do it all over again, even if just for one solitary night making mad, passionate love with Lord Robbie Keith, Viscount of Kintore.

"Wake up!" she told herself.

"Tired?" Robbie asked. "Perhaps you should retire early tonight."

Alone, Mechi thought. If only the queen had her own quarters!

Mechi laughed. Imagine wishing you didn't have to sleep with a real live honest-to-goodness queen! Why, most people would die for the chance. She hoped that wasn't what was in store for her!

Chapter XXXV

Mechi tossed and turned fitfully all night long. She felt like the weight of the entire world was bearing down on her shoulders. Truth is, she admitted, it was. Well, maybe not the whole world, but at least the whole country.

As if he could hear her thoughts all the way down the narrow corridor, Robbie quietly tiptoed to her room and knocked softly on her door.

Mechi, knowing instinctively who it was, hurried to open the door. There, dressed in his deep indigo robe, stood Robbie, more handsome than ever, Mechi thought.

"Would you like to join me in my solar for a cup of tea?" he asked, his eyes twinkling. "I promise I'll not leave my sash behind."

Mechi felt herself blush. It had been a long time since she had first arrived at Dunnottar Castle and had tucked Robbie's sash into her corset.

So much water under the bridge, she thought, then glanced out the window at the crystal blue water which sparkled in the moonlight. Appropriate metaphor, she decided.

"I would be honored, my lord," she said softly so as to not disturb or awaken Queen Mary.

She slipped out of the room and down the hallway with him, carefully feeling her way as she went. The candle Robbie had in his hand did little to illuminate the way.

Inside Robbie's chambers, Mechi looked around. It was a definite masculine-influenced room. On the wall above the bed was a huge bow and arrow, which Mechi knew was not there for decorative purposes. She wondered if he had ever used it on anyone. God help the woman who tried to entice Lord Robbie Keith against his will!

"'Tis for hunting," he said, reading her thoughts again. "Does it frighten you?"

"No," Mechi said. "Well, not too much." After a brief pause she added, "As long as I'm not the hunted one."

"I've already captured you as my prey," he said, pulling her to his hard, warm body. "Least I think I have."

"Oh, yes," Mechi said. "I'll be your captive for life."

She laughed. Suppose her women's lib friends heard her now. They would kick her right out of the association. Not that she was a card-carrying member, but she had supported several of their rallies in the past. Or in the future. Or whenever!

"That's what I like," Robbie said. "A good submissive lady."

Mechi had a hard time not giggling. One of the few secrets she had learned about men in her brief experiences with them was that you could get them to do anything you wanted, as long as they thought it was their idea. Robbie Keith was no different. He was exactly where she wanted him. At least for the moment.

"Are we doing the right thing?" she asked softly.

"Absolutely," Robbie answered, kissing her passionately, lighting the fire of desire in her entire body.

"No," Mechi said, pulling away from him. "I don't mean that. I mean Queen Mary. And poor Mrs. McGrath! What if she actually dies in Mary's place! How can we ever live with ourselves, knowing that we caused her death?"

"'Tis her choice," Robbie said. "You do not understand the depth of devotion we Scots have to our kings and queens, me thinks. When Robert the Bruce was reigning, people begged to die for his cause. 'Tis what we call a war. Do you mean to tell me that in America in your day you do not have wars?"

Mechi shook her head. Oh, that it was so. She had always detested war. She had been so afraid when Brian was in the middle of Desert Storm that he would never come back. Was time really so different then than it was now? The more things change, she thought, the more they stay the same.

"Yes, we have wars," Mechi said. "I hate wars. People die in wars. Innocent people. Men, women and children who just happen to be in the wrong place at the wrong time."

"People like Mrs. McGrath?" Robbie asked.

"People like Mrs. McGrath," Mechi said, realizing just how much they were asking from the poor woman. Was it too late to back out? What would it take to call off the whole thing?

"She can fend for herself," Robbie said. "You, on the other hand, might need a little help."

Before Mechi knew what had happened she was secure within his arms, their flesh melting together as they became one. Rivers of deep passion and desire flowed over her. She had no idea how long it was before she exploded and felt Robbie's release fill every part of her being.

Mechi slept soundly when she returned to her own room.

The morning, with the first light of dawn, came all too soon. She turned over, wishing she could sleep for at least another hour, but she knew there was a busy day waiting for her.

Ann was busily scurrying about, arranging the clothes for the day for both Mechi and their honored guest.

"Good morning, Ann," Mechi said, stretching her hands high above her head. She always loved the feeling of freedom she got from a first-thing-in-the-morning stretch. It was better than aerobics, she thought.

Mechi looked at Queen Mary, who was already sitting up on the side of her bed. She tried to picture the queen doing jumping jacks and running in place with Richard Simmons.

Mechi laughed. Actually, she could imagine the queen and Richard Simmons hitting it off quite well. They were, in some crazy way, a lot alike. Spontaneous. Fun-loving. Sensitive. Yes, she would make quite a guest on his infomercial.

"Are you ready to go down to breakfast?" Mechi asked Mary.

"Nay, my lady," Ann said. "I'm afraid her majesty will have to break the fast here in her quarters. I had strict orders from Lord Keith that *no one* is to know she is here. Not even Lady Keith."

Mechi's breath caught in her throat. Was it possible that Lord Keith had not told his wife anything at all of their plan? Did he trust his wife that little?

Mary motioned for Mechi to come over to her. Mechi went, anxious to please the queen. Yes, Robbie was right. She did instill a sense of deep and true devotion from everyone around her.

"'Tis all part of the plot," Mary told her, as if she had dreamed up the whole scheme by herself. "I thought that if Mums Keith did not know of it, it would be the perfect way to test it after we…"

Mechi waited for her to continue. When she did not, Mechi offered, "switch places?"

"Yes," Mary said. "There are very few people who know me the way she does. If Mrs. McGrath can convince her that she is me, we will know that we have succeeded."

"Brilliant," Mechi admitted. "I just hope it works."

"It has to work," Mary said, a deep authority in her tone of voice. "For my sake, and the sake of Scotland, it must work."

In little more than an hour Mechi, Robbie and Queen Mary were on their way to the cottage deep in the forest of Boscobel. No one would ever have recognized the queen as their devoted leader. She was in a plain tan high-necked flax dress, her hair pulled back tightly behind her neck in a bun, and a scarf tightly fastened around her head. She looked like any peasant who might be wandering the land early in the morning in search of berries and ferns.

Mechi was surprised, and somehow pleased, that the queen was such an expert horsewoman. She rode like it was her favorite sport. Perhaps, Mechi thought, it was. That and golf.

"Maybe we can go out into the clearing one day and put in a few rounds of golf," she said to Mary. "You will have to teach Mrs. McGrath how to play. I would love to help you. It is what I do…"

Robbie's sharp eyes caught her attention. She dare not tell the queen that teaching golf is what she did for a living. She was going to have to be more careful. They had enough to worry about without her having to explain her whole life to the queen of Scotland. It was far too complicated.

"You are quite right," Mary said. "It has been far too long since I've enjoyed a round or two." She watched Robbie for his reaction as she said, "I thought of asking to stop at St. Andrews as we passed."

"'Tis a good thing you did not," Robbie said, laughing. "I'd have been between a rock and a hard place to know what to do. As your subject, I am bound to fulfill your every wish; as your protector, I am sworn to protect you." He looked directly at Mechi. "You with your wonderful logic, what is one to do when faced with such a dilemma?"

Mechi scratched her head. She was still trying to figure out who first said "between a rock and a hard place." She always thought it was probably one of the quotes from Ben Franklin's *Poor Richard's Almanac*. She wondered if he had ever been sued for plagiarism; maybe all of his famous quotes were nothing more than things he heard his grandmother say.

"I suppose one could always order everybody off the golf course so the queen could have it to herself. That way you would fulfill her wishes to golf, yet keep her away from anyone who might cause her harm."

"And who would she play with?" Robbie asked. "'Tis not very entertaining to play by oneself."

"It's far better than playing dead," she said. She burst into uproarious laughter. She thought of the dog she had when she was a little girl. It was not much of a dog, pedigree wise. "Purebred mutt!" her dad used to say, rubbing him behind the ears just the way he liked. She had tried to teach him to do some tricks, and he always did the exact opposite of what Mechi ordered him. When she told him "Play dead" he would roll over. When she told him to "Heel" he would sit as still as a log.

"I wish I could figure you out," Robbie said. "You laugh at the craziest things."

Mechi wiped her hand across her mouth in an attempt to remove the smile. With her best deadpan expression she said, "Better?"

Robbie laughed.

"I didn't know it bothered you," Mechi said. "I'll try to refrain from laughing in the future."

"Oh, no you won't!" Robbie said, running over to her and tickling her furiously.

Mechi wiggled and giggled. She had always been extremely ticklish. She had never told him that little secret, but then the subject had never come up. Before. Now, she was being tickled half to death by the man of her dreams—literally—right in front of the queen of Scotland.

She had been right when she told him that maybe she belonged locked up in the loony bin. She had to be crazy! If she tried to tell anybody this whole episode, they would certainly agree with her.

That settled it. No matter what happened, when—no, if—she ever got back to the future the first thing she would do would be to book an appointment with a resident shrink. She definitely needed it. For that matter, if Robbie could go back with her, he would no doubt benefit from a few sessions too, just to learn how to cope with *life in the fast lane.*

As they entered the cottage, Mechi saw right away that Genevieve was there alone.

"Where is Mrs. McGrath?" she asked, afraid of the answer she might receive.

"I don't know," Genevieve answered. "She left a long time ago. She said she was going out to gather some firewood, but she hasn't come back."

Mechi's eyes filled with fear. She looked at Robbie. They were both thinking the same thing. Together, in unison, they said… "The ring…

Chapter XXXVI

Robbie and Mechi ran out towards the woods.

"Stay with Genevieve," Robbie called back to Queen Mary. "We'll be back as soon as we find her."

"Mrs. McGrath!" Robbie bellowed in his loudest tones. "Mrs. McGrath! Can you hear us? Mrs. McGrath!"

Neither Mechi nor Robbie dared to put their fear into words. What if they didn't find her? What if she had been transported back—or ahead—to Mechi's time? It would have been better, Mechi thought, to have warned her of what the ring could do. She might not have believed it, but at least it would have done a little in preparing her for it in the event that…

Safely tucked inside the little cottage, Genevieve stared at Queen Mary with her mouth agape.

"What is it, child?" Mary asked.

"You—you are really the queen of all Scotland?" she asked, running her fingers over Mary's face, tracing her features. She was spellbound by such greatness. Finally she curtsied deeply.

"Aye, lassie," Mary said. "And you are Genevieve."

"You know about me?" Genevieve asked, her face lighting up with a smile. "They told you?"

"Of course," Mary said. "Why wouldn't they? We will get to know each other well while I am here with you."

Tears brimmed over in Genevieve's eyes.

"They—they are not ashamed of me?" she asked.

"*They*?" Mary asked. "Who are they?"

"Why, the Keiths, of course," Genevieve said.

"They have been good to you?" Mary asked, her heart reaching out to this innocent child. They had obviously found a place in their own hearts for her, providing her with a place to live and a woman to care for her in spite of the malady they claimed she had. A very noble gesture for some poor forsaken orphan.

Genevieve shrugged her shoulders, her voice indifferent.

"You call this *good*?" she asked, sounding like a wounded animal. "You do not see any of the other Keiths living like this, do you?"

"Nay," Mary said. "You imagine yourself to be a Keith? Surely just because they took you in…"

"Oh, no, your majesty," Genevieve said, proud of the royal manners Robbie and Mrs. McGrath had taught her in preparation for the queen's visit. "You do not understand. I *am* a Keith, through and through. I was born a Keith, and I shall die a Keith. 'Tis the only thing I have…"

Mary pitied the poor disillusioned child. Had they treated her perhaps too well? Did she really believe that she was a member of one of the most powerful clans in Scotland? Well, be that as it may, it was not Mary's place to set her straight. She would, however, have a chat with Robbie to tell him that she should be told the truth.

"Over here!" The voice was faint and weak, but fortunately loud enough that Robbie and Mechi could follow it. They hurried to its point of origination, calling "Mrs. McGrath!" as they went.

Soon they came upon Mrs. McGrath, lying in a heap on the ground. Her skirts were pulled up nearly around her waist and the *platforms* they had created for her were still on her feet.

"What happened?" Robbie asked, kneeling down beside her.

"'Tis me ankle," she said. "I do not think it is broke, but it is mighty sore. I tried to make it back to the cottage, but I could not. Not with *these* on!" she said, pointing to her shoes. "I should never have come out here with them, but I thought it would be a good way to get used to them. Now I may never walk again! Of all the bloody foolish ideas!"

"I'm sure you will," Robbie said. "It will just take some time to get used to them." He laughed as he added, "Perhaps it would be wiser to begin *inside* the cottage for a time first. Then, when you have mastered that, you can go roaming about in the forest."

"I suppose," she said, suddenly realizing that her pride was hurt almost as much—if not more—than her ankle. She quickly tugged at her skirt, pulling it down to make her at least partially presentable.

"How are we going to get her back to the cottage?" Mechi asked. "Do you want to go get a horse while I wait here with her?"

"Nay," Robbie said. "There's no need for that." He gathered Mrs. McGrath into his arms and headed for the cottage. "Hold on tight," he told her. She obediently placed both arms around his neck.

If you had an ounce of brains in your head, Mechi thought, *you would be insanely jealous. Yes, even of Mrs. McGrath. No woman belongs in his arms except you.*

"Coming?" Robbie called to her.

"Aye, my lord," she said. She knew it was ridiculous to even think such things. If the only woman she had to worry about for competition was Mrs. McGrath, she had it made. Yes, she was safe with her Robbie.

Robbie smiled as he entered the cottage, Mrs. McGrath still in his arms, in spite of the way his back hurt. For such a short woman, her stoutness was more stonesweight than Robbie had realized. But, he was not about to admit to his own weakness. He deposited her on the bed and went to where Queen Mary and Genevieve were busily occupied with a game of sticks and stones.

"So she has captured you as well, has she?" he asked the queen.

"Aye," Mary said. "She's a charming lass, just as you said."

"Aye," Robbie agreed. "That she is." He leaned over Genevieve and kissed her tenderly on the cheek.

Mary, seeing how fond he was of the child, walked over to the far side of the room, motioning Robbie to join her.

"The poor dear is delusional," she said, watching the innocent look on Genevieve's face.

"How so?" Robbie asked.

"She—she thinks she is a member of the clan."

"The clan?" Robbie asked.

"Aye, the clan Keith," Mary said. "She claims to be a member of the clan Keith."

Robbie threw his head back and laughed. Mechi turned to see what was so funny. Their conversation to that point had been too soft for her to hear, but there was no mistaking the amusement Robbie found in something. There was no way to silence that wonderful laugh.

"Gen," he said, going back to her. "The queen seems to be a mite confused."

"Her majesty—confused?" Genevieve asked. "But she cannot be confused. *She is the queen*, and surely there must be a law against someone confusing the queen."

"Nay," Robbie said, mischief glistening in his bright green eyes. "'Tis no law which says one cannot confuse the queen. And you, my little princess, have succeeded in doing just that."

"Me?" Genevieve asked, looking horrified at the mere idea that she had done something wrong towards the queen.

"But I have not done anything to her."

"She is confused because you told her you were a member of the clan Keith," Robbie explained.

Genevieve's face fell. She looked, Mechi thought, like some poor little puppy who had just been scolded for piddling on the new white carpet. So they had not told the queen who she really was. Genevieve looked at Mechi. Maybe she didn't know who she really was, either. She had so hoped that they had finally accepted her, at least a little, rather than being so ashamed of having her as a member of the clan. It wasn't her fault she was the way she was!

Robbie picked his sister up and set her on his lap. She was, Mechi knew, twelve years old, yet she was very small for her age. She looked perfectly comfortable on her brother's knee. Mechi wondered if she would feel as comfortable if she was on his lap.

"Mary," Robbie said, rubbing Genevieve's back as he spoke, "I would like to introduce you to the missing member of the clan Keith. Queen Mary, may I present Genevieve Keith, my sister? Genevieve, meet Mary, Queen of the Scots."

Mary felt her mind go into a tizzy. Could it be? Someone as high and mighty as the clan Keith could have borne a child like this? So innocent, so pure, yet with fits and seizures that could turn her into a raving lunatic at any moment? How could it possibly be?

"Are you certain?" Mary asked. "But I never heard…"

"Nor did anyone else," Robbie said. "I'm afraid Mums was quite embarrassed by her. She had her hidden away here in Boscobel to prevent anyone from learning of her existence. She pronounced her new baby dead on birth, if you recall."

"I am afraid not," Mary said. "I was in France at the time."

"Aye, so ye were," Robbie said. "Well, at any rate, Father hired Mrs. McGrath to come here and tend to her." He paused, then explained, "Father was nearly heartbroken when she left Dunnottar. But Mums would not have it any other way." He gave Genevieve a big hug. "I come nearly every day—when I can—to visit her. Aye, she is a Keith, and proud of it."

"Father does not like it," Genevieve added. "He comes to see me often, too. He says he loves me. He calls me his *little cuckoo bird*. He says I sing as pretty as one."

How sad! Mechi thought. If only they had all been born a few centuries later how different little Genevieve's life would have been.

Genevieve began to giggle, her eyes sparkling just like Robbie's did when he was up to something.

"What is it?" Robbie asked.

"I dare not say," Genevieve said, refusing to tell them what was so funny.

"Gen!" Robbie said. "We have no secrets, you and I. Mechi and I have let you in on the biggest secret in all Scotland, your knowing of the plot to protect Queen Mary. Surely you can trust us."

"I promised…" Genevieve insisted.

"Who did you promise?" Robbie asked.

Genevieve answered before she could stop. She should have been more careful, but Robbie had a way of getting anything he wanted from her. She did dote on her big brother.

"Mumsy," she said. "I promised her."

They all exchanged puzzled glances. What could she be talking about? They all knew that Lady Keith had practically banished the child from her very memory.

"Mums?" Robbie asked. "But how could you promise her anything? She doesn't… She won't… She…"

"She what?" Genevieve asked. "She comes to see me at least twice a week. She always has. Only she made me and Mrs. McGrath promise that we would never tell."

Mechi felt a lump form in her throat and tears well up in her eyes. What a complex woman! It would take a shrink an entire lifetime to figure out the complicated mind of Lady Keith. *The Two Sides of Eve*! she thought. Or was it three? Whatever! Maybe on their way back to the twentieth century, if they ever did return, they should stop and pay a visit to Sigmund Freud. This would be one for the books!

Before any of them could ask about Lady Keith's visits, the sound of fast-approaching horse beats sounded outside.

"Quick!" Robbie ordered Queen Mary. "Out the back door! No one must know you are here!"

Mary ran outside just as the front door opened, without so much as a knock. Mary was peeking through the window. She felt her heart leap into her throat as she set eyes on the most handsome, dark-haired man she had ever seen. Maybe life in Boscobel, away from her devoted subjects, wouldn't be so bad after all. Not if she could find some way to persuade this fellow to "stick around," as Mechi put it.

Chapter XXXVII

"Uncle David!" Genevieve exclaimed excitedly as the man entered the room. "You came back!"

"I promised you I would, *mi amore*," he said, giving her a big hug. "Have you been good while I was gone?"

"I promised you *I* would," Genevieve said, mocking his own smart retort. "And were you good?"

"I fear the child knows me too well," the man said.

Mechi wondered if this David was truly an uncle, as Genevieve called him. He did not resemble any of the other Keiths Mechi had met. Besides, his speech had a definite Italian accent. *David Rizzio*, she thought. Robbie had said that Mrs. McGrath had a cousin from Italy who was visiting her. So this was to become Queen Mary's personal secretary and supposed lover. Well, no wonder! The man looked as handsome as Dean Martin, only he appeared to be quite sober.

Robbie studied the man. He had no reason to trust him, nor to doubt him, but he found himself liking him immediately. Their first encounter had been only a momentary exchange, so this was his first real up-close-and-personal meeting.

Robbie saw that Genevieve was completely entralled by the foreigner. He had learned long ago to trust her instincts. If David Rizzio was trusted by Genevieve, he could be trusted by anyone. Yes, he was perfect for the job of protecting Queen Mary.

"Might I have a word with ye outside?" Robbie asked.

"Of course," David replied. He, too, liked the brawny Scotsman. He had, even before they had met. His cousin had told him how kind he had been to both herself and to the little girl who was her charge. A man who is kind to women and children, he had decided, was worthy of his friendship.

David headed for the back door.

"No!" Robbie nearly shouted. "Out this way!"

"Wild boars await us from behind?" David asked, laughing cheerfully.

"Nay," Genevieve said. "But the queen of all Scotland does!"

David stopped dead in his tracks. Had the child gone mad? Surely a small humble cottage in the midst of a forest called Boscobel was no place fit for a queen.

"She speaks the truth," Mrs. McGrath said. "'Tis a most honored thing we've been called upon to do. I'm sure Robert will explain it to you." Mrs. McGrath, who up until now had never even smiled as far as Mechi knew, suddenly broke into wild peals of laughter. "'Tis for the queen that I'm fitted in these." She pulled her skirt up just slightly to reveal her somewhat crude homemade platform shoes. Just a few minutes ago she had been cursing them, but now she boasted them proudly. "I dare say I'm the only woman alive who has ever worn such fare."

Mechi laughed. It was probably true. She wondered how she would have managed in the 1960's with spike heels.

"Come then," David said to Robbie, going to the front door. "Enlighten me."

Robbie turned back to face Mechi.

"Fetch Queen Mary," he said. "'Tis quite safe for her." He looked towards the tiny leaded window at the rear of the house where he had seen Mary peeking inside. "Although it might not be necessary." He winked at the queen, revealing that he knew all along that she was there.

"Consider it done," Mechi said. She began whistling a little tune. Drat! She thought. I wish I could remember the words. Frustrated, she sang, "*Consider yourself…*" She hummed the next couple of notes, then went on to "*Consider yourself—part of the family.*"

Robbie smiled warmly at her. "Consider it done!" he said, his words not part of the song, but a definite lilt to his voice.

He could put a song in your heart! Mechi thought as she went to bring the queen back inside.

Robert filled in all the details—at least as many as Mechi had revealed to him—of Queen Mary's future. David Rizzio listened intently, absorbing every word, trying to comprehend this strange turn of events. Who would have thought a simple visit to his favorite cousin would put him right in the center of such a scheme? Still, he had always loved a challenge.

"What does this have to do with me?" he asked Robert.

"My father has been searching for someone who could stay here to protect her majesty," Robert explained. "Since you are already here, and since you know Mrs. McGrath, and since she trusts you, you seem like the perfect man for the job."

"And if I refuse?" David asked.

Robert sat a few moments, contemplating the situation, before he spoke. Finally he said, "Well, since you are privy to the information which could destroy the queen, I suppose I shall just have to dispose of you in any way I see fit." He grinned at his new friend and confidante. "What is your preference? A duel? Swords? Or a simple hanging?"

"You don't leave a gent much choice, do you?" David asked, knowing full well that you couldn't keep him out of this whole plot with any of the threats. He had always been a pushover for a fun adventure, and this one promised to be the biggest and best he'd participated in yet.

"I thought that was a very good choice," Robert said. "There were three options."

"I believe I'll accept the fourth," David said. "Falling in place in your proposal is much more appealing than the alternatives."

"Shall we inform the women?" Robert asked, standing up and going back to the cottage. David followed close on his heels. Only one question remained in his mind: how did Mechi Jeanotte know what would happen in the future? He'd heard of the gypsies, but she didn't measure up to the image he had conjured up of such characters. Still, looks can be deceiving…

"So you are to be my constant companion?" Queen Mary asked David Rizzio. *It suits me fine*, she thought, her eyes dancing at the mere idea of it. *Certainly far more desirable than that damned Darnley Mechi wants to get me hooked up with!*

"So it would seem," David said.

"And if I do not choose to have you by my side constantly?" Mary asked.

"Then I shall have to chain you to the bed and see that you remain there." There was a gleam in his eye, Mechi noticed, that would match any Robbie had shown in the past. What a pair they would make!

"The queen of Scotland will not be shackled!" Mary said, showing her spunk as she spoke. "Not by you nor by anyone else."

Except your cousin, Queen Elizabeth, Mechi thought. I wish I could remember how many years she kept you a prisoner. Well, with a little bit of luck the queen would be spared such a fate.

Mechi glanced at Mrs. McGrath. She wanted to go and hug her. She wanted to say she was sorry for what they were about to do to her. She wanted to go back to where she came and take them all along with her so they could be spared a fate worse than death. Well, for Mrs. McGrath it was a fate which would include death. Or for Mary, if their plan failed.

"*With a little bit*," she sang. "*With a little bit. With a little bit of bloomin' luck.*"

"I do believe," David said, "that if what Lord Robert has told me is true, we shall need more than just a little bit of your bloomin' luck!"

"I fear you are quite right," Robert said. "May God grant us His protection as we proceed."

"Amen!" they all entoned together.

"I will tell her everything I have ever done," Queen Mary said as she bade farewell to Robbie and Mechi. "I shall even endeavor to tell her what I think."

Mechi nodded her approval. This had to work. If it did not, her entire trip back here was for nothing. That is, of course, if you forgot about Lord Robbie Keith, Viscount of Kintore. But forgetting him would take a lifetime. Or centuries. Or whatever it was that she would have in the future.

Chapter XXXVIII

Robbie rode like the wind on his way back to Dunnottar. He seemed oblivious to Mechi's presence with him. The truth was, he was *too* conscious of her. As they left the cottage in Boscobel he was overwhelmed with the sense that Mechi's mission was almost completed. They had found the replacement for Queen Mary. *A clone*, she had called it. Mrs. McGrath was being thoroughly indoctrinated by the queen, and with a little bit of luck she would be able to portray her perfectly. In a little over a week, they had decided, they would escort Mrs. McGrath to Dunnottar for the final test: to see if Lady Keith would detect that she was a fraud.

Mechi, picking up on the vibes that he needed time alone, stayed back a ways, giving him the space he desired. Suddenly she felt a pull towards him, like a huge magnet had dropped down from the trees and wrapped itself around her, pulling her to him. She dug her heels into the side of her mount and raced to catch up with him.

"With a little bit," Robbie was singing at full voice as she neared him. *"With a little bit. With a little bit of bloomin' luck."*

Mechi laughed. He was extremely adept at memorizing the snippets of songs she was so fond of singing. Fact is, she very often sang without even being conscious of it. *Habit,* she thought. *It's hard to break. The only habit I really want is being near Robbie Keith. I don't know how I will ever be able to survive without him.*

The same sense of doom Robbie had felt had also come over her. She knew, somehow, that fate would return her to the future. She had no control over it. She could always avoid the cursed ring, but she was not sure she would even need it.

"Mission accomplished!" she shouted as she rode. Then she made a loud "Boom" sound, her mind replaying the noise of the briefcase from Mission Impossible.

"No!" Robbie said, turning his horse around so they were face to face. "Don't say that!"

Mechi looked at him. The green eyes which usually sparkled so were filled with fear. She wanted to jump from her horse onto his, to put her arms around him and hold him so tightly that nothing—not even fate or the gods who had deemed her to come to this time—could separate them. Instead she slowly reached out for his hand and gave him a knowing nod. *Maybe*, she thought, *if neither of us put our fears into words we can avoid the inevitable.*

"Dunnottar lies just ahead," he finally said, avoiding the dreaded subject. "We must tell Father at once."

"You are certain this Rizzio can be trusted?" Lord Keith asked the duo.

"Aye," Robbie replied. "Mrs. McGrath says he is the most loyal member of their family. And I know you trust her." He paused momentarily. "Ye trust her with Genevieve."

Mechi wondered if these two strong, take-charge men would accept her input into the situation at hand. A woman dabbling in politics, religion or whatever else was not exactly the name of the game in 1651. Still, they had befriended Queen Mary…

"Queen Mary seemed quite smitten by Mr. Rizzio," Mechi said. "I dare say she would trust him with anything. Surely more than she would trust Darnley."

Lord Keith looked at Robbie. "Does she speak the truth?" he asked.

"Aye," Robbie said. "I did notice that Mary's eyes were nearly bulging out of her sockets at the mere sight of him. He is a very handsome chap."

Mechi sat, slouched in the huge oak chair. She was dazed, in sort of a semi-conscious state. She had not realized how tired she was. It was a terrible burden—bearing the future of an entire country and its monarch—on one person's shoulders. Granted, she had Robbie and Lord Keith's help, but she knew if *she* failed the entire plot would collapse.

Mechi cleared her throat and sat up erect. The two men looked at her, waiting anxiously. They had both learned that when she had something to say, it was almost always noteworthy.

"There is the matter of Lady Keith," Mechi said.

"We have already discussed her role in this matter," Lord Keith said. "There should be no problem."

"Not unless she goes to Boscobel before we are ready to bring Queen Mary—alias Mrs. McGrath—here for their encounter," Mechi said.

She watched Lord Keith for his reaction. He and Lady Keith seemed to know each other so intimately, yet she wondered if he knew this part of her life, or if it had been kept a secret even from her husband. She didn't need to wonder long, as the color drained from Lord Keith's face and he drew in a huge, deep breath.

"To Boscobel?" he asked, his fingernails digging into the wood on the desk in front of him. "Why would you even suggest such a thing?"

Robbie nodded to Mechi, indicating that he would pick up the story from there.

"It seems, Father, that Mums has been paying nearly weekly visits to Gen."

"And you have this on whose word?" Lord Keith asked.

"Gen's herself," Robbie said. "And it was confirmed by Mrs. McGrath."

"I cannot believe it," Lord Keith said. Surely there would have been some indication that she had made such visits. A hint. A dropped word. Something that would have told him. How could they live so close and yet have secrets from each other after all these years?

"I'm sorry, Father," Robbie said. "Truly I am." The corner of his lips, nearly hidden by his bushy red beard, curved up into a broad grin. "Or perhaps I am not. I think it is most admirable that Mums has been doing that. I really found it quite deplorable that she had abandoned the child. Her very own child. Somehow this makes Mums—so much more human. More compassionate. More loving."

Mechi smiled at him. Maybe there was another side to Lady Keith, as Robbie said. She seemed so stiff, so formal, so taken with her post in life. Maybe all she was trying to do was protect her own. Genevieve was so small, so vulnerable. She needed her mother's protective hand. But Robbie? He was so strong, so virile, so capable of defending even the very throne of Scotland. Yet Mechi realized in a flash that to Lady Keith, Robbie was as vulnerable as his sister. To Lady Keith, Robbie needed his mother's protection from—from *her*! The thought struck her like a loud clap of thunder. She was as normal a mother as any in the twentieth century. The only thing different about life in this era, she concluded, was that it was so much the same.

"I shall find a way to deal with your mother," Lord Keith said.

"I have an idea," Robbie said. He hesitated, to see if his father was really listening to him. Convinced that he had his attention, albeit divided with his thoughts, he said, "It has been far too long since Aunt Elanor visited Mums. She has spoken often of late of how she longs to see her sister."

"I dare not send her away with so much turmoil over the queen," Lord Keith said.

"Nay," Robbie said. "I did not mean for that. But what if I rode out to escort Aunt Elanor here for a spell?"

"A splendid idea!" Lord Keith said enthusiastically. "With her here, your mother will be too busy entertaining her and catching up on all the gossip of home to even think of going to Boscobel." He rubbed his head thoughtfully. "But just in case, I shall have one of the guards keep an eye on her to be sure."

"Then our plan is ready to go into Phase Two," Mechi said, yawning and stretching lazily. Oh, this brain drain was really getting to her. She could do with a good old-fashioned Sunday afternoon nap. Even on a Tuesday.

Chapter XXXIX

Daily, Mechi and Robbie made their way to Boscobel to oversee the sessions between Queen Mary and Mrs. McGrath. Mechi left most of the coaching to Robbie, fearful that she would insert things into the conversation which had not yet occurred.

Genevieve spent long hours playing with the toys Mechi fashioned for her from spindles, string and paper. She was content in her little corner of the room. Often Mechi would wander over to her and tell her stories. Stories which had not yet been written, such as *Alice in Wonderland* and *Little Red Riding Hood* and *Anne of Green Gables*. Stories Mechi had heard years ago, but which were still years ahead in their making.

Genevieve sat, spellbound, as she listened to the yarns Mechi spun.

"They dropped bread crumbs as they walked," she said, relating the story of *Hansel and Gretel*.

Suddenly Genevieve's head flew back and she began tossing about in the chair, nearly falling to the floor.

"Robbie!" Mechi called out. "Help!"

Robbie and Mrs. McGrath came running. Robbie placed his big strong, brawny arms around his little sister, overpowering her in his protectiveness. Mrs. McGrath ran soothing fingers through the child's hair, trying to calm her. Mechi again grabbed a small stick and placed it inside Genevieve's mouth, holding the tongue secure. In a few moments the episode passed, leaving Queen Mary dazed.

"This is a common occurrence with the child?" the queen asked when she was sure the spell was over.

"Aye," Robbie said, hanging his head in shame.

"And there is nothing can be done for her?" Queen Mary asked.

"I'm afraid not," Robbie said, still not daring to look up. "If there was, do you not think we'd have tried?"

"Perhaps in Paris…" Queen Mary suggested.

Yes, perhaps in Paris, Texas. In 1997, Mechi thought, knowing she could not speak such farfetched ideas. *If only there was some way...*

When they were sure Genevieve was all right, Queen Mary, Mrs. McGrath and Robbie returned to the task at hand. Mechi, staying beside Genevieve, heard them off in the distance. They seemed like they were light years away as Robbie reminded Queen Mary of childhood pranks and events which had occurred at Dunnottar.

"These are the kinds of things Mums will remember and is likely to bring up when you go to Dunnottar," Robbie told Mrs. McGrath. "If you can pass the scrutiny of me Mums, ye can do anything."

Mrs. McGrath twisted the ring on her finger nervously. It was one of Queen Mary's rings which she had been presented so she would appear as the exact clone.

Mechi watched them in awe. Mrs. McGrath might be a commoner, she thought, but she would make a wonderful actress. *She is playing her role to the hilt. If I did not know myself which one was which, I would be hard pressed to tell.*

She glanced down at Mrs. McGrath's shoes, which were just barely visible beneath her full, flowing crinolines and skirts. That was the one sure giveaway. But, with both of them seated, staring at each other across the table, anyone would have had a very difficult—if not impossible—task to identify them.

"I think she's got it," Mechi said, shaking her head in disbelief. "Mrs. McGrath, you're a miracle. Truly you are. I am sure even Lady Keith will not be able to tell you are not the real McCoy."

"I most certainly am not!" Mrs. McGrath snapped, her voice full of anger and hatred. "Do ye not know that I'm a kin to the Hatfields? And the Hatfields and the McCoy's are the bitterest of enemies!"

"Whatever would make you say such a thing?" Robbie asked, puzzled by Mechi's choice of words.

Mechi scratched her head, trying to remember what she knew about the feud between the Hatfield's and the McCoy's. She finally decided she knew nothing of the history between the two clans, but that it was—in her day—a common expression. She wondered who was the real McCoy, anyway, and why would anyone care about a fake.

"I don't know," Mechi said. "I guess it's just something I heard some time or other. I'm sorry, Mrs. McGrath. I didn't mean to insult you."

"It's past," Mrs. McGrath said. "Besides, I should be apologizing to all of you. If I have another outburst like that, everyone will know I am no more the queen of Scotland than a Hatfield. And God knows we could never have a Hatfield on the throne of Scotland!"

Mechi glanced at a small cupboard. Her eyes caught the sunlight sparkling off the jewel of the sapphire in the magical ring. She wondered if she should go and grab it, or if she dared leave it there. It was clearly exposed for everyone to see. She knew no one had worn it, or they would have disappeared. She was convinced of that. But why was it not wrapped, as she and Robbie had left it?

Suddenly it dawned on her that there was one member of their happy party missing. Rizzio! Had he rubbed the ring the wrong way and been hurled through space and time? She was just about to ask about his whereabouts when he walked in.

"Thank God you are here!" she said, beads of perspiration popping out on her forehead.

"You missed me?" he asked, his dark eyes glistening like the black of his oil-slicked hair. He grinned at her, making Mechi feel uneasy. She wondered if he could be trusted any more than Darnley.

"We all missed you," Queen Mary said. Her deep admiration and infatuation with this man was obvious just by the way she looked at him. "You were...?"

"Just out to enjoy the crispness of the air," he said. "Not to worry. I will not venture outside the perimeter. And your secret is safe with me. In fact, I have determined that I shall not leave your side once you leave the cottage."

"But I am not leaving!" Queen Mary said. "It is her." She pointed at Mrs. McGrath. "She's the one who must face the piercing eyes of Lady Keith."

Soon, when they realized what had just happened, the entire group was howling with laughter. The tears ran down Queen Mary's face. Robbie's eyes were aglow with delight. Mechi, who had been the originator of the whole plan, was relieved beyond words. Even Mrs. McGrath's very own cousin could not tell the difference. He had chosen the wrong one!

"It is finished!" Robbie declared gleefully. "We are ready to tackle Mums! Mechi, me dear, ye have your clone. Well done!"

In an instant Mechi was in his arms and he was kissing her passionately—right in front of the queen of Scotland! Or in front of *two* queens of Scotland! They might think it was a congratulatory action, but she knew it was far more than that.

A feeling like that of a huge boulder dropping settled in the pit of her stomach. She looked sideways at the ring on the counter. If she got half a chance alone she would toss the thing as far as she could, never to be seen again. If her work was done, did she have any right to stay here? Would she be sent forth, even without the ring, to spend eternity alone? She knew without Lord Robbie Keith, Viscount of Kintore, she would never find true happiness.

Chapter XL

Queen Mary sat facing Mechi and Robbie in the carriage as they wove their way over the rough terrain back to Dunnottar. At least to anyone—friend or stranger—they might encounter on the trip, that is how it would seem.

Lord Keith had explained the queen's absences in the country of late as a "return to France to finalize the death of her late husband." It seemed perfectly logical, and no one had questioned him about it. After all, Lord Keith was known as perhaps the most honest man in all Scotland, as well as the wealthiest.

"Welcome home, your majesty!" Lord Lindsay called out as they passed each other on the road.

Queen Mary gave a royal wave, much like the ones Mechi had seen Queen Elizabeth—the Second, that is—present on television.

Mechi snickered, quietly, but just loud enough so Robbie heard her. She looked up and saw him staring at her intently. She heard the warning of his head, forbidding her to speak of such things as boxes with people in them and steel chambers that cooked without fire and…

"Don't worry," she assured him, setting her hand atop his. "I won't *freak her out* with the truth."

Robbie smiled at her. *Freak her out* was one of her crazy expressions that she had tried to explain to him. He still *didn't get it*, which was another one of her mysterious quotes, but at least that was one he understood.

Robbie's expression sobered. Suppose she would have to leave them, if her part in protecting Queen Mary was complete? How could he ever survive without her? He had come to depend on her. No! He knew that was not being honest with himself. *He had come to love her!* This crazy woman from someplace that hadn't even been discovered yet who came to him from some time that didn't even exist and who was to his mother an honest-to-god witch had cast his spell over him like a giant cobweb when it entrapped a tiny fly. He was madly in love with her, and if there was any way to do it, he would follow her to the ends of the earth—or the world—or time itself. Which is exactly what he might have to do, if it was possible.

One carriage wheel dropped suddenly into a hole, causing them to nearly upturn.

"Well, that's par for the course," Mechi said. "We are almost home and we take a spill."

In true Mechi-fashion, she began whistling "*Jingle Bells*." When she got to the words "*..and we, we got upsot!*" she sang them, causing both Robbie and Queen Mary to laugh.

"You do know some of the strangest little ditties!" Queen Mary said. "But your speaking of *par for the course,* we really must take a ride over to St. Andrews and putt a few rounds. I do so miss the game. I'm afraid I've been off the course so long, I may end up in the sandtrap more often than not."

"I'm sure you will do fine," Mechi said, looking sympathetically at her. "It is like riding a bicycle," she said. "Once you learn, you never forget."

"A bicycle?" Queen Mary asked. "I've not heard of such a thing. Tell me what it is, please do."

Mechi began describing a bicycle when she realized, suddenly, that their plan was working so well that she herself had forgotten that the woman who was talking about her golf game was not her fellow-pro, but was a rank amateur who up until two weeks ago had never even seen a gold club and who thought an "iron" was a rod you used to secure the door.

"Robbie!" Mechi cried out. "Isn't it wonderful! She is so good she even fooled me! And I know who she is!"

"Hush!" Robbie said, grabbing both her hands and squeezing them as if the flow of blood might stop. "We must not talk about this. We never know when someone might be within earshot of us. We must be very cautious."

"I'm sorry," Mechi said. "Of course you are right." She thought about adding "You're always right," but she didn't want to give him that much power over her. He already exuded far too much control over every part of her being—body, soul and spirit. "I will be more careful, I promise."

"I'm sure you will," Robbie said.

Mechi was glad and relieved when she saw the warm smile return to his mouth.

"However, you are quite right. She has done a wonderful job of becoming Queen Mary."

Queen Mary—alias Mrs. McGrath—or was it the other way around?—turned her nose slightly upward in a very regal manner.

"Why, Lady Mechi! If I didn't know better I would say that we even have you fooled. You did not know that we switched places at the last minute? Mrs. McGrath, the poor dear, was just not certain that she was prepared to face Lady Keith quite yet."

Robbie's face turned ashen. So they had the *real* Queen Mary with them. Then they might as well turn around and go back to the cottage in Boscobel. There was no point in pursuing an experiment that couldn't be done.

Robbie missed the wink that passed between the two women, which caused Mechi to lean forward slightly and lift her skirts just a trifle. Just enough to expose her heavy platform shoes.

She reached over and tapped Robbie's knee, then pointed to the shoes.

"Got you!" she said, laughing. Soon the trio was howling, just as they began the sharp ascent up the rocky crags to Dunnottar Castle.

"Be it ever so humble," Mechi sang, *"there's* no place like home!"

"It is wonderful to have you back with us!" Lady Keith said warmly to Queen Mary as they entered the keep.

The dowager and the monarch embraced, and Mechi noticed that Lady Keith's nose fit in just the right place on the queen—right into her bosom. Yes, the platforms were exactly the right height. Mechi held her hand over her mouth to stifle a grin, wondering how many men in the nation—besides Darnley—would give everything they owned to have their nose in the place of Lady Keith's.

"It was fine in France," Mary said, "but there is no place like Scotland. It's home."

Much to Mechi's amusement, Mary repeated the phrase in a sing-song tone of voice, *"Be it ever so humble, there's no place like home."*

"And our home is your home any time," Lady Keith said. "Do you remember the time when you were about three or four and William was telling you about Robert the Bruce...?"

"And he ended up by taking me to the walkway at the top of the keep and I nearly fell over?" Queen Mary asked, finishing the story, much to the delight of all.

She was nearly finished with the tale when Lord Keith walked in. He did not interrupt, but listened carefully as the queen spoke. When she was finished, he said—quite gruffly—"Robert, might I have a word with you in my library?"

Robert stood obediently and headed for the library. Mechi followed. She was going to be in on this, invitation or not. It was *her* plan, and if Lord Keith was going to lower the boom, she was going to be there to catch her share of the blame, too.

"How could you do this to me?" Lord Keith demanded. "Do you both take me for some sort of a fool?"

"Whatever do you mean, Father?" Robbie asked, his shiny green eyes looking as innocent as a four-year-old boy who just threw a hammer at his sister and claimed he didn't know it was wrong.

"You were to bring Mrs. McGrath here to try to fool your mother. Why did you not follow the plan?"

"Mechi?" Robbie asked.

Mechi knew instinctively what he wanted. She went to the door and returned to the salon where Lady Keith and Queen Mary were still deeply engaged in reminiscing.

"Begging your pardon, your majesty," Mechi said, curtsying to Queen Mary, "but Lord Keith desires your company with us for just a few moments."

Queen Mary stood and joined Mechi.

"I shan't be long," Queen Mary said to her hostess. "I have not had such fun since…"

"…since the kitten crawled up under your petticoats?" Lady Keith asked.

"Aye," Queen Mary said. "And she would have stayed there until I disrobed, if only that sheepdog hadn't come sniffing around me!"

They all laughed, even Lady Keith, at the sights the story conjured up in their minds.

"I shall be right back," Queen Mary said as they all three disappeared into the laird's library.

"Why have you come instead of sending your imposter?" Lord Keith bellowed. "I have risked a great deal to go along with this scatterbrained idea of theirs to try to protect you. I swore to your father that I would defend you with my dying breath. But I can do nothing if you will not co-operate with me!"

Queen Mary went to her guardian and embraced him warmly.

"Do not be afraid," she said. "It will all work out as you had planned. I shall be spared." She looked him straight in the eye as she said, "Now, will you please turn away from me?"

Lord Keith looked at her, puzzled and shocked by such a demand.

"Please, William, for me. Just for a moment," she said, repeating the request. "Please turn away from me."

He followed his queen's orders, turning his back to the wall, staring at the rows and rows of leather-bound volumes he had always found so fascinating. Today, with the queen standing directly in front—well, now behind—him, they held no appeal at all.

Queen Mary bent over and unlaced her boot. She then held it out for Mechi to pull off. Once it hit the floor with a *thud*, she repeated it with the other boot. As soon as she stood in her stocking feet, she returned to stand directly behind Lord Keith.

"You may turn around now," she instructed him.

As soon as he was facing her, she quickly gave him another hug. This time, though, she had to stretch her arms as high as she could to grasp him about the neck.

"Satisfied?" she asked him, grinning like Sylvyster after he set Tweetybird free from his cage.

"Whatever…?" Lord Keith asked.

"It worked!" Mechi exclaimed excitedly.

"It did indeed!" Robbie said, grabbing Mechi by the hands and twirling her around as he danced a few steps from the highland fling.

"What are you talking about?" Lord Keith asked.

"My lord," Mrs. McGrath—alias Queen Mary—said. "It is so good to see you again."

She reached up and pulled his ear down to her mouth, then whispered a secret only Mrs. McGrath would have known about their original agreement about her care of Genevieve.

Slowly the corners of Lord Keith's mouth turned upward. He was convinced, in a way no one but Mrs. McGrath could have done, that their plan had truly worked.

"So it has!" he said. Much to Mechi's surprise, Lord Keith took Mrs. McGrath and they, too, danced a jig.

"Welcome back to Dunnottar, your majesty," he said.

"The pleasure is all mine," Queen Mary said.

When they finished their spin, she went to gather her shoes. She held them up for Lord Keith to see.

"Very clever!" he said as he knelt on the floor in front of her. "It is an honor to assist your majesty with her…"

He turned to Mechi.

"What in heaven's name do you call these things?" he asked.

"Platforms!" Mechi said. "They're really quite the rage…back in Paris."

"How a woman can walk in such things!" Lord Keith said, shaking his head in disbelief.

"He should see the spike heels of the sixties!" Mechi muttered to herself. "Now that would really cause him to wonder!"

"I think it is time we tell him the rest of the story," Mechi said softly to Robbie as they all left to rejoin Lady Keith.

"Soon," Robbie said. "Very soon."

Chapter XLI

The day seemed to fly by, and before she knew it Mechi glanced outside to meet a silvery moon casting an eerie shadow over the slightly rippling inky water which surrounded the fiddlehead.

As she stared out at it, she wondered if she would be more alone if she were at the bottom of that huge expanse of water.

"Lost in thought?" Robbie's deep resonant voice questioned.

"Yes," Mechi said, turning to look at him. He was, she thought, more handsome now than when she had first laid eyes on him. Certainly far more comely than the image she had seen in her dreams. Of course that wasn't really a fair comparison; the man in her dreams had only shown himself to her from behind.

Mechi, giggling, walked around behind Robbie and tilted her head, first to one side, then to the other, surveying the *real* posterior to the one in her nighttime visions. Yes, indeed, they were one in the same. No one could mistake those buns! She wondered how he would look in a tight pair of Levi's.

"You find my backside amusing?" Robbie asked, trying to sound put-out.

"Extremely," Mechi said.

"And just how is it so?"

"You see, I had a preview of your—buns," Mechi said, suddenly aware that this explanation could land her in deep trouble. It would be bad enough trying to explain it to someone who knew all the right terms and intentions, much less to a man who might as well speak a foreign language.

"You saw my—*buns*?" Robbie asked, completely confused. "What has a loaf of bread to do with anything?"

He threw his head back and laughed that wonderful completely-enveloping laugh of his.

"You do *have a thing* for bread, don't ye now, lassie?" he asked, his eyes full of mischief. "Like with the horses. And now it's me own turn for a fling at the bread. What do ye plan to do with me? Feed me some of your moldy crusts to see if I will turn over and die?"

"No," Mechi said. "*Buns,* when used in my day in the sense I meant it, is a word applied to mean your bottom. Your behind. Your rump."

"*Buns?*" Robbie asked, amused at the image it conjured up. True, they were round and rather squishy, quite like the mass of dough he had seen Cook prepare often enough. His eyes twinkled at the sight of Mechi's buns which were so well-hidden beneath all the layers of petticoats and fabric.

"You do not wear such clothing in your day?" he asked, picking up a corner of Mechi's dress and holding it up in the air. "You wear only such things as those which you sported when I—found you?"

"Primarily, yes," Mechi said. "Oh, we do wear dresses for special occasions."

She wondered what he would do or say at the first viewing of a mini skirt! While his head was quite obviously filled with imaginary pictures at the discussion of *buns,* such a garment left nothing to a man's imagination.

"I think I prefer your—what do you call them—*jeans?*" Robbie said, surprising Mechi by this revelation. "It gives me a better idea of your—*buns.*"

Mechi blushed. This conversation had taken a dangerous curve, and it was up to her to steer it back on course.

"When we leave…" she said, then stopped, her mouth agape. "I mean…"

Robbie took her hand in his. "Don't be afraid," he said, trying to offer her assurance. "If you leave…" He paused, watching her eyes for a reaction, "…I will leave with you. If that is possible, of course."

Mechi felt her heart leap with joy. Was he saying that he didn't want to live without her any more than she did without him? Was it somehow in the realm of feasibility to transport him back—or ahead—through time with her? The only way to find out was to try it.

"Don't think it!" Robbie said, seeming to read her thoughts. "Come with me." He took her by the hand and led her out to the kitchen, which was housed in a completely separate building from the keep, or the main part of the castle. Inside, tiny red embers still glistened in the huge fireplace.

"Do you mind?" he asked her.

"Mind?" She smiled. "It all depends on what is on your mind."

"You are, m'lady," he said, bowing deeply to her. "I know this sounds sort of…" His brain sought for a word, which wouldn't come.

"*Kinky?*" Mechi asked.

She didn't have to define the term; Robbie knew she understood what he meant.

"Okay," he said, "*kinky.*" For the first time since Mechi had met him, he seemed uneasy, nervous.

"When I was a little boy, this was my favorite part of the castle. Cook would come here and make delicious feasts. Every day we had wonderful fare." His green eyes danced. "Her buns were wonderful!"

Mechi laughed.

"I always imagined that the most wonderful place to make love to the woman I loved would be in the kitchen, with all the good smells and the wonderful memories there to make the moment perfect."

Mechi stood inside the kitchen, dazed. Had he just admitted that he loved her? Or did he make wild passionate love to every woman he conquered in the kitchen? Somehow, she doubted it.

"Does it seem too strange to you?" Robbie asked. "I did not mean to insult you. If you would rather not...."

"No!" Mechi nearly shouted, then clapped her hand over her mouth. She certainly didn't want to call anyone's attention to the fact that they were here. But she didn't want him to stop, either. Not if he was going to do what he promised to do.

"If you would rather, we could go somewhere else," he suggested.

"No," Mechi said. "The kitchen is fine. In fact, the kitchen is perfect." She snickered. "After all, it is the most appropriate place to set your buns."

They laughed together. Finally she looked up into his bright sparkling eyes and asked, "Did you mean what you said? Do you mean to tell me that you love me?"

"Of course I love you!" he said, pulling her tightly against his body. She could feel every muscle in his body tighten at the sense of her nearness. His pants produced bulges that let her know exactly what she was doing to him.

He pressed his lips against hers, leaving her struggling for breath, but not caring if she was starved for oxygen or not. His tongue poked its way into her slightly separated lips and she felt the blood tingle all the way from the roof of her mouth to the deep caverns of her innermost womanhood. She wanted him so bad she could taste it. If this was the last time they had together, she wanted it to last forever. What a memory she could take back with her, even if that's all that could safely come away with her when her time was up.

"And do you love me?" Robbie asked. When Mechi didn't reply, he said, his voice filled with hurt, "Is this whole thing just a game with you? Don't you care for me at all? Has it all been just one big charade?"

"Of course I love you!" Mechi gasped between attempts to recover her breath. "That's the problem. Don't you see? If—no *when* I leave, I want you to come with me. But I don't know if that is possible. If you can't come with me..." She looked at him. "Or if you choose not to come with me..."

"Of course I will come with you!" Robbie insisted. "I cannot imagine my life without you. I would run myself through with my own sword before I would live without you."

"Romeo and Juliet, here we come!" she said.

"Who?" Robbie asked.

"Nobody," Mechi said. "At least nobody important. Just a couple of silly, foolish young lovers."

"Who cares?" Robbie asked, picking Mechi up in his arms and setting her on the big old wood baking table.

Mechi wriggled and squirmed. There were little pieces of dough lodged here and there in the table top. She almost got a sliver.

Robbie took the plaid from around his shoulders and laid it gently out on the table. He transferred Mechi to the wool fabric, then gently guided her body to a lying-down position. Soon he was beside her, and he was unfastening all the tiny bone buttons to free her from the encumbrances of her garb.

"Don't know why women have to wear so many layers of clothing!" he sputtered as he kept fumbling with the buttons.

"Neither do I," Mechi said. "In my day, women wear only one or two—at the most—layers of anything."

"I think more and more I am getting to like your time better than mine," Robbie said. "Perhaps this will be our last time…"

"Then we better make it good!" Mechi teased. Nothing seemed very amusing right now. If this was to be the last time they would be together, she wanted it to last forever. Or at least until Cook arrived early in the morning. If she could not cling to Robbie Keith himself, at least she could hang onto this time of lovemaking. On the kitchen table in the Castle of Dunnottar, Scotland in 1561!

Mechi awoke in the arms of her lover. She was vaguely aware of being in the big four-poster bed in her own solar in the castle, but she could not remember moving from the kitchen to the keep itself. Or had she dreamed that they had made love on the kitchen table?

She laughed as she reached out to run her fingers through the deep mass of red coarse curls on Robbie's chest. There was no question about it; this man was as real as they come! As she felt his manhood jab her leg beneath the wool quilts, she knew just how real he was! If the kitchen episode was merely a dream, she wondered if he was having the same dream.

"Good morning!" she said, amazingly alert and bouncy as he slowly opened his eyes and gazed at her.

"Good morning to you, too, " he said, fondling her shoulders and breast with his big strong hands. "What a wonderful way to greet the day."

"It is, isn't it?" she said, agreeing completely. She would love to greet every new day in Robbie's arms. For the rest of her life. However many centuries that transcended.

"I do believe we should arrange for Father to come to Boscobel today after we have returned," he said, suddenly becoming very business-like. It reminded Mechi why she was here; it was not *just* for her own pleasure. In fact, she knew that whatever pleasure had been offered her in the process of saving Queen Mary's life was merely a *perc* of the job. Like health insurance.

"I think it is time we tell him the truth. *All of it*. I don't know how he will handle it, but he must know. We cannot leave without someone knowing what has become of us. Mums would die from the not knowing. It will be much easier for Father to tell her once we have gone."

Mechi's heart cried out to him. She wanted so desperately to believe that he really could come with her when she left. She knew, deep within, that her days here were numbered. Maybe, if she didn't admit the dual trip might not work, it could somehow or other prevent the inevitable from occurring.

So, she did not speak. She kissed him instead. Kissed him like there was no tomorrow.

Chapter XLII

"Father will join us later this afternoon," Robbie said to Queen Mary and Mechi as they neared the cottage in Boscobel.

"I shall be sad to see this whole thing come to an end," Queen Mary said. As if she had a premonition of the future, she said to Mechi, "Will we ever see each other again?"

"I don't know," Mechi admitted. She had become very fond of the queen during their time together. She almost seemed, Mechi reflected, like the sister she had always longed for. "But if not, you will always be very near and dear to my heart."

"And you to mine," Queen Mary said.

Mechi looked at her friend and confidante and caught sight of a tiny tear trickling down her cheek. She bit her lip to keep from bursting out into loud sobs. Such behavior would be most unbecoming in the presence of a queen. Then it struck her that this was not the queen she had become so close to at all, but was in fact Mrs. McGrath. Yes, she would miss Genevieve's caretaker as well.

Inside the cottage Queen Mary, Mrs. McGrath, Robbie and Mechi were all sitting around in a circle when Lord Keith put in his appearance.

"What is so important that you must discuss it with me no later than today?" Lord Keith asked.

"I think you had better sit down," Mechi said.

"You have heard bad news about the queen?" he asked, his face laden with fear.

"No," Mechi said, trying to comfort him. "Well, yes, in a way. But it will not happen for quite a few years."

"You speak in riddles," Lord Keith said. "Please make your point."

'I know none of you will be able to understand this. I do not understand it myself." She paused. If she was a religious person, she thought, she would pray for guidance. Maybe she should, anyway. A silent plea for help went heavenward.

The room was filled with a deafening silence. You could have heard a feather fall.

Feathers! Mechi shivered at the image of the strange golf ball at St. Andrew's Country Club—the one just outside Aberdeen, Maryland—as it had burst into a million pieces with feathers flying everywhere.

Suddenly she was confused. Which was the amulet, anyway? Was it the ring, which was still safely resting on the cupboard? Or was it the old golf ball and its feathers? Or would they need both objects to take them back to the future? Just to be sure, she must be certain she got hold of her green nylon jacket before she needed it. She knew there were a couple of the feathers still in the pocket. When they returned to Dunnottar, she would have to make sure she had her original clothing with her on her horse at all times.

"I'm waiting," Lord Keith said impatiently, looking at Robbie for an explanation.

"Mechi?" Robbie said, giving her the floor. "It's your turn."

"Like I said," Mechi said, "I am sure you will find what I have to tell you hard—if not impossible—to believe." She stopped. She had never been so scared in her life. She knew that deep below the surface of the castle at Dunnottar was a dungeon. She could imagine spending the rest of her life there, never to see such a simple thing as sunshine again.

Robbie reached over and took her hand, offering her the encouragement and strength she needed to continue. She smiled weakly at him.

"I know what will happen to Queen Mary because I have been sent here for one purpose and one purpose only. To protect her."

"You will singlehandedly fight the forces of mighty armies?" Lord Keith asked, laughing the same hearty laugh she had heard from Robbie so many times.

"No," Mechi said. "I will not fight anyone. But I will tell you a story so farfetched you will no doubt think I am a witch, as Lady Keith has insisted upon countless occasions."

"Are you?" Lord Keith asked pointedly.

"No," Mechi said. "At least I don't think so." She felt Robbie squeeze her hand tightly. "No, I am not. I was sent here from the future to warn Queen Mary, and you, as her guardian, of the danger which lies ahead of her."

"So you have said," Lord Keith said, thumping his fingers impatiently on the table. "From Darnley."

"From Darnley," Mechi said, "and others."

"What others?" Lord Keith asked.

Mechi looked at Queen Mary. She was taking in every word Mechi was speaking, trying to comprehend exactly what it was that she was supposed to fear. She detested Darnley, but she wasn't afraid of him. He was far too stupid to fear.

"From Queen Elizabeth," Mechi replied. "She has sent Darnley to entice Mary to forsake the idea of gaining control of the throne of England as well as that of Scotland."

"But it is rightfully mine," Queen Mary—the real one—insisted. "She has no right to anything. Certainly not to my life."

"Darnley, however, has plans of his own," Mechi said, hoping she could make them understand what all was involved in their futures.

They waited, silently, for her to continue.

"He will persuade Queen Mary to marry him," Mechi said. "It will be a terrible marriage."

"I should think so!" Queen Mary—the clone—said. "Why, I can think of nothing worse than being bedded by the rat!"

"And bedded you will be," Mechi said. "Queen Mary bears a son, James. He will grow up to do what Elizabeth will never accomplish. He will reign over all of Scotland, England, Wales and Ireland."

Queen Mary looked almost frightened. "Will he be a good king?" she asked.

"One of the best," Mechi said, smiling warmly at her. "One of his major accomplishments will be to translate the Bible into the English language so every person will be able to read the scriptures for themselves."

Mechi stopped. She wondered just how much she should reveal. Finally, she jumped in with both feet.

"I told you I was sent here from the future. When I left America—a land which has not yet been inhabited by Europeans—the year was 1997."

The entire group stared, their mouths hanging open like a crocodile ready to strike its prey.

"I know," Mechi said. "I told you you would not believe me. I don't understand it at all."

She got up and walked to the cupboard. She picked the ring up, carefully holding it in the cloth Robbie had wrapped around it for fear she would disappear. She had a mission to accomplish first; she had to tell them the rest of the story.

"My mother, who said she was descended from Darnley—but not Queen Mary—said Queen Mary was raped by Darnley. Considering his personality and the feelings of both of you Queen Marys, I dare say it is likely true."

Mechi breathed a little easier when none of them questioned the fact that she was descended from Darnley, but not from Queen Mary. That was one part of the puzzle she had not been able to decipher herself yet.

"I'm sorry that I don't remember the dates these things occurred, but I think I can tell you which event happened first."

"I wed Darnley?" the Queen Mary clone asked.

"Yes," Mechi said. "Although you were not at all happy. In fact, you were quite close to Rizzio. So much so that Darnley became insanely jealous."

"Not far to go," Robbie remarked. "He's nigh there already."

"Rizzio was murdered. Stabbed, I think. Mary was pregnant at the time. She was convinced that Darnley arranged the murder."

"Would you mind telling us which one of us does what?" Mrs. McGrath— now Queen Mary—asked.

"I'm afraid I can't," Mechi said. "For all I know, the real Queen Mary carried out all of these things herself. I do not honestly know if we can change history or not, but we will certainly try."

Queen Mary looked at Mrs. McGrath. She tenderly placed her arm around her. "I cannot ask you to do these things for me," she said, her hands trembling. "If this is the fate that is meant for me, I must handle it alone."

"But you did not ask," Mrs. McGrath said. "I offered. I would do anything for my country, and for you. Even if it meant death. There is no sacrifice too great for my beloved Scotland."

Mechi felt a cold chill run up and down her spine. Did Mrs. McGrath somehow have a premonition of what lay ahead? The fate that awaited her was the worst that could be imagined.

"Go on," Lord Keith said. Mechi saw the skepticism that filled his mind. She couldn't say she blamed him. If she was in his shoes, she would probably not have believed a word of what she was saying, either.

"Queen Mary," Mechi continued, "separated from Darnley after Rizzio's death."

"Where do I go?" Mrs. McGrath asked.

Mechi was amazed at the lengths to which this humble citizen was willing to go for her sovereign and her country. She wondered if she would change her mind when she learned that Mary… Well, it was a death worse than hell itself.

"You stay on at Holyrood," Mechi said. She said a quick silent "thank you" to her mother for her insistence at telling the story of poor Mary, Queen of Scots, over and over when Mechi was just a little girl.

Still, Mechi pondered, there was the mystery of how she could be descended from Darnley but not from Mary.

Suddenly, like she had been struck by a gigantic bolt of lightening, Mechi knew the answer.

"I can't say for sure," Mechi said, "but I do think that Darnley eventually found out about the switch you two make."

"How do you know that?" Lord Keith asked.

"I think—and this is just a guess—that Darnley came after Mary when he found out that the woman he had been married to was an imposter, a fraud."

"What would he do?" Mary asked.

"I think he probably came here to Boscobel where you, the real Queen Mary, are staying. He raped you, just as he had done to Mrs. McGrath. I believe you both ended up bearing a child at almost the same time."

"So whose child became King James?" Mary asked.

"I imagine it was really your son," she said to the queen. "I don't know how, but I think Mrs. McGrath must have raised your child and Mrs. McGrath's son... well, I am not certain, but it would have been too risky for him to have stayed here with you. I think the children were probably switched, just as the two of you are."

"If that should happen," Lord Keith said slowly, "I would be most honored to raise your son at Dunnottar, just as you have cared for Genevieve all these years. It is the least I could do for you."

"I could just kill that damned Darnley!" Queen Mary shouted. "He is not fit to live!"

"And that is exactly what you will do," Mechi said. "He will live outside Glasgow at a place called Kirk o'Field. He gets sick and you go to visit him. I think you were attending a wedding there, if my memory is correct."

"Who will get married?" Queen Mary asked.

"I don't know," Mechi said. She huffed and puffed a bit at the unimportant question. There were much bigger issues at hand. "It doesn't matter. What is important is that you leave Darnley and his page at the cottage at Kirk o'Field. There is a terrible explosion, and everyone thinks they both died in it."

"They escape?" Queen Mary asked.

"No!" Mechi exclaimed. "Hardly! In the morning they were both found hanged in the garden."

"Who hanged them?" Queen Mary asked.

"People said you did," Mechi answered. "Moray found some letters that were supposed to have been written by you, claiming that you arranged the whole thing."

"And did I?" Queen Mary asked. "Or will I?"

"It was never proven," Mechi said. "There have been handwriting analysts who have examined the letters and they seem to think it was not your handwriting."

Mrs. McGrath, still looking for all the world more like Queen Mary than Queen Mary herself did, jumped to her feet. Up until now she had been silent.

"Of course it is not her handwriting! Don't you see? I will kill Darnley! For all the evil things he has done to me. *To us*! If he found out there were two of us, he would have exposed us. We could not allow that. So I did what I had to. I killed him!"

Mechi could feel the rage that was welling up within Mrs. McGrath's very heart and soul. To attack her, to rape her, to leave her with child, it was more than any woman should have to bear.

Mechi's mind, for the first time in ages, returned to the twentieth century. Things really never changed that much. If a woman, under the same circumstances, killed a man who mistreated her that badly, she would most likely be sent to prison for murder. In fact, she had watched case after case on Oprah and Jenny Jones and Sally Jesse and…

"Well?" Lord Keith was saying when her thoughts landed.

"I'm sorry," Mechi said. "What did you say?"

"After Darnley is killed," Lord Keith repeated, "what happens to Mary?"

Mechi froze. How could she tell them the terrible end of Mary, Queen of Scots? Whichever woman it was who carried out this charade to the end would be dealt the final blow when the henchman lowered the axe on her neck, severing her head and leaving it to fall into a basket below her.

"I'm—not—sure," Mechi said, stammering.

"You must know!" Lord Keith said. "You must tell us."

"Queen Elizabeth has Mary imprisoned," Mechi said, hoping that would be the end of the subject.

"For how long?" Queen Mary asked.

"I—don't—remember," Mechi admitted. That, at least, was true. She knew it was quite a few years, but she could not remember exactly how long it was.

"Days? Weeks? Months?" Mary asked.

"Years?" Mrs. McGrath added.

"I think years," Mechi finally said.

"Do I die in prison?" Mary asked.

Mechi felt her head reeling. She had never had to do anything as hard as she was being called on to do now.

"Are you all right?" Robbie asked, putting his arm around her to support her.

"I—I will be," Mechi finally managed to say.

"What happens to me?" Queen Mary asked. "I have a right to know."

"Tell her!" Lord Keith ordered.

"You…" Mechi's eyes welled with tears. They spilled over onto her cheeks and down onto the bodice of her dress.

"What?" Lord Keith demanded. "Tell us!"

"You are executed by the order of Queen Elizabeth," Mechi finally manages to say.

"How?" Mrs. McGrath asked.

"You are beheaded on the balcony at Fotheringhay Castle," Mechi said, her voice so low they had to strain their ears to hear her.

"No!" Lord Keith shouted, jumping to his feet. "I will not allow it! I am your guardian. Your protector. I will stop them!"

"I am afraid you cannot," Mechi said. "They had a trial. It was all done legally."

When Mechi finally looked at Queen Mary, she saw that her face was as pale as a ghost's. Maybe it was a mistake to tell her, but it was too late now. The word was out, and there was no way she could take them back.

"You don't know which of us it is?" Queen Mary asked.

She turned to Mrs. McGrath. "I cannot allow you to carry this out," she said. "It is more than anyone has a right to demand from anyone. I forbid it!"

"I am sorry, your majesty," Mrs. McGrath said, "but you have no choice. It has already been decided. If it means my death, so be it. I have pledged you my allegiance, and I shall not reverse that."

Queen Mary was weeping. "It is more than I deserve," she said. "I will not allow it."

"You are my queen, my sovereign, my ruler," Mrs. McGrath said. "I will carry out the plan to the end. You have no choice in the matter. It is settled."

"Greater love hath no man than this," Lord Keith said. "That he lay down his life for his friend."

Mechi recognized it as a quote. *Sounds like it came straight from the King James Bible*, she thought, even though it had not yet been translated.

Mechi, without realizing what she was doing, broke out into one of her witty songs, this time sung in a very English accent.

"Thank you very much,
Thank you very much.

"That's the nicest thing that anyone's ever done for me."

The words escaped her, but the melody lingered on. She hummed the next few measures, then ended with a rousing,

"Thank you very, very much."

"I think I like that," Queen Mary said. "Sing it again."

Mechi obeyed, repeating the musical ditty. When she was finished, Queen Mary—the real one—began to repeat it. Mechi felt like plugging her ears. She might be the queen, and she might be the most powerful woman Mechi could ever hope to meet, but she would never make it on Broadway! She couldn't carry a tune in a bushel basket. *Only her head*, Mechi thought, ashamed of such a gruesome thought.

Even Mechi, who knew what lay ahead of them, could not envision Queen Mary standing in the midst of the crowd on February eighth, 1587, quietly singing *"Thank you very much, thank you very much, that's the nicest thing that anyone's ever done for me"* as she watched her clone take her place to the ultimate extreme.

"I think I had better get back to Dunnottar," Lord Keith said softly and slowly. His head was bowed. He felt like a complete failure. According to Mechi Jeanotte, he would be unable to stop the process which would end the life of the woman who was like a daughter to him. Whichever woman it was, they were very special to him. The thought of such a horrible doom for either of them was enough to make him sick.

He nearly ran out the door of the small cottage. Genevieve was playing near the edge of the woods. His eyes were so blurry he did not see her. She, however, saw her father as he vomited just a few feet away from her. As soon as he was mounted on his horse and rode away, she ran inside.

"Father is sick!" she said, rushing through the door.

The atmosphere inside the cottage was as heavy as if the execution had already occurred. For all practical purposes, it had. It was as sure as death itself.

Genevieve, overcome with fear, went to a corner of the cottage and curled up on the floor. No one seemed to even notice when she went into one of her spells until Mechi finally saw her and ran to cradle her head in her arms.

"Robbie!" she called out. "Bring a stick for her tongue!"

Robbie ran to her aid. He heard her tell Genevieve, "Don't worry, pumpkin. If I get out of here, I promise I will take you with me so we can get you all better."

Robbie's heart froze. He had imagined that if Mechi was forced to leave this world for a future one, she would take him with her. He thought she loved him, as he loved her. The thought of living the rest of his life without her was more than he could bear. Now, was she telling him that she would take his little sister and leave him there alone? Like Queen Mary, he felt that life was totally unfair. There had to be a way…

Chapter XLIII

The silence hung between Robbie and Mechi like the heavy fog over St. Andrew's the day Mechi had disappeared. The ride from Boscobel to Dunnottar seemed far longer than usual. Mechi recalled days when she and her father had visited relatives in Houston; it always seemed ten times farther to get there than it was to get home. The same sense closed in around her now. She wondered if they would ever arrive.

At last the fiddlehead came into view and they began the long ascent to the castle at the top.

"I'll miss you when I'm gone," she said under her breath.

She knew that, inevitably, her days here were numbered. She wondered if Robbie felt the same thing.

She cast a sideways glance at him. His eyes, usually so bright and full of life, were glazed over. Was it the news of Queen Mary's death that cast the shadow over them? Or was it the fear of being alone after she was gone?

Finally, breaking the deadly silence, Mechi said, "I do wish there was a way to get the modern cures to Genevieve."

Robbie shuddered. Was that really all she was concerned about? He had been so sure she felt the same tug at her heart strings for him that he felt for her. Was he so mistaken that all she really cared about was the betterment of mankind? No wonder she had been cast back over the centuries to protect the queen. Who else would be so selfless?

When he didn't answer, Mechi dropped the matter. She would have to talk to him, but it would have to be later. Perhaps tonight, after everyone else had retired...

Mechi remembered the first night she had spent at Dunnottar. She smiled slightly as she thought of Robbie's robe sash which she had so carefully tucked into her bosom for safekeeping until she could slip it—unnoticed—to him. The memory made her breasts feel the heat of his touch. She wanted to jump off her horse onto his and wrap herself in his big, strong muscle-bound arms. She wanted to stay there—forever.

As they reached the top, Robbie led the horses over to the stable and gave the reins to one of the boys. He reached up and placed his arms around Mechi's waist, lifting her down from her mount.

Mechi felt her heart pounding like it would explode. His hands on her, touching so gently yet so firmly, did that to her. She wrapped her arms around his neck and before they knew it, they were kissing like there was no tomorrow. Maybe, she thought, there will not be. She vowed, then and there, that if this was to be their last day together they would make the most of it. She didn't have a second to lose. If all she had to take with her was a memory, it would have to be a humdinger!

As they entered the keep, Lady Keith greeted them. Mechi was surprised by her warmth and cheerfulness. Maybe there was hope yet. Maybe Mechi should just forget about going back to her own life. She could live without such modern conveniences as electricity and indoor plumbing if she had Lord Robbie Keith, Viscount of Kintore, with her. She could survive anything for that reward.

"I have had a special banquet prepared for the sup," Lady Keith said.

Mechi cringed. She felt like she was a prisoner on death row being offered their final meal. *The Last Supper!* she thought. Now she knew what Jesus must have felt like when he dined with his traitors—Judas Iscariot who would betray him and Simon Peter, who would deny him.

Funny, she thought, how religious thoughts have entered my head so often lately. Maybe I won't return to the future. Maybe I will just disappear into an eternal oblivion. My purpose on earth has now been fulfilled and God—or whoever—doesn't need me any more.

She looked at Robbie. Maybe he doesn't need me, either. But God, how I need him! Life without him would be so incredibly boring.

Mechi's thoughts returned to the discussion earlier at the cottage. If what she suspected was true, and if her mother had her facts straight, that was the only logical conclusion. It meant, in effect, that Mrs. McGrath was Mechi's umpteen times great grandmother. And if Lord Keith took the child in to raise him, perhaps he would even give the boy the Keith title.

Robbie and I are related—almost—Mechi reasoned. Would their relationship be considered incest? She shook her head in disgust. It was acceptable, even in the twentieth century, for two people who were at least third cousins to marry. There was no actual blood relationship between Mrs. McGrath and the Keiths, so it was a dead issue, she decided. Even if the offspring of Mrs. McGrath and Darnley should be adopted by Lord Keith at some point in his life, it would not make them blood kin. No, she was safe.

"Could I see you in my solar?" Lord Keith asked Robbie. "Alone?"

Robbie looked at Mechi. Whatever it was his father wanted to discuss with him, he wished she could be a part of it. But, he knew an ultimatum from his father was not to be taken lightly. He followed his father down the long, dark corridor.

Mechi watched the two of them disappear. She was tempted to follow and put her ear tight against the door, but with Lady Keith there she knew better than to try it.

The two Keith men, so alike in every way, sat staring at each other. They could hear each others voices through the stillness.

Finally, breaking the silence, Lord Keith spoke.

"If she goes, you're going with her, aren't ye, laddie?"

Robbie sat at attention, stunned. Had Mechi told her father where she had come from? Of course, at the cottage she had enlightened all of them. How could he have forgotten?

"What makes you think she is going to leave?" Robbie asked.

"Just call it a feeling," Lord Keith answered. "It is nothing she said; it is just that her work here is finished. Mrs. McGrath, God bless her, will carry out her part of the plan, no doubt about it. I can't say I value the loss of her, but neither do I dare to think what would happen if Mary herself was destroyed."

"What good will it do for her to live if she cannot be the queen?" Robbie asked.

"It is quite simple," Lord Keith explained. "She can still rule the land through James. He will certainly be trustworthy to keep the secret of her survival to himself."

Robbie studied his father. He was a kind man, filled with compassion to everyone he met. No wonder he had such a loyal following. He hoped that someday he would be respected as much as his father.

"You did not answer me," Lord Keith said. "You will follow her?"

"I do not know if it is possible," Robbie said, the doubts putting voice to his thoughts. He had so feared that he would be left behind. Somehow, sharing it with someone else made it seem less threatening.

"And if it is?"

"Oh, Father," he exclaimed, "I would follow her anywhere! Never have I known such a deep desire and love for anyone. I dinna ken if I could live without her."

"I understand," Lord Keith responded. "I would follow your mother to the ends of the world." He threw his head back and laughed. "I guess that is what you would be doing, isn't it? The end of our world, and the world of generations after us, to a strange time when you would not understand anything."

"She has told me a great deal about life in her time," Robbie said. His eyes danced with excitement. "Do you know that they have big metal birds that carry hundreds of people through the sky? And little boxes with images of people in them. You can actually see what people all over the world are doing at the very instant they do it! And things that stick into the walls and cook things in just a few seconds without any fire. And…"

"Whoa!" Lord Keith nearly shouted. "Enough! It is more than I can bear! It is a time for you to enjoy, if you can. I am perfectly contented here with my life just the way it is."

"You would not be upset or disappointed if I went with her?" Robbie asked.

"I would be more disappointed if you did not," his father replied. "The love of a good woman is hard to find. It is to be treasured above all else. I know; I was fortunate enough to obtain it. I would trade all of Dunnottar for your mother's love and devotion."

Robbie laughed. "I doubt Mums would give up Dunnottar for anything. She loves the place like she was born here."

"Aye, that she does," Lord Keith said, a twinkle in his eyes. "At times I forget that she was not. She is a natural Keith, just as if she had been born one."

"And Mechi, should we have such a lifetime together, will be as fine a Keith as has ever been born."

"Aye, that she will," Lord Keith said. He spoke with such certainty that Robbie fully believed, for the first time, that they could really have such a life together.

"My only regret," Lord Keith said, "is that I shall never see your bairns." He smiled warmly at his son. "Of course I know they shall all have red hair!"

"And green eyes," Robbie joked.

"Aye, and green eyes," his father agreed.

"Go, and God be with you. I do not suppose that you shall ever be able to return here once you have gone."

"But if we have the ring…" Robbie said.

"Nay, it is too great a risk," Lord Keith said. "Ye must not dare to venture outside your own circle."

"How will you explain it to Mums?" Robbie asked.

"I shall tell her that you had to take a trip to…" He paused. "I do not know. Perhaps there is no way to make her understand." For the first time in Robbie Keith's life he saw fear in his father's face. He knew he was asking the impossible of his father. He was his mother's firstborn, and she practically idolized him. He could just imagine the devastating effect his disappearance would have on her.

"Tell her we had to travel to Paris," Robbie said. "She would accept that."

"I cannot lie to your mother," Lord Keith said. "She would know it was not the truth."

"But it would not be a lie," Robbie said. He began to explain to his father about the new world which was inhabited by thousands of British subjects. He told him of the town in Texas, called Paris, where Mechi grew up.

"I suppose it is the best I can offer her," Lord Keith said. He took his son's hand in his. "Thank you, my son."

"For what?" Robbie asked. "'Tis I should be thanking you. You have been the best father anyone could ever hope for. If I can do as well with my own children, I shall have succeeded in life."

"And I must thank you for being such a fine son." He gazed into Robbie's eyes. "I could never hope for any better. I just wish I could be there from time to time to sneak a peek at you. Even if you could not see me, it would satisfy my fatherly curiosity."

His voice dropped. "Whatever you do, always be kind to Mechi. One of the most valuable lessons I have learned in our marriage is that you must not only love your mate; you must also like her. There is a great difference."

"I do love her," Robbie said. "And I like her far more than anyone else I have ever known. And yes, you are right. There is a difference."

Robbie ran his finger nervously back and forth on his father's big oak writing desk. "Like Agnes and Moray," he said. "It is clear that she loves him. But I can't for the life of me imagine that *anyone* could ever like him!"

"You definitely understand the difference," Lord Keith said. "I must say, I agree with you wholeheartedly."

The two of them laughed together. One day, when Mary was locked away, Agnes's marriage to Moray would promote her to the position of the wife of the regent of Scotland. Had they known that, they no doubt would have agreed that even such an honorable place as that would not have been worth the price of an eternal boredom from living with such a man as Moray.

Lord Keith walked around to his son. He was not a particularly expressive man, but he embraced his son, knowing that it may be the last time he could ever take him in his arms. So many things to say, but the words would not come. Instead, the tears flowed.

"Don't cry, Father," Robbie said. "It is what I must do." He knew, as did his father, that it would work. Even if the power of the ring was not strong enough to transport him along with Mechi, his love would carry him across the realm of time.

Robbie turned to leave the room. As his hand clutched the shiny brass doorknob he turned back to his father.

"Does it not seem odd that no one has inquired about the queen's absence?" he asked.

"Aye, people's tongues have wagged," Lord Keith said. "I have merely told them that she had some unfinished business to attend to in France. When she returns, it will be with Mrs. McGrath in her stead, but no one will know that. Why, even your mother could not detect the difference."

"Aye, she has done her job well," Robbie said. "I just wish there was some way to spare both of them." He stopped, then said, "For Gen's sake, if nothing else."

"She will be fine with the queen," Lord Keith said. "I have briefed Anne on what must be done, and have dispensed her to attend to them there."

"Good thinking," Robbie said, smiling. Suddenly his countenance changed. "My God, but I shall miss her!" He had not stopped to think about the daily visits and to his little sister which would never again occur.

Robbie told his father about the medicines which had been discovered to control the disease which plagued the little Keith lass. How he wished he could find a way to whisk them back through time to control the malady.

"I must find Mechi," Robbie said as he left. "I must tell her that I wish to accompany her on her return voyage."

"*Bon voyage!*" Lord Keith said. He did not speak any further words. He could not. The lump in his throat was far too big for a sound to escape.

Chapter XLIV

"I am so glad that is over," Robbie said as he sat by the fireplace in the dining hall. "It seemed like everyone was a little tense."

"A *little* tense?" Mechi said, howling with laughter. "If a rope had been pulled any tighter, it would have split in two from the sheer force."

Robbie looked deep into her eyes. He felt like he could see into her soul. What he saw encouraged him. If he read her right, she did not want to leave him any more than he wanted to be apart from her.

"When do you think it will be?" he asked.

Mechi contemplated playing dumb, but decided against it. This was far too serious to fool with. It was a matter of life and death. Or at least sanity. She was afraid she would lose both if she lost Robbie. She knew exactly what he meant.

"I don't know, exactly," she said. "But I am afraid it is soon."

"How can you tell?" he asked.

"I don't know," she said. "It is just a feeling I have. Like my job here is finished. Like I am free to leave."

"And if you were free to stay…?" he asked.

"I don't know," she said. "I don't think I am."

"Do you think I could go with you?" he asked at the same time as she asked, "Would you consider coming with me?"

They laughed, the tension broken.

"Yes," they both answered simultaneously.

"What if it doesn't work?" Mechi asked, shaking like a windblown autumn leaf.

"In that case," Robbie said, "we had better enjoy what time we have." He took her by the hand and led her up the winding staircase, down the corridor and into her bedroom. Once they were safely inside, he secured the big giant lock on the door, swept her into his arms and carried her to the bed.

Mechi did not argue. If there was anything she wanted in her *final hours*, it was to be lost completely in the loving arms of Lord Robbie Keith, Viscount of

Kintore. Even if she lost him forever, she would carry him in her heart for the rest of her days. Even if she could never tell a soul, knowing that they would have her declared "insane" if she dared to mention this whole crazy affair.

"Are you making me your prisoner?" she asked laughingly as she pointed at the locked door.

"Absolutely," he replied. "Do you object?"

"No problem!" Mechi said, imitating the oft-repeated popular phrase of the 90's.

"Good," he said, grinning impishly at her. He stood over her, admiring the perfect specimen of humanity which was resting on the bed. He wanted tonight to be perfect, just in case... His desire, which was burning deep within him, urged him to cast aside his own clothes and rip hers from her with no thought for anything except how much his entire body ached for her.

"What are your wishes, my lord?" Mechi asked, using a put-on tone of voice.

"My only wish is to be here with you forever," he said. "Or wherever—as long as it is with you."

"Your wish is my command, my lord," she said, climbing up onto her knees on the bed.

Mechi reached up and unfastened the belt which held his plaid in place. She thought of the age-old question of whether a Scotsman wore anything beneath his kilt or not. If luck held out for her, he would be completely bare once she pulled his plaid from him.

Robbie did not flinch. Not a muscle on his steely-hard body rippled. The only thing which had remained well hidden from view by his plaid was his manhood, which was already standing at full attention.

"Are you saluting me, my lord?" Mechi teased.

"Aye, my lady," he answered. "I'm at your disposal, as you can see. Take me. I'm yours."

Mechi gently reached up and rubbed her index finger up and down the hardened shaft which stared at her. She felt the blood rush through her entire body as she touched him. Robbie's body shivered from her caress. He reached down and began to undo her long row of buttons.

"Damned women's garb!" he muttered, struggling to get his clumsy fingers to manipulate the tiny buttons.

Mechi was tempted to offer to help him, but the fight he was enduring to get to her was far more fun.

When he finally released the last button, he slid the gown from Mechi's shoulders. It fell to her waist, and he quickly untied the straps of her camisole, freeing it to fall freely onto the bed behind her.

"Thank God you don't have a corset on!" he said, pulling impatiently at the mountain of crinolines she had on. He released the tie at the waist from them, one by one, then forced them down to her knees, which were still pushed into the feather mattress on the big four-poster bed.

"Get up!" he ordered, tugging at the garments.

Mechi stood up on the bed, waited patiently while he removed them, then toppled onto a heap on the bed.

"It's so soft," Mechi said. "It's hard to keep your balance on it."

Robbie laughed. He looked down at his bulging manly tool and winked at her.

"I didn't think it was soft a bit," he said. "Would you care to prove it?"

Mechi turned over onto her back on the bed and Robbie lowered himself down beside her. He began to fondle her breasts, causing them to stand as erect as he was. His mouth sought hers, then gently moved his tongue into her welcoming mouth.

Mechi groaned from sheer ecstasy. Never had she felt anything so deeply warm and wonderful. When at last he entered her, she shuddered and shivered from the excitement. Yes, this was a night she would remember for the rest of her life, whichever century it was in.

As they arrived at their mutual climax, Robbie lifted himself off her and lay on the bed, his chin resting on his hands, and stared at her. He had to capture the way she looked this very instant, in case it was the last time he ever saw her.

In true *Mechi form*, she began to sing. *"Memories are made of this…"*

"Do you always sing?" Robbie asked, amused by her actions after such an intense time of passion.

"Only when I'm deliriously happy," she said.

"You seem to sing a lot when we are together."

"Of course," she answered. "You always make me happy." She giggled. "Or maybe you just make me delirious!"

"Well, you did seem to swoon quite often when you were first in my presence," he kidded. "I thought it was because of your—*trip*."

"That stupid oak root!" Mechi grumbled. "If it hadn't been for that…"

"You would never have found me," Robbie said, suddenly extremely serious. "Nor I you. I owe my life to that stupid oak root."

"I guess you're right," Mechi said.

Abruptly, she changed the subject. If they were going to leave this world before too long, she better make sure he was prepared. She had spent endless hours telling him about modern inventions, but she knew he could not possibly comprehend what it would really be like.

"Do you trust me?" she asked him.

"Of course I do," he said.

"Completely?"

"Aye, with my life," he replied.

"Good. If it does succeed for us to leave together, when we return who knows how long I will have been missing. The police might be out looking for me in full force. Besides, I have told you about so many things. Things which are so strange to you. I know you think you understand them, but believe me, it will be a great shock for you to land in the 1990's. Nothing I can say or show you can possibly prepare you fully for such an adventure. You must just trust me. If I tell you to do something, please do as I say and I will explain later."

She grinned at him as she said, "Besides, I have to figure out how to explain you to Brian." She shrugged her shoulders. "I guess I can always say I found you out on the golf course at St. Andrew's."

"Which is, of course, completely true," Robbie said, returning a smile. "Different era, different country, different world, but who's counting...?"

Mechi laughed, then sobered almost instantaneously.

"There is one other matter," she said.

"Which is?" Robbie asked.

"Genevieve," Mechi said, causing a puzzled look to come over his face.

"What does Gen have to do with any of this?" he asked.

"Do you suppose it would be possible for us to take her back, too?"

Robbie looked at her in surprise.

"Why?" he asked.

"Don't you see?" she said, agitated by his lack of understanding. "It would be perfect! We could get the medicine she needs for her epilepsy so she could live a long, normal life. Then, when she is cured, we could give her the ring and send her back here."

Robbie pondered the possibility.

"Perhaps I should discuss it with Father," he suggested.

"No!" Mechi said. "He would never allow it."

"You are probably right," Robbie said. "If it is possible, we will try it. We must talk to her first, to prepare her in case it does work."

"First thing in the morning," Mechi said. The next thing Robbie knew, she was sound asleep, snoring, with her head on his chest.

Chapter XLV

When Mechi awoke in the morning, she turned over. The only hint that Robbie had been there the night before was his scent, which lingered on the pillow. She buried her head in it, hoping that he had not disappeared. Maybe the hope she clung to of his going with her was too much. Was it possible? Or was it all a dream? Just wishful thinking.

"Hurry!" Robbie said as he rushed into her room. "You must get dressed at once!"

"What's the hurry?" she asked, stretching lazily.

"I mean it!" Robbie shouted at her. "Queen Elizabeth has heard that Queen Mary was spotted here at Dunnottar. Someone must have seen us when we brought her here for the visit with Mums."

"What does that have to do with us?" Mechi asked innocently.

"They have ordered Mary to be found and brought to her," he explained. "It is, I fear, the beginning of the end."

Mechi thought back to their discussion at the cottage yesterday. She was so afraid of what lay ahead for both of the women she had become so fond of.

"We must go get Genevieve," Mechi said, getting up and collecting her old, once-familiar blue jeans, GUESS sweatshirt and green nylon windbreaker.

"And the ring," Robbie added.

"Naturally," Mechi said. She began dressing as she explained, "If today is the day, I should wear my old clothes. I know you don't find them particularly appealing, but I will call much less attention to us if I am dressed so I fit in."

She snickered, adding, "It will be hard enough explaining a *hunk* like you—to Brian, or anyone else we might happen to meet."

Robbie laughed. She had, long ago, explained a *hunk* to him. He puffed his chest up and took a deep breath. If he was going to play the role of a *hunk*, he had better start rehearsing now.

As they went downstairs, Robbie rushed them out the side door and over to the stables. He said "Good bye" to Duncan and lit off at a breakneck speed.

Mechi, clinging to the reins for dear life, was glad she was an expert horsewoman. She found it easy to keep up with him.

"Halt!" the governor of the castle called out to Robbie.

Fearing bad news, Robbie stopped, with Mechi following suit.

"Elizabeth has spies all about," the governor said.

Mechi took note that the governor, like almost all Scots, refused to recognize Elizabeth as the queen of *anything*. To them, Mary was the queen. That was the end of that.

"What should we do?" Robbie asked nervously. "We must get to Boscobel."

"I would suggest that you go on ahead, perhaps towards St. Andrews. You could go to the cathedral there, and no one could touch you."

"But I told you," Robbie insisted, "we must get to Boscobel first."

The governor eyed Mechi suspiciously. "Could she do what must be done there?" he asked, skeptical, but not seeing any other solution. "You would have already diverted the attention from her by going alone."

"I can do it," Mechi said, sounding much more confident than she felt.

"Please be careful," Robbie pleaded. He came very close to her, both of them still mounted, and whispered, "Be careful not to expose the ring."

Mechi heard his words and understood his warning. If she should happen to rub the ring the wrong way, and if Genevieve was with her, they might both disappear—forever—leaving Robbie behind.

"Don't worry," she assured him. "I do not want to leave until…"

"Go!" the governor urged, knowing how close danger was to them.

Mechi waited for about five minutes, although it seemed more like eons. Finally she loosened the reins and headed off towards the woods at Boscobel. She knew there was no time to waste.

"Gen!" Mechi called out as she ran into the cottage. "Come here, quick!"

Gen ran to greet Mechi with a warm hug. They had bonded, Mechi thought gratefully.

"Robbie sent me to get you," Mechi explained. "We are going—on a trip. We want you to come with us."

"Really?" Genevieve asked excitedly. She had never been allowed to leave the little cottage in the forest. She had tried to imagine the "outside world," as she had called it to Mechi.

Mechi realized that it would be much easier for Genevieve to deal with and accept than it would be for Robbie. He was a man of the world, while Genevieve was a mere sheltered child—but she knew it. That made her anticipation so much more acceptable. She was so vulnerable, Mechi thought. She would have to keep a very close eye on her. There were so many things to endanger such an innocent person—in Mechi's world.

"We must take her with us," Mechi told Queen Mary. "If luck is with us, she will one day return. Without her physical problems."

"I do hope so," Mary said. "I have become very fond of the child. I shall miss her greatly."

Queen Mary turned away from Mechi. "I shall miss you, too," she said sadly. "You have been the best friend I have ever had."

"And you have been the same to me," Mechi said. She laughed. "Imagine, me, calling the Queen of Scotland my closest friend! No one will ever believe me!"

Mary spoke slowly, deliberately. "You are returning…to *your world*?"

"We are going to try," Mechi said.

"We?" Mary asked.

"Yes," Mechi said. "Robbie, Genevieve and I."

"I wish you all godspeed," Mary said, her words nearly choking her. "I shall think of you often."

"And I you," Mechi said. "I hope, for your sake, that our plan is successful."

"For the sake of the country, so do I. Although I must admit that for the sake of poor Mrs. McGrath it might be better if it failed."

"Where is she?" Mechi asked. "I did so want to tell her good bye."

"She and Rizzio have gone for a walk in the woods," Mary said. She chuckled as she said, "She has learned to handle her *platforms* quite well." Her laugh gained steam as she told Mechi, "She has managed the whole thing most amazingly. Why, one day we played a trick on Rizzio. We switched places again—back to ourselves. I went for a walk with Rizzio in the forest, and he thought I was her. Oh, the secrets he told me! I was tempted to tell him, but it was just too enjoyable. I will never reveal to Mrs. McGrath what he said."

Mechi saw that Mary was blushing. Had he, as Mechi supposed, admitted to the woman he thought was his cousin that he was deeply, madly, head-over-heels in love with the queen? What's more, it appeared that Mary was just as smitten with the handsome Italian.

"I promise I will not tell a soul," Mechi said. "Not that anyone in my lifetime would be that interested."

Mechi glanced at her watch, which she had put on when she dressed for the first time in weeks.

"I would like to wait for them," she said, "but we really don't have time. We are going to meet Robbie at St. Andrews." Mechi gave Queen Mary one final hug. They clung to each other, knowing that this was their final farewell. Neither said another word, but she waved as Mechi and Genevieve rode off on the horse.

"Are you frightened?" Mechi asked Genevieve, sensing that she had perhaps never been on a horse before.

"Oh, no, Mechi!" she exclaimed. "I am not afraid. Not as long as I am with you and Robbie." Her voice warmed as she said, "I rather like that you call him Robbie. All my life—until you—he was simply Robert. Robbie fits him much better."

"I agree," Mechi said. Her old fiancee, now that was a *Robert*! And this, her beloved Scotsman, was definitely not a *Robert*. Nosireebob! He was a *Robbie*. And she wouldn't have it any other way.

Chapter XLVI

Mechi held onto Genevieve's hands tightly as she lowered her to the ground. She watched in awe as Gen stared at the cathedral, her mouth wide open. It was the first time she had ever seen any building other than the tiny cottage where she and Mrs. McGrath had lived.

"We have to be quiet," Mechi said as she fastened the reins of the horse around a tree, fastening it tightly. "Come on. Robbie should be inside."

Mechi stood still inside, allowing her eyes time to focus in the near darkness. Soon she heard voices. She would know his voice anywhere. Even if she could not see them, she could follow the sound and find them.

She held Genevieve's hand as she felt along the pews to the front of the sanctuary. Flashes of the night she had spent here popped in and out of her head.

"*Ay, mon dieu!*" the priest exclaimed. "Surely you are not the woman he speaks about!"

"You know each other?" Robbie asked.

"Yes," Mechi said. "I spent one night here. The night I was on my way to help you with the horses."

"She was a lifesaver!" Robbie explained to the priest. "She was able to cure the horses. We didn't lose a single head."

The priest lifted his head heavenward. He knew he needed divine help. There was something very strange about this woman. Besides her apparel, that is. He felt that she was not to be trusted, but he could not explain why. Not even to himself.

"If we could have just a few moments alone?" Robbie asked the priest.

"Certainly," the priest said, obviously relieved that he could escape the clutches of the strange woman. He disappeared behind a closed door, making the sign of the cross as he exited.

"Now what?" Mechi asked.

"Do you have the ring?" Robbie asked.

"Right here," Mechi said, reaching into her green nylon jacket pocket. She pulled out the tiny object, still securely wrapped in the piece of cloth Robbie had put it in. A tiny feather seemed to stick to it.

Mechi shook the package, but the feather stuck, undaunted, as if it had a mind of its own.

Mechi slowly unwrapped the ring. She put it on her finger, then grabbed Robbie's finger and Genevieve's finger. She pulled them towards her until they all touched the bright shiny blue gem. The feather had made its way under the ring, causing Mechi to giggle from the way it tickled her.

"Ready?" Mechi said as they all made contact with the jewel. In a few seconds the whole world began to spin around and she felt like she was inside a giant ball as it was rolled down a bowling alley.

Thump! Mechi felt like she had landed upside down. She rubbed her eyes and looked around. She was lying on the ground—at St. Andrew's Country Club—near Aberdeen, Maryland. Her head was resting in Robbie's lap, and Genevieve was sitting beside them, clinging to her brother with every ounce of strength she had.

Mechi looked up into Robbie's face. His red beard and his brilliant green eyes were now a familiar sight. She reached up and ran her fingers over his cheek.

"We did it!" she shouted gleefully. "We are back!"

"Now what?" Robbie asked.

"Now is the time to trust me," Mechi said. "You said you did, remember?"

"I did," Robbie said, smiling at her. "And I do."

"Come on," she said, taking each of them by the hand. "Gen, don't be afraid. You are going to see a lot of things you don't understand. Like right now, we are going to find my car. We will all get inside it and it will make a lot of noise. Don't be afraid. It will begin to move and it will take us to my apartment. That's where I live."

"Let's go!" Genevieve said, her voice full of wonder and amazement at such strange things.

Mechi opened the door to her car. She pulled the ashtray open and took out the key. She put it in the ignition and it began to purr like a kitten. The radio was still on, and Robbie and Genevieve both looked all over to see who was talking.

"*Take me on a sentimental journey…*" the songster crooned.

"I think you already did," Robbie said, laughing. He had tried to imagine these things, but it was far more than he had ever dreamed. He watched as they rode past other cars, looked at the funny-looking buildings, blinked at the stop lights, then began waving at people as they passed them.

His head leaned backwards and he laughed, that wonderful, delightful laugh Mechi had grown so fond of.

"This is wonderful!" he shouted. "It is so much more than you said it was!"

"You are not afraid?" Mechi asked.

"Afraid?" Robbie asked. "Of what? I trust you, remember? There is nothing to fear."

Mechi pulled the car into the underground garage at her apartment complex. As soon as it was parked in her own spot, she showed them how to open the door. Together they got out.

Mechi led them to the elevator. She tried to find the words to explain how it would happen. She wished Mr. Otis, whoever he was, was there to help her.

They began to rise, and they rode, speechless, to the fifth floor. When they reached it, the door opened and Mechi pulled them out into the hall.

Robbie blinked at the brightness from the electric lights. Genevieve just stared, trying to take everything in at once.

When they got to Mechi's apartment door, she realized that she didn't have her purse. She must have lost it someplace at St. Andrew's when she tripped over that stupid oak root. To her surprise, she heard noises inside and the door seemed to be slightly ajar.

Mechi pushed the door open. Brian was sitting on the sofa, his feet resting on the coffee table, and he was watching TV.

"Come on in, Sis," he said. "I found your purse at the club. I waited around for you to show up, but when you didn't, I figured I would just mosey on over here and wait for you. Where you been, anyway? You've missed almost a whole day."

One whole day! Mechi gasped. How could so much have happened in one single day? Time stood still while she was gone. That had to be it.

"You won't believe where I've been," she said.

Brian, noticing Robbie and Genevieve, said, "Nice to meet you, whoever you are. Hope you don't think I'm rude, but this is really exciting."

"What are you watching?" Mechi asked.

"Geraldo," Brian answered. "It's more fun than when he claimed he'd found Jimmy Hoffa!"

"What's it about?" Mechi asked.

Robbie, who had heard about televisions, gazed at the tiny box in disbelief. There were, just like Mechi had said, tiny people inside it.

"So you opened the tomb of Mary, Queen of Scots?" Geraldo asked.

Mechi almost shrieked. What on earth was going on?

"Yes, we did," the woman on the stage said. "We had to get special permission from Queen Elizabeth, of course. She was quite reluctant at first, but when we told her what we suspected, she finally agreed."

"And what did you find?" Gerald asked.

"The body inside—the head was separated from the body, of course—was about five inches shorter than Queen Mary was supposed to be," the old gentleman with the gray beard said.

"How do you explain that?" Geraldo asked.

"The rumor that has recently arisen that there was an imposter who took the place of Queen Mary was apparently true," the old gent said. "From the bone structure, there was no way that woman in that tomb is Queen Mary."

"You are sure?" Geraldo asked.

"We have the best archaeological team ever assembled," the man said. "We all agree. We have studied Mary's life very carefully. We have no idea whose body that is, but we can say without a single doubt that it is not the body of Queen Mary!"

Mechi looked at Robbie. His green eyes were brighter than she had ever seen them. He grinned so broadly even his bushy red beard couldn't hide it.

Robbie ran to Mechi and grabbed her, dancing around in circles.

"We did it!" he shouted. "It worked!"

"Aye, so it did!" Mechi said in her best Scottish accent. "It worked."

"Quiet!" Mechi ordered. "Listen to what they are saying."

"There appears to be some strange foreign object in the casket," the head archaeologist said.

Geraldo laughed. "Besides her head?"

"Yes," the archaeologist said, not at all amused by the TV talk show host's attempt at humor. To him it was very serious business.

"I'm sorry," Geraldo said. "I guess it is just that I have to protect my reputation, too. I can't have it all serious. Bad for ratings."

It was obvious the man did not agree with this point of view, but it was Geraldo's show.

"So what would your guess be as to the object you found?" Geraldo asked, returning to the serious matter at hand.

"They were, of course, very fragile after so many years," the archaeologist explained. "But it seemed to be two blocks of wood."

"Blocks of wood?" Geraldo repeated.

"Yes, and it makes no sense that something as simple as that would be important enough to bury with the queen."

Mechi and Robbie laughed, delighted that their secret, after more than four hundred years, had still not been found out.

"Mrs. McGrath's shoes!" the chimed in unison.

"Sis, you've really lost it this time," Brian said. "You make no sense at all."

Suddenly Mechi froze with fear. "You are not sorry that you came here with me?" she asked Robbie.

"Not in a million years," he said, kissing her passionately.

"Well, actually," Mechi said, trying to calculate the time in her head, "I think it was only four-hundred and thirty-six years."

They laughed together hysterically.

"Okay," he said. "Whatever. It doesn't matter. We are together. That is all that matters."

For the first time, Brian noticed what Robbie and Genevieve were wearing. He thought back to the strange Liz Stuart who had turned up—late—for her golf lesson.

"Sure never know what you are going to pick up at the golf course these days!" He shook his head, turned the volume on the TV up and ignored them.

Robbie and Mechi were too busy with each other to notice that Genevieve had gone over and sat down beside Brian.

"You think I am odd?" she asked him openly. She had known all her life that people considered her odd. Strange. Different. Out of control.

"No stranger than my sister," Brian said, looking at Mechi and shaking his head again. "I think I'm going to need more than a three-day leave to figure this whole thing out."

"You'll need a lifetime to understand what has happened," Mechi said. "Or not." She winked at Robbie. He winked back.

As if on signal, the TV screen went blank.

"It is still not time for the world to know what the blocks of wood are," Robbie remarked. "What made the people in the little box disappear?"

"Lost the cable," Mechi said.

Robbie shrugged his shoulders. There were so many things he would have to learn. It seemed like she was talking a foreign language.

"Don't worry about it," Mechi said. "Just figure it is *par for the course!*"

EPILOGUE

"Are you sure she is ready?" Robbie asked Mechi, his fingers twitching nervously. "She's so…"

"…well," Mechi finished his sentence for him.

"She does seem to be," he agreed. "I guess I need to trust you—one more time."

"I have the ring," Mechi said. "And the feather. We will explain to her that she can return to her mother and father if she wants to. We will leave the decision up to her."

"You are sure she can survive okay back there?" Robbie asked. "I would not want her to have her seizures again."

"With the formula the pharmacist wrote out for her, she should be able to live a long, healthy, normal life," Mechi assured him. "Even back there. They are all ingredients that were available in 1561. They just didn't know how to use them. With her written information, there should be no problem."

Genevieve walked into the room where Robbie and Mechi were discussing her.

"What's up?" she asked, sounding very much like a teenager of the nineties.

"We were discussing you," Robbie said, patting her gently on the back as she sat down between them on the sofa.

"Whatever it is," Genevieve said, "I didn't do it. Promise."

"Nobody said anything about doing anything wrong," Mechi said. She watched her, admitting that the girl reminded her very much of herself at that age. She always seemed to have a guilty conscience, too. Like the time the horses all got loose and they found out somebody had opened the corral gate deliberately. The first words out of her mouth to her father had been, "I didn't do it. Promise."

"So what's up?" Genevieve repeated.

"You have a decision to make," Robbie said. "You don't have to answer right away."

"What is it?" Genevieve asked.

"You have not had any of your *fits* for a long spell," Robbie said. "Mechi thinks perhaps it is time for you to return."

"Return where?" Genevieve asked.

"Back to Boscobel. To Mrs. McGrath and Queen Mary."

"And Mums and Father?"

"Especially to Mums and Father," Robbie said. "I am sure they are nearly dying from worry over you."

"And over you, too," Genevieve reminded him.

Robbie took her hand in his. "Father knows," he said simply.

"He knows?" Genevieve said, surprised by such a revelation.

Robbie nodded his head. "Now, do you want to return to them?"

"Aye, Robbie. I have had a good time here, but I do miss them. You were made for this place, but I belong there."

Genevieve turned to Mechi. "Will it work again?"

Mechi stood up and went to the desk drawer where she had put the ring. She took it out and went back to Genevieve. The one stubborn feather, she noticed, was still stuck to it.

"Put it on," she told Genevieve. "But be careful not to touch the sapphire until you are ready to leave."

Genevieve slid it on her finger, but it was far too large for her. It slipped off, falling to the floor.

Robbie quickly retrieved it from under the sofa, where it had rolled.

Mechi took the ring and got a ball of string from the desk. She wrapped several layers of the string around the ring, then put it back on Genevieve's finger. It held in place securely now.

"I'm ready," she said, looking at first one of them, then the other. She stood up, and they did likewise. She gave each of them a huge hug, then carefully, slowly rubbed her finger across the blue jewel. In an instant she was gone.

"I have one wish for us," Robbie said as they prepared for their wedding ceremony.

"A long, happy life?" Mechi asked, grinning. "I think you, Lord Robbie Keith, have had that more than anyone else who ever lived."

"No," Robbie said, appearing far more serious than she had ever seen him. "I know we will have that." He hesitated a few moments, then said, "I would like to go back to Boscobel. To the cottage. Just to see what is there."

Mechi looked at him. She wondered if he, like Genevieve, missed the "good old days." Did he, if he was honest, rue the day he had followed her to the ends of the earth?

"What do you expect to find, after all these years?" she asked.

"I don't honestly know," he said. "But it is just a feeling I have. Like there are unanswered questions that hold the key to our lives back there. Would you mind terribly?"

"Of course not," Mechi said. "We could go to Dunnottar for our honeymoon. I have read that it is being restored and is open for the public."

She reached over to the end table for the tour guide of Scotland she had bought.

"I wanted it to be a surprise," she said. "I found the phone number for Dunnottar Castle listed in here." She paused. "I called it."

Robbie stared at her in disbelief. She was, without a doubt, the most wonderful woman any man had ever found.

"And?" he asked.

"And we have a reservation to stay at the castle for five days." She smiled at him, relieved that he seemed pleased. "It was to be my wedding present to you."

"Let's get this show on the road!" he said, pulling her to him and kissing her in appreciation.

Mechi laughed at him. He sounded like the most modern Scotsman she had ever imagined.

"You've got it!" she said, going to her desk and getting out their marriage license.

"You know," she said, mischief in her eyes, "I have done things for you I have never done for anyone else."

"Like?" he asked.

"Lying to get a fake birth certificate for you," she said. "And that's just for starters."

"You didn't exactly lie," Robbie said, chuckling. "They asked what year I was born. You just gave the last two numbers of the year. That only added four hundred years. It was the clerk who wrote in '19' instead of '15.' She never asked about it, so why should you have answered?"

"You are wonderful," Mechi said, kissing her groom-to-be.

"For a man my age," he bantered back to her.

They walked, hand in hand, through the woods at Boscobel. They said very little, but the air was filled with anticipation.

When they reached the clearing, there was no sign of the old cottage. It had, Mechi supposed, been demolished years ago. Maybe hundreds of years ago. It was not built to endure for centuries, like Dunnottar, and even it had been nearly destroyed.

Mechi's heart went out to Robbie. The look on his face had been devastating when he saw the ruins of the castle, his home. "At least," she had told him, "they are working to restore it now."

He had not replied. He could not. While they had slept in Mechi's old solar, it was certainly not the same. Still, there had been a sense of *deja vu.*

"Over there," Robbie said, pointing at a grassy spot on the grounds.

Together, anxiously, they went to examine it. Grass and weeds were overgrowing the area, but in the midst of it were two stone slates. "Here lies the body of Mary Stuart, Queen of Scotland," it read. Below it, in very small letters, it said, "The real one." The date of her death was "1604," seventeen years after her supposed death.

"She's here!" Mechi said.

"Awesome!" the thoroughly modern Robbie added.

"Look!" Mechi cried excitedly. "Over here is another one."

They knelt down together, clearing the grass and dirt from the smaller marker. "Genevieve Keith," it declared. "1549-1617."

When she could finally speak again, Mechi said, "You got your wish."

"Aye, I did indeed," Robbie said, a tear sparkling in his eye. "She had a good, long life." He ran his hand softly over Mechi's cheek. "Thank you," he said.

"You're welcome," Mechi said simply.

"Let's go home," Robbie said.

"It is good to be at Dunnottar again, isn't it?" Mechi asked.

"No," Robbie said. "I mean *home,* to our apartment. I'm ready."

Mechi smiled at him. "I'm ready, too," she said.

About the Author

Janet Elaine Smith is the author of 10 novels, several which are based on her genealogical digging. She weaves truth with fiction in such a way that her readers often ask, "I loved the book, but which characters were real historical people and which ones were imaginary?" Janet has been a well-known magazine writer for 25 years, and now she is winning the hearts of readers with her fiction. *Dunnottar,* her first historical novel, was a best-seller on many venues. She lives with her husband, Ivan, in Grand Forks, ND, where they operate a charitable "Helps" organization. They have 3 adult children.

Dear Readers,

You have asked for more Keith clan stories after reading *Dunnottar* and *Marylebone.* Now you have it, in *Par for the Course.* As always, some of the Keiths were real and others are figments of my imagination. The basic story, however, is based on actual historical facts—and then left to wander. I hope you will enjoy it.

Please take note of this: any experiments included in *Par for the Course* such as the production of penicillin, etc., are purely for fictional purposes and should not be duplicated by the readers.

I always love to hear from readers. It makes writing all worth while. You can reach me at janetelainesmith@yahoo.com or P.O. Box 126, East Grand Forks, MN. 56721. To see more about me and my other books, check out my website at http://www.janetelainesmith.com .

Happy reading!

Janet Elaine Smith

Printed in the United States
88958LV00006B/85-93/A